NIGHTS OF SWEET DELIVERANCE

"I think it's time we talked," Dominic said, taking her hand. "About last night," he began.

"It was wonderful, Dominic, but . . ." Catherine swallowed hard. She looked at his beautiful dark thick-fringed eyes, the sensuous curve of his lips. In the deep vee of his shirt, smooth brown skin rippled over taut muscle and she remembered how it felt beneath her hand. She needed to tell him they could never touch each other as they had last night, but instead her fingers came up to touch his cheek.

"Catherine," he whispered, his hands already moving down her body. He raised his head to look at her. "I've never wanted a woman the way I want you." He kissed her, plunging his tongue into her mouth.

She could now feel the heat that was building inside of her, and nothing else mattered. When he broke away to shed his clothes, Catherine clung to him.

"I want you," she told him. "Now. This minute." Knowing the risk she was taking only made her more desperate . . .

"A rich read, memorable characters, a romance that fulfills every woman's fantasy."
                                                                    —Deana James

"Kat Martin's *Gypsy Lord* is . . . throughly delightful!"
                                        —Catherine Hart, author of *Temptation*

"An irresistible treat sure to delight, captivate and enchant."
                                                                    —*Romantic Times*

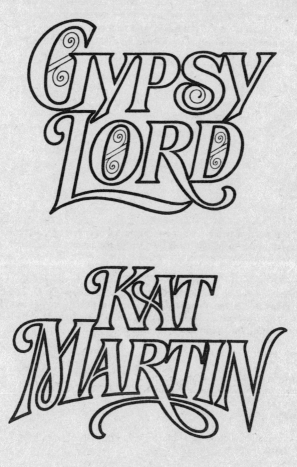

GYPSY LORD

KAT MARTIN

St. Martin's Paperbacks

This is a work of fiction. All of the characters, organizations, and events portrayed in this novel are either products of the author's imagination or are used fictitiously.

Some of the gypsy poems used in this book are from *Gypsy Sorcery and Fortune Telling* by Charles Godfrey Leland. Copyright © 1962 by University Books, Inc. Reprinted by permission. Other gypsy poems are from *In Sara's Tents* by Walter Starkie, Litt.D. Copyright 1953 by E. P. Dutton & Co., Inc. Reprinted by permission.

GYPSY LORD

Copyright © 1992 by Kat Martin.
Excerpt from *Sweet Vengeance* copyright © 1992 by Kat Martin.

For information address St. Martin's Press, 175 Fifth Avenue, New York, NY 10010.

ISBN: 978-1-250-04074-9

Printed in the United States of America

St. Martin's Paperbacks edition / September 1992

10 9 8 7

For my friends, those dear and trusted people who have stood with me through the bad times and rejoiced with me through the good.

My best friends, Diana, Martha, Debbie, Ronetta, and of course my husband, Larry.

My writer/reader friends, Olga, Brenda, Sue, Wanda, Ruth, Debbie, and a score of others whose help and guidance I treasure.

Friends in Tulare, California, where I was born and started school.

Friends in Santa Barbara, Silvio, Reno, Sally, Pam, who helped me grow from girl to woman.

Friends in New Jersey, Donna, Jane, Bev, Marge, Doris, who taught me to appreciate the finer things in life.

Friends in Bakersfield, who helped me believe in myself and were always there when I needed them.

For Russ, Mike, and Ron. For Gary, Richard, Kris, Larry, Tracy, Leslie, Jeff, Denny, John, Sherian, Tommy and Judy, Ed and Martha, Ron and Janythe, Sam and Kim, Lawton and Aloma, Mary and Carl, Kenny, Butch and Mariann, and at least a dozen others.

This one's for you. I love you one and all.

Chapter One

"THEY SAY HE'S a Gypsy."

"Bah! All those rumors about his tainted blood? Half of London's heard the gossip—only makes him more intriguing."

Lady Dartmoor laughed, covering her mouth with a delicate white-gloved hand. "I suppose you're right. The scandalmongers always adore such tales and yet. . . ." She appraised the dashing figure in immaculate black frock coat and snug gray breeches standing across the marble-floored ballroom. Smooth dark skin and bold black brows stood in contrast to the white of his stock and cravat.

She eyed him wistfully, smoothing an unseen wrinkle from the front of her green silk gown. "God's truth, I think Dominic Edgemont is one of the most dangerously attractive men in all of London."

The stately woman standing next to her, Lady Wexford, seemed to agree. She said something in a whisper, then both of them laughed. Their next words were lost in the music and gaiety of the elegantly garbed ladies and gentlemen who surrounded them, but the rosy hue of the younger woman's cheeks made the meaning of their words more than clear.

Lady Catherine Barrington, Countess of Arondale, watched their smiling departure, a little guilty for having overheard but curious nonetheless.

1

"I wonder, Amelia, who was it those women were talking about?" She surveyed the room once more, but couldn't decide which of the well-dressed men he was. "They seem to be quite taken with the gentleman under discussion."

Wearing a high-waisted white beaded gown that set off her pale complexion and unusual golden-red hair, Catherine swung her attention to Amelia Codrington Barrington, Baroness Northridge, her cousin Edmund's wife and Catherine's closest friend.

"They're such busybodies," Amelia said with irritation. "I don't know why they can't mind their own business."

"Tell me," Catherine persisted. "The way they keep tittering, it would seem he is all the vogue."

A servant walked past just then, a silver tray balanced on his shoulder, and the crystal beads on the chandelier above their heads jingled lightly. Across the marble floor, black-clad musicians played a lively roundelay, and through the doorway in the distance, several gentlemen sat playing cards at a green baize gaming table, smoke from their cigars curling thickly around their heads.

"They were speaking of Dominic Edgemont," Amelia told her. "Lord Nightwyck, heir to the Marquess of Gravenwold." Five years older than Catherine, Amelia smiled knowingly. "He's the man standing at the end of the ballroom beside that big gilt mirror."

Catherine's eyes searched the lavish salon, looking past silk-gowned women aglitter with flashing jewels and men in expensive frock coats and breeches. Ornate candelabra flickered against gold brocade walls while tables spread with silver and linen and laden with foodstuffs scented the air with a savory aroma. Trays of crystal champagne goblets sparkled like prisms to the left of the group she spotted near the mirror.

"Which one is he? There are at least a half-dozen people standing there."

"Nightwyck's the tall one. The man with the wavy black hair. He's really quite something, isn't he? Half the women in London have already fallen prey to his charms and the other half would if they weren't more than a trifle afraid of him."

Catherine located him instantly, since he towered over the others, but the man her cousin spoke of faced away from her. She could see only the back of his head, his hair a glistening blue-black that gleamed in the light of the candles, and the broad width of his shoulders, outlined perfectly by the cut of his immaculate black frock coat. High-ranking ladies and gentlemen of the *ton* stood around him, the women looking enraptured, the men more envious than amused.

"Do you know him?" Catherine asked, still unable to see him, but noting the skill with which Lady Wexford had maneuvered to a place at his elbow. Every few moments, she fluttered her hand-painted fan.

Amelia shrugged. "We've met on occasion. Nightwyck prefers the country, though he maintains his social obligations whenever he feels it necessary for propriety."

Elegant and statuesque, with short blond hair that framed a fine-boned face, Amelia Barrington had the kind of beauty Catherine envied. Six years ago, her cousin Edmund had fallen in love with Amelia practically on sight. They had a four-year-old son named Eddie whom Catherine adored.

"Is the gossip about him the truth?" she asked, watching the seductive glances cast his way by a dark-haired woman standing across from him.

"Of course not. But no one really knows much about him, and Nightwyck prefers to keep it that way. He's quite a catch, though. Intelligent, handsome, wealthy. At one time, your father hoped for a match between the two of you."

Catherine's head came up. "Surely Father didn't approach him."

"Only by subtle suggestion through a very close friend. Nightwyck wouldn't hear of it, of course. He says he's not interested in marriage to anyone. Now or ever."

"But he's bound to marry one day. If he's the marquess's heir, he'll have to." Until recently, Catherine's quiet life in the Devon countryside had kept her too busy for the London social whirl and quite well sheltered from the gossips. Though at nearly nineteen, she was a little bit older than she should have been, tonight was her coming-out ball, her first real introduction into the fashionable world of the *ton*.

"It's a long story," Amelia told her. "Since the two of you would hardly suit, it's really of no concern."

Catherine opened her mouth to pursue the subject, but Jeremy St. Giles approached to claim the dance she had promised. With a smile at the handsome young man she had only met that evening, Catherine accepted his arm.

"I was afraid you might have forgotten." Warm brown eyes moved over her face.

"I rarely forget a promise," she said simply.

Jeremy seemed pleased at that, smiling as he led her onto the dance floor. The heavily beaded train of her white silk gown, attached at her wrist, came up when she rested her hand on his shoulder. A gift from her uncle, the Duke of Wentworth, the gown fell in a straight line past her hips to the floor, the sleeves puffed softly, and the square neckline revealed the rounded tops of her high, full breasts.

"You look enchanting, Lady Arondale," Jeremy said, holding her as if she might break. "An absolute vision."

Catherine made an appropriate response to the flattery, though that was hardly the word she would choose to describe herself. She was not a fragile beauty like Amelia. Not slender and delicate, but ripe-figured, with a tiny waist and amply rounded curves.

Her skin was smooth and clear, except for a smattering of freckles across her nose, but her eyes were a little too large and a little too green, and her lips were a little too full. Even the simple braided coronet of her hair did nothing to disguise its thickness and striking golden-red color.

Enjoying the rhythm of the dance, Catherine smiled

politely as she whirled about the dance floor, catching an occasional glimpse of the two of them in the mirrors that lined the walls. But her thoughts kept drifting to the intriguing Lord Nightwyck. Again and again, she found herself searching for him, curious to see his face, but to her chagrin, she caught only a glimpse of his tall retreating figure as he disappeared out on the terrace.

"What is it, Dominic?" Rayne Garrick, Fourth Viscount Stoneleigh glanced from the tall dark man beside him to the wax-sealed envelope the slender sandy-haired footman had just brought in.

"A missive from Father." Dominic tore it open, slid out the letter, and scanned the finely scrawled words. "It says he's taken a turn for the worse, and I'm to attend him forthwith."

"Maybe this time it's true."

"And maybe horses can fly." Dominic's black brows drew together. "We both know it's just another of his attempts to control me. The man is nothing if not determined, I'll give him that."

"You're terribly hard on him, Dom. The man is old and sickly. Maybe he's trying to make up for all the years he ignored you."

Dominic worked a muscle in his jaw. His mouth, usually full and sensuous, narrowed to a thin, grim line. "And maybe he's twenty-eight years too late." Crumpling the note into a small ivory wad, he tossed it to the footman and started to walk away.

"Is there a reply, Your Lordship?" the boy called after him.

"I'll give him my reply in person." His expression hard, long brown fingers balled into fists, Dominic strode off in search of the cloakroom.

Rayne watched him go, noting several of the women who stopped him along the way. He grinned as he watched Dominic's skill in dealing with each, the prac-

ticed smiles, the words of flattery that could land him in
just about any lady's boudoir he set his mind to.

There was something about him women found fascinating. A dark, elusive quality they couldn't quite grasp.
Dominic tired of them easily, leaving them to pine away,
replaced by another for an equally short period of time.
The fact that none could hold him only seemed to entice
them more.

Rayne watched his friend quit the room, just missing
an encounter with the reigning beauty of the evening,
Lady Arondale. If her innocence hadn't been so obvious—
and her uncle so powerful—it might have been an inter-
esting contest with Nightwyck for the lady's attentions. As
it was, Dominic would probably be away for the balance
of the season, and the lovely young woman's all too obvious charms posed too much of a threat to Rayne's bach-
elorhood.

He watched her conversing with her cousin Edmund
and his pretty wife, Amelia. Rayne had never liked the slender, slightly effeminate, too-foppish man, though the
woman could be quite charming. He wondered if the
baron resented his young cousin's recent inheritance,
the earldom of Arondale, which would have been his had
her father not petitioned the crown to make Catherine his
legal heir. Whatever Northridge felt, he hid it well, for it
was obvious the girl was quite fond of him.

Rayne watched her a moment more, wondered at her
untried passions, and felt his body stir. With a soft sigh of
regret that neither he nor his friend would be the one to
sample her charms, he turned away from the innocent
temptation she posed and melted into the crowd.

"I believe Catherine's come-out has proved quite success-
ful," Amelia said.

Edmund Barrington, Baron Northridge, watched his
young cousin being led once more onto the dance floor.
Far different from his wife's fragile, patrician beauty, Catherine's small frame exuded a lush sensuality few men

could resist. All evening they'd been drawn to her like bees to a vibrant red blossom.

"She's caught the eye of three earls, a baron, and a duke," Edmund said. "Old Arondale would have been pleased. Too bad he couldn't have lived to arrange a match." Since the two had been raised together as children, Edmund had always been fond of Catherine, protective as a brother might be of a younger sister.

She was a sweet young thing, though always a bit too spirited. And she worried overly much for the people in her service. It was silly, really, such a sense of responsibility in one so young.

Edmund watched her now, her silvery laughter turning the heads of several young blades who stood nearby. As she passed by him, she smiled as if to say thank you for all he had done. Always, she had been close to him.

"She seems to like young St. Giles," Amelia said. "The way he keeps looking at her, he's bound to make an offer. A shame he's only the second son and not the heir."

Edmund nodded. "We must be careful. See only to Catherine's best interests." But then hadn't they always?

When her father, Christian Barrington, Earl of Arondale, had died, Catherine had begged Edmund and his family to come to Devon, to stay with her at the castle. They had gone to her, of course, since Catherine held the purse strings, and her uncle, the duke, had been pleased. Immersed in affairs of his own, Gilford Lavenham, Duke of Wentworth, had encouraged the relationship. With his sister, Catherine's mother, long dead, the duke believed Amelia would be a good influence, that a young girl needed an older woman's guidance.

The arrangement had suited everyone except Edmund, who loathed the country and missed the excitement of the city. Several months later, Edmund had finally prevailed in moving them into Catherine's London town house.

Her uncle the duke was ecstatic.

"It's time you found a husband," Wentworth said. "You've the Arondale name and estates to think of. When your father made you his heir, he expected you to marry and bear him a grandson."

Though Catherine in her innocence had blushed at the old duke's words, she agreed. "I could use your counsel in this," she said to him, sure her uncle would allow her great latitude in choosing a proper mate.

"Of course, my dear."

"Amelia and I will do our best to help you select wisely," Edmund had put in.

That was when he knew the end of his dreams loomed close at hand.

And that was the moment he determined to do something to stop it.

Catherine finished her first London season and rumor had it she was "all the vogue." Strangely enough, as the days wore on and she attended one soiree after another, endless costume balls, house parties, and nights at the theatre, she began to weary of all the excitement and yearn to go back to her simpler life at home.

By then she'd had several offers of marriage, men from the finest families in England, and there were a dozen other likely prospects. Still, none of them really stood out as the man she wished to marry. Instead, she begged her uncle to let her return to Arondale with Edmund and Amelia for the holidays, and Uncle Gil agreed—as long as she came back to London with the first likely break in the cold winter weather.

Now, as she crossed the floor of her bedchamber in her family's London town house, snuffed the light of the whale-oil lamp beside her big four-poster bed, and climbed wearily beneath the covers, she sighed to think of the days ahead.

Edmund, of course, was delighted to be back in the social whirl, but Catherine had found this evening's soiree just another round of endless flattery and meaningless conversation. And choosing a husband seemed more a matter of eliminating unsuitable prospects than finding a man with whom she could happily spend the rest of her life.

What about falling in love? she thought, staring bleakly up at the sculpted ceiling above her head. It was hard to believe she had actually imagined that could happen. Just because her father and mother had been in love, didn't mean it would happen to her. She had known that, accepted it as a possibility when she had accepted the responsibility of the Arondale title and fortunes, and yet . . .

Catherine sighed into the darkness. She needed a husband to produce an heir, and though Edmund and Amelia had been patient—even encouraged her to take plenty of time and make the right choice—sooner or later, she would have to accept the inevitable. Beyond that, the faster she made her decision, the sooner she could go home.

Lying beneath the satin counterpane, Catherine pulled the blankets up to her chin against the chill that had crept into the chamber. The fire in the hearth had burned low and her white cotton nightrail wasn't heavy enough to be much protection. Distantly, she knew she should ring for a servant to bring an extra blanket, but her mind was on her problems and their impending solution.

As the clock ticked into the silence, weariness slipped over her and Catherine's eyes closed. Once her breathing had slowed and her worries began to dim, the darkness and quiet in the room dragged her into a heavy slumber. Even when she heard a faint stirring, the creak of the inlaid parquet floor, she couldn't seem to force her eyes open.

Not until she felt rough, blunt fingers clamp over her mouth and the biting grip of a man's huge hand on her shoulder, jerking her up from the deep feather mattress.

God in heaven, what is happening! "Edmund!" Catherine cried out, but the man's callused palm muffled the sound. "Help me!" Fear sent her heart into a madly beating staccato. Catherine struggled wildly, thrashing her arms and legs, her green eyes wide and frightened.

"Quiet!" the man hissed, shaking her roughly in warning.

Whoever it was, he was big and strong, and even as she fought to twist free, her jaw exploded in pain. Catherine whimpered softly as the room began to spin; then the world around her faded, and darkness engulfed her.

Slumping into the arms of her attacker, her head falling limply against his shoulder, Catherine struggled no more.

Chapter Two

**Outside Sisteron, France
April 20, 1806**

CATHERINE PULLED THE ROUGH WOOLEN SHAWL more tightly around her against the biting chill of the wind. Beneath the thin fabric, her shoulders were bare above the low-cut neckline of her simple white peasant blouse. Strands of her thick golden-red hair whipped against her cheek as the wagon jolted into a pothole and she bounced against the stout, barrel-chested man who sat on the hard wooden seat beside her.

"Soon the weather will change," Vaclav promised. "In a few days it will begin to warm."

Catherine cast an eye to the gray clouds above that to her boded storm. "And pray tell, why is that?" she asked sarcastically, tired of the cold and the rain, but more tired still of Vaclav and his boorish manners and lust-filled glances.

The beefy man just shrugged his thick shoulders. "I tell you only that I can feel it. It is our way to know these things."

She wanted to argue, to say there was no way he could possibly know, but in the last eight weeks she had learned there were things Gypsies knew no one else did, things about the land and the weather. Things about the future.

Catherine straightened on the cold wooden seat and adjusted her full red skirts, pulling them down over her bare legs as far as she could. She wished she owned a pair of sturdy shoes instead of her thin leather sandals. But then most of them owned no shoes at all.

"We will reach my people soon," Vaclav told her, scratching his hairy chest through the opening of his frayed blue silk shirt. Over it he wore a moth-eaten sweater he had picked up along the road.

"We're nearly there?" Catherine's pulse picked up. She would have to make plans, preparations. She would have to start watching again for the chance to escape.

"They will be camped somewhere along the river. That is all I know."

It was as much as she would get from him. Gypsies never cared about exact time or place, had no desire to know even what month it was. They lived from day to day, moment to moment. She sighed thinking how much she had learned of them since the night eight weeks ago when someone had stolen into the bed-chamber of her town house, knocked her unconscious, and carried her away.

Catherine leaned back against the wooden seat of the *vardo*, the brightly painted, barrel-roofed house on wheels Vaclav lived in. In English, one of the many languages most of them spoke, he called it a caravan, so proud of it he fairly beamed when he looked at it. He was one of the richer Gypsies, one who no longer lived in a tent.

More and more, he'd once told her, his people had begun to build and live in the wagons. They were warmer in winter, tighter against the rain. She should be grateful, he had said. Once they were married, the *vardo* would provide a wide comfortable bed for the two of them.

Catherine's stomach tightened. How much longer before he found out the truth? That she had no intention of marrying him and never had. That it had been just a ploy, a trick of survival. One among many she had learned in the last few soul-crushing weeks.

She thought of the beatings she had taken, the miles she had walked, shoeless, her tender feet bloody and torn from the sharp stones that cut through skin unused to going without protection. She thought of the cruelty of the women, who treated her as an outcast, a servant, little more than a slave.

Most times, she could scarcely remember her life as a pampered young lady, or see the faces of people who had once been her family and friends. That was another time, another world. *The present is all that matters,* she told herself. *Don't think of the past. Let it slip away.*

Again and again, she had fought back her tears, which at first had been endless. But she had learned quickly all they earned her were beatings, or a night without something to eat. Now they refused to come at all, and for that Catherine was grateful.

She would survive, she had vowed as she faced each agonizing day moving farther and farther away from the home and family she loved. No matter what she must endure, she would live to return to England. She would discover who was responsible for her abduction, for her sale to the Gypsies, and she would make him pay.

"Domini! Leave the horses and come in to supper. I have fixed you a nice hare soup."

His mother stood on the edge of the shallow depression, her small weathered hands resting on the bright yellow skirt that hung on her tiny, too-slim frame. *She looks so much older this year,* he thought, wondering for the first time how many more winters the fragile old woman would live and feeling a sudden tightness in his chest at the thought.

He would miss her when she was gone. He would miss this way of life.

With a wave in her direction, Dominic tethered the dappled gray mare alongside the string of horses grazing among the trees at the edge of the grassy meadow where his people had camped, and started walking toward her.

The night air felt chilly and damp, but the days would soon warm. Already through the flat gray clouds, he could see the twinkling of stars, harbingers of sunny days ahead. At least the break in the weather would ease his mother's aches and pains, the weariness he could see in her eyes.

"You will go to Yana tonight?" she asked him when he reached her side and they moved through the tall grass back toward the wagon.

Dominic arched a thick black brow. "Since when have my nights with Yana become your concern?" A hint of amusement laced his voice. Would she ever stop seeing him as the small boy who tugged at her skirts?

"Yana sets her snare for you. She is not worthy."

Dominic smiled indulgently. "Always so protective. You worry for nothing, Mother. The woman warms my bed, but I have no plans for *rommerin.*"

"That is what you say now, but she wants marriage, and she is clever, that one. Just ask Antal, her first husband."

Dominic's smile grew thin. "No wench is that clever. Besides, she knows I'll soon be leaving."

His mother's weathered face looked suddenly older, her thin gray brows drawing together over wrinkle-creased eyes. "I will miss you, my son. But as always, it is for the best."

She had been saying that since he was a child of thirteen. Since his father had come for him. She'd been saying the marquess's English blood was stronger than that of his Gypsy mother, that it called to him and he must obey.

For a short time he had hated her for it.

Now, fifteen years later, it seemed to Dominic that his mother had been right.

He moved to the fire, which blazed orange and yellow into the darkness of the night, warmed himself a moment, then sat down on a small wooden bench he had fashioned from a fallen tree several years earlier. His mother placed the steaming bowl of soup in his hands, and the heat eased the stiffness from his icy fingers.

At Gravenwold, his father's palatial estate in Bucking-hamshire, being cold was never a problem. Nor was an empty belly or escaping the winds and the rain. Yet here, in the chill and damp of Provence, camped beneath the towering granite citadel of Sisteron, Dominic knew a peacefulness he never felt in England.

He would miss it when he went back home.

Catherine spotted the distant flickering lights of a dozen campfires, glowing red embers bright against the black-ness of the night. An occasional melancholy sigh of violin drifted on the currents of the wind. Gypsies. The Pin-doros—traders of horses. Vaclav had told her about his people when he had bartered her away from that other wandering band.

"I have bought you," he had said that first night. "You belong to me now." Dressed in baggy, coarse brown breeches and a tattered, cast-off linen shirt, he ran a sau-sage-thick finger along her cheek and Catherine shivered.

"You are full of passion and heat"—he stroked her heavy flame-red hair—"like Mithra, goddess of fire and water. I desire you above all others—tonight I will take you to my bed."

Catherine stepped away from him. "I will not go," she said with a bravado she used to protect herself but didn't really feel.

When Vaclav moved toward her, Catherine fought him—like a tigress. Scratching and clawing, kicking and screaming, calling him vile unladylike names that only weeks before she wouldn't have believed could cross her lips. Vaclav slapped her, threatened to beat her, but still she would not submit.

"I'll not lie with you like some harlot whose favors you have purchased. I will sleep only with the man who is my husband."

His eyes roamed over the curves of her body, all too

clearly displayed by her scoop-necked blouse and simple gathered skirt. "If it is a husband you want, then I will marry you."

"You would marry a *Gadjo*?" A non-gypsy. It was unheard of, she knew. The Rom were a world unto themselves. Outsiders were not accepted.

Vaclav's thoughts seemed to mirror her own. For a moment he looked uncertain. Then his wide jaw tightened and his eyes grew dark. "This I will do, if you will willingly come to my bed."

Catherine's mind whirred with possibilities. If she agreed to the marriage, maybe she could keep him away a little longer, gain a little more precious time. "What about your parents? Your family? Surely you would want them to attend the wedding?"

"Even now we are traveling to meet them. Two weeks' journey, maybe three. The wedding could take place at Sisteron."

Sisteron. Southwest. Far away from the Turkish pashas of Constantinople. Away from the white slavery she had been meant for. Closer to England and home. "Then I accept your offer. Once we're married, I will do as you wish. Until then, you must promise not to touch me."

Vaclav had grudgingly agreed. The days had flown by and he had kept his word. If only she could keep hers.

"Pindoros," he said, snapping her thoughts from the past. "We are almost there."

"Yes," Catherine whispered. *Love of God, what would she do now?* She'd have to tell him the truth before he revealed his marriage plans to his family. He'd be madder than ever if she caused him to lose face with his people.

Catherine's stomach balled into a hard tight knot. What would he do when he found out he'd been duped? He'd be angry. Furious. He would take her, she was sure, with or without her permission. She could almost feel his blunt hands on her breasts, his thick, hairy body thrusting brutally between her legs.

If only she could have run, found some means of escape.

But there had been no place to go, and he had watched her, kept her tied to the wagon at night. There'd been no time then. There wasn't time now.

The wagon rumbled toward the camp, the wooden wheels churning up mud that puddled on the road. A dozen ragged children and several barking dogs raced up to greet them, heedless of the chill in the air or the wet black earth beneath their shoeless feet. Feathery plumes of thin white smoke rose up from cook fires in front of each wagon.

"We will make camp in the trees, away from the others," Vaclav said with a look she could only describe as hungry. "As soon as we are settled, we will seek out my family and tell them the news of our wedding."

As soon as they were settled, Catherine would tell Vaclav news of her own—that there would be no wedding. She looked at his bulky arms and shoulders, remembered the feel of his heavy hand when she had angered him before. His fury would go unchecked this time. Catherine shuddered at the thought.

Dominic stretched full length on his comfortable eiderdown mattress in the back of his *vardo*. He and his mother had the finest wagons money could buy. In fact all of the people in his tribe had benefited from his great wealth in one way or another. He'd had to do it with subtlety, of course. They would hardly accept his charity. Just a gift here and there, something someone "found" and claimed as his own.

Dominic admired them for it. They didn't need riches to be happy. They had their freedom. It was the greatest wealth of all.

He stirred in the wagon, hearing some distant sound he couldn't quite discern. It was faint, at first, just the merest whisper in the breeze. There it was again, louder this time. He could have sworn it was the voice of a woman.

Dominic swung his long legs to the floor of the wagon, grabbed his full-sleeved white homespun shirt, and pulled his boots on over his tight black breeches. Jerking open the door to the wagon, he descended the stairs to the ground and made his way across the short space between the wagons. His mother stood over the cooking fire in front of her own wagon, stirring a big black kettle of *gulyás*, a rich meat stew. The aroma wafted toward him, and his stomach gnawed with hunger.

"Supper is almost ready," his mother said. Usually they ate before darkness fell, but tonight Pearsa had been tending a sick child, and Dominic had been working with one of his horses.

"Did you hear someone?" he asked. "I thought I heard voices down near the stream."

"Vaclav has returned," his mother said simply, stirring the bubbling stew. It smelled of herbs and spices and the venison he had brought into camp.

"He usually camps near his parents. Why—"

Voices raised in anger, one male, one distinctly female, drifted through the chill night air, cutting off his words. "He was traveling alone when he left," Dominic said, the statement clearly a question.

His mother glanced away. "He journeys with a woman now." There was something furtive in her manner, the way her eyes kept sliding away, that made Dominic uneasy.

"What woman?" he asked. Just then came her high-pitched scream. The voices grew louder, one pleading, the other raised in fury. The sound of a hand against flesh echoed across the clearing, and Dominic tensed. "He beats her."

"She belongs to him. It is his right."

It occurred to him then that the two were arguing in English. *English*, not French, or Romany, the language of his people. Dominic started walking in the direction of the sound, away from the circle of wagons, close to where his horses were tied.

"Do not go, my son." Thin gold bracelets jangling, Pearsa hurried to his side and caught his arm. "This is none of your concern."

"If you know of this, then tell me."

"She is a *Gadjo*. They are saying that she is a witch."

Dominic started walking again, Pearsa's small bent frame hurrying to keep up with his long-legged strides.

"Remember your promise. You must not interfere."

Dominic just kept walking.

"She has already bewitched Vaclav. She might bewitch you, too."

He openly scoffed. Years ago he might have believed it, but endless hours of schooling had wiped out most of his superstitions. "I won't interfere. I just want to see what's going on. Go back to our camp. I'll join you there soon."

Pearsa watched after him, wringing her gnarled old hands as he strode off into the darkness. He could feel her eyes on his back, feel her censure—and her worry—but still he kept walking. A true Gypsy would have ignored the sounds, privacy of utmost value among those who had none, and the fact that he could not made Dominic's features turn hard.

Moving with a stealth that came as naturally as breathing, he walked past the horses with only a calming word or two, and finally reached Vaclav's wagon. From the darkness beside it, he stared across the clearing, past the small fire which had burned to low red embers, mesmerized by the scene unfolding before his eyes.

The stout, hairy Gypsy he had known since childhood stood over a beautiful flame-haired woman who glared at him with a mixture of loathing and defiance. Vaclav's shirt hung in tatters, his hair, shaggy and mussed, fell into his dark brooding eyes, and his heavy-browed face was distorted with rage.

A few feet away, the woman faced him squarely, her small hands bound at the wrists, feet splayed, her eyes locked with his. Her fiery hair tumbled around her shoulders while her blouse, torn and dirty, exposed all but the peaks of her high, lush breasts. Even the imprint of Vaclav's hand across her cheek couldn't disguise the beauty of her face.

"You lied to me!" he roared. "You meant to cheat me of that which I bartered with every last ounce of my gold!"

"I've told you a dozen times, I can get you money, more gold than you can carry, if you'll just let me go."

"What a fool you must think me." Vaclav slapped her again; she stumbled but did not fall.

Dominic's stomach tightened, but he didn't move. Half of him was Gypsy. He must abide by Gypsy law.

"I do not want your money!" Vaclav shouted. "It is your body I burn for. I have offered you marriage. You have refused me, shamed me in front of my people. Now you will learn to obey."

Grabbing her bound wrists, he dragged the woman toward a tree. Dominic stood transfixed as Vaclav draped a length of rope over a limb, secured her hands to it, and hoisted her up until her arms stretched high above her head. He grabbed the back of her blouse and roughly tore it open, exposing the palest, smoothest skin Dominic had ever seen.

"You will learn to heed my commands. You will learn to submit. If it takes the taste of the lash, then so it will be."

Dominic's mouth went dry. If Vaclav owned the woman, it was his right to discipline her as he saw fit. Dominic's hand tightened around the wheel of the wagon, but still he did not move.

Vaclav turned to retrieve the long leather whip he used to command his horses, and the woman's eyes, a bright, clear green, seemed to burn into his back just as the lash would soon burn into hers.

"I'll never submit, do you hear me! I loathe you and every foul Gypsy I have ever met! You're animals—all of you. All you know is cruelty and violence." Her voice broke on the last word, but she stiffened her small shoulders against the first whirring crack of the lash.

A thin line of blood appeared, marring the perfect whiteness of her skin, but she made no protest, only pressed her face against the rough tree bark with a look of resignation.

When her heavy fringed lashes slid closed against the pain she knew would come, the last slender thread of Dominic's control snapped. He stepped from beside the wagon just in time to catch the second brutal thrust of Vaclav's whip.

He forced himself under control. "It would seem, my friend, that you are having some difficulty subduing your woman." He spoke the words in English, continuing to converse as they had. Though he managed a cordial note in his tone, it took an iron control not to yank the whip from Vaclav's hands.

The stout man whirled to face him. "Stay out of this, Domini, this is none of your concern."

"I merely came to extend a welcome. It has been some time since we traveled the same road."

"The time for greeting is not now. As you can see, I have others matters to attend."

"So it seems." But he made no move to leave.

"The woman deserves a beating," Vaclav added, but part of him seemed uncertain, and even a little defeated.

"That may be true. If she is yours, you are certainly within your rights to do with her as you wish."

"Then why do you interfere?"

"I thought I might be of help. Maybe there is another way for you to solve your problem." Dominic shrugged his shoulders in a thinly veiled gesture of nonchalance. "But of course you are not interested in gold."

For the second time Vaclav seemed hesitant. He glanced to the woman tied to the tree, and Dominic read his conflicting emotions. He didn't really want to hurt her, but she had left him no choice. Unless he taught her obedience, he would lose face among his peers.

"I thought maybe—for a considerable profit—you might rid yourself of your burden."

Vaclav looked at the woman and the hunger he felt for

her glittered in the depths of his eyes. The woman spat at his feet.

"How much of a profit?" Vaclav asked.

"I'll give you twice what you paid for her."

"A king's ransom. The red-haired witch has cost me a fortune in gold."

She looked to be worth it. "Three times," Dominic said softly.

"You buy trouble, Domini. More than you will ever know."

"I'll take my chances. I offer four times the price you paid."

Vaclav's face, already flushed with anger, reddened even more. "You and your money. You can buy anything you want, eh, *didikai?*"

It was an ugly Gypsy word—half *Gadjo*, half Romany. Always an outsider fighting for acceptance. As a child, Dominic had heard it often, but over the years he had earned a place among his people and he heard it no more. Now it pierced his insides like a scythe.

"You want the woman?" Vaclav taunted. "I will sell her to you for six times the price I have paid."

It was a challenge, a cruel reminder of his heritage. No true Gypsy could have afforded such a price. Dominic fixed his eyes on the girl. Over one pale shoulder, she watched him warily. Blood from the whip had darkened what little remained of her blouse and the leather ties she hung from bit cruelly into her wrists. His mother had been right—he should not have come. Now he could not walk away.

"Done," he said. "Cut the woman down."

Vaclav smiled in triumph, and Dominic felt bitter resentment well up inside him. Vaclav had won and both of them knew it.

"Your *Gadjo* blood makes you weak," he prodded, knowing none of the others would have stopped him. Romany men believed in absolute domination of their women. So did Dominic. He just didn't believe in using force to get it.

Vaclav tossed him a knife, the blade glistening in the light of the fire. "She is yours now. You cut her down."

Dominic closed the distance between himself and the woman, and used the knife to slice through her bonds. She stumbled and swayed against him. Dominic's arm went around her tiny waist to hold her up.

"Don't touch me!" Jerking free, she backed away.

Dominic grabbed her chin and forced her to look at him. "You had better learn to curb that wayward tongue of yours," he said, recalling several oaths he had heard her throw at Vaclav. "You're through giving orders. You belong to me now; you'll learn to do as I say."

"Go to hell!"

"Very likely. But it won't be you who sends me there." Dominic turned and started walking. When she didn't fall in behind him, he paused to look at her. "I own you, but the choice is yours. You may stay here with Vaclav or you may come with me."

Catherine's eyes ran from the top of the Gypsy's raven-black hair to the toes of his scuffed black boots. Eyes the color of obsidian bored into her. He stood so tall she had to crane her neck to see his face. When she did, it occurred to her, as it had the moment he had stepped into the clearing, that as hard as he looked, she had never seen a more handsome man.

Without waiting for an answer, he turned his back and walked away. Shoulders the width of an axe handle, narrow hips, and long muscular legs disappeared into the darkness surrounding the wagon. Catherine took one last look at Vaclav, who still clutched the whip in a blunt hairy hand, and hurried into the woods behind him.

"Get into the wagon."

Catherine eyed him warily. "I don't care how much you paid for me. I won't lie with you any more than I would him."

The tall Gypsy's eyes ran over her, burning into her with an intensity that sent a hand to her breast to pull the torn peasant blouse more closely around her.

"If I wish it, little one, you will lie with me. Make no mistake about that. But if you do, it won't be at the threat of a whipping."

Then it will never happen, she thought, but didn't say so. She had learned the hard way that arguing with these people did no good, nor did pleading, nor did tears.

"Get in," he repeated.

"Why?"

"So I can tend to the wound on your back."

It burned like the fires of Hades. What would it have felt like if Vaclav had continued with the beating?

Catherine climbed the wooden stairs and sat down on a soft, wide eiderdown mattress. "Vaclav called you Domini. Is that your name?"

He turned her so her back faced toward him. "One of them. Dominic is another." Just the single word. Names meant as little to them as time or place. Most had two or three which they might change when someone died or married—or was wanted by the law. "And you?" he asked.

"Catherine."

"Catherine," he repeated. "Catrina. It suits you, I think." Long brown fingers slid across her back, spreading something thick and sticky.

The pain receded at once, and Catherine sighed with relief.

"How did you come to be with him?" he asked.

"He bought me from a caravan of Gypsies traveling north of here. Vaclav offered them a fat price and they took it."

His hand stopped moving. "You speak well; you're obviously no peasant. What was an English woman doing alone in the north of France in time of war?"

"You're not French, either. And your English is quite remarkable. I could ask the same of you."

"I am Gypsy," he said simply. "We are at war with no one. For you it's different."

"I wasn't in France. I was in England." If only she could tell him the truth, ask him to help her. But she had tried that before. For a price, the northern Gypsies had promised the man who had abducted her that they would carry her far from England—they weren't about to let her go.

Others she had told—including Vaclav—hadn't believed her story. They had called her "my lady wench" and "her high and mightiness." It had only made her life a whole lot harder.

She thought of how she looked in her ragged peasant clothes, her hair wildly disheveled, her bosom half exposed. She looked about as much like the Countess of Arondale as the old woman bent over the cooking fire outside. She could almost hear the tall Gypsy's laughter, and the thought of it squeezed a tightness in her stomach.

"I ran away from home," she lied. "A man took me prisoner and sold me to the Gypsies." *That part was true.* "There was a pasha in Constantinople who had a taste for pale-skinned women and apparently he paid very well."

White slavery. It was better than being dead—or at least that was what the man who had taken her believed. He had a conscience of sorts. "Vaclav had money, a great deal of it." *Probably stolen.* "He offered it to them and they took it." Selling her to another Gypsy wasn't the same as letting her go, they had reasoned.

"And all this time you've kept him out of your bed?" Dominic eyed her from top to bottom in a way that made the heat rush into her cheeks. "No wonder he went a little crazy."

She ignored his comment, refusing to be led in that direction. "Vaclav's gone, now it's you I'm forced to deal with. What will happen to me now?"

What indeed, Dominic thought. The last thing he needed was a woman. At least one he owned. He'd be gone in just a few more weeks, returning to his life in England. Back to duties, responsibilities. He didn't need any more.

"That depends upon you, I suppose. For now, I suggest you get some sleep. You look as though you could use it."

She eyed him like a wary kitten. "Here?"

"I think you'll find it comfortable."

"Where will you be sleeping?"

"On the ground beside the wagon." Dominic assessed the woman's smooth white skin, her tiny waist and ample breasts. "Unless you're inviting me to stay in here with you."

Green eyes, bright as emeralds, narrowed in irritation. "I told you before, I won't willingly lie with you or any other man."

Dominic chuckled, amused more than he should have been by her defiance. He had never seen a woman quite like her—all fiery will and determination. Certainly not an Englishwoman. She was a tempting package indeed, one that intrigued him more by the minute.

"We will see, fire kitten. We will see."

She moved just then and her tattered white blouse fell open, revealing the underside of one ripe breast. It looked heavy and smooth, rounded perfectly to fit a man's hand. Dominic's groin tightened. He'd sleep on the ground, all right—after a tumble with Yana to ease the powerful ache he'd begun to feel.

"I'll see you get something to eat," he said, his voice a little husky.

"Thank you."

Taking a pouch of gold coins from one of his trunks, Dominic left the wagon to settle his debt with Vaclav. His mother stopped him at the edge of the circle of firelight.

"You have bought Vaclav's woman." Pearsa eyed the pouch with a look of accusation. "What will you do with her?"

"I haven't quite decided."

"She is trouble. I can feel it. You should not have interfered."

Dominic's jaw tightened. He thought of the beautiful flame-haired woman in the wagon. Thought of how good she would feel moving beneath him, her shapely legs locked around him. He thought of how much Vaclav had wanted that same thing.

"I know," was all he said.

Extend to me the hand so small,
Wherein I see thee weep,
For O thy balmy teardrops all
I would collect and keep.

Gypsy Poem
George Borrow

Chapter Three

CATHERINE FINISHED THE LAST of the stew the old woman brought her, grateful for an end to the gnawing in her stomach. Afterward, she climbed beneath the bright patchwork quilt that covered the soft eiderdown mattress, comfortable and warm for the first time in weeks.

Her eyes searched the interior of the wagon lit by the warm glow of a candle. Cupboards lined each side of the *vardo*, and everything was neatly put away. A full-sleeved, frayed homespun shirt hung on a peg beside one of shiny red silk. A yellow silk scarf, a worn pair of black breeches, and a vest stitched from bright scraps of gold-embroidered tapestry, a row of small gold coins glittering on the front, hung nearby.

The *vardo* looked like others she had seen, only neater and cleaner, and built of penny-farthing boards so that it fit more tightly together. The only thing that seemed out of place were the several leather-bound books jammed in a slot beside the carving of a tiny wooden horse.

Since Gypsies couldn't read, why had he bought them? Or more likely, stolen them? She wondered, too, if the intriguing man named Domini had carved the small wooden horse.

Catherine blew out the candle, rolled to her side, and stared into the darkness inside the wagon. Her eyelids felt heavy, her body bruised and fatigued, but she dared not fall asleep. Instead she listened to every small sound outside, waiting for the footsteps of the man she was certain would come.

Why had he bought her, if not to warm his bed?

Catherine jumped at the hoot of an owl, then lay back with a sigh of relief when she realized what it was. Occasional laughter drifted across the camp from distant wagons, but it slowly faded away. As the night wore on, she identified the snorting of the horses, the last crackling embers of the fire, but no man's footsteps came. Just before dawn, she finally fell asleep, only to be awakened at first light by the tall Gypsy's husky male voice.

"The sun moves high, Catrina. Rouse yourself—unless you want company." He jerked open the low wooden door and Catherine bolted upright, tugging the covers up to her chin.

"Do you always barge in on a lady in her bed?"

"Not always," he replied with a rakish smile, "but often enough to find the pastime pleasant." His eyes raked her, taking in her disheveled appearance, the smudges beneath her eyes, the tightness around her mouth that betrayed her sleepless hours. "You look worse than you did last night. You didn't find my bed to your liking?"

Catherine bristled, her chin coming up, but a hand lifted self-consciously to shove back strands of her sleep-tousled hair. "I was afraid you would try to . . . I thought you might change your mind about our sleeping arrangements."

He certainly didn't look any the worse for wear, she thought. In fact he looked very well rested indeed. He had the most incredible features: straight Aryan nose, smooth dark skin, and thick-lashed obsidian eyes. His mouth could have been carved in stone, it looked so perfectly sculpted, and when he smiled, he flashed the whitest teeth she had ever seen.

"Disappointed?" he mocked, arching a heavy black brow. He was handsome, but not in the usual sense. There was an overall hardness about him, a leashed quality she had sensed from the start. It only made him more attractive.

"Hardly."

Dominic smiled as if he didn't believe her. Such arrogance! But then he was a Gypsy.

"There's a pitcher and basin of water in the cupboard on your left." He tossed her a blouse much like the one Vaclav had torn up, this one brightly embroidered. "My mother has coffee, bread, and *brynza*—sheep cheese. Make yourself ready and join us."

She held up the blouse. "Your mother's?" It looked much too big for such a frail little woman.

Dominic flashed a smile of amusement. Today he wore a silver earring in one ear. "I borrowed it from a friend. Would you like me to help you put it on?"

"Certainly not!"

"Then I suggest you hurry. If you're not out here by the time I finish my coffee, I intend to come back in." With a last bold glance, he turned and left the wagon.

Catherine hurriedly rolled from the bed, tugged off the tattered remains of her blouse, and quickly pulled on the clean one. At first she had been scandalized by the lack of clothing the Gypsies wore, just a skirt and blouse with no undergarments at all. In winter, they merely layered several sets of clothing one on top of another to keep them warm. It all seemed perfectly sensible now.

Using her fingers to work the tangles from her hair, Catherine washed her face, did her best to smooth out her wrinkled red skirts, and descended the stairs from the wagon.

"Much better," Dominic exclaimed with a look of approval. "You may find some privacy off to your left." He glanced in that direction.

Grateful he had understood her need, Catherine walked off that way and completed her ablutions. She knew better than to try to escape. That was no easy task, alone and penniless, and unsure even which way to go. Instead she returned to the camp, and Dominic handed her a blackened tin cup filled with steaming hot coffee.

"Later today," he said, "after you've helped my mother with her tasks, you will rest. Tomorrow you'll feel better." He smiled at the frail old woman. "This is Pearsa, my mother. I expect you to do whatever she tells you."

Pearsa said nothing, just flashed her a look so cold it could have frozen stones. Another hateful old hag, Catherine thought. She could almost feel the bite of the willow switch slicing across her back and legs.

Not this time, she vowed. She was stronger now, not frightened as she had been in the beginning. Then she had been just an innocent young girl, too terrified to stand up to them. But during the months since she had been forced to leave her home, she had changed. She had lost her innocence, all but one last remaining vestige, but she had learned to survive.

"If she tries to beat me, I shall fight her," Catherine warned, thinking of others who had treated her badly. Better to let them know where she stood right from the start.

Dominic eyed her a moment, then set his tin coffee cup down and crossed to the place in front of her. He tipped her chin with his hand.

"No one here is going to hurt you. You just do your share of the work and stay out of trouble. At night you may sleep in peace." The long-boned fingers beneath her chin moved upward across her cheek, cupping her face and sending a tremor of warmth along her spine. "When I'm ready to claim what is mine, you will know."

Dominic caught her sharp intake of breath, the rosy flush that colored her cheeks, and found her responses enchanting. He almost smiled. Though it hadn't been his intention when he bought her, claim her he would—sooner or later. Every time he looked at her, he felt his body stir. There was something about her. Something different. Fascinating.

Last night in Yana's arms, his hardness thrusting inside her, it was the flame-haired woman he thought of. The flame-haired woman he wanted. Where had she come from? What secrets did she keep?

That she had suffered at the hands of his people was becoming more and more apparent. Some tribes were more violent than others, some stole more, some strayed farther outside the law. And after the hundreds of years of the prejudice the Rom had suffered, all of them feared and hated outsiders. A *Gadjo* woman, bought and paid for, might be treated worse than a slave.

He looked at her now, eating the bread and cheese, sipping the sweet black coffee, and watching him furtively from beneath her heavy lashes, their color far darker than the fiery shade of her hair. He could see the tops of her high round breasts, gauge the narrow span of her waist, guess closely at the fullness of her bottom. When her lips parted to accept a bite of cheese, her small pink tongue touched the corner of her mouth, and Dominic felt the blood rush through his veins. His body tightened, and a sharp ache pulled at his loins.

How many men had taken her already? Used her brutally with no regard for her pleasure? Surely more than a few men had fallen prey to such splendid temptation.

He would have to go easy with her, let her get used to the idea of sharing his bed. He would give her some time, not much because he had so little remaining. Just enough to ease her fears and let her warm to him.

Dominic had no doubt he could bed her—quite willingly.

After all, *Gadjo* or Gypsy, she was only a woman.

Catherine worked beside the old Gypsy, gathering firewood, scrubbing pots and pans, mending a handful of well-worn clothing. She didn't mind the tasks, in fact she had come to enjoy the small daily chores that made her feel useful. She stretched against an ache in her back, reached over and plucked a small yellow wildflower from a clump near the base of a tree. When she straightened, she saw the old woman watching.

"You may pick some if you like," Pearsa said. "My son enjoys them, too." That the woman spoke English came as little surprise, since most of them spoke several languages besides their own. Their wanderings took them through many different countries. It was necessary for them to move easily from place to place.

"These are the first I've seen." Catherine sniffed the delicate petals, then bent to gather several more stalks.

Pearsa merely grunted and walked away, leaving Catherine alone. Which was just as well, since the old woman's words about her son had sent Catherine's thoughts in that direction. She couldn't imagine the handsome, arrogant Gypsy enjoying a bouquet of flowers. He was probably just as hard and cruel as the others she had known. She remembered the words he had spoken, the way he had looked at her. *When I'm ready to claim what is mine, you will know.*

Catherine shivered, and not with the cold. Traveling with the caravan to the north, she had been protected by the Gypsies' lust for gold. To the Turkish pasha, an untried woman commanded a small fortune, and they were determined to claim the reward.

And Vaclav had been easily duped, a feat she wasn't really proud of but a necessity just the same.

This one, this dark mysterious Gypsy, was something else entirely. She had known this morning—without the slightest doubt—that he meant to take her to his bed. No man had ever looked at her the way he did. No man had ever made bending her to his will sound so easy.

And he was far too intelligent to fall for her trickery. She could see it in his bold dark eyes, feel it in the way he gauged her every movement.

Until this latest turn of events, Catherine considered in a way she had been lucky. Though she had been cruelly abused, she was no longer destined for a life of white slavery, and her virtue remained intact, a prize she would one day offer to her husband—once she returned to England. She had been lucky; *bahtalo,* the Gypsies called it.

But one glance across the clearing to where the danger-ous-looking man called Domini worked patiently with his horses, and Catherine knew her luck was about to run out.

As Dominic had ordered, Catherine napped all afternoon and awoke feeling stronger than she had in weeks. She ate some cold venison the old woman gave her, freshened her-self at the stream, and felt a growing readiness to face the challenge of making her way back home.

It would be difficult, she knew, nearly impossible. But she was no longer guarded every moment, or bound to the wagon at night. If she kept a watchful eye, waited, and prayed, sooner or later she was sure to find a chance to escape.

It came even sooner than she had hoped.

At dusk the following evening, a tinker rolled into the *kumpania*, the campsite, hoping to sell a few of his wares or sharpen some knives or scissors. Green paint peeled from the sides of his wagon, the once-bright sign of his trade now faded and old, but the wheels looked sturdy and the mule was sound.

"Armand is *Romane Gadjo*," Dominic told her, walking to where she stood watching from the edge of the meadow. "He and old Jozsef are friends." Most travelers didn't venture near the Gypsy encampments, but this man was many years on the road and apparently he knew their leader. "Come. We'll see what he has to offer."

Dominic flashed one of his winsome white smiles and took Catherine's hand. His fingers looked long and dark, gripping hers. She could feel their warmth and strength as he helped her step over the wagon tongue.

When she glanced up at his profile, she noticed the way the firelight outlined the hard planes and valleys of his face, giving him that hard-edged, dangerous look she had noticed before. His features were stronger than most of the English men she had known, his skin darker and smoother. In fact everything about Dominic seemed larger and more powerful than any man she had ever known.

"Domini! Bring the *Gadjo* woman. It is time we got a look at your prize."

Dominic led her in the direction of the man's reedy voice. Ducking beneath a rope strung between two wagons and draped with tattered but freshly washed clothes, they stopped in front of a group of people that included a tall, gaunt older man; a flat-faced, obese woman with a downy mustache; and a young pregnant girl. All sat laughing and talking around a small warm fire.

"Catrina, this is Jozsef, our leader," Dominic said, "his wife, Czinka, and his daughter-in-law, Medela."

"Hello." Catherine forced an uncertain smile. All of them merely assessed her, their dark eyes running the length of her, then returning to her face. Not her face, she realized, her hair.

"*Bala kameskro,*" Jozsef said with what seemed approval. "Maybe she will bring us good fortune."

"What does *bala kam . . . kam—*"

"*Bala kameskro—*" Dominic repeated. "Translated, it means *sun-haired,* but to us it means *red-haired,* a red-haired woman. It's believed to bring good luck."

Now that she thought about it, once during her time with the northern Gypsies, someone had approached her while she slept and cut off a lock of her hair. For luck she now understood, though at the time she'd been torn between anger and fear.

The pregnant girl came forward and touched the heavy golden-red mass almost with reverence, her hand stroking slowly down the thick, shiny strands. The woman's long black hair, like that of her mother-in-law and every other married woman, was covered by a scarf, a *diklo,* which she tied at the back of her neck.

"It is very beautiful," Medela said as a heavy burnished curl wrapped itself around her finger. She smiled softly, almost shyly, so unlike the other Gypsy women Catherine had known.

"Thank you." Catherine's eyes swung to Dominic's. "If she would like, I could cut some off and give it to her."

A warm smile touched his face. "Medela would be pleased." Dominic looked pleased as well, his features less severe as he watched her in the firelight.

"If you would do this, I would wear it here, against the child," Medela said, patting her swollen belly.

Dominic propped his boot on the wagon tongue, reached inside the top, and slid out a slender, bone-handled knife. "Turn around."

Catherine didn't like the gleam of the wicked-looking blade, but did as he told her. Dominic lifted away the top strands of her hair and sliced off a small lock from beneath. He handed the hair to Medela, who fairly beamed.

"*Mandi pazzorrhus,*" she said, "I am in your debt."

Czinka shifted her huge girth, jingling the bells that dangled from her fat-lobed ears, her full skirts bunching around her hips. "It may yet be that the price you have paid was not too high after all," she said to Dominic, who looked uncomfortable at the reminder, but made no reply.

The four of them talked of the weather, of the warming that would soon ease their days, of the coming horse fair to which they would journey, and finally of Armand the tinker's arrival.

"As always, he comes to sell us his cheap wares for too high a price," said Jozsef, but there was affection in his voice.

"It will be good to see him again," Dominic put in.

They said their farewells, and Dominic once more took her hand, his grip warm and solid as he led her off toward the tinker. The Frenchman's wagon sat a goodly distance across the meadow, surrounded by Gypsy men and women engaged in lively bartering. Several mangy dogs yapped and frolicked nearby.

"Domini!" the old man called out to him. "It has been too many years, *mon ami.*" The little man grinned, exposing a mouthful of rotting teeth, but his smile was one of friendship, and Dominic responded with a warm smile of his own.

"You have not changed," Dominic told him in the same

French the tinker used. "You are still the only *Gadjo* who could ever outwit the Gypsy." The two men laughed and spoke of the past as if it had been merely days.

Catherine felt Dominic's hand at her waist, his touch lightly possessive. When she tried to move away, his hold tightened and he flashed her a cool look of warning.

"You have taken a wife, I see," said the tinker. "It is certainly way past time."

Dominic's hand fell away. "She is English," he said, as if that should be explanation enough. "She is not my wife."

Merely my possession were the unspoken words, and Catherine stiffened. *You may think so, but you are wrong.*

"How long will you camp with us?" Dominic asked.

"I cannot stay. I eat and drink with Jozsef, listen to Ithal play his violin, then I go. I have business in Arles that cannot wait."

Dominic merely nodded. From among the tinker's metal pots and pans, bells, knives, and other sundry items, Dominic picked up a tiny tin box fashioned in the shape of a heart.

"For you," he said lightly, his good humor restored, "to hold the pretty ribbons I shall buy you."

Catherine looked down at the object he held out to her. She wanted to tell him he could keep his foolish presents. If the box were made of purest gold, it wouldn't be enough to buy her favors. Instead she smiled sweetly and accepted the small tin heart.

"Thank you."

Dominic's hand found her waist again. Catherine felt the heat of it and a matching warmth slid through her body. She wasn't sure exactly what caused it, but she had her suspicions, and she didn't like them one little bit.

"I think I'll enjoy buying you gifts, fire kitten." His husky voice rolled over her like a caress, and Catherine's heartbeat quickened.

"Shouldn't we be getting back? Your mother will need my help preparing supper."

She knew by now that where his mother was concerned, Dominic was overly protective. He had been greatly pleased by the amount of Pearsa's work Catherine had done these last few days. And to her surprise, as his mother had said, he'd enjoyed the bright yellow flowers.

"I suppose you're right." He tossed the old French tinker a coin for the heart-shaped box. "*Au revoir,* my friend. I wish you *bahtalo drom* until next we meet."

It meant *lucky road,* a Romany farewell Vaclav had often used. Catherine released a wistful sigh, wishing she were the one headed off toward the coast—closer to England and home.

That was the moment it struck her. An idea so simple, so amazingly uncomplicated it just might work.

It took all her will to subdue her whirling thoughts and let Dominic guide her back to the wagon. Along the way, several small children ran beside his long legs. He stopped to pick one of them up and hoisted the child up onto his broad shoulders.

"Janos, this is Catrina," he said to the shirtless, barefoot boy. It was amazing the way the children never seemed to notice the cold.

"Hullo." The boy smiled shyly.

"Hello, Janos," Catherine said. She loved children, always had. At home she had been involved with a group called the Society for Bettering the Condition of the Poor, working to educate children of the lower classes. Thanks to her efforts, and those of her father before he died, children of the villagers at Arondale attended school regularly. She had stopped by often. Seeing the little boy reminded her of her homeland, the family she hadn't seen in weeks, and a hard lump swelled in her throat.

She glanced away from the child, who rode Dominic's wide shoulders by holding on to a handful of his wavy black hair. When she looked back at the tall dark Gypsy, he was watching her with an odd look in his eyes.

He set the boy on his feet, and the child raced off with the others. "You like children?"

"Yes," she said softly. "Very much so."

Dominic said nothing more.

They ate a supper of fried potatoes, cabbage, and roasted chicken—one of those taken from the cage beneath Pearsa's wagon. Catherine had learned that Gypsies kept chickens of every color so that if a nearby farmer should come in search of a stolen one, there would be others of that same kind to disguise the one that had been taken.

Dominic sat beside her—a little *too* close to suit her—conversing pleasantly about the weather, which, though the nights remained cold, had begun to warm just as Vaclav had said. He spoke of his horses, which he seemed quite passionate about, and the trading he would do at the upcoming horse fair.

"I think you'll enjoy it," he said. "It's quite a colorful gathering."

He certainly spoke proper English for a Gypsy, she thought vaguely, but in truth had trouble keeping her mind on the conversation. She was thinking of exactly which moment she should choose to steal off to the tinker's wagon, praying she wouldn't be too late, and working to ignore the muscular length of thigh that pressed far too boldly against her own.

"I'm still a little tired," she finally said. "If you don't mind, I believe I'd like to get some sleep."

"You're certain you don't want company?" he teased. Jet-black eyes swept over her and something fluttered in Catherine's stomach.

"Quite certain."

His hand came up, and he lifted a heavy lock of hair away from her face, barely brushing her skin with the side of his finger. Catherine felt it like the wings of a moth, and her heart speeded up even more.

"Good night, little one," he said. With a last too-thorough glance, he turned and walked away.

Catherine hurried up the stairs, opened the door to the

wagon, and stepped inside the candle-lit interior, seeking
its scant protection, but from what she wasn't quite sure.

A little while later, she blew out the candle and lay down
to wait and listen in silence. She didn't think the tall Gypsy
would come. He wasn't the kind of man to break his word.
He would let her know when he meant to take her—only
Catherine wouldn't be there.

Waiting for the long minutes to pass set Catherine's nerves
on edge. Dogs barked, horses whinnied, children scrambled about, but eventually the Gypsy revelers began to
quiet. She hadn't heard the rattle and clang of the tinker's
wagon as it left the camp, so she figured she still had time
to steal inside. She would ride with the wagon as far as
she dared, then leave and find some other means of travel.

Catherine left the warmth of Dominic's soft bed with
some reluctance and moved through the night's chill air
to the low wooden chest on the right side of the wagon.
She had seen him remove the coins he needed to pay his
debt to Vaclav—she prayed there were more to be found.

Digging through an assortment of blankets, bits, bridles,
curry combs, and other gear he used to tend his horses,
she finally reached the bottom of the chest and found
another pouch heavy with coins, more money than she
ever would have dreamed.

She wished she didn't have to steal, but there was really
no other choice. Once she reached home, she would find
a way to see the money returned. Taking only what gold
she would need, Catherine stuffed the coins in the pocket
of her skirt then grabbed her tattered woolen shawl and
draped it around her shoulders. She listened to be certain
no one was near, opened the door to the wagon, and
quietly descended the stairs.

Pearsa slept in a wagon on the opposite side of the fire,
but Dominic was nowhere to be seen. With a sigh of relief
she hoped wouldn't be short-lived, Catherine crossed the
open spaces between the wagons, skirting the dying

embers in each glowing fire and creeping quietly along in the shadows.

The tinker's wagon sat at the edge of the camp, the tall meadow grass nearly obscuring it on one side. Approaching the wagon from the rear, Catherine crouched low among the stiff blades, lifted the canvas flap and climbed in.

From her uncomfortable position behind a wooden crate on the cold wooden floor, she could hear old Armand in the distance, speaking in French to Jozsef. The music of the violin had stopped some time ago; she hoped he'd soon leave. Wishing she'd had the foresight to bring a blanket, Catherine rested her chin on her knees, wrapped her arms tightly around them against the cold, and settled in to wait.

Dominic stood in the shadows beside Yana's wagon. At first he had been baffled by Catherine's appearance outside the warmth of his *vardo*, but after watching for a moment, her intentions became only too clear.

"Domini?" Yana's sultry voice drifted down from the back of her wagon. She stuck her pretty head out the opening, and her almond-shaped eyes, black as the darkness around them, fixed on his face. "Why do you not come in? You have kept me waiting far too long already."

Glossy black hair hung heavily around her shoulders, bare above the low-cut neckline of her blouse. Her breasts rose and fell with her breathing, the dusky nipples forming tight, stiff peaks against the cold.

"I'm afraid you'll have to wait a little longer," Dominic said. "Something has come up."

Yana smiled seductively. "That is as it should be. Come inside, my love. Let Yana please you." She stretched out her arms, graceful and beckoning, but Dominic ignored them.

"Later." Turning, he walked away. In truth, he had been standing outside her wagon for some time, deciding whether or not to go in. He had meant to join her as he had promised, but had dallied instead, sipping *palinka*, a strong Gypsy brandy, smoking a thin cigar, checking the horses, delaying his meeting with the voluptuous Gypsy woman when he should have been looking forward to it.

Dominic swore softly, knowing it was Catherine, not Yana, he had wanted again tonight. Catherine, not the woman who for weeks had been warming his bed. Catherine—the flame-haired minx who was right now trying to escape him.

Dominic crossed the open field, jerked open the door to his wagon, and entered the dark interior. Among the Rom, there was no need to worry about thievery—a man did not steal from his brothers. But the *Gadjo* woman he had saved at the cost of his pride was something else altogether.

Lighting the white wax candle on the shelf, he went straight to his heavy wooden chest and flipped open the lid. Though his hand groped the bottom, first one side and then the other, in his heart he knew he would not find the gold. He'd been a fool to trust her—and the woman's betrayal tasted bitter in his mouth.

He rummaged farther, his face growing harder with each passing second. At the moment his search was to end, his fingers closed over the rough leather pouch. He drew out the bag and hefted it. Lighter, but only by a little. Why hadn't she taken it all?

He didn't have an answer, but the fact that she hadn't, lightened his dark mood considerably. He took a deep breath, inhaling the scent of her that still lingered in the wagon. Clean, like the soap she had used, yet honeyed by some sweetness he couldn't quite name. He thought of her hiding in the back of the wagon. She had to be cold and uncomfortable.

Good, he thought, but found himself smiling instead of scowling as he should have been. It took courage to leave the warmth and comfort of his *vardo*, the certainty of a fire and a belly full of food, to steal off in the night by herself.

Not that he wouldn't give her a good dressing-down when he brought her back. Still, she had spirit, and an English woman with courage and spirit like hers was a treasure worthy of the outrageous price he had paid.

Dominic left the *vardo*, saw that the tinker's wagon had already pulled out, and headed off toward his horses. He relished the look on Catherine's lovely face when he caught up with her. Looking forward to the challenge, Dominic could hardly wait.

Pots and pans clanging, the wagon creaking and swaying, they rumbled along the dusty road toward the distant city of Arles in the French Camargue. Catherine worked her way toward the rear of the wagon and peeked beneath the canvas flap, looking back the way they had come. Gypsy campfires burned in the distance, but soon they would disappear out of sight. It would be hours until dawn, when Dominic would find her missing. Hours away from the Gypsy encampment and the man whose dark looks stirred something peculiar inside her she would rather not explore.

Catherine leaned back against the rough wooden side of the wagon and let the first real taste of freedom wash over her. The air smelled sweeter, the sounds of the night more serene. For the first time in weeks, she allowed the feeling of hope to enter her heart and drowsily settled back to pass the hours until morning.

Chapter Four

CATHERINE WASN'T SURE if she had slept for hours or merely a few minutes, so deep and pleasant were her dreams. She roused herself slowly, taking a moment to realize the wagon had stopped moving, another to identify the brush of something soft and warm against her skin.

Catherine gasped when she sensed the tall Gypsy's presence beside her, his mouth nibbling softly on the nape of her neck.

"You are safe, fire kitten," he soothed when she tried to twist away. "I've come to rescue you from old Armand's lecherous clutches."

"You!"

"Surely you weren't expecting your old friend Vaclav?"

"Let me go!" She tried to jerk free, but his arms tightened like manacles around her. There was nowhere to run, and he was already lifting her up, carrying her toward the rear of the wagon. With an easy grace, he jumped to the ground, holding her tightly against his chest.

"Shall I challenge my old friend?" he taunted. "Kill him for stealing you away? Surely that is what happened—Armand came into my wagon and forced you to leave with him?"

Catherine stiffened, pressing her palms against the bands of muscle across his chest. "The tinker knew nothing of this. Leaving the camp was my doing. Mine alone."

At her honesty, he flashed a look that might have been surprise or approval. "Did you really think I would let such a prize slip away from me? I find it highly unflattering that you would choose the company of a toothless old tinker to mine."

Dominic let go of her but kept an arm wrapped firmly around her waist. Catherine flushed as she slid slowly down the hard-muscled length of his body.

"What did you expect? You're a Gypsy."

That brought a scowl to his face, and Catherine felt glad. She didn't like the way he was looking at her. She didn't like the warm, light-headed way he was making her feel.

"*Merci beaucoup, mon ami,*" he called to the tinker.

"*Au revoir,* Domini." The old man waved, clucked his mule into a trot, and the wagon rumbled off down the road.

Dominic took Catherine's arm and guided her to a big gray stallion tied to a tree beside the road. Taking a blanket from behind his flat leather saddle, he draped it across her shoulders, then lifted her up and settled her sideways on the seat. As he swung up behind her, Catherine wondered with a shot of despair how he had found her so quickly.

She surveyed the starlit blackness around them. Not the slightest graying of dawn. He shouldn't have discovered her missing for hours.

"Have you nothing to say in your defense, little *tschor*?"

"What does that mean?" she asked sullenly, torn between anger and gloom. She did her best not to lean against him, which was nearly impossible with the sway-ing motion of the horse as it plodded along the dirt road.

"*Tschor* means *thief*. It means I know about the money you stole from me."

"I only took what I needed to get away. I meant to repay you just as soon as I could."

"Why did you wish to leave? Were you being mis-treated? Was I starving you? Beating you?"

Catherine ignored his jibes. "If anyone deserves to be called an ugly name it is you. Since you discovered so soon

I was missing, then you must have gone into my wagon.
If you went in—breaking your word—then we both know
your intentions—and exactly why I wished to leave."

He laughed at that, and she wondered why he didn't
seem angry.

"I saw you go," he said simply. "I was standing in the
shadows."

"I don't believe you."

"Why not? I believe you."

Why not, indeed? So far he hadn't lied to her. At least
she didn't think he had. There was some comfort in the
thought, and a little of the tension eased from her body.
She let herself lean against him, noticed the warmth and
strength of the hard arms around her, heard the even beating of his heart.

When he moved in the saddle, the muscles expanded
across his chest, and Catherine's heartbeat quickened.
Unwillingly, she imagined how his smooth dark skin might
feel beneath her fingers and soft heat curled in the pit of
her stomach.

Catherine sucked in a breath, startled at the unfamiliar
sensations and amazed at the direction of her thoughts.
She tried to pull away from him and nearly unseated them
both.

"Take it easy, Catrina. It isn't far back to camp, but I
would surely rather ride than walk." He settled her against
his chest once more, and grudgingly Catherine gave in to
its hard protective warmth.

"Were you really so frightened of me that you decided
to run away?" he asked a little later. "Or was there another
reason you wished to leave?"

Catherine thought of her homeland, of Arondale and her
friends at the castle. She thought of her uncle the duke and
wondered if he still searched for her. She thought of
Edmund. Dear, dear Edmund, who had been like a brother.
Edmund who was now the Earl of Arondale—the man
most likely responsible for her abduction. Or was some-

one else to blame? Could Edmund and Amelia be missing her as much as she missed them?

"I wanted to go home," she said softly, a hard ache swelling in her throat. She had allowed herself to hope. Now that hope was gone.

"But you told me you ran away from your home. Are you telling me now that you wish to return?"

"I . . . I made a mistake," she hedged. "All I want is to see my family again."

"If you wanted to return to England, Catrina, all you had to do was ask."

Catherine's face swung to his but his expression fell into the shadows beneath the branch of an overhanging tree. "You would let me go home?"

Long brown fingers came up to cradle her cheek. "I will do even better than that. I will take you there myself."

Catherine eyed him warily. "Why would you do that? You paid a fortune for me."

"My reasons are my own. If you wish to go home, I will see that you get there."

"You're telling me the truth?"

He smiled. "I swear it on the grave of Sara-la-kali—the patron saint of the Gypsies."

"When?"

"Soon enough." Dominic watched the play of emotions on Catherine's pretty face. He saw the uncertainty, saw the despair that changed to a tiny glimmer of hope, and something moved inside his chest.

His hand sifted through the heavy strands of her fiery red-gold hair, the texture like flame-colored silk, and his arm tightened around her. Moonlight brightened the curve of her lips, the sweep of her thick-fringed lashes, dark against her pale skin. Only a small purple bruise, a remnant of her confrontation with Vaclav, marred the creamy perfection.

Dominic's jaw tightened a fraction, along with his hold on her waist. The heavy weight of Catherine's breast rode softly against his arm, and the clean sweet scent of her drifted up from her hair. Dominic shifted in the saddle, trying to ease the uncomfortable swelling in his breeches.

A glance ahead revealed the glow of dying Gypsy fires, and he drew back on the reins.

"We'll walk the rest of the way so we won't wake the others." He swung a long leg over the horse's rump, stepped to the ground, and lifted Catherine down, his hands nearly spanning her narrow waist.

They walked along the road, then disappeared into the trees, where the rest of his horses were tied. He unsaddled and tethered the gray, then walked back to where Catherine waited beneath a thin-branched poplar.

He laced her fingers through his, but didn't start walking. "Since I've promised to take you home, it seems only fair that you should thank me properly."

Catherine's look turned guarded. The woman was surely no fool.

"And just how, pray tell, might that be?"

"I ask only the price of a kiss."

Green eyes fixed on his face, searching for the truth.

"Just a kiss," he repeated. "Surely that's not too much to ask."

"If your promise is real, I don't suppose it is." She leaned over and kissed his cheek.

Dominic couldn't help but smile. "That isn't exactly what I had in mind." How could she possibly be so fiery and at the same time seem so innocent? But then maybe in a way she was. It was one thing to be used, another to be seduced. Dominic intended the latter.

"The kind of kiss I want takes a little more effort," he said. "Just close your eyes and I'll do the rest." She hesitated a moment, and he read her uncertainty. "You're sure going home is what you want?"

Catherine squared her shoulders and her eyes slowly closed. Dominic admired the perfection of her features as she stood in the moonlight, but only for a moment. Cupping her cheeks with his hands, he slanted his mouth across hers, gently at first, then with an insistence that sent a fresh flood of warmth to his loins. Catherine's big green eyes flew open, and she tried to push him away, but he only increased his assault. When she opened her mouth to protest, his tongue invaded the warm interior. She tasted as sweet as her scent, he thought fleetingly, wishing he could taste her all over.

Catherine tried to break free, but something seemed to war with her will. From the moment of their first meeting, she had been drawn to Dominic's dark good looks. That he had come to her rescue had increased the attraction, and in the short time since, she had felt his powerful masculinity as she never had another. She felt it now as his lips moved gently over hers, his tongue tasting, invading, compelling her to accept him.

As if her heart lay just beneath her skin, Catherine noticed every too-rapid flutter, the blood that seemed to pound through her veins. She couldn't think straight, could barely remember to breathe. Dominic shifted his hold, clasping her wrists and pinning her neatly between a stout tree trunk and the muscular length of his body.

When he looped her still-rigid arms around his neck, corded muscle bunched beneath her hands. His tongue felt silken, his hands like velvet fire, skimming over her body. Long sinewy thighs pressed against her, making her tremble, and her breasts pushed into the bands of muscle across his chest.

Catherine moaned. Dear God, this couldn't be happening! Could not possibly be allowed to happen. And yet some little-known feminine part of her wanted it to.

Her arms tightened around his neck and her tongue touched his, tentatively at first, then more boldly. Through a hazy awareness that threatened to retreat completely, she felt a hand cupping her breast through her thin cotton blouse while another caressed her bottom as he molded her against him.

When Catherine felt his decidedly masculine arousal, a dash of cold water couldn't have jolted her more. She jerked away from him, her eyes alive with outrage, drew back and slapped his face.

Dominic looked stunned.

"How dare you take such liberties!" It was the Countess of Arondale speaking. A lady of good sense and breeding. A lady of propriety who should never have allowed a common Gypsy to kiss her in the first place, who vowed never to let it happen again.

Dominic eyed her thoughtfully, one hand rubbing his cheek. "I could beat you for that," he reminded her, but there was no anger, only disappointment in his voice. "It would be my right."

"Then why don't you? If that is what it takes to make you feel like a man."

Dominic smiled thinly. "What it takes, fire kitten, I was just about to show you. Not, I might add, without a good bit of encouragement."

Catherine flushed to the roots of her flame-colored hair. Sweet Jesus, the man was right! Why hadn't she stopped him? Why had she let him kiss her in the first place? How could she have behaved that way? It took a will of iron to meet those jet-black eyes.

"You're right, of course. My conduct was quite unpardonable. I hope you will forgive me for any wrong impression I might have given you. I've never . . . I mean, I was rather taken off guard."

Dominic's black brows shot up. He watched her a moment, assessing her, it seemed. Then one corner of his mouth curved up. "You continue to surprise me, Catrina. An apology from you was the last thing I expected."

"One from you would not be remiss."

Amusement flickered in his eyes, then he made a sweeping bow. "Please accept my most humble apologies, milady." He lifted her hand to his lips and brushed it in a courtly manner that would have passed in the king's drawing room. "I'm afraid that's the best I can do, considering I enjoyed the kiss most thoroughly."

Catherine fought a smile and lost. So did she, for the

most part, though she would be loath to admit it. She thought of his apology. *Milady,* he had called her, never guessing how close he was to the truth. Inwardly, she mocked herself. She certainly didn't look like a lady—she hadn't behaved like one, either.

Hoping he couldn't see the flush that stole into her cheeks, she took the arm he offered and walked with him back toward the wagon. The moon had come out from behind a cloud, only a sliver but enough to light the path through the trees and show them the way. Dominic stopped at the edge of the circle of firelight, and Catherine noticed that the fire had been rekindled. Several feet away, a black-haired woman stood with her arms crossed over her breasts awaiting their arrival, it seemed.

"Good evening, Yana," Dominic said pleasantly, but an edge of irritation laced his voice. "You wished to see me?"

"So this is the *Gaðjo* woman you have bought from Vaclav. What a fool I was not to have come sooner."

"This is Catherine," he said, and she felt a surge of gratitude that he had used her English name. There was something unsettling about the woman who faced them with such menace, her anger boiling just beneath the surface.

"Catherine," Yana repeated with a dark-eyed look so vile it sent a shudder down Catherine's spine. "A haughty name for a woman who is no more than a slave."

"Now that you've seen her, why don't you go back to your wagon?" Dominic suggested, the words clearly a warning.

"Without you? Surely you mean to go with me, to lie in my arms and take your pleasure as you have each night since you came."

"You knew from the beginning this time would come."

"That is true. You were always a man who enjoys his women. Still, I am surprised you would desire this pale-skinned creature over me. Surely she cannot warm your blood as I can. Even now she looks as though she can barely remain on her feet."

The words were only too true. If she hadn't felt rooted

to the spot, Catherine was sure she would have swooned. Was this woman Dominic's wife? His lover? Whatever place the woman held, Dominic had obviously wronged her.

"I will see you well settled, have no fear of that."

"Money is always your way out, isn't it, Domini?"

"I only meant to see you cared for."

Yana turned to Catherine. "You think you have won, but I warn you—he will tire of you, just as he has me."

Dominic took an ominous step in her direction. "I've had enough of your ranting, Yana. Go back to your wagon, before I drag you there myself."

Catherine glanced from the beautiful Gypsy woman to Dominic, whose face had grown dark with rage. *He will tire of you, just as he has me.* The bile rose up in her throat. Dominic would return her to England, to be sure—after he had taken his pleasure. Once he'd had his fill, he would gladly discard her. Or maybe he would sell her again.

"If the two of you will excuse me," Catherine said with a lift of her chin that took every ounce of her will. "I find I'm really quite tired."

Yana glared at her with such loathing Catherine had trouble forcing herself to move. The Gypsy girl obviously believed Dominic had taken her to his bed, that she had allowed it, maybe even enjoyed it! The heat of humiliation washed over her. Dominic's hand went around her arm, staying her movement, then he let her go.

"We'll talk about this in the morning," he said.

Catherine just kept walking. She had to pass close by the Gypsy girl in order to reach the stairs to the wagon. When she did, the woman's fingers bit into her arm. Yana spun her around and slapped her hard across the face.

"Yana!" Dominic started toward them.

Two months ago, Catherine would have been mortified, too stunned and outraged to move. Now she grabbed the woman's thick black hair, jerked her head up, and slapped her back even harder. With a look of disbelief, Yana reeled backward, landing on her backside in the dirt. Her bright green skirts slid up to her thighs, showing a pair of shapely legs, while her long dark hair tumbled forward into her eyes.

"I don't want *him* or any other man," Catherine said to her with a pointed glance at Dominic. "I want nothing but to be away from here, nothing except to be left alone."

"Liar!" Yana climbed to her feet, brushing dirt and twigs from her clothing. She hadn't taken two steps forward when she tripped and sprawled back into the dirt.

Pearsa walked from the shadows. "The girl has done nothing to you. My son has a mind of his own. If he wishes her company over yours, that is for him to decide."

"Stay out of this, old woman."

"Go home, Yana," Dominic softly warned. "I intended we should part friends. If you leave now, we still can."

"I am not like the *Gadjo*—I am not yours to command."

"Go back to your wagon," Pearsa ordered, "before I put a curse on you. How would you like to lose all of that pretty black hair?"

Yana clutched at the shiny dark strands and scooted away, the dust puffing softly around her. "You have always hated me. But I never thought you would take the side of a *Gadjo* over one of your own."

"Scat!" Pearsa shouted, waving a shriveled-up chicken leg she had pulled from the pocket of her skirt, its long black talons flashing in the light of the fire. Yana scrambled to her feet and started backing away from the camp.

She looked hard at Dominic. "You will pay for this—far more than you paid for the girl. You will all pay." In a whirl of bright green skirts and the sound of jangling beads, she raced off into the darkness.

Dominic turned his attention to Catherine. She looked pale and shaken, but she still held her ground. "Catherine." He started toward her, but she lifted her hand as if to ward him off.

"Please . . . I should really like to go in."

"Let her go," Pearsa told him, and at last he relented. Woodenly, Catherine turned and climbed the stairs.

"Already she brings trouble." Pearsa sat smoking a long-stemmed brass pipe while Dominic drew on a thin cigar and sipped a tin cup filled with *palinka*. The scent of smoke mingled with burning poplar chips to sweeten the late night air. A small white owl hooted above them in the trees.

"What happened with Yana was not Catherine's fault."

"No, it was yours. You and your women. When will you settle down, my son?"

"We've talked of this before. I refuse to discuss it again."

They sat in silence for a while, grudging at first, but soon comfortable again, as they usually were.

"She is not like the other women of your blood I have known," Pearsa said, breaking into his thoughts.

Dominic's mouth curved up. "She's not like any I've known, either."

"She works hard and does not complain."

Dominic arched a bold black brow. High praise indeed, coming from his mother. "You like her?"

Pearsa scoffed. "She is *Gadjo*. That in itself is enough to make me despise her."

Dominic stared into the flames, thinking how close the color to Catherine's fiery tresses. "She gave a lock of her hair to Medela for the baby."

"She knew it would bring good fortune?"

Dominic nodded.

"Medela must have been pleased." She drew on her long-stemmed pipe and puffed the sweet-smelling smoke into the thick night air. "Why did she run away? We have not treated her badly."

He leaned back against the side of his mother's bright-colored *vardo*. Red and yellow serpents climbed a green-leafed trellis painted around the door. "She wants to go home."

"Back to England?"

"Yes."

"Then you will take her with you when you leave. After the horse fair."

He nodded. "I'll see she gets home." *Sooner or later,* he thought. "I'm thinking of staying a little longer." Pearsa shot him a look of speculation, but didn't pursue the subject, to Dominic's great relief. There were things at Gravenwold that needed attending: his father's lands, the people who worked for him, the horses he raised. Until Catherine's arrival, he had been fast becoming restless to return—a fact he bitterly resented.

Each year as a boy, when he had come home to his mother's people, he had dreaded the thought of his leaving. But little by little, he found himself looking forward to the books he had learned to read, to the vast new world his father had opened up for him.

The cost of his new life had been high. Years of loneliness away from the people he loved. A youth darkened by whispered scorn from those few his father had trusted with the secret of his birth—his tutor, his nanny, the servants who lived in the marquess's distant country home—the abuse of a father he could never come close to pleasing.

The pain his mother had suffered because of his leaving.

As always, Dominic tasted the bitterness of hatred for the man who had caused him such despair. The man who still caused him grief whenever he got the chance.

"If you want the woman," Pearsa said, "—and I can see that you do—why do you sleep on the ground while she sleeps in your bed?"

Dominic chuckled softly. "It seems my Catherine prizes her virtue, no matter how tattered it might be. She has been mistreated. She needs a little time to get used to the idea."

Pearsa seemed surprised. "She duped Vaclav with tales of her virtue, but I am surprised that a man of your experience would be so easily fooled."

Was it possible? Dominic thought of her kiss, so sweetly

passionate, the way she blushed whenever he touched her or looked at her with desire. Her maidenhead might have been breached, but this was no woman of experience. He would bet his life on it.

"A few days one way or another makes no difference. In the end the result will be the same. The woman belongs to me. When the time is right, I will claim her."

Pearsa puffed on her pipe, watching her son through the thick black smoke billowing around her. Had the woman bewitched him as she once had Vaclav? Or was it something else?

At least the girl had rid Domini of Yana's sinful manipulations, and if her presence in the camp meant her son would stay a little longer, Pearsa would put up with her. Besides, as she had said, the girl worked hard and so far she hadn't complained.

Chapter Five

CATHERINE AWOKE TO A WARM SPRING MORNING far brighter than her mood. Outside the wagon, sparrows chirped, and insects buzzed over the blossoms of the first fragrant flowers of the spring. Below the ancient stone-walled fortress of Sisteron, the world looked sunny and inviting, but Catherine hardly noticed.

She had spent the night tossing and turning, replaying her conflict with Yana and the kiss she had shared with Dominic in the woods.

Back at Arondale, she had been kissed just once before, by the son of a friend of her father's. It had been sweet and warm, and she had thought how nice it must be to share such a kiss with a husband each night before sleep.

Dominic's bold invasion brought thoughts far more wicked.

It had taken several hours and a good deal of will, but Catherine had finally subdued them, explaining the episode away as little more than a bout of curiosity. Amelia had hinted at the passions a man and woman might share, and Catherine had seen displays of such untoward behavior among the northern Gypsies she had traveled with.

When Dominic had kissed her, she had simply been intrigued by the unfamiliar sensations. Curiosity had overcome her better judgment. It wouldn't happen again.

Yawning behind her hand, Catherine hooked sleep-tangled strands of heavy red-gold hair behind an ear, climbed out of bed, and tried to straighten her clothes. With nothing else to sleep in, her skirt was wrinkled and dirty, her blouse rumpled nearly beyond repair, but she wasn't about to lie naked in Dominic's bed.

Catherine stood at the door to the *vardo,* hearing the sounds of an awakening camp: kindling being chopped to start a fire, water sloshing in pails brought up from the stream, children laughing as they rolled up their bedding or stepped down out of their wagons. Already the sun warmed the windows; soon Pearsa would be grinding beans for the morning's sweet black coffee.

Catherine descended the narrow wooden stairs, her leather sandals touching an earth much drier than the day before. Though the fire had already been started, neither Pearsa nor Dominic were about, which suited Catherine just fine. She was determined to bathe, no matter how cold the stream.

In the days following her arrival in the first Gypsy camp, the Rom had educated her in their strict rules of sanitation. Areas for drinking and cooking water lay upstream, next came water to clean the utensils, that for the horses, bathing water—men's and women's—then the water used by pregnant women and those who had their monthly flow. *Marimay,* they were called. Unclean.

Catherine headed downstream to a spot among the boulders which had been designated for women's bathing. Leaving her sandals at the edge of the pool, she waded, clothes and all, into the frigid, slow-moving water. Ignoring the goosebumps that fanned across her skin, she washed her hair with a small piece of soap she had found in the wagon, then used the soap on her clothes. By the time she had finished, the full red skirt looked bright once more, the blouse white and clean-smelling.

Satisfied that she again looked presentable, she climbed up on a sun-baked rock to wait for them to dry enough to return to camp. The sun felt so warm and inviting, and Catherine had slept so poorly, she drowsed a little, enjoying the heat and the few puffy clouds overhead. Then a shadow fell over her eyes, and Catherine bolted upright.

"Sorry," Dominic said, "I didn't mean to scare you."

"I—I must have fallen asleep." She glanced at her blouse, which had dried enough to satisfy her modesty. "I only meant to stay long enough for my clothes to dry."

"Who could blame you on a day like this?" He handed her a steaming tin mug. "I went to bathe and when I finished, I noticed you'd had the same intentions. I thought perhaps you'd be ready for a cup of coffee."

Catherine started to thank him, but one look in those unwavering black eyes and her mind flashed on the awful scene in camp the night before. She thought of the beautiful Gypsy girl named Yana, thought of Dominic's cruel betrayal, and all the hostility Catherine had felt last night rose up like a towering beast.

She started to tell him exactly what she thought of a man who would do such a thing, but her eyes locked on his wide bare chest, covered only by the gold-trimmed patchwork tapestry vest she had seen in his wagon, and the words died somewhere in her throat.

Catherine swallowed hard. Though she worked to ignore the burning in her cheeks and think of something scathing to say, she thought only that she had never seen skin so smooth or so brown, and that she desperately wanted to touch it, to know if the powerful body that loomed above her was really as solid as it looked.

"I'm sorry about what happened with Yana," he was saying, and for once she was grateful his eyes were on her body and not her face. "I should have spoken to her sooner."

At the sound of the woman's name, the spell was broken. Catherine tossed back her still-damp hair, the heavy mass falling well below her shoulders. "You mean you should have gotten rid of her sooner, don't you? Before she became an embarrassment? Is the woman your wife?"

His lips quirked into an unpleasant smile. "Hardly. Yana and I have known each other since childhood. Given the circumstances, it was only natural, sooner or later, for things to happen as they did."

Catherine sat up straighter on the rock, her hold on the cup growing tighter. The sound of the water bubbling over the rocks seemed to have suddenly grown softer. "Given what circumstances?"

"Yana is a woman of . . . shall we say . . . rather large appetites. Her husband, Antal, recently discovered that small failing and divorced her. She found a certain comfort with me at a time when she needed it."

"You're telling me you took no advantage?"

"None whatever. As a matter of fact, it was Yana who came to me, not the other way around."

It was hard to argue with that kind of logic. If the woman behaved so shamelessly that her husband had divorced her, it was difficult to summon much sympathy for what Dominic had done. "I suppose if she offered herself freely . . ."

"At last—a woman of reason! I had thought there were none to be had. Does this mean you're no longer angry?"

"It means I think you've made a grave mistake in giving her up. Unless you intend using force, you'll have no one to warm your bed."

Dominic's eyes ran over her. "Just looking at you, Catrina, makes me warm all over. Can you not imagine how good it would be between us?"

He leaned toward her and Catherine instinctively moved away. "Don't! Don't talk like that. Don't even think it."

"Why not? Would it be so terrible?"

"Of course it would!" But her mouth had gone dry just thinking about it, and the hand holding the cup had started to tremble.

Dominic laughed softly and took the mug from her fingers. "You'll burn yourself." Eyes the color of midnight suggested the fire he could stir would be far hotter than the coffee.

"Dominic, please. . . ."

"Please what, Catrina? Please kiss you and make you feel like you did last night?"

Catherine lifted her chin. "I meant, please—let's discuss something more civilized."

His mouth curved upward. He watched her a moment more, set the tin cup down on the rock, and stepped away. "Tomorrow we leave to trade horses. Today we pack and ready the wagons. When we have finished, I wish to show you Sisteron."

For days she had been craning her neck to look up at the rock-walled fortress, looming like a granite giant among the rugged, boulder-strewn hills. "I should like that," she found herself saying, and the fact that she meant it made Catherine's insides churn.

Dominic touched her cheek and tiny goosebumps rippled across her skin.

"We'd better be getting back," he said softly.

"I need a moment more," she hedged. Anything to get him to leave.

"All right. I'll see you back at the wagon." With a last warm look, he turned in the direction of the camp, his long legs carrying him away from the boulders and into the trees at the edge of the meadow.

Catherine numbly stared after him, trying not to notice the width of his shoulders, the smooth bulge of muscle in his arms. Sweet Jesus—how in the name of heaven could the man affect her so?

She thought of England and home. Thought of Arondale, and the sons she must bear for her father, the title he had worked so hard to give her. She imagined Edmund as the newly titled earl, knew a sharp stab of betrayal, followed by one of guilt for blaming him without proof. Whether or not Edmund had planned her abduction, it was her place, not his, to carry on the Arondale title. It was what her father wanted, what she wanted above all else.

Then she thought of the tall dark Gypsy who set her heart to pounding with a single hungry glance. Each day brought him closer to the time he would claim her.

Catherine vowed it would not happen—it was time she went home.

Catherine worked beside Pearsa, straightening and packing the wagons then gathering berries and slicing potatoes for supper. Dominic finished cleaning and storing his horse gear. With so much to do, the day passed swiftly. They ate an early meal, the women washed and stored the tin plates and heavy pots they had used, then Dominic returned—thank God he had put on his shirt—and took Catherine's hand.

"We should climb to the top before we lose the light," he said, urging her forward. They headed along a well-worn path that led to the ancient granite-walled citadel, Dominic leading the way.

"Is that a church I see way up there?"

"A cathedral. Twelfth-century Romanesque. It's been sacked, but it's partially restored and it's still being used."

Catherine eyed him with a mixture of surprise and interest. A Gypsy who knew French history? How could that be? Then she thought of the books that lined the shelves of his *vardo* and stopped dead in her tracks. "You can read!" It was almost an accusation.

Dominic smiled dryly. "Did you believe there was something in our blood that did not allow us to learn?"

"No . . . it's just that I've never met a Gypsy with any formal education. I didn't think they believed in schooling. Does your mother read as well?"

Dominic shook his head and tugged her forward.

"Then how is it that you do?"

He stopped with a sigh of resignation and turned to face her. She noticed his earlier lighthearted expression had been replaced by a scowl. "I suppose someone will tell you sooner or later, so it might as well be me. I'm only half Gypsy. My father—a *Gadjo*—insisted I have an education. Among the Rom, it's nothing to be proud of, so I'd prefer you didn't bring it up."

Gypsies hated any intrusion from the outside world, she

knew. Reading would allow them to glimpse another way of life, other people's goals and dreams. They probably saw it as a threat. "I knew there was something different about you from the moment I met you."

Dominic's black brows drew together even more. "I've been told that all my life, Catrina. I certainly don't need to hear it from you." His grip on her hand grew tighter and he strode the path as if he could walk away from the grim reminder of his parentage, practically dragging Catherine along behind.

"Dominic, please," she finally said, digging her heels in until she forced him to stop. "I thought I was supposed to be enjoying this."

He swung to face her, saw the flush of exertion in her cheeks, and his black look eased to a slow-curving smile. "Sorry. My past is hardly your problem. It just isn't my favorite subject."

"I'll remember that." But already she was trying to figure a way to learn more about him. If he wouldn't tell her, maybe his mother or some of the others would.

Catherine mentally shook herself. What in heavens was she thinking? She wasn't going to stay here any longer than she had to—the less she knew about him the better.

Dominic helped her over a boulder that had rolled into the trail, his hand strong and solid around her waist. Catherine eased herself away and prayed he would think her rapidly beating heart was merely a result of the climb.

They continued along the path toward the fortress, the Durance River winding along below them. Skirting the tiny town, they followed narrow stone passages that led them beneath flying buttresses, which propped up rock houses along the way.

"Spanish Gypsies call these trails *andrones*," Dominic told her, stopping again to let her rest. He seemed not to notice the difficult climb, his muscular legs absorbing the steep trail with an easy grace that seemed as natural to him as the way he sat his horses.

"Such a powerful language," Catherine said.

"Do you speak it?"

"No."

He flashed her a knowing glance. "But you do speak French, *n'est-ce pas?*"

Catherine's head came up. "Yes, but how did you—"

"The tinker, remember? You wouldn't have known when he was leaving if you hadn't understood him."

Catherine smiled. She'd been right about him. He wasn't a man who was easily fooled.

"What other secrets do you keep, Catrina?"

More than you could ever guess. "What makes you think I'm keeping any?"

He laughed. "You are easy to read, little one. I think you have far more to tell than you wish me to know."

Catherine didn't answer. She didn't like the probing way he looked at her, or the feeling that he somehow knew her thoughts.

As dusk settled in, they broke away from the town and traveled upward through the ancient citadel itself. There were grassy plateaus then steep stone staircases that seemed to climb into the very sky itself. Below them the river looked no more than a narrow blue ribbon.

Finally they reached the top—a granite platform, long and walled with a small steepled church rising upward at one end. Rocky peaks surrounded them as the last rays of the sun slid into shadow. They stood quietly in the fading light, watching tiny pinpricks of illumination begin to brighten the heavens.

"Look!" Catherine pointed upward. "There's a shooting star."

Dominic grabbed her hand and pulled it down against his chest. "The Gypsies believe a falling star is a thief taking flight. If you point at it, it means the man is caught."

Catherine looked into his face and noticed the way his jawline fell into shadow beneath the curve of his cheekbone. His lips curved so beautifully it took her breath away. He was different from any man she had ever met. Different—and totally unsuitable.

"Your people think so vastly unlike mine. We would want a thief captured. The Gypsy sees the guilty man as the victim."

"They always take the side of the disadvantaged," Dominic said simply. "They know how hard life is . . . what a man must do to survive."

"Even if his actions hurt someone else?"

He shrugged his broad shoulders. "It's a game to them. It rarely involves hurtfulness."

"That's where you're wrong, Dominic. The Gypsies I traveled with were callous and cruel. They enjoyed hurting me, making me suffer because my skin was lighter than theirs."

"I have known such people, though mine are not that way. The Rom have suffered great prejudice throughout the years. Since they came to Europe in the fifteenth century, they've been enslaved, condemned as sorcerors, and burned at the stake, even executed for cannibalism."

"Cannibalism!" A chill touched Catherine's spine.

Dominic nodded. "In Austria, just a little over twenty years ago. Forty Gypsies were hanged before Emperor Joseph the Third abolished the trials—he discovered that none of the monks supposedly eaten was actually missing."

"Dear God."

Dominic looked resigned. "Some of the tribes have suffered worse than others, which may have been the reason they treated you so badly. In truth, just as with any group of people, some are more cruel, some kinder. You won't have to worry as long as you are here." He lifted her fingers to his lips.

Catherine felt the warmth of it, the reassurance, and a promise of something more. "It's getting awfully late," she said, easing her hand from his. "Will we be able to find our way down in the darkness?" Dominic stood beside her, his body not quite touching, but close enough she could feel his powerful presence almost as if he were.

"It's easier going back. We'll be fine."

Catherine looked down at the tiny yellow lights sparkling from the windows of the town below. "It's beautiful here."

"My people make this same journey each year. Every time I come to this place, I love it a little bit more."

"It feels almost sacred," Catherine agreed. "Timeless. As if it's just humoring those of us who pass inside its walls."

He smiled at that. "I hoped you would like it." His eyes ran over her face. Catherine's own eyes met them. There was hunger in those bottomless depths and something else she couldn't quite name. Still she did not back away.

"I want you," he said, moving closer. "I've wanted no other since the moment I saw you." The husky note in his voice swept over her like a breeze.

Catherine's throat went dry. "What you're asking cannot happen. Not now, not ever."

Dominic arched a brow, his look becoming one of amusement. "Have you forgotten so quickly, little one? Should I decide the time is right, you will have very little say in the matter."

Catherine moistened her lips, which felt as dry as her throat. He could do it, she knew. He had the strength and the will. She should have been afraid of him, but she was only afraid of herself. "You said you would not force me."

He turned her to face him, pulling her even closer. One hand settled at her waist while the other slid upward into her hair then skimmed over her throat until he cupped her cheek with his palm. His thumb moved along her jaw, teasing, stroking, coaxing.

Catherine's legs turned weak.

"Do you really believe I would have to?" Onyx eyes raked her, knowing eyes that took in the blush in her cheeks, the heightened beating of her heart. Her breasts rose and fell with each too-rapid breath.

"If you think I will submit, you are mistaken. There is nothing you can do or say that can make that happen."

"No?" He watched her a moment more, his eyes holding her, daring her to move away. Catherine stood transfixed.

Dominic's mouth came down over hers, feather-soft and meltingly gentle, his tongue brushing her lips, warming her yet not demanding entrance. Catherine swayed against him just as he pulled away.

"As you said, little kitten, the hour grows late. The descent is long, and tomorrow will be a difficult day."

Catherine bristled. Dominic turned away, his face falling into shadow, but she had no doubt of what she would have seen. He was toying with her! So sure of himself and her responses it brought a fresh rush of heat to her cheeks.

Damn him! Did he really believe she was that easily swayed from her convictions? That a lifetime of plans and dreams would be so readily cast away? And for what? A moment of passion in the arms of a man she hardly knew. It was insane!

What did it matter that Dominic attracted her as no man had? Made her feel things she never dreamed she could feel? She had responsibilities, commitments. Besides, to him she was only a plaything, just another woman to warm his bed. She wasn't about to be used and discarded like the rest of them.

His arm went around her shoulders, guiding her back toward the steep rock stairs. This time she felt nothing but bitter resentment. Tonight he had shown her again the power he believed he could wield. Catherine had yet to show him the force of her resistance.

Dominic descended the steep stone path smugly satisfied with the course of the evening. His campaign of seduction was working just as he planned. He was winning her confidence, and Catherine's desire for him was even greater than he had expected. Though she hadn't meant for him to know, the frank approval with which she'd looked at him, the breathless tone of her voice had given her away.

He found her guilelessness intriguing, refreshing in a way that had been missing from his life for some time. Most of the women he knew wanted something from him—his money, his title, the passion he could stir in

them. Catherine knew nothing about his wealth and position, and did her best to deny her attraction.

Then again, maybe she was trying to deceive him as his
mother had said, dangling her sweet little body in hopes
of gaining his prolonged attention, or even his name.

He watched her walking along beside him, and noticed
the stubborn tilt of her chin. She looked different than she
had just minutes ago up on the mountain. Harder, more
determined. If it was a game she played, he'd soon discover her next move and he would be ready.

Dominic found himself smiling, enjoying the anticipation. She was a challenge, an enigma. He would find out
more about her, find the key to her passions, and woo her
into his bed.

His eyes ran over her, taking in her simple garments, the
low-cut, loose-fitting blouse and bright red cotton skirt.
What would she look like in expensive silks and satins, he
wondered, her fiery hair artfully arranged? Beautiful, he
had no doubt, and very much the lady. He wished in that
moment that he could see her that way, then cursed himself for the thought. How greatly he had changed since
he'd left the simple life of his people. And not all for the
best.

He thought of the words he had spoken to Catherine
about his heritage and wondered if her attitude toward
him would soften if she knew that he was half English—
and a nobleman into the bargain. He wouldn't tell her, of
course. Just the idea that it might affect her manner
toward him left a sour taste in his mouth.

"What does *didikai* mean?" she suddenly asked, and he
frowned to think that an English woman might read his
thoughts as easily as the Gypsies believed they could.

"Where did you hear that?"

"Vaclav said it the night you came to his wagon."

Dominic felt the same revulsion he always did when he
heard that word. "It's what the Rom call a man of mixed
blood. He was reminding me of what I am. That a true
Gypsy would not have interfered on your behalf."

Catherine didn't miss the bitterness that had crept into his tone. "I'm grateful for what you did. More so, now that I know what it must have cost you." To help her, he had gone against Gypsy beliefs, knowing he would face their contempt. Why? she wondered, but did not ask. When Dominic said nothing more, she asked, "Does your background really matter so much?"

He tossed the pebble he'd been toying with and it skipped against another rock, echoing softly into the night. "It probably shouldn't. Maybe to some it wouldn't, but to me . . ."

But to him it meant everything. Catherine could read it in the sudden slump to his usually straight broad shoulders, the hardness that had settled around his mouth.

"What about your father's people? Couldn't you have stayed with them?"

He scoffed at that. "I lived with them—*existed* might be closer. They hated Gypsies almost as much as I hated them."

Catherine's heart went out to him. She could easily imagine what he must have looked like as a child, all raven-black hair and splendid dark eyes. There was something caged beneath his cool exterior that spoke of vulnerability. Gypsy or not, how could anyone have hated a young boy like that? "So you left your father and came back here."

A flicker of hesitation touched his eyes, then it was gone. "For the most part these people accept me. As long as I live by their rules."

His hard look reminded her that he had broken those rules by protecting her from Vaclav. As curious as she was to know more about him, his silence, and that last burning glance, warned her not to ask.

They continued along the trail and finally reached their camp to find the fire had been doused and Pearsa had retired to her bed. Dominic walked Catherine to his wagon, bent down and brushed her lips with a kiss before she could pull away.

"Good night, fire kitten."

"Good night, Dominic." He waited at the foot of the stairs for her to go inside. She could almost feel his eyes on her back, and her mouth still tingled from his soft, brief kiss.

Catherine stepped inside the *vardo,* closed the low wooden door, and leaned against it. God in heaven, she'd be glad when she got home.

The moon was round!
And, as I walked along,
There was no sound,
Save when the wind was long
Low bushes wispered to the ground
A snatch of song.

Gypsy Poem
Walter Starkie

Chapter Six

IT TOOK TWO DAYS OF TRAVEL ALONG THE DURANCE, then inland, to reach the small French village of Reillanne, outside of which both Gypsies and peasants had gathered for the horse fair.

For most of the journey, Catherine sat beside Dominic, enjoying his love of the country. He told her Gypsy legends, one about a castle named Great Ida, defended by Gypsies who lost their lives in a last fruitless battle. Gypsies still mourned the day, he said. They sang melancholy songs about it, and wept when they heard them.

He taught her the Romany name for certain flowers and trees, and the name for different animals. When a small bird sang to them from the branch of a budding poplar, he pointed to it and smiled.

"A pied wagtail. He's called *Romany chiriklo*. It's said that when you see one, you will soon encounter Gypsies."

And they did. A few hours later, another wandering band turned onto the road just ahead of them, trailing horses for the fair just as Dominic was, their bright-painted wagons rolling in the same direction.

"They follow the *patrin*—leaves or twigs arranged at the crossroads as a signal of where we should meet." He smiled again and the warmth in his look was contagious.

"Do you love this life so much then?"

He surprised her with a shrug of his shoulders. "Once it meant everything to me. Now things are different. I'm different. I enjoy the comforts afforded by my wagon while the others care nothing for the simplest convenience. I find myself thinking of the future, but the Rom live only in the present. They praise lavishness and abhor carefulness or any need to consider security, outside of plain survival. To the Gypsy, the candle isn't made of wax, it's all bright flame."

Catherine felt a small surge of warmth that he had trusted his thoughts to her. "From the day of my arrival, I've been amazed by their indifference to hardship. Sometimes I wondered if I'd be able to survive living as they did."

"But you have, Catrina. Even my mother is beginning to approve." He grinned roguishly. "I heard her telling Czinka that you had a strong back, and thighs of a firm consistency. She said you made a very good worker."

Catherine blushed from head to toe. "You are the most infuriating man," she told him, angry at his indelicacy. "Sometimes I think you're the devil himself."

"*Beng,* we call him, and I think it is you who tempt me into behaving like one, *gula devla.*"

"I'm afraid to ask what that means."

He laughed again, such a rich male sound. "It means *sweet goddess,* and never have I spoken truer words."

She *was* sweet, he thought, so charmingly interested in the beauty of the world around them. Every time he taught her a Romany word, she repeated it until she got it right—as if to her it really mattered. She had laughed at several of his stories, and her eyes misted with sadness at the legend of Great Ida. Why? he wondered, when the Gypsies had treated her so badly.

His eyes drifted down to the curve of her breast. The tempting mounds rose upward as she took a steadying breath. It was all he could do not to reach out and cup one. As if he had, her nipples hardened, the firm little buds pressing against her thin cotton blouse.

"Getting cold, Catrina?" he teased.

Catherine's face flushed even redder. "You *are* a devil! Rude and mannerless into the bargain! Stop this wagon. I'd rather walk than sit here with someone as uncouth as you."

Dominic chuckled softly, but didn't slow down until Catherine threatened to jump. "I should have thought, after this long, your sensibilities would have dimmed. I can see I was mistaken. My sincere apologies."

Strange, but he found he meant it. He shouldn't have teased her so mercilessly, but he had been curious to see her reaction. That she'd been gently reared, he had witnessed again today. For the past several months, she had done what she had to in order to survive, but still she behaved like a lady. She deserved to be treated as one.

"I'm sorry," he repeated, as if she might not have heard him.

"I still want down."

He felt a thread of irritation. "Fine," he grudgingly agreed, pulling the wagon to a halt. She'd probably break her pretty little neck if she jumped, and he knew without doubt she meant to. "Let me know when you get tired."

"Thanks to your people's *kindness*," she said sarcastically, "I can walk this road all day."

His mouth turned grim at the reminder. Dominic waited for her feet to touch the ground then slapped the reins against the horses' rumps, and they leaned into their harness. As soon as she had faded from his view, he eased them back to a walk and watched her walking beside him from the corner of his eye.

What was there about her that made him want her near? Made him tell her things he rarely admitted, even to himself? What he'd confessed to her had been startlingly true. While part of him still yearned for the feeling of freedom the Gypsy life gave him, another, larger part felt an eagerness to set down roots, to achieve something, build something. As his mother had long predicted, his English blood had grown strong.

He thought of his past, and the same fierce resentment he always felt rose up inside him. At thirteen, after years of abandonment by a father he had vaguely known existed, he had been forced to leave his mother, his grandparents, and the rest of the people he loved. In England, he'd been a victim of prejudice, a lonely, desolate youth yearning to return to his home. He didn't because his mother had begged him to remain, and a Gypsy child always obeyed his parents.

He saw even now what that decision had cost her. Without her son, Pearsa's beauty had faded and she'd grown old before her time, beaten in a way that broke his heart. Still, for Pearsa he remained with his father. And no matter how barren his existence, he survived, growing stronger with the challenge of each passing day.

By the time he'd reached twenty, Dominic had changed so much he hardly knew himself. He was a man split apart. No longer completely accepted by the Rom, nor wholly a part of the English world he by then spent most of his time in. And because of his torment, his hatred of his father had blossomed even more.

Today, at twenty-eight, Dominic Edgemont, Lord Night-wyck, was a man fully grown. He knew what he wanted, knew where he belonged, knew this would be the last year he would live in the world of the Gypsy. Oh, he would always take care of his mother, see her whenever he could. But this was the last time he would travel their road, live as they did.

It made him sad—and yet it ended a portion of his torment.

He glanced around him, inhaling the sweet-smelling air, determined to remember each of these last precious days. Amidst schools of white clouds and lofty blue skies, the spring sun warmed the land, inviting the emergence of new growth and brightening the landscape with colorful flowers.

There were flowers at Gravenwold, too, he reminded himself.

But no fiery woman with thick red-gold hair.

Catherine walked the dusty road for most of the afternoon. She no longer felt angry at Dominic—with his soft, warm glances, he was a man hard to stay mad at—it was just far safer being away from him. Besides, she was enjoying herself. Along with the melee of bright-painted Gypsy wagons, men, women, children, goats, cows, pigs, and straggly-haired dogs, little Janos walked beside her, sometimes holding her hand. He was such a darling little boy, no more than six or seven, probably looking much as Dominic had with his big dark eyes and smooth olive skin. His father had died, she discovered, then his mother. He lived with a big Gypsy named Zoltan his mother had taken as a second husband.

Janos didn't much like him.

"He is always so cross," he said. "And he drinks and he often beat my mother. You are lucky to have a man like Domini."

"You don't think Dominic would beat me?" she asked, with mock seriousness, for even she no longer believed he would.

"Oh, no. He likes you very much. Medela says she can tell by the way he smiles when he talks of you."

"Dominic talks about me? What does he say?"

"He says you are different from other *Gadjos.* That you do not hate Gypsies as they do."

But she did, didn't she? She loathed everything about them. She would never forget their cruelty, the abuse she had suffered at Gypsy hands.

She would never forget the way Dominic had come to her rescue. The way Pearsa had protected her from Yana. The words of gratitude Medela had spoken for the gift of her hair.

"What else did Dominic say?"

"Why do you not call him Domini, as we do?"

Why didn't she? Because *Dominic* didn't sound nearly

so foreign, so very Gypsy. But she couldn't tell the child that. "I guess I just liked his other name better."

That night they made camp outside Reillanne. Even before the fires were lit, she could hear the sound of laughter and violins.

"*Patshiva* tonight," Dominic said. "They will feast and celebrate, sing, and dance the *czardas.*"

"What are they celebrating?" Catherine asked.

Dominic shrugged. "Nothing in particular. Someone has money, he gives a feast. Tomorrow they trade horses, tonight they celebrate seeing old friends. My people live from *patshiv* to *patshiv.* They survive on meager fare then lavish themselves with overabundant feasts. They care nothing for any day except this one."

Even after the months she had spent with them, Catherine had difficulty understanding their ways. "Will you take me?"

Dominic smiled. "I'm looking forward to it."

They finished setting up camp, Pearsa having left to visit old friends, then wandered off toward the distant cluster of wagons. Fires of pine and peat scented the air, iron caldrons stood on tripods over the flames, and dogs waited patiently for any scraps they might be thrown.

There was a lightness in this new camp that had been missing in the one before, Catherine noticed. Since the weather had changed and they'd left Sisteron, a feeling of anticipation had accompanied them. Catherine also discovered that besides casting off their dreary mood, they'd shed their ragged layers of winter clothing for bright silk shirts, gold bracelets, and colorful swirling skirts.

Dominic arrived wearing his silver earring, snug black breeches tucked into his boots, and his gold-trimmed tapestry vest. He looked so handsome her heartbeat quickened. Where Vaclav's chest had been dark with thick black hair, Dominic's was mostly smooth, sleek muscle. She wanted to reach out and touch it, see if it felt as hard as it looked. His arms were thick with sinew and his stomach flat and firm.

When he caught her appraising glance, she forced her eyes to his face and accepted the handful of small gold coins pierced with holes that he handed her.

"I hope that look was one of approval," he said with a wicked grin.

Catherine blushed, but said nothing. Just sat down and began braiding the coins into her hair.

She noticed Pearsa and most of the other women had decked themselves out far more lavishly, wearing bracelets of gold or silver, or draping chains of gold around their waists.

"Gypsies always seem so poor, yet they never appear to lack for gold," Catherine said, walking with Dominic toward the center of the neighboring camp where the music was being played.

Tents of black mohair dotted the open field beside the wagons. The smell of garlic mixed with cigars and the faint odor of musk filled the air. At one camp, several black-bearded men crouched on their haunches, smoking hand-rolled black cigarettes.

"They wear the gold for its beauty. Money means little to them." Dominic smiled, white teeth brilliant against his dark skin. "When they run out, they fleece the nearest *Gadjo* and get some more. Tomorrow I'll show you how it is done."

"You're going to steal something?"

He smiled indulgently. "There was a time when I did. Not anymore."

Relief surged through her. "Why not?"

"Because I don't have to, and because I know I can. I no longer need to prove myself."

She wasn't sure she liked that answer, but by then they had reached their destination. Her eye caught the man and woman dancing in the circle beside the fire and the music began to wash over her. Across the way, she recognized old Jozsef, sitting beside Czinka, whose huge girth swayed in time to the heady rhythm of the song.

Standing not far away, Medela, even heavier with child

than before, looked nearly as big. The black-haired girl smiled and waved, then patted her weighty stomach. Catherine waved back and Dominic smiled.

"You see, you have made another friend."

"Another? Who is the first?"

"Why, I am, of course."

She liked the way he looked when he said it, and just for tonight she would pretend to believe it.

"I'll be right back." He brought her a cup filled with *pastis,* an anise-flavored liquor from the southern French countryside, and Catherine enjoyed the warm licorice flavor.

"They say you can make a peasant drunk on water and Gypsy violins," Dominic said when he saw her swaying to the music. One man accompanied the violinist on a flute, while another played a *cymbalom,* an instrument shaped like a small piano with open strings struck by a felt-tipped hammer.

Catherine felt Dominic's hand at her waist, his body close beside her, but the *pastis* had relaxed her, and the music was so hypnotic that she didn't move away. Dance after dance continued, until Catherine's head buzzed with the effects of the drink and the sensuous exotic rhythm. Her feet moved in time to the beat, her palms tingled from clapping, and her breasts felt overly warm.

Unconsciously, she slid a hand into her thick flame-red hair and lifted it off her shoulders. When she turned, she saw Dominic watching her, his black eyes glittering. Holding her with the warmth in his gaze, he backed away from her, into the circle of firelight. Around him, Gypsies clapped and cheered, calling him *pral,* brother, and shouting his name.

Dominic seemed not to hear them. Though he clapped his fine dark hands above his head, arched his back, and stamped his feet in time to the music, his eyes, so black they glistened, remained fixed on her face. The memory of every touch they had shared, every brush of his mouth against hers, seemed etched in the hot look he gave her.

He moved forward, then retreated, so graceful and yet so masculine, denying and beckoning all at once.

When he held out his hand, she might have gone to him, but Yana stepped between them and picked up the dance. When she thrust her full breasts forward and laughed into his handsome face, Catherine felt a wild stab of jealousy. Fury pumped through her as she turned to leave. She had taken just a few short steps before Dominic's hand closed over her wrist.

"Come," he said softly, "it is you I wish to dance with."

"But I don't know how. I couldn't possibly—"

"Just let yourself go," he coaxed, leading her forward. "Let your body feel the music."

What about Yana? she thought, her eyes searching the firelight. As Dominic pulled her into the circle, she saw the woman standing next to Vaclav, so furious her eyes fairly gleamed. Dominic ignored her. Instead he began his slow sensuous dance for Catherine, lifting his hands, thrusting his pelvis forward, tossing his head back, daring her to meet the challenge in his sensuous dark eyes.

Catherine glanced at Yana, saw the smugness, the certainty that she would surely look the fool, forced a smile and lifted her skirt up out of the way. Though she didn't know the steps, all evening she had watched the others and felt the beat of the music. If she closed her eyes and gave herself up to it, her body would do the rest.

And so she did. She ran her hands through her hair, tossing it back, and began to move as Dominic did. She swayed when he did, clapped her hands and stamped her feet. In minutes the crowd became only a colorful blur, her attention fastened on the man whose hard-muscled body glistened with exertion in the firelight. Naked sinew tightened across his chest as his hands rose once more above his head, and his long legs moved with a sensuous grace matched only by the poignant notes of the violin.

Once he caught her up in his arms, lifting her above his head, then dipped her low and bent her back over his arm. Catherine let her head fall back, her golden-red hair shimmering to the ground in the firelight. Seeing only Dominic, she danced with raw abandon, running her hands over her breasts and along her throat in age-old invitation she was only vaguely aware of.

How long they went on she could not guess. One moment they were dancing, twirling amidst the surging crowd of Gypsies, their feet pounding, spoons clapping against palms, tongues clicking, knuckles rapping on wood. The next moment Catherine's feet left the ground and she was caught up in Dominic's arms.

He was striding away from the music, heading back toward his wagon, the cheers and laughter of the Gypsies following in their wake. When they reached the shadows beside his *vardo,* he let go of her legs and she slid down his body till her feet touched the ground.

Catherine's eyes went wide at the feel of his hardness pressing against her, a shaft so thick and pulsing she could not mistake it even through the layers of her clothes.

"I want you," he said, his eyes blazing. "I have never seen anyone dance the way you did. I have never wanted a woman more."

He kissed her then and lightning careened through her body. It was a hard, demanding kiss that matched the fever of their dancing. Catherine moaned. Dominic's hand cupped her breast and he pebbled the peak through the fabric. His tongue found its way into her mouth and Catherine felt scorched by the heat of it.

She wanted to slide her arms around his neck, to run her fingers through his hair. She wanted to touch his hard-muscled chest, feel his hands on her body. She wanted to get as close to him as she possibly could, to be one with him and never let him go.

Instead she jerked away.

"What's wrong?" he asked, his breathing harsh and ragged.

Catherine's own unsteady breaths nearly matched his. "Does your word mean nothing?"

"What—what are you talking about?" He ran a hand

through his wavy black hair, working to gain some control. "We'll go inside, is that it? You're afraid someone will see us?" He reached for her, meaning to help her into the wagon, but Catherine backed away.

"I told you this isn't going to happen. Do you think I'm a fool? Do you think I don't know where all of this leads?"

Dominic's eyes took on a different glint. "It will lead to my bed, Catrina. Exactly where we both wish to be."

"You're wrong, Dominic. You may wish it, but I do not."

"You deceive yourself. You want this as much as I do."

God in heaven, it was the truth! "I want no part of you." She started to turn, spotted the whip he used to train his horses, reached over and picked it up. "You said if we came together it would not be at the threat of a whipping. Forcing me is the *only* way it will happen. If that is what you intend, do it now."

Dominic's jaw clenched and his face turned hard. He stared at the whip, looked at her, and grabbed it from her hand. She thought of the way he had kissed her, the way she had responded. She imagined what it must feel like to lie with him, to kiss him, to feel his fine brown hands on her body. She glanced at the whip and in that moment she almost wished he would use it, force her to do what they both knew she wanted.

He tossed the whip away. "It appears, my love, I'm a bigger fool than you are." With a last angry glance, he stalked off into the darkness.

Catherine watched him go. It was all she could do not to follow, to rush into his arms and beg him to kiss her again.

She forced her eyes to stop searching the darkness, forced down the lump in her throat. How long it had been since she'd allowed herself the cleansing relief of tears? She had never fought the urge harder and yet it was a weakness she could ill afford. Certainly not now, maybe not ever.

Catherine wearily climbed the stairs. Tomorrow they would go into Reillanne for the horse fair. With renewed determination—and any luck at all—she would find a means of escape.

Dominic worked to cool his raging temper. He had never been more furious in his life. He felt like throwing open the door to his wagon, climbing into Catherine's bed, and thrusting into her firm little body. He didn't believe for a moment that she wouldn't bloody well like it. But he'd never forced a woman in his life and he wasn't about to start now.

He patted the muzzle of his sleek little dapple-gray mare. "Easy, pretty one." She nickered and nuzzled his hand for sweets. "Tomorrow, if you behave yourself, you will get your treat." He would be trading some of the others, but not Sumadji. She was too precious. Along with her mate, the big gray stallion, Rai, she'd be an asset to his stable back in England.

"Why couldn't my Catherine be more like you?" he asked, thinking of the willful little vixen he had left back in camp. Even now his body throbbed for her; the ache would be hours in leaving. He could almost feel the weight of her breasts in his hand.

The power of her resistance still amazed him. When they had been dancing, she had been on fire for him. Her every movement spoke of her desire—no man on earth could have missed it. He'd been sure she would come willingly to his bed.

Instead she'd refused him, just as she had before.

His grip grew tight on Sumadji's lead rope. God's breath, the woman made his life a living hell. He thought of the way he had kissed her, then remembered with satisfaction how fiercely she had kissed him. If he found himself tied in knots, how must she feel? He could bet she wouldn't get much more sleep this night than he would. Time was what he needed. She couldn't resist much longer. If only he had a few more days. . . .

For the first time, Dominic smiled. Maybe he did have. He'd already decided to lengthen his stay, and after that, he'd be traveling with her to England. He had promised to return her, but he had never said exactly what he would do with her when they got there.

It crossed his mind he might barter her passage for her willingness in bed, but he discarded the idea almost immediately. If he had to pay a bribe to win her passion, he didn't want it. No, he would wait a little longer, play the game a little while more.

Catherine was a passionate woman. Sooner or later, she was bound to give in.

For every gypsy that comes to toon,
A hen will be a-missing soon,
And for every gypsy woman old,
A maiden's fortune will be told.

                              Gypsy poem
                              Charles Godfrey Leland

Chapter Seven

CATHERINE AVOIDED DOMINIC all morning. He was working
with his horses, feeding them, grooming them, braiding their manes and tails and tying them with ribbons. She
was certain he was still angry, and she wasn't yet ready
to face him.

Besides, after their heated encounter, she'd spent the
oddest, most uncomfortable night. She had tossed and
turned, dreamed of Dominic, replaying the way he had
kissed her, and awakened several times damp with perspiration. Even this morning, her breasts felt achey and sore.

Maybe she was coming down with an ague of some sort.

"Watch where you are walking," Pearsa scolded, snapping her out of her thoughts. "You will wind up in the
cooking fire."

She stood dangerously close to the tripod that held a
heavy iron kettle containing leftover *bokoli*, pancakes and
meat, part of the morning meal.

"I'm sorry. I guess I was thinking of the horse fair.
Dominic promised to take me." After what happened last
night, he would probably go by himself.

"I should have known it was my son who held your
thoughts. He is very handsome, no?"

There seemed no reason to deny it. "Yes, he is."

"You like him."

"He's been very kind to me."

"That is all he is to you? A man of kindness? I do not think so. Domini is a strong, virile man; you are a woman of passion. You want him. Why do you not welcome him into your bed?"

Catherine felt the warmth creeping into her cheeks. "He is not my husband." It was a simple answer, and yet those few short words brought the truth home in a rush. Though they shared a strong attraction, Dominic wasn't her husband and never would be.

He was a Gypsy, she a countess. Soon she would leave him, leave his way of life. Once she reached England, she would find the man who had betrayed her and see justice done. Then she would choose a suitable mate, bear his children, and carry on as the Barringtons had done for generations.

"Vaclav offered you marriage," Pearsa was saying. "Why did you not stay with him?"

"Because I didn't love him." This was the longest conversation she and Pearsa had ever had. The older woman's tone seemed less biting today, though no less wary.

"And you love my son?"

"No! Of course not. It's just that he came when Vaclav would have hurt me. He saved me and for that I feel grateful."

"He will not marry you. He swears he will never marry."

Catherine absorbed that news with a bit of surprise. "Surely he wants children, a woman who will love him?"

"His reasons are his own. I am telling you this so that if you go to him, you will know the truth."

"I won't go to him—at least not by choice. Dominic knows that. He swears he will not force me."

Pearsa flashed a look Catherine couldn't quite read. "A woman is wise not to sell herself cheaply."

"I don't intend to sell myself at all."

"My son can be very persuasive."

"And I can be very stubborn."

Pearsa chuckled softly. "So I have seen."

Catherine said nothing more, but when she lifted the

heavy iron kettle and started down to the stream to wash it, Pearsa waved her back.

"You have done enough. Go on with my son. Enjoy the horse trading. If you keep your eyes open, you might learn something of value."

With a smile of thanks, Catherine wandered away from the wagon, but she didn't seek out Dominic. Instead she strolled toward the yellow-painted *vardo* where Medela worked airing blankets. She glanced up at Catherine's approach.

"It is good to see you, Catrina." A smile of welcome beckoned Catherine forward.

"Good morning, Medela. How are you feeling?"

The dark-haired girl rested her palms on her lower abdomen, so swollen now each cumbersome step seemed an accomplishment. "*Mi cajori* comes soon. He will be healthy, as I am. Your charm works well."

"I'm glad," Catherine said, not believing for an instant a lock of her hair had anything to do with the matter.

"Where is Domini?" Medela asked. "He has not left for the fair without you?"

In truth, she wasn't sure. "He promised to take me, but he may have forgotten." That wasn't quite the case but it would have to do.

"Domini would never forget a promise. He will come for you."

As if she had conjured him, he strode through the space between the wagons. Catherine heard the sound of his heavy footfalls distanced by his long-legged stride and turned in his direction.

She had expected to see his displeasure marked by an angry scowl, but saw only a determined look and something of a smile lighting his handsome face. Today he wore his full-sleeved red silk shirt open nearly to his waist, and Catherine had to concentrate to keep from staring at the sleek bands of muscle across his chest.

"You're looking fit, Medela. I trust you're feeling passably well."

She smiled and patted her belly. "It is because of the charm."

Dominic nodded, his expression mildly indulgent. He swung his attention to Catherine. "The fair awaits, Catrina. Are you ready?"

"Yes. I was hoping you would . . . I mean . . . after last night . . . I was afraid you might be——" Catherine felt a flush stealing into her cheeks. "Why don't we go then?"

One corner of his mouth curved up in amusement. "Why don't we?" He took her hand and led her back to where his horses were tied. Five had been groomed and readied, one of which wore a saddle, but his dapple-gray stallion and a pretty little gray mare remained tied among the trees at the rear of the camp.

"You aren't selling all of them?"

"Rai and Sumadji are for breeding." Hands clasped firmly around her waist, he lifted her sideways onto the saddle of a tall white-stockinged bay then swung up behind her. She could feel the heat of his body, the arms that rested just inches below the curve of her breast.

"Can't I ride one of the other horses?" she asked, hoping to put some distance between them.

"You know how to ride?"

"Of course." Any woman of breeding knew how to ride, though Catherine had always enjoyed it so much she had become far more proficient than most of her friends.

"You never cease to amaze me, Catrina. I'm beginning to fear there's a lady beneath those simple garments, and I'm not at all certain I like the prospect."

"Would it really make a difference?" Catherine's heart started thudding with a quick jolt of hope. "If I were a lady in truth, would you stop making improper advances, would you see that I was safely returned to my home?"

Dominic arched a brow. "Considering your present circumstances—and the fact that you've been bought and paid for—I would say my advances have been quite mild indeed. As to my returning you home, I've told you on more than one occasion that is exactly my intention."

"When?"

"Certainly not today." He clucked the horse into a trot, "We have trading to do."

And certainly not tomorrow—or any other day before you've spent time in my bed! Well, it wasn't going to happen. As Dominic urged the horse toward the activity in the distant fields, Catherine renewed her vow to leave.

She eyed the peasants walking beside them, the dozens of Gypsies in bright plumes and ruffles who also led horses, the children, goats, and mongrel dogs. Dust rose up from the fields and wagons rumbled in every direction. As they rode closer, several *vardos* bore signs that promised fortune-telling, there were jugglers and food vendors, men selling second-hand harness, blankets, saddles, and bridles. One man fashioned whips and curry combs, and several sat carving mouthpieces for flutes and hubble-bubble pipes.

All in all, it was a setting of friendly chaos, and one that would serve Catherine's purpose most admirably.

"There is much to learn about the *graiengeri*—men who trade horses," Dominic told her, helping her down from the bay. "For instance . . ."

He led his string of animals toward a tall, thin Gypsy speaking rapid French to a fat *Gadjo* villager. At the end of the Gypsy's rope danced a little sorrel mare, its head lifting proudly, nostrils flaring as it sucked in great breaths of air.

"Are you interested in that one?" Catherine asked. "She certainly has plenty of spirit."

Dominic chuckled. "She has plenty of spirit because old Tibor has given her a small dose of arsenic. It affects the animal's nerves. More often they give them a dose of salt to heighten their thirst. Either way, the animal shows itself off to its best advantage."

Catherine's eyes went wide. For a moment she fell silent, her mind searching wildly for a word strong enough to relay her outrage. "That is the vilest, most deceitful—"

"Only one of the most deceitful," Dominic corrected,

"definitely not the most deceitful." He had the audacity to grin. "They usually save that little trick for the *Gadjos*. A gypsy would easily spot such a simple ploy."

"Simple!"

"Another approach is to flog a horse while shaking a bucket of stones. The horse learns to fear the sound. When the owner wants a show of spirit, he simply rattles the bucket."

"Do you use these tricks?" She let him tug her along, but her respect for him had begun to dwindle.

"I would never abuse an animal, though as a boy I used many other such ploys. Still, as a trader of the *grast*, my knowledge of *janjano*—that means trickery—gives me an advantage." He urged her toward a pudgy, flat-faced Gypsy bartering three matched blacks that looked handsome indeed.

"Domini!" the squat man called out, reaching up to clap him on the shoulder. "I see you bring another batch of winded horses. A pity you do not own horses like these."

"Catrina, this is Adolf." The plump man tipped his floppy-brimmed hat, unleashing unruly thick black hair.

"Hello," Catherine said.

"What do you think?" Dominic asked her. "Shall we trade for these?"

There was something in the way he said it. Catherine stepped closer to one of the blacks, patted his sleek neck, and carefully looked him over. "Let me see his teeth."

Dominic's brow went up in a look of approval. Adolf stepped forward, opened the animal's mouth, and Catherine noted the hollows in its teeth, not yet worn smooth with age.

She knew something of horses, not all that much, but the animal's hooves looked sound, his chest, rump, and legs showed nice conformation. "I see nothing wrong with him."

"He appears to be sound," Dominic agreed, "and I believe he is. Unfortunately, he won't be for many years longer." He drew the long slender knife he carried in his boot, forced open the animal's mouth, and pried out a piece of tar from one of its teeth. Beneath the spot, the animal's tooth had been worn smooth. "You see, he's a whole lot older than he seems."

Adolf looked stricken. "May my eyes drop into my hat if this horse is more than six or seven. He must have eaten something—"

"Like tar?" Dominic supplied.

"But he has no white hairs," Catherine put in. "His coat is as black and sleek as a yearling's."

"Potash," Dominic told her, "rubbed into the hair to cover the gray."

Catherine shook her head. "I can scarcely believe it." But of course she did.

"Take a look at this." Dominic gripped the halter of the second black horse and lowered its head. "See this?" He pointed toward the animal's eye.

"What? I don't see anything."

"This little pinhole. The eyelid's been punctured. A tiny reed is inserted then blown full of air. It takes away the hollow-eyed look of an aging horse."

Adolf sighed dramatically. "You wound me, Domini. May my life dissolve if this horse is not a wonderful beast."

"Save it for the *Gadjo,* my friend."

"May my fingers and toes disappear—"

With a good-natured wave good-bye, Dominic led Catherine away.

"I can scarcely credit what you've shown me. How on earth do you ever find an animal that's worth buying?"

"I'm not looking for the best of the lot. I'm looking for horses that are incorrigible, those that have been poorly trained, ill-treated, or abused. The price goes down if an animal has sores from a badly adjusted harness, or if it's overly skittish. I buy them cheaply, feed and care for them until they're in good health, work with them until they're properly trained, then resell them for a profit."

Or at least I do whenever I live as a Gypsy. Since he'd been in France, he had occupied his time as he always did, enjoying his work with the *grai,* bringing them to their peak of performance. The gray pair he had run onto north of Sisteron when he'd first joined the caravan. The animals would make quite an addition to his stable at Gravenwold, one of the finest in all of England.

They strolled among the crowd, stopping several times to hear offers for one or more of Dominic's horses. He wouldn't buy more, since his time with the Rom would soon end. Catherine walked beside him, asking questions, making comments, enjoying herself as she always seemed to. Dominic found he was enjoying himself, too. Her enthusiasm sparked his, making the hours fly past in a blur of excitement and gaiety. The only fly in the liniment came from the hot jolt of desire he felt whenever she brushed against him, and the heavy tightness in his loins he had suffered since they had first met.

"Dominic, isn't that Pearsa?" Catherine pointed toward a red-painted *vardo* he recognized immediately. "Is your mother a fortune-teller?" She had hung a sign above the door, inviting all comers.

"She tosses beans into circles drawn on the head of a drum. Mostly, she sells potions. I've a few things left to do. Why don't you sit with her a while? Watch her at work."

Catherine's interest piqued. "You don't think she would mind?"

"Not if you're quiet."

Catherine climbed up in the wagon behind a brawny peasant with thinning gray hair. Pearsa glanced up at her entrance, but when Catherine sat down in the corner, she turned her attention to the man on the low wooden stool in front of her.

Nervously mopping his brow with a worn red handkerchief, he told Pearsa his wife had threatened to leave him so he needed a love potion. She held out her weathered, veined hand, and he placed a coin in her palm.

"Mix a handful of beans and the blood of a cow with the hairs of a loved one," Pearsa instructed, "a child or a mother or father. Let the mixture dry, then grind it into a powder and sprinkle it into your wife's food. After that, for three days, tell her how much you love her."

"You are certain this will work?" the peasant asked.

"It will work."

"Thank you," the man said, looking relieved as he left the wagon.

"Will the potion really work?" Catherine asked.

"If his wife still loves him, it will work. It is not often enough a man tells a woman that he loves her."

Catherine laughed at that, and Pearsa chuckled softly. Another man came in, and Catherine listened to Pearsa tell his fortune.

"At one time you have had great trouble with your relatives and friends," she said, carefully reading the position of the beans she had cast onto the drum.

The little man's mouth dropped open. "Why, yes. My mother-in-law hates me. She tried to prevent my marriage to her daughter."

"You have three times been in great danger of death," Pearsa droned, her brows knit, her face dark and serious.

The man thought for a moment, then his eyes went wide. "Once as a child I had the small pox. The second time I was injured when my wagon slid into a ditch, and once I was knifed in a tavern brawl. You are a wise woman, indeed."

From her place in the corner, Catherine smiled. What Pearsa had told the Frenchman would fit almost anyone. But the man flipped her a coin and left the wagon convinced of her sorcery.

Catherine glanced outside the wagon. She had thought Dominic only meant to be gone for a moment, but he still had not returned and the light was beginning to fade.

Catherine's hopes began to rise. Outside the wagon, the trading continued with even more fervor, the men beginning to drink, music being played.

"I think I'll look around a bit before it gets dark," she told Pearsa, stooping to climb from the wagon.

"Do not go far. My son will be worried."

Only as far as England, she thought but merely nodded and smiled. All afternoon she had gauged the area, spotting which road led out of town, which might provide the best avenue of escape.

Once, when Dominic had left her a moment to barter one of his horses, she had gone so far as to approach a well-dressed woman from the village.

"I'm terribly sorry to bother you," she'd said, "but I'm in a good bit of trouble and I wondered if you might be able to help me."

"Trouble?" the woman asked, arching a fine blond brow. "What sort of trouble do you mean?"

"I was abducted, taken from my home in England. Now I'm trying desperately to return. Is there someone in the village who might help me?"

The woman's light blue eyes strayed toward the colorful wagons, the menagerie of horses, animals, dark-skinned women and men. "The Gypsies are holding you? They have taken you against your will?"

Catherine hesitated only a moment. "Yes. I was sold into slavery. My family will pay handsomely for my return."

The woman inspected her from head to foot, taking in her simple garments, the heavy reddish hair that tumbled unkempt around her shoulders. Her expression was less than encouraging. "I cannot help you. Maybe someone else can."

"But surely—" The woman's brisk departure silenced her words. What had she expected? She was an English woman in a country at war with her homeland. On top of that, she looked no more than a peasant, certainly not a woman of means who could pay a lavish reward. The same thing had happened before.

Catherine took a last wistful glance at the woman's retreating figure just as Dominic returned to lead her away. As she had known from the start and knew again now, any chance for escape would be by her own efforts.

With that thought foremost in mind, Catherine rounded the wagon, spotted Pearsa's pair of sturdy bays tied behind it, and saw instantly the chance she had been seeking. In the hazy dusk, she could disappear with ease, and even if someone followed, once she got far enough down the road, she could ride among the trees and hide if she had to.

She still had the gold she had taken from Dominic's trunk, now sewn tightly into a handkerchief and hidden in an inside pocket of her skirt. Why Dominic hadn't remembered to take it back she could not say, but whatever the reason, it gave her a small ray of hope. She would travel to Marseilles, find a ship, and eventually make her way home.

Whatever happened, she would be away from the Gypsies, away from Dominic and her dangerous attraction— and a whole lot closer to a safe passage home.

Dominic returned to his mother's wagon a little after dark, his mood no longer pleasant. It had taken him more time than he had planned to sell his horses, and he had been chafing at the bit to get back and see Catherine.

Pearsa climbed down from the back of the *vardo* at his approach. "You look tired, my son. The trading did not go as you expected?"

"It just took longer than I planned." He glanced toward the rear of the wagon. "Where's Catherine?"

Pearsa looked up at him in surprise. "She left some time ago. I thought she went to find you."

"I haven't seen her since I brought her here."

Pearsa shrugged. "There is much to see. Perhaps she found something of interest."

"Perhaps," he said, but he was beginning to have his doubts. "I'll take a look around."

He hadn't gone three paces when he realized there was just one horse tied to the rear of the wagon—one horse, not two, as there should have been.

"Damn!" He swore several other oaths and finished with "the bloody little witch." Untying the second animal's halter, he grabbed a handful of mane and swung himself up on its back, then rode around the wagon to where Pearsa stood.

"She's taken one of the horses. I'm going after her."

"The roads are dangerous," Pearsa said, "but she has not been gone long. She can't have gotten far."

Just far enough to get herself into trouble, Dominic thought, remembering the drunken peasants and rowdy Gypsies who roamed their surroundings.

"Little fool," he grumbled, digging his heels into the big gelding's ribs and urging him off down the road at a gallop. There were two roads leading away, but one passed through open fields while the other traversed the woods.

Catherine had never been a fool. She would guess he'd come after her—she would travel the road that provided the best cover, the best chance for escape.

If she wanted to go so bloody much, he ought to let her. Why should he care what happened to a hard-headed little minx who thwarted him at every turn? But he did care, and the farther he rode and the darker it got, the more he worried that something terrible might have already happened.

Had she run across bandits or thieves—they always lurked nearby whenever there was chance of gain. A good deal of money traded hands at the horse fair. They would be waiting for the unwary along the lane.

Dominic thought of Catherine, imagined her lying in the forest, her simple garments torn away as she fought off her attackers, her small womanly body bruised and hurting. The idea of another man touching her, violating what she guarded so well made his heartbeat quicken and he urged the big bay faster, cursing himself for a fool, cursing her willfulness even more.

There was no sign of her up ahead, but he hadn't noticed any tracks where a horse had left the road. Thank God, the moon shone bright this night—he would thank Him even more if he found Catherine before something happened.

The stout bay's hooves thundered against the hard-

packed earth, the animal beginning to lather. But the gelding was sturdy and sound; Dominic pounded on. Several
times the road ahead curved to the right or left, and he
prayed he would find her around the bend just out of
sight. Instead he found nothing.

He wasn't sure which was causing his heart to thud so
painfully, his worry—or his temper. But with every passing minute, his anger heated up a little more. How dare
the cunning little wench put him through this! How dare
she cause him so much grief!

When he found her, he would give her a dressing-
down she wouldn't soon forget. When he found her, he
amended, his fury growing hotter, he would throttle her
within an inch of her life!

When he found her, he finally admitted, he would be
so bloody relieved, he wasn't sure what he would do.

He neared another bend and a sound up ahead caught
his attention. He pulled the bay to a halt. Hoofbeats, rapid
then slowing as the rider left the road. Catherine! He
would bet his last ounce of gold.

Dominic smiled grimly, cold determination setting in.
She was a sly little fox, but he had years of experience on
his side. Reining the horse off into the woods, Dominic cal-
culated the angle he would need to cut Catherine's trail.
If he erred, or if the rider was in truth someone else, he
would be losing precious time.

Dominic prayed his instincts were not wrong.

Catherine heard the hoofbeats. Dominic? Or was it someone else? Either way, she needed to elude them. She reined
the stocky horse off through the trees, riding as fast as she
could but the going a whole lot slower than it would have
been on the road.

Her legs ached miserably from riding in the uncomfortable position astride. Even the woolen blanket she had
thrown over the animal's back did not help. Branches
scratched her cheeks and tore at her hair; her knees, bare
with her skirts hiked up, were bruised and scraped, but

still she rode on. Sooner or later, she would find a place to hide, use shrubbery to erase the tracks of the horse, and wait for the rider to pass.

Once he had given up the search, she would go on.

Catherine ducked another low-hanging branch, made a sharp turn down a slope, and came to a small trickling stream. She smiled at her good fortune—the creek provided a perfect way to disguise the direction she planned to take. Feeling a surge of renewed confidence, she urged the animal forward. She had just entered the water when a shot rang out from somewhere to the rear.

Catherine's breath caught and held, and her heart lurched wildly. Who would be shooting? And who were they shooting *at*?

Ignoring a voice inside her head that urged caution, Catherine dug her small heels into the sides of the bay and rode back the way she had come until she could listen for the hoofbeats she had been certain meant Dominic followed. Instead she heard men's voices, garbled and too far away to make out their words, but the hostile tone more than clear.

Ride on, said the voice in her head. *Now is your chance for escape. Just follow the streambed as far as you can, then ride out and gallop away.*

What if it's Dominic? another, more urgent voice asked. *He helped you, you can't just leave him.*

Maybe it isn't Dominic at all, the voice argued. *Maybe there's some other explanation.* Any number of things could have happened yet she found herself unwilling to take the chance. Instead she turned back along the trail, her palms damp, her heartbeat thundering its worry for the man who might be in danger.

As the harsh male voices grew near, Catherine rode the bay off the trail, dismounted, and tied the horse to a tree. She crept through the undergrowth, ignoring the sting of branches and rough stones that scraped her arms and legs, until she came to an open spot in the forest.

Catherine's stomach knotted. Across the clearing, two

men held Dominic at gunpoint. Blood trailed from the corner of his mouth, and his arms were wrenched behind him by a third, powerfully built man who stood even taller than he did.

"God in heaven," Catherine whispered. What on earth could she do?

Glancing around, she searched frantically for something to use as a weapon, or something that might distract the men long enough for Dominic to get away. Grabbing a handful of pebbles and a short, stout dead tree branch, she edged as close as she dared and tossed one of the small rocks against a tree on the opposite side of the clearing.

"What was that?" one of them asked, a tall rawboned man with several missing teeth. Thieves from the look of them. "I think I hear some'sing."

Catherine lobbed another stone, which landed with an ominous clatter across the way.

"'Ave a look, René," said the one who held Dominic, apparently the leader, and a third man, a stocky Frenchman who wore his trousers way too short, strode off toward the sound.

"I will ask you only once more, Gypsy, where is the money? We saw you trading horses—we are not fools to believe what little we found is all that you 'ave." The huge Frenchman's pistol, stuffed into the waistband of his breeches, pressed into Dominic's ribs. "Where is the rest?"

"I told you, it's back in my wagon. Unless you wish to ride into a Gypsy camp, this is all you get."

The rawboned man stepped forward and punched him hard in the stomach. Dominic gasped at the heavy blow and tried to jerk free, but the bigger man only wrenched his arms even higher. The other cocked the hammer on his gun, the rasping click the most ominous sound Catherine had ever heard.

"What do you say, Pierre, shall I kill him?"

The huge man chuckled. "We will be doing the country a favor, *n'est-ce pas?* Ridding the land of another filthy Gypsy."

Catherine could wait no longer. Forcing aside her fear, she stepped from the woods and swung the stout branch hard across the arm of the man holding the pistol, knocking the gun from his fingers. When he spun toward his attacker, she used the stick to trip him and he sprawled into the dirt. In the same instant, Dominic made a move toward escape. Taking advantage of the Frenchman's surprise, he jerked an arm free, drove an elbow brutally into the big man's ribs, doubling him over, then spun and punched him hard in the jaw.

Catherine grabbed the fallen pistol, aimed it in the direction of the third robber, racing toward them from the woods, closed one of her eyes and fired. With a look of confusion and a muted grunt of pain, he clutched his bloody shoulder, sank to his knees, and pitched forward into the dirt.

When Catherine swung back toward the others, she saw Dominic had grabbed the pistol that had been stuffed in the big robber's belt and pressed it, cocked, beneath the man's beard-stubbled chin.

"If you do not wish to die," Dominic said, wiping the blood from his mouth with the back of his hand, "I suggest you make no too-sudden moves."

Pierre's fists clenched at his sides, but he stood stock-still. So did the man Catherine had disarmed, once he had staggered to his feet. Dominic dug into the huge man's pocket and removed the coins the thief had taken.

"Since there's a lady present, I'm not going to kill you." Catherine sucked in a breath. "I'm going to turn you loose. When I do, I expect you to move very slowly, take your two friends and leave."

Perspiration dotting his forehead, the big robber nodded. "We will do as you say." He glanced to the man across from him. "Gaspar, see to René. As the Gypsy says, I do not wish to die this night."

Gaspar edged carefully toward the wounded man, who groaned pitifully a few feet away.

"*Un moment,*" Dominic warned. "Fetch his pistol, Catherine. It's lying beside those bushes." He inclined his head toward the weapon.

Letting the spent pistol she still held slide noiselessly to the ground, Catherine forced her legs to move. Thank God she hadn't killed him, yet in that moment knew she would have, if it meant saving Dominic's life. She picked up the heavy weapon lying in the dirt and walked back toward the others.

Dominic released the burly Frenchman and stepped away, leveling the pistol on the man's wide chest. Catherine did the same with the gun she held, though her hand shook so much she could barely hold it steady.

"Go!" Dominic commanded the men. "And if you want to live, I suggest you keep on going."

With a low-muttered oath from one of them, the two men draped the injured man's arms across their shoulders and dragged him off into the woods. Catherine could hear them cursing, their heavily burdened movements awkward as they stumbled farther and farther away.

Releasing a sigh of relief that they were both safe at last, she turned her attention to Dominic. The cold, hard fury that darkened his eyes to glittering jet made Catherine's face go pale.

Unconsciously, she backed a step away.

Chapter Eight

"WHY?" DOMINIC ASKED, far too softly, moving toward her with a stealth that conveyed the anger he didn't bother to disguise.

"Why what?" She took another step backward. "Why did I come back? Or why did I run away?"

"Both," he said as he reached for her, his arm snaking out, grasping her before she could flee. He hauled her against him, his hands coming up to grip her shoulders, biting into her tender flesh. He shook her so hard her teeth rattled. "You little fool—don't you know you could have been killed?"

Catherine jerked free.

Dominic swore something she would rather not have heard and raked his long brown fingers through his hair. "Damn you, woman—are you so bloody determined to get home you're willing to risk capture by the likes of that bunch?"

"I'd have made it if I hadn't come back for you," she countered, her own temper rising.

"Made it? You wouldn't have gotten another two hours down the road. Dressed as you are, you've the look of a peasant wench—a tasty little morsel that would whet even the sanest man's appetite. You'd have fallen prey to the first rogue you passed by."

Of all the nerve! Catherine thought, her anger mounting. She had saved him and he dared to treat her like this. "I'd rather take my chances with any rogue but you!"

Dominic grabbed her again. "Is that so?"

"Yes!"

His eyes blazed with fury and a muscle twitched in his cheek. "You little hellion. You're in need of taming in the worst way, and I'm just the man to do it." He kissed her then, so savagely she might have fallen if he hadn't been holding on to her. She beat on his chest, tried to jerk away, but Dominic's grip only tightened.

One minute she was standing, fighting against his savage embrace, the next he had dragged her down in the grass, his hard body pressing her into the soft, damp earth beneath them. His kiss, so hot and demanding, seemed to steal the very air from her lungs. Instead of fighting him as she knew she should, she found herself kissing him back, her flesh tingling every place it pressed against his.

Dominic pinned her wrists beside her head and continued his assault, gentler now, his tongue sliding over her lips, coaxing them apart, then gliding into her mouth. No longer angry, he teased and stroked, sampled and tasted until Catherine moaned. When he let go of her wrists, she meant to push him away, but instead slid her arms around his neck and twined her fingers into his hair.

"That's right, fire kitten," he whispered into her mouth, "you want this, too."

She wanted to deny it, but his hand was cupping her breast, keading it, molding it through the thin cotton fabric. Her nipple rose up in his palm, and he teased the stiff peak between his fingers. She could feel his hardness pressing against her thigh, thick and throbbing, but his mouth tasted so hot and male and his tongue plunged so deeply that she arched against him instead of pushing him away.

She felt his hand slip into her blouse, felt the roughness of his palm against her skin, and her body heated until it turned to flame. When he moved his mouth from hers, lowered his head and captured the tip of the breast he held in his hand, Catherine thought her heart must surely pound its way through her ribs.

One hand cupped her bottom, moved down along her thigh, then lower. He began to shove up her skirt.

"No," she whispered. "You promised."

But he only covered her lips and kissed her. The hand on her calf moved up her thigh, and Catherine began to squirm. She wore nothing beneath her skirts—there was no protective barrier to save her from his warm, probing fingers. She felt them on the inside of her leg, felt them moving higher until they brushed against her sex.

"Dominic, please," she whispered, trying to stop him, but his hands had a will of their own. They touched where no man had, stroked and separated the satiny petals of her flesh and his finger slid inside.

"Oh God," Catherine sobbed, knowing soon he would take what he wanted—soon she would want it just as much as he.

"You said you would not force me," she pleaded, turning away from the lips that sought to stop her words. "I saved you—and you take what I am not willing to give."

Dominic's fingers stilled, and Catherine trembled at the sudden loss.

"You want this as much as I do," he said roughly, sensing her growing need.

Dear God in heaven, there was nothing on this earth she wanted more. "We can't always have what we want," she whispered.

"Let me love you, Catherine." The fingers slid inside again, working their magic, tempting her, promising pleasure she could only begin to dream.

Catherine squeezed her legs together against the fiery sensations. "No. I beg you, do not repay my deed by taking me against my will." The hand moved gently, sliding inward, stroking. Catherine unconsciously arched against the knowing fingers.

"Against your will?" he softly taunted.

"Take me back to your camp, if you must, but do not force me to do something I will forever regret."

For the first time he seemed uncertain. "Why would you regret?" He straightened. "Because I am a Gypsy?"

Because you're the devil himself. "Yes!" She would have said anything—anything to get him to stop. "I'm English— you're nothing but a worthless Gypsy!"

Dominic's hard gaze raked her. Eyes that moments ago held a fiery caress now looked at her with loathing.

"Your pardon, milady. I had not thought you found my company so distasteful." With an expression of disgust that could have shattered stones, he dragged his hand from beneath her skirts and rolled away, coming gracefully to his feet. The heavy thrust of his sex still pressed boldly against his breeches.

Catherine sat up too, her faced flushed with unspent passion, embarrassment, and guilt for the cruelty of her words. Afraid of the contempt she would see in his eyes, she climbed to her feet and started walking toward the woods where the horse was tied.

"Where do you think you're going?" Dominic snapped, gripping her arm as she tried to brush past him.

Catherine tossed back her hair in a gesture of defiance meant to cover her troubled emotions. "To get the horse. Yours appears to be missing."

"So it is, thanks to you." But he let her go, and she walked into the forest, grateful for the minutes to compose herself. By the time she returned with the bay, she was ready to face him, but her heart felt heavy, her breasts still tingled, and the place between her legs throbbed and burned.

There was no denying the passion she had felt, no denying she felt it even now.

There was no way to mend the destruction of her words.

Besides, she reasoned, her life lay ahead of her, a life as the Countess of Arondale, a life back in England. Passion for a man—any man except the one she would marry—could not go unchecked.

One glance at Dominic, one look at the bitterness on his face, the heavy toll her words had taken, and Catherine knew she had found a way to make it end.

Why did the truth always have to hurt so badly? He had known there was a reason for her rejection—had known she wanted him and yet denied him. He just hadn't wanted to believe his Gypsy blood had been the cause.

But he should have known—should have guessed it from the start. There wasn't a decent woman in England who would welcome a Gypsy into her bed. It was one of the reasons his father had guarded his secret so carefully. There had been speculation, of course, rumors that had traveled throughout the *ton*. But no one gave them credence. Instead they only enhanced his mystique, making him even more desirable.

Back home women flocked to his bed. Now the truth became clear as it never had before: Dominic Edgemont, Lord Nightwyck, might make an acceptable lover—Domini, the black-eyed Gypsy, would not.

Not even to a ruined woman without a shred of virtue.

He watched Catherine now as she looked off into the woods, afraid to meet his eyes, afraid because she had finally admitted the truth.

He could almost believe she *had* bewitched him, just as Vaclav once predicted. He thought about what had happened between them. Given the same set of circumstances, the way she had responded, there wasn't a woman on this earth he wouldn't have taken—whether she hated his Gypsy blood or not.

Her desire for him certainly hadn't been lessened by the fact of his heritage. She was a woman of fire and passion, and whatever virtue she'd once possessed had long ago been stolen, so there was no need for his restraint.

Had her cutting words alone been enough to sway him

from his goal? What was it about her that kept him at bay yet bewitched him almost to the point of madness?

"Will you search for the other horse?" she asked, leading the one she had ridden up beside him.

"With any luck, when he gets hungry, he'll find his way back to the wagon." His hands gripped her tiny waist and he swung her astride the horse's broad back, her skirts protectively bunched beneath her. He didn't miss her wince of pain.

"Sore?"

"I've never ridden astride before."

"The ride I would have given you would have left you sorer still." Catherine's pretty face turned red, and Dominic felt a jolt of satisfaction. Gripping a handful of the horse's mane, he swung up behind her, reached down and adjusted her leg over the horse's neck so she rode sideways in front of him.

"Better?"

"Yes. Thank you." Catherine swallowed the tightness that had risen in her throat. Dominic was angry, furious in fact. But even after her hurtful words, he concerned himself with her comfort. Though the ploy had worked far better than she would have dreamed, she already regretted her words. The fact he was born half-Gypsy was no fault of his, and there was nothing about him that was worthless—nothing at all.

They rode in silence the long way back to the wagon. Dominic said nothing even as she opened the door and stepped inside the *vardo*, but he looked at her with such bitter disappointment it nearly broke her heart.

That night she slept poorly, arising at first light to find Dominic already returned to the fair, and Pearsa working over her cooking pots. She straightened at Catherine's approach.

"Good morning, Pearsa."

The old woman's face, always lined and weathered, looked even more haggard and grim. "What have you done to my son?" Any trace of the warmth she had shown yesterday had fled with the morning's breeze.

"Done to him? I've done nothing. I don't know what you're talking about."

"I do not believe you. From the moment you came, you have been nothing but trouble. As long as you made him happy, I did not care. He is not happy now."

"Maybe he's having trouble with his horses."

Pearsa snorted in disbelief. "Do not imagine me a fool. I know my son well. Whatever you have done makes him feel less than a man. The others know he sleeps on the ground outside your wagon. They know you ran away from him—Vaclav saw you. Yana made certain all in the *kumpania* knew. They whisper that his Romany blood is not strong enough to keep a mere *Gadjo* woman in her place. Vaclav has them laughing behind his back."

"Vaclav is a fool!" Catherine spat. "Dominic is more of a man than Vaclav, more of a man than any in this camp. If the others cannot see it, they are blind."

Pearsa's dark brows shot up. She eyed Catherine with a hint of speculation. "Then you will tell him so," she demanded with cool authority. "You will mend whatever damage you have done."

Catherine licked her suddenly dry lips. "No."

Pearsa started to argue, but the high-pitched wail of her name stopped her short.

"Pearsa!" the shout echoed again. Coming from the space between the wagons, Czinka waddled as fast as she could in their direction, beads, spangles, and bright gold coins jingling with every step. She spoke in Romany, the words tumbling out with each rapid breath, her hands flailing wildly, urging Pearsa to follow.

"What is it?" Catherine asked as the old woman started away. "What has happened?"

"It is Medela. Her time has arrived. The baby is coming much faster than we expected."

Catherine hurried along beside the two women. "Is that bad?"

Pearsa smiled, but kept walking. "It is very good. She will suffer little pain. You have indeed brought good fortune—"she stopped at the entrance to the black mohair tent beside Czinka's wagon, where Medela and her husband, Stavo, Czinka's son, resided—"at least for some of us." She ducked beneath the tent flap.

With a heavy grunt, Czinka stooped to follow.

"Is there anything I can do?" Catherine asked before she could step inside.

"You can put a few more logs on the fire. It will keep the evil spirits away."

That wasn't what she had in mind, but Catherine agreed. "I'll keep it going until the baby comes." She smiled to think she was growing accustomed to their odd beliefs.

"Until the child is baptized," Czinka corrected, and barged inside the tent.

Baptized, Catherine thought, amazed as always at the Gypsies' mix of ancient superstitions and modern religion. What a melting pot of odd beliefs the Romany were.

Shaking her head at the notion, Catherine bent to the task, tossing a heavy log on the fire outside the tent, then she started into the woods to renew the dwindling stack. Halfway there, little Janos raced up and caught her hand.

"Medela is having her baby?" he asked.

"Yes. Very soon, it seems."

There was dirt on his nose and chin. He wore only a ragged pair of pants, no shirt, no shoes. Kicking a stone with his small bare foot, he looked up at her a little oddly. "Is it true what they are saying? That you stole one of Domini's horses and ran away?"

Catherine toyed with the folds of her skirt but forced herself to look at him. "I borrowed the horse. I would have seen it returned."

"Why do you wish to leave us? Domini said you were not like other *Gadjos*. He said you liked Gypsies."

What would he say if Janos asked him today? "I like a great many of your people. I like you and Medela. I like Jozsef and Czinka."

"Do you like Domini?"

Catherine's heart constricted. *Like* was hardly the word. What *did* she feel for Dominic? she wondered, but when the truth threatened to surface, Catherine firmly tamped it down.

"Of course I like him. Dominic's been very good to me."

"Then why did you run away?"

Catherine brushed tousled black strands of hair from the little boy's cheeks. "I want to go home," she said softly. "Back to England. I have family there, just as your family is here."

"Domini lives there sometimes. Maybe he will take you."

Catherine smiled wanly. "Maybe."

"Where is he?" He glanced back toward the wagons.

"He's gone back to the horse fair," Catherine answered.

"No he hasn't. He rode off by himself. I think he is sad because you ran away."

Catherine stopped walking and knelt at Janos's feet, the tops of their heads now even, one glistening black, the other sun-shot crimson. "Why do you say that?"

"Because when Vaclav laughed at him and called him a fool, he said only that for once he agreed."

Dear God, what had she done? "Do you think you might guess where he went?"

Janos thought for a moment, his small black brows drawn together. "To the pond, maybe." He pointed through the trees. "Sometimes he likes to catch fish."

"Why don't I go and see?" Medela was in good hands with Pearsa, and they wouldn't let her inside the tent anyway.

Janos grinned and nodded. Instead of asking to go along as she had thought he would, he turned and raced back toward his wagon. What a wise little boy he was, she thought, and started off toward the lake among the trees.

As her steps cut a path through the long-bladed grasses, Catherine's thoughts remained on Dominic. Her cruel words had stopped his advances, but the cost to him had

been high. There had to be another, less destructive way
to deter him, a way that would leave them both with dignity.

Squaring her small shoulders in a gesture that said no
matter what happened, she had no intention of giving in
to his demands, she marched onward, believing somehow
she would find the right way to thwart him.

Knowing even more strongly that whatever happened
between them, using hurtful untruths about his heritage
would not be the way.

Dominic tossed a dry blade of grass into the water. It
floated on the surface, drifting, drifting, just as his
thoughts had been.

Needing time to himself away from the knowing
glances, the smug insinuations that he could not handle
his woman, he had ridden the gray until both were
exhausted, then come here to the pond.

His woman. Vaclav had called her that. Dominic scoffed
at the notion. He had paid a fortune in gold—and yet she
defied him as no woman had.

He should have bedded her long ago, slaked his desire,
and been done with it. If he had shown her her place from
the start, kept his feelings in check, her words could never
have hurt him.

What did it matter? he told himself firmly. In a few more
days he would return to England. He had work to do at
Gravenwold, responsibilities he couldn't ignore. If this
hadn't happened, he would have delayed his departure as
he had planned, hoping Catherine would come to him,
admit her passion, her desire.

That this was his last chance to know the freedom of
the Rom had been part of the reason he had decided to
stay. He would never feel guilty about spending these last
few precious weeks with his mother, roaming the landscape with his people. Once he returned to England, he'd
be doing battle once more with his father, fighting the old

man's bitter domination, or observing the strict code of ethics of the *ton.*

Over the years, he had come to accept his place in society, even enjoy it. But this last taste of freedom he would savor the rest of his life.

All except for Catherine. The deceitful little wench had made his life a living hell.

He thought of the way she'd come back for him, the way she'd endangered her life for a chance to save his. He had never felt such pride in a woman, such a fierce desire to protect one.

Why had she done it, he wondered, when she felt the way she did?

He remembered again the cruel words she had spoken, words he had heard a thousand times, yet coming from her cut his insides like a blade. He had believed she was different. Special. He should have known she was not.

He wasn't fishing, Catherine saw, but he sat near the edge of the water, his broad shoulders propped against the sturdy trunk of a tree. His big gray stallion grazed on the end of a tether in the soft green grass in the distance. A mockingbird sat in the branches above him, making occasional forays out over the pond.

"May I join you?"

Dominic turned at the sound of her voice. His expression held no warmth, only cold resignation. The mockingbird screeched down at her with the same disapproval she read on his face.

"You've nothing better to do than spend time with a worthless Gypsy?"

She ignored the barb and instead sat down on the log beside him, looking out onto the tiny pond. A fish broke the mirror-smooth surface, sending minuscule ripples dancing back to the shore.

"It's very pretty here. It reminds me a little bit of home."

His look remained cool, but a small measure of interest

sharpened his features. She could see him struggling with his curiosity, just as she had hoped.

"You lived by a pond?"

She nodded. "A lovely little lake not much larger than this."

"Where?"

"In Devon, not far from the coast. When I was very small, my father used to take me fishing. I thought it a great deal of fun." She smiled at the memory, remembering the knee breeches she had borrowed from Cook's little boy. They were too big in the waist and too snug in the seat, but she wore them with pleasure for a time. "Of course, I was soon too much of a lady for those sorts of things—or at least thought I was."

His mouth curved sardonically. "Too much of a lady for a lot of things."

She let that comment pass, trying not to recall the very unladylike way she had responded to his kisses, the magic he had worked with his hands.

"By the time I was six or seven," she continued as casually as she could, "I preferred dolls to fishing. I liked to dress them up in the beautiful gowns my mother helped me sew and give them miniature tea parties."

"Tea parties?" He looked faintly amused.

"I always loved the feminine things in life. A whiff of perfume, the feel of a piece of silk against my fingers." She smiled then, a bit wistfully. "If my parents could see me now, they wouldn't recognize me as their proper little girl."

Dominic arched a brow, his tone dry and not the least forgiving. "I'm afraid I beg to differ. Given the circumstances, I believe you've retained your English sense of propriety most admirably."

The way he said *English* made her suddenly wish she weren't. "Is that what you think, Dominic? That saying what I did to you last night was the proper thing to do?"

He looked at her hard, a challenge in his eyes. "What do you think?"

"I think it is something I shall always be ashamed of—especially when I didn't mean a word of it."

His head came up at that, strands of shiny black hair blowing softly across his forehead in the breeze. "You meant it. You wouldn't have said it if you didn't."

"I only meant to stop you. I wouldn't even have thought of it except you brought it up. At the time, it seemed a good way to . . . to . . . set things back on a more stable course."

He scoffed at that. "A more stable course, Catrina? Like returning to your bed alone—without the company of a worthless Gypsy?"

Catherine watched him a moment, saw the anger—and the pain. Impulsively, she leaned over and kissed him softly on the mouth. "I don't care that you're a Gypsy. And there is nothing worthless about you."

He didn't move to touch her. She prayed that he would not.

"You're a fine man, Dominic. I won't soon forget the way you saved me from Vaclav. Even last night, I believe you came after me because you thought I might be in danger."

She touched his cheek, willing him to believe her. "I've seen you with Janos and the rest of the children. I've seen your patience with them, the way they look up to you. I've watched the way you care for your mother, the kindness you've shown old Jozsef, even Yana. You never wanted to hurt her, even I could see that."

"Catherine," Dominic said softly, reaching out for her. She only moved away.

"I admire you, Dominic, for your strength and your courage . . . your gentleness. But I must return to England, to my family."

"To your parents? Your brothers and sisters?"

She shook her head. "No. My parents are dead. I have no brothers or sisters."

"I'm sorry," he said. He straightened on the bench beside her, looking larger, more in control than he had just moments ago. "But I still don't understand. If you have no family, why is returning so important?"

If only she could tell him the truth, ask him to help her. But an offer of gold would mean nothing—he seemed to have plenty already. And her title would mean less than nothing. In fact it might only make him believe she really did think him beneath her. Certainly now was not the time to broach the subject, not when she was trying to repair the damage she had done.

"Is there someone . . . ?" he coaxed when she didn't answer soon enough. "A husband or a lover?"

Catherine hesitated only a moment, then grasped the idea like a drowning man clutches at straws. "Yes. Yes, there is." Unconsciously, her chin came up, the lie demanding all her concentration. "You see, I'm engaged to be married. We quarreled and I ran away. I'm certain he's been searching, waiting and praying for my return."

"This man . . . are you in love with him?" Black eyes held green, probing, searching.

Say yes, the voice demanded. *Make this madness end.* "He's very kind and generous," she answered with a glance away. "We've made great plans for the future."

Dominic eyed her with a touch of tenderness. "I know something of society, Catherine. Do you truly believe this man will want you after all that's happened? The scandal alone would drive most men away."

"This man will want me." Dear God, he spoke the truth. It would take all the machinations in the kingdom, the wealth of Arondale, and the hand of her powerful uncle to repair her ruined reputation. Somehow, some way, she vowed, they would succeed.

"Tell me about such a man," Dominic pressed, leaning back once more against the tree. He looked confident now, the shadowed look in his eyes had fled. Catherine felt a rush of relief that he had decided to believe her.

Which left her right where she'd been before. "He's very handsome," she said, hating to continue the deception, but seeing no way out of it, "and strong, of course. He's very much in charge of things." She tried to envision her made-up lover. "He can sometimes be demanding, but also he can be gentle."

Dominic's heavy brows drew together. "He's wealthy, I assume—since he's so perfect. Is he titled as well?"

She shook her head. "No. And he isn't all that rich, either, just merely comfortable."

"What does he do for a living?"

Catherine worried her lip. This was really getting sticky. "He . . . ah . . . he raises horses. Yes, he's a landowner and he raises beautiful horses. He's always loved the country, you see. And children, of course, he definitely loves children."

"I see." His dark eyes touched her face. There was a flicker of something there that hadn't been there before. "Quite a man you've described. A woman is bound to love a man like that one."

"I suppose that's true." A man like that would indeed be to her liking. It struck her then, like a bolt of lightning— the man was very much like Dominic. In fact, with the exception that her imaginary lover lived a quiet life in England—he *was* Dominic.

She silently prayed he hadn't noticed the similarity.

"What about you?" she asked, hoping for a change of subject. "Your mother says you never intend to marry. Don't you want a wife and family of your own?"

"That, my sweet, is the last thing I want." The edge had returned to his voice.

"But why not?" Why did she feel so crestfallen?

"It's a long, ugly story, and I'm hardly in the mood to discuss it now." He took her arm. "It's getting late. We ought to be getting back."

He was brooding again, though for the life of her, she couldn't fathom why. "Dominic?"

"Yes?"

"Do you forgive me?"

For the first time he smiled, a flash of white in a face so handsome it made her knees go weak.

"Ah, fire kitten, when you look at me that way, I would forgive you almost anything. Just promise me you won't put yourself in danger again—even if it means my worthless hide."

He was teasing her now, and Catherine laughed at the sound. "Were you worried for me, then, out there in the darkness? Maybe just a little?"

"Worried? If you hadn't looked so damned beautiful standing there holding that pistol, I would have throttled you within an inch of your life."

"Is that a thank you?"

He smiled again. "Yes, I suppose it is."

"My pleasure." She gave him a soft look in return.

Dominic took her hand. "None of this would have happened, my love, if only you would trust me to return you to England. Behave yourself and I give you my word I shall get you there."

"Back to my betrothed?" she couldn't resist, then saw by the narrowing of his eyes that she shouldn't have.

"If that is indeed your wish."

Catherine said nothing more, and as they strolled through the grass Dominic grew pensive as well. *Little fool,* he thought, no man in England would marry a young woman who had spent months with a band of Gypsies, to say nothing of her lost virginity.

Strangely enough, it angered him. Virgin or not, Catherine was a prize worthy of any man, no matter his wealth or position. If things were different, he would not be put off by her slightly soiled condition. He wasn't put off now.

In fact, after her startling confession, her concern for his feelings, and the way she had humbled herself to him, his desire for her burned hotter than ever. Her Englishman wouldn't want her—but Dominic did.

And now he believed she did, in truth, want him. He brushed off her involvement with the Englishman. Catherine might think she still loved him, but the way she responded in Dominic's arms said it just wasn't so.

He smiled to himself. In light of this new information,

the idea he'd been considering seemed even more appealing. He would bed her, make her see that her feelings for her betrothed had long since faded away, return with her to England, and make her his mistress.

The next time the opportunity presented itself, nothing Catherine could do or say was going to make him stop. Once she discovered the delights he could show her in bed, the rest would be easy.

The breeze blew a gust of cool air and beside him Catherine shivered. "Cold, my love?" he asked.

She shook her head. "Only in the shade. I'll get my shawl then I need to check on Medela, she's already begun her labor."

A *Gadjo* concerned for a Gypsy. He still couldn't quite fathom it. But it only made him more certain that Catherine's words of apology had been sincere.

Dominic smiled with satisfaction. Catherine wanted him no matter who he was. He wondered if tonight would be too soon to renew his campaign.

*There's night and day ... sun, moon, and
stars ... wind on the hearth. Life is very
sweet....*

George Borrow

Chapter Nine

CATHERINE RETURNED TO MEDELA'S TENT while Dominic fed
and watered his horses. Pearsa's big bay had not yet
returned, so Dominic had decided to ride back along the
road they had traveled last evening to see if the animal
might have stopped somewhere to graze.

Holding her shawl together against the brisk late afternoon breeze, Catherine made her way toward the circle
of wagons.

Earlier, on their return from the lake, she and Dominic
had gathered a load of firewood, which now lay neatly
stacked beside the low-burning flames. They had known
immediately all was well—Stavo, Medela's lanky black-
haired husband, sat beside old Jozsef and several other
men, grinning and swilling great draughts of *palinka.*
There was laughter and hearty congratulations, several of
which were directed to Catherine for the gift of her hair.

"The little *Gadjo* brought *kushto bacht.*" Good fortune.
"Too bad, my friend," Stavo said to Dominic, "that she has
not done the same for you!" Stavo laughed and Dominic
scowled, but only for a moment, then he shrugged off the
comment as nothing more than a result of his friend's
intoxication.

"You may not be feeling so fortunate when your little
bundle of luck keeps you up half the night," he replied

good-naturedly. The men guffawed, slapped Stavo on the back, and took another swig of their fiery brew.

"Never were truer words spoken," old Jozsef said, grinning, wiping the liquor from his mouth with the back of a wrinkled thin-veined hand.

Inside the tent, Dominic and Catherine found Medela resting comfortably—her strapping black-haired baby cuddled securely in the crook of a dark-skinned arm.

"You've given Stavo a fine-looking son," Dominic told her. "You should both be proud."

"He's a beautiful baby," Catherine agreed as the tiny infant began to root at its mother's plump breast. She meant to walk off, allow Medela some privacy, but the young woman merely lifted the blanket, exposing her milk-ripe bosom until the tiny searching mouth found the nipple and covered it from view.

Catherine felt the heat creep into her cheeks, which flushed even more at the look of amusement on Dominic's handsome face.

"I think we should let Medela rest," Catherine said, turning away to cover her embarrassment. "I'll come back a little while later."

Dominic followed her out. "There is nothing to be embarrassed about, Catrina. A child nursing at its mother's breast is only nature's way."

Catherine looked at him and suddenly felt foolish. "You're right, of course. It's just that things are so different where I come from."

"Different, yes. Still it seems you've managed to adapt. If it should come to it, I think you could adjust to almost anything."

There seemed some point to his words, though Catherine didn't bother to pursue it. Instead, they had walked back to his wagon so Catherine could retrieve her shawl, and Dominic went in search of the bay.

Now, standing once more outside the tent, Stavo and Jozsef snoring soundly off to one side, Catherine smiled to think of the contented mother and tiny child lying on their sheepskin pallet within. One day she would love to have children of her own. Boys or girls, it would make no difference as long as they were healthy.

She thought of the child *she* had once been, of her mother, a slightly taller image of herself who had always been there to comfort her, and of her father, knowing what a grandchild would have meant to him. She imagined, if he were alive, how worried he would be for her now, how fearful for her safety. Then she thought of the man who had abducted her from her town house and forced her into a day-by-day fight for survival.

Who would do such a thing? she asked herself for the thousandth time, and for the hundredth time swore she would discover the truth of who it was and make the villain pay.

Catherine stooped to pick up a log, which she added along with several dry branches to the fire in front of the tent, filling the air with the odor of pine. Then she bent over and lifted the tent flap. Pearsa had not returned, but Czinka sat near where Medela lay sleeping.

"How is she doing?" Catherine asked.

"Medela is fine. Her *cajori* is fine. She has named him Sali, our word for laughter, because already he smiles and plays."

"Sali," Catherine repeated, "it's a fine name."

"As fine as the child," Czinka said. "Your magic is strong. There are few *Gadjos* who would help a Gypsy mother bring another child of darkness into the world. We are grateful."

Children of darkness. Catherine had heard them called that before. It seemed a sad prophecy of the life the tiny Romany boy would live.

And yet they were happy. Carefree in a way men envied. Catherine wondered if that were not part of the reason for their persecution. Gypsies had never formed a government, never waged a war, and never owned a territory. It was sometimes said there were only two classes who were

truly free—the nobility, who were often above the law—
and the Gypsies—who were below it.

"Tell Medela I'll stop by again tomorrow," Catherine
said. "If you need anything, just let me know."

Czinka smiled, rocking forward on her heavy thighs, the
coins below her fat earlobes jingling. "I will tell her, but
she will already know. Good night, Catrina."

Always they referred to "knowing" or "seeing." Maybe
they did possess some special powers. Whatever the truth,
the belief had been instilled in them for hundreds of years.

"Good night, Czinka."

By the time Catherine left the tent to return to
Dominic's wagon, the sun had gone down and campfires
burned into the clear black sky. It was a pleasant time of
evening, when violin music drifted through the cool
spring air and laughter floated up from distant wagons.

The woman were serving the evening meal. In most
families the men ate first, served from behind, the women
careful never to lean across them. Women never walked
between two men, but always walked around, something
Catherine had trouble accepting in the beginning, but
now did without conscious thought.

She had almost reached Dominic's wagon, usually set
up on the perimeter because of his work with the horses,
when a man's thin hand clamped over her mouth. Catherine tried to scream and started to struggle, but he urged
her to silence with a finger to his lips.

When she nodded her understanding, the thin man
released his hold. "What is it you want?" she asked in
French, recognizing the man for a peasant. He stood a
good foot taller than she, spare to the point of gaunt, his
face a study in angles and planes.

"We have come to help you, mademoiselle. It was
learned in the village that the Gypsies are holding you prisoner. We have come to see you safe."

Another man stepped from the trees, this one thick-
chested, with beefy thighs and hands. He wore a leather

vest over a homespun shirt, dark brown breeches, and a
soft brown slouch hat pulled low across a wide forehead.

"Come, mademoiselle, we must hurry," he said. Each
man took an arm and urged her forward.

Catherine looked from one man to the other, gauging
them, her mind spinning with thoughts of leaving—and
the promise Dominic had made to see her safely home.
The villagers looked scruffy and unclean, and there was
something in the way their eyes ran over her that warned
her to beware.

"The story you've been told is wrong," she said. "I'm
here by my own wishes. I do not need your help." She
tried to stop but the beefy man shoved her forward.

"You will come, pretty one. With us you will be safe."

Catherine's heartbeat quickened. Again she tried to halt
their forward progress, digging in her heels—already they
were leaving the camp behind. "Let me go! I don't want
to go with you."

The lean man chuckled. "You will go, *chère Anglaise.*
You will give to us what you give to the filthy Gypsies."

Catherine screamed then, as long and as loud as she
could. The beefy man slapped her, gripped her arms, and
jerked her hard against him. She could feel the scratchy
fabric of his shirt, smell the sour odor of stale red wine.
Heart hammering, Catherine tore free and started to run.
She stumbled over several loose rocks, fell and scraped
her knees, stood up and started running again.

"Dominic!" she screamed. "Somebody please help—"
But the man's thick fingers cut off her plea. She was breathing hard, struggling against his heavy frame. The Frenchman merely wrapped an arm around her waist and
dragged her deeper into the woods.

"Do you think someone will come?" the gaunt man
asked his friend, craning his neck toward the camp with
a look of unease. Catherine thought she heard the sound
of voices shouting in the distance, but couldn't be sure.
"You worry for nothing, Henri. They will be far too busy
to worry about the *Anglaise.*" Both of them laughed.

As they dragged her deeper into the woods, Catherine twisted against the iron hold of the beefy Frenchman, clawing, kicking, and biting to no avail. He only squeezed the arm that encircled her, cutting off her air supply until the world spun crazily and small black circles danced with menace in front of her face.

The Frenchman hauled her down behind a clump of bushes, and Catherine felt her legs kicked out from under her. She landed with a jolt of pain beneath the barrel-chested man, his heavy weight once more making it hard to breathe. She heard the slight rending of fabric as he jerked her blouse off one shoulder, baring a breast, then thick blunt fingers dug into her flesh. When he removed his hand from her mouth, Catherine tried to cry out, but he silenced her with his hot sticky lips.

The bile rose up in her throat. Love of God, she couldn't bear it!

With a fresh surge of will, Catherine fought against him, struggling to free the arms he pinned between them, kicking her legs, and twisting her mouth free of his. At another muffled scream, he raised his arm to slap her, but the hand stopped in midair and his heavy weight jerked backward. He stumbled but Dominic's grip on the back of his vest held him up.

"Mon Dieu," the Frenchman growled as Dominic whirled him around. A hard brown fist punched him solidly in the chin, and the Frenchman staggered backward. Catherine pulled her blouse back up to cover herself, struggled to her feet, and stumbled out of the way.

"Henri!" the big man yelled, searching wildly for his companion.

"Your friend has fallen asleep," Dominic said with sarcasm, glancing at the gaunt man lying on the ground a few steps away. Only the telltale bruise on his cheek and the blood that trickled from his mouth conveyed the truth of his fate.

"I will kill you!" the big man roared. Lowering his head, he charged, but Dominic sidestepped, jerked him upward

and slammed a fist into his stomach. The Frenchman
grunted in pain and outrage, and swung a hard blow to
Dominic's middle, doubling him over. He spun away,
regained his balance, and delivered a reeling blow to the
bigger man's jaw. Two quick jabs followed by another
crushing blow to the face, and the beefy man went down.

Blood ran from his nose and his eye had begun to puff
closed. Still, he climbed to his feet. Several blows were
exchanged, then Dominic threw a powerful punch that
snapped the big man's head back. He staggered and
swayed then crumpled toward the earth, landing with a
groan face down in the dust. For a moment, Dominic
stood over him, his face a dark mask of rage, his hands still
balled into fists.

At last he turned and his black eyes fixed on Catherine.
She saw his look of concern, the fear for her he couldn't
disguise, and started running toward him. He caught her
up in his arms, pressing her against him, his hand lacing
into her hair as he cradled her head with his palm. He
pressed his dark-skinned cheek against her softer fair one.

"Dominic," she whispered, clutching his neck, holding
him as if he were all that saved her from the raging fires
of hell. "I didn't think you would hear me."

He swept back heavy locks of her golden-red hair, clearing away the dirt and twigs with a shaky hand. "Are you
all right?"

She nodded. "Thank God you came when you did." A
lump swelled up in her throat and her voice broke on the
last word.

"I found the bay. I was just leading him back to camp
when I heard you cry out." Dominic tightened his hold
and squeezed his eyes closed against the image of Catherine struggling beneath the bulky peasant, her blouse
pulled down, her lovely milk-white breasts spilling into
the Frenchman's hands.

Her body trembled against him. Dominic tipped her
chin with his hand and realized she was crying. It was the

first of her tears he had seen and something tightened around his heart.

"Hush," he soothed, "you're safe now. No one's going to hurt you—not as long as I'm alive to stop them." It surprised him how much he meant the words.

Catherine only clutched him tighter. "Why did this have to happen? Why can't I ever feel safe anymore? I always felt so protected, so loved. Now . . ." She wept quietly into the hollow between his neck and shoulder. "Every day seems harder than the last."

He cradled her against him, his hands sifting through her silky hair. Tilting her chin up, he brushed a tear from her cheek with the tip of his finger.

"Fear is a way of life for my people," he said, his voice still rough with emotion. "They never feel safe, no matter where they are." His thumb moved gently back and forth along her jaw. "But you soon will. I shall see you returned to England, back where you belong."

"Yes," she said softly. "Back where I belong."

She spoke the words, but he could have sworn they rang with a note of hollowness. Did she hate to leave him then? Would she miss him if he let her go? He prayed the answer was yes and that she would accept his plan to keep her with him.

Catherine sniffed and wiped away the balance of her tears with the back of her hand. "I'm sorry. I never cry anymore. I guess I was just . . ."

"It's all right, *cajori,* women are supposed to cry."

Catherine smiled tremulously and released a weary breath. "I found out long ago crying is just a waste of time. There is very little in this world worth my tears."

He wanted to argue, to tell her there was much besides sorrow for a woman to cry about. There was beauty and laughter, and times of joy with the people who really mattered.

"We'd better be getting back," he said instead. "Those two ruffians will be waking up soon enough. I don't think they'll bother you again, but they may cause trouble in the village. We'll have to tell the others what happened, pack up and leave just as soon as we can."

Catherine looked surprised for a moment, then resigned. What she might have said got lost in the sound of gunshots coming from the *kumpania.*

"God in heaven, what now?" she whispered.

There wasn't time to answer. "Come on." Grabbing her hand, Dominic raced back in the direction of the camp.

As they drew near, he could hear Gypsy voices raised in anger, the terrified neighing of horses, the crack and groan of timbers and the heavy thud of wood as it crashed against the earth. Smoke billowed into the clear night sky, French villagers shouted in triumph, and Dominic ran faster.

By the time they reached the wagons, the villagers were leaving the camp, pitchforks and lanterns in hand, some on horseback, some walking, dust rising up from their heavy boots as they trod the fields back toward their homes.

The destruction they had left behind clenched Dominic's stomach into a hard, tight knot.

"Dear God," Catherine whispered.

The camp lay in shambles, cooking pots overturned, sacks of flour and sugar trampled into the dirt, clothes and bedding scattered from one end of camp to the other. Babies wailed and stiff-haired dogs slinked, tails between their legs, beneath the wagons. One *vardo* lay on its side over a smoldering campfire, the flames now beaten to blackened wood and smoking embers. A sign in big red letters had been hastily nailed to the side: STATIONNEMENT INTERDIT AUX NOMADES—GYPSIES FORBIDDEN.

Dominic walked straight to old Jozsef, who stood wringing his hands, looking haggard and far older than he had just hours ago.

"Is anyone hurt?" Dominic asked.

"Stavo tried to stop them. He nurses a bloody nose and his ribs are cracked. The others are older, wiser. They knew better than to try to fight back."

"Medela and the baby?" Dominic asked.

"They stayed inside the tent. Luckily the villagers were more intent on destroying the wagons. But Ithal lost his violin."

Dominic glanced across to where the white-haired old man cradled his dearest possession, the two halves of the instrument resting in his arms like a stricken child, the broken strings trailing over his weathered hands.

"How did this happen?" Catherine asked, moving to Dominic's side. "Who would do such a thing?"

As if he had awakened from a trance, Jozsef swung his gaze in her direction, his eyes, dull and listless just moments ago, now burned with a furious light. "You!" he shouted. "You have brought this curse upon us."

"Me!" Instinctively, Catherine stepped back, but Dominic's arm around her waist held her firm. "What have I done?"

"Do you deny you asked the villagers to help you escape? That you told them the Gypsies held you captive?"

Dominic let go of her waist. He turned to face her, his eyes no longer gentle, but dark and strangely accusing. "You were trying to leave again? That's what you were doing with those men in the woods?"

Catherine wet her lips, which suddenly felt so parched she could barely speak. "It—it wasn't that way. I told them what they heard in the village was wrong. That I was here by choice. I didn't want to go with them, but they forced me." She looked up at him, her green eyes pleading. "You must believe me, Dominic. I never meant for anyone to get hurt. I just didn't know. . . ."

He didn't know either—didn't know if he believed her, couldn't have imagined how much he wanted her words to be true. One thing was certain. As she glanced at the destruction around them, he had no doubt about the sorrow she felt, her regret at what had happened. He could read the anguish in the depths of her lovely green eyes.

"But you did speak to the villagers," he pressed, because

he had to know for sure. "You told them you wanted to leave."

"That was before . . . before I believed you would help me go home."

"Surely you are not fool enough to believe her." This from Yana, hands on hips, raven hair tumbled around her shoulders, thick black strands blowing wildly in the breeze. "The *Gadjo* woman brings trouble. If Dominic cannot control her, then she must go!"

"What Yana says is true," Vaclav put in, coming to stand in front of Dominic. "You believed yourself man enough to tame the witch, but you have failed. You stopped me from doing what should have been done from the start. Take the woman in hand, Domini. Prove you are a man."

There was relish in Vaclav's words. Yana's face glowed with triumphant satisfaction.

"He is right," old Jozsef said. "It is the men of this camp who must see to the safety of the others. Either you are one of us, my son, or you are not. Will you see to your woman?"

"She does not know our ways," Dominic argued, seeing Catherine's stricken face, the way her hands gripped the folds of her skirt. "She is not one of us."

"She is your responsibility," Vaclav argued. "Yours and yours alone."

Pearsa stepped from the shadows of the overturned wagon. "The woman came to us as a slave. She acts as any of us would whose freedom has been taken. She has worked side by side with the rest of us. She has been a friend to Medela—she has brought her and the child good fortune."

"Yes," Medela put in, thrusting her head through the opening of her tent, her babe in her arms. "Catrina would not wish us harm. She did not understand."

"Hush!" Stavo warned her. "This is men's business. Get yourself back inside the tent and see to our child." Medela hesitated only a moment, then ducked back into the tent.

"The gift of her hair brought your babe into this world."

Czinka waddled toward her son-in-law, gold bracelets jangling. "You should be grateful."

"She also brought me these!" He pointed toward the bruised ribs visible through the remnants of his bloody, tattered shirt. "It is a wonder no one was killed!"

"I warned you, *didikai*," Vaclav sneered at Dominic. "I told you she would bring trouble. Now we will see—are you a man, or has she turned you into something less?"

Catherine glanced at the smoldering wagon, the crying children and scattered remains of the camp. Though the women, all but Yana, seemed to side with her, the men wore hostile, unforgiving expressions that clearly blamed her—and ultimately Dominic—the man responsible for her conduct.

She looked up to find his hard black eyes fixed on her face. "They expect me to beat you," he said with soft menace, and Catherine's insides churned. "It is the way of the Romany male to rule his woman." His hand came up to touch her cheek. "For the trouble you've caused, you probably deserve it but I . . . in the name of Sara-la-Kali, I cannot bring myself to lay a hand on you." He glanced toward the men who muttered their displeasure around them. "Maybe Vaclav is right—maybe you have bewitched me."

She hated the defeat she heard in his voice, the condemnation she saw on the face of the others. She knew how much Dominic's Gypsy heritage meant to him, how badly he ached for acceptance, and in that moment she could not bear the thought of him being rejected.

She tossed back her hair and squared her shoulders, cold determination setting in. "What's the matter, Domini? Can't you handle a lowly *Gadjo* woman?" A smile of challenge curved her lips. "Maybe you're afraid of me, afraid of my powers—is that it?"

Dominic's jaw clamped hard and a muscle ticked in his cheek. "Have you lost your mind?" he hissed between clenched teeth.

"Maybe you're afraid I shall run away and leave you,"

Catherine taunted, drawing each of the men's attention. "Maybe you couldn't bear to live without me."

Blazing black eyes, so dark they seemed bottomless, bored into her. Dominic grabbed her arms and jerked her up on her toes. "I'm warning you, Catherine."

Catherine swallowed hard, met his frightening dark look, and willed him to know what she was doing. "Why should I listen to you, Domini—you're nothing but a worthless Gypsy!"

Something flashed in Dominic's eyes, then it was gone. For an instant, she thought he had understood, then the grip on her arm grew tighter and she knew that she had been wrong. He turned to the men who still clustered around them, said something in Romany which made them all laugh, and dragged Catherine toward the center of the circle of men.

Sweet Jesus, what had she done? Dominic's fury rippled through every muscle and sinew. Catherine strained against his powerful grip, for the first time truly afraid. He was a big man, stronger than any she had ever known. And his eyes—God in heaven, she had never seen such anger. An image of the beefy Frenchman, reduced to a mound of battered flesh, rose up in her mind.

Catherine closed her eyes, certain she would feel the bite of his fist at any moment, then her world turned upside down. She landed with a grunt of pain across Dominic's sinewy thighs, and several layers of her skirts were tossed over her head. He had seated himself on an overturned crate, and pulled her across his lap.

"Scream, damn you," he warned, so low that only she could hear, "and a few more tears would not be remiss."

"Let me go!" she shrieked, never meaning anything more. "Damn you! Damn you to hell!" She felt his palm through the last remaining layer of petticoat, but the powerful blow she had expected felt little more than a playful sting.

"Scream," he warned, and this time, though the blow made her gasp, it was only meant as a warning. *He knew!*

she realized with a wave of relief and began to scream her lungs out. From the corner of her eye she watched the furious-looking blows he delivered that were in truth quite bearable.

All but the last two, which he delivered with what must have been relish. He was grinning when he jerked her to her feet and the men around them were cheering. Catherine rubbed her bottom and gave him her very best glower.

"From now on you'll do exactly what I tell you," he commanded. "Isn't that right, Catrina?"

She tried to look meek and repentant. "Yes, Dominic."

"Tell these people you're sorry for the trouble you caused."

"I really am sorry. I never wanted anyone to get hurt." This she said with sincerity, for it was the truth.

Vaclav turned to Yana. "Maybe Domini is smarter than I thought," he said. "You would do well to heed this lesson, or you may receive a little of the same."

Yana's dark eyes went wide. "You would not dare!"

Vaclav stepped toward her with a look of menace. "Should you doubt it, I will show you. Now get back to your wagon. I will join you there in a moment."

When she didn't move quickly enough, Vaclav grabbed her arm, swung her around, and gave her a hard swat on the bottom. Yana hurried away with a backward glance that could only be deemed respectful.

Even Stavo seemed satisfied. "I shall remember this, my friend. I have always dreaded the day my pretty wife might come in need of direction. Now I believe I will look forward to it!"

They all laughed at that, and Catherine left them laughing. She smiled a little herself. Dominic's pride had been saved, and the men seemed satisfied as well.

Catherine kept on walking, thinking the sacrifice had been little enough to pay for the sake of the man she loved. She stopped dead in her tracks, appalled that a thought so absurd could have somehow crept into her mind.

Sweet Jesus! It was just that the violence she had witnessed had left her emotions in turmoil, she told herself
firmly, and pushed her musings in a safer direction. There
was much to be done back at the wagon if they would be
leaving this eve. When she reached it, she found Pearsa
already at work. Catherine silently joined in, uprighting
spilled barrels of flour, shaking out trampled bedding,
refilling the water supply. Thank heavens neither of their
two wagons had been badly damaged, just a board broken
loose here and there.

They had just about finished storing everything away
when Pearsa reached over and took her arm. Eyes as dark
as midnight touched her face. "I am grateful," she said, "for
what you did for my son."

Catherine just nodded, feeling a sudden tightness in her
throat. For the first time, she realized how much the old
woman's approval had come to mean. Though she had
tried her best not to, Catherine had worried what her
taunting words to Dominic might have done to the wom-
en's nebulous relationship. She smiled now, thankful Pearsa
had understood. With luck, the old woman would see that
the others did, too.

It wasn't much later that Dominic arrived with the
horses, hitching them up to the wagon—Pearsa's lost bay
among them. She climbed up on the wagon seat, and Catherine started to join her, but Dominic took her hand.

"You'll ride with me," he said simply, leading her back
to his wagon instead. He helped her up on the seat, then
climbed up beside her. Pearsa pulled her team of horses
in behind the other wagons, and Dominic drew his in line.
They rode along in silence for a while, Catherine wondering at his thoughts.

"Why did you do it?" he finally asked, turning to look
at her. "I don't understand."

Catherine smiled softly. "I know how much it means to
you, being one of the Rom, being accepted. I didn't want
you to be hurt."

He raked a hand through his hair, but several shiny

black locks tumbled back across his forehead. "It was you who might have been injured. For God's sake, Catherine, I'm more than twice your size. What were you thinking to do such a thing?"

"I hoped you would know why I was behaving as I was. I believed you would not hurt me and I was right."

Dominic studied her face, his eyes moving over the curve of her cheek and coming to rest on her mouth. "Catherine . . ."

One hand cupping her face, he leaned over and kissed her, softly at first then with greater and greater urgency. She could feel his need for her and it kindled a need inside her. Catherine parted her lips for him, allowed his tongue to slide in, tasted it, and touched it with her own. Dominic groaned.

She felt a sudden slowing of the wagon as he pulled the animals to a halt, and dust from the lane swirled up around them.

"We'll catch up with them later," he said, his voice husky.

"No! It's dangerous here. There are those men you fought with earlier, to say nothing of the villagers who came to the camp."

Dominic hesitated a moment, then he sighed with resignation. "I suppose you're right. The last thing either of us needs is more trouble." With an expression that looked none too pleased, he slapped the reins lightly on the horses' rumps and they leaned against their harness, quickly catching up with the rest of the wagons. "Besides, you've had quite enough excitement for one night."

His broad chest rumbled with laughter.

"What's so funny?"

"You thought for certain I was bound to commit murder, didn't you?"

"You ought to be on the London stage."

"Every Gypsy learns to act by the time he's three years old. *"Mong, chavo, mong!* Beg, boy, beg!" He grinned, white teeth flashing. "When it's necessary, we can play any role from a beggar to a king."

Catherine rolled her eyes skyward. "You certainly had me fooled."

"I didn't really hurt you, did I?"

"No, but I credit you enjoyed yourself far too thoroughly."

He laughed again, such a rich male sound. "All too true, fire kitten, all too true."

Catherine poked him playfully in the ribs, and he grunted in imagined pain. She smiled and leaned back against the seat, then she sighed, beginning to feel the stressful events of the evening. Resting her head against his shoulder, she felt the strength there, the warmth of his body, and closed her eyes.

Beneath her, the wagon creaked and moaned, rumbling toward the distant horizon. She wondered where they were going, but as long as they traveled closer to England, she didn't really care.

England. Back to her life as the Countess of Arondale, a life away from the Gypsies and their constant fight for survival.

Away from the warmth and protection of the man who sat beside her.

A hard knot balled in Catherine's stomach. For the first time since her ordeal began, she wondered what it would be like to go on without him.

And knew without doubt that without him, she would never be quite the same.

Far up the dim twilight fluttered
  Moth wings of vapour and flame
The lights danced over the mountain
  Star after star they came

              In Sara's Tents
              Walter Starkie

Chapter Ten

"**W**HERE ARE WE GOING?" Catherine finally asked.

Dominic shifted his position on the hard wooden seat, trying in vain to get comfortable. They had traveled throughout the night, Catherine asleep on his shoulder until he finally woke her and insisted she go inside and lie down in his bed. Even then she had stayed just a short while, returning to the seat, demanding to take over the reins, which she did for several hours, allowing him to rest just as she had.

"We're traveling to Ratis in the Camargue, to the festival of the Saint Maries. For years Gypsies have been going there to celebrate their patron saint, Sara Kali."

"Tell me about it."

He smiled. "No one knows exactly when it started. No one even knows exactly why the Gypsies started coming. But the Saint Maries—two sisters of the Blessed Virgin who bore witness to the resurrection of Christ—were said to have arrived there after their ship foundered on the rocks off shore. They say it was their Gypsy hand-maiden, Sara, who saved the women's lives."

"Go on," Catherine urged.

"In the twelfth century a church was built called Notre Dame de Ratis. Since the early thirteen hundreds, every year at the end of May, Catholics pilgrimaged to the church to celebrate the Saint Maries, but no one knows exactly when the Rom began to make the journey. It just seems that year after year more Gypsies come, and except for a few years during the Revolution when the church was pillaged and sacked, they still do."

"To celebrate Black Sara," she confirmed.

Dominic nodded. "It's said she tends the sacred fire for the Wandering Race. They believe her body is entombed beneath the church and come to pay homage."

Dominic grinned. "It's also a damned fine excuse for a gigantic *patshiv.*"

Catherine laughed. "They never miss the chance for a party."

"No, and this one brings Gypsies together from all over the world. It's quite an occasion."

Catherine found herself looking forward to it. "How long before we get there?"

"If we keep on as we are, we should arrive some time tomorrow."

"And afterward . . . after the festival? Then will you take me home?"

He hesitated only a moment. "Yes."

When Catherine sighed with relief, Dominic almost felt guilty. Then he thought of the uncertain future she would face back in England, the ruin and the heartbreak, and renewed his resolve to do as he had planned.

Except for a few brief stops for food and a short night of exhausted slumber, the small band of wagons continued along the road. They crossed a fertile region of crops and vineyards in the south of Provence and entered the wild Camargue, the marshy plain that reached the shores of the sea. Scrubby tamarisks dotted the landscape, sea ravens circled overhead along with plovers, herons, ducks, and even an occasional blue ibis.

The cloudless sky did nothing to block the sun, which would have been hot except for the chilly wind that swept down across the plains from the central plateau.

"It's called the mistral," Dominic told Catherine when she remarked on it. "It blows one day out of every two."

"I don't think I would like that."

"At least it keeps away the mosquitoes and helps to dry up the mud."

They passed clumps of stout low trees and an occasional cypress, saw great roaming herds of black cattle and shaggy white horses, and in the salt moors, rabbits, beaver, and small land tortoises.

"Look, Dominic!" Catherine pointed excitedly toward a huge flock of pink flamingos, their vibrant feathers in bright contrast to the stark white limestone hills. From their lazy attitude perched on one leg, they burst into the sky in a shower of color that left Catherine breathless.

Dominic watched her with what seemed warm admiration, pleased at her interest in this desolate expanse of reeds and salty marshlands. "There is beauty almost everywhere," he said, "if only we take the time to look for it."

A few short months ago, Catherine wouldn't have understood his words the way she did now, traveling like a carefree child among a band of Gypsies as wild as the creatures around them. In some ways she would miss this life, she realized, and found the notion surprising.

As their destination grew near, they passed more herds of cattle and horses.

"Those white shaggy-maned horses are Arab," Dominic said. "They may be small, but they're hard-hoofed, and sure-footed, and they've a great deal of stamina." The men who attended the horses and the great herds of stout black bulls wore bright-colored shirts, brown cloth breeches, and black coats lined with velvet.

"Guardians," Dominic called them. "The great long trident they carry is called a *ficheiroun*—it's used together with a rope to help with the herding."

In Ratis, the city of the Saint Maries, they passed white plaster buildings with red-tiled roofs and traveled down narrow streets paved with granite. The women wore their hair in high chignons tied with a strip of velvet or lace, and many of the men wore white garments with a wide red sash and a black string tie.

In the distance, the huge steeple of the fortress church rose up over the flat arid land with its stiff grass and reeds. There were battlements and a watchtower, and church-bells chimed news of a wedding. They camped at the rear between it and the sea.

"Every year by tradition," Dominic explained, "the same families camp in the same space."

For the Pindoros, Dominic's band, it was a fortunate cus-tom indeed, for every inch of the barren landscape was already filled to overflowing with wagons and tents.

"Les Caraques!" a Provencial called out to the passing caravan.

Dominic wove his way expertly through the melee of vendors selling their wares, trough makers, coppersmiths, leather craftsmen, horsetraders, and kettlemenders. Women wove blankets and mats from marsh reeds, sold carved wooden clothespins and bundles of wildflowers, and children shined shoes. There were men who offered to pull teeth, or catch rats—just about anything that would earn them a coin or two.

Once camp had been set up, Catherine working hur-riedly, eager to take in the sights, Dominic led her around the encampment. By afternoon, the entertainment had begun—a variety of circus performers, jugglers dodging knives, puppets, dancing bears, violinists, and fortune-tell-ers. Street musicians played flutes, panpipes, and tambou-rines.

Near the center of the camp, a fat lady and her tiny trained dogs, all of them dressed in matching pink satin dresses, performed for a crowd of laughing children. One of the dogs, a spotted mongrel with patches of fur missing from its ragged coat, perched on a stick held off the ground by two dark-skinned men. The animal seemed to be smiling at its own finesse.

"Domini!" someone called out. It was old Armand, the

tinker. "I see you made it at last." He flashed Catherine a toothless grin. "And you didn't even lose your lady."

"After her little adventure with you," Dominic teased, "I kept a much closer watch on her."

His rheumy old eyes moved over her with a look of appreciation. "A wise move, *mon ami,* a very wise move, indeed."

They ate from at least half a dozen food stands, then laughing and sated, Dominic returned her to their wagon.

"I've a friend I need to see in the village. Why don't you rest for a while? Tonight there will be singing and dancing—you'll enjoy yourself more if you're not tired." *Besides, I intend you'll get very little sleep.*

Feeling Catherine's warm fingers entwined with his own, watching the soft way she looked at him, he knew he had waited long enough. Dominic shifted to hide his growing arousal. Tonight, at last, Catherine would be his. "I'll be back by the time you awaken."

Catherine started to protest that she wasn't tired at all, but Dominic's determined expression gave her pause. Besides, how would he know what she did?

Dominic pressed a hard kiss on her mouth, then waited for her to climb up in the wagon. As soon as he left, she climbed down. Pearsa had set up a fortune-telling booth near the front of the encampment. She would go and watch her working for a while. Catherine started in that direction then stopped short.

She had seen Pearsa at work before and remembered each of the old woman's tricks, as well as how to read the customer's expression and use it to make him believe. Wouldn't it be fun to try it?

Already she was being called *bala kameskro*—the sun-haired Gypsy. She believed people would come. And she could earn money for Dominic and his band, just the way the other women did! For the first time she could be an asset instead of a liability.

Catherine hurried back to the wagon, searched the shelf behind the bed, and found the small gold coins with the

holes in them that Dominic had given her to braid into
her hair. She also found several bright ribbons and wove
them into the lace trim on her blouse to make herself look
more colorful. This time she *wanted* to be noticed—she
wanted people to pay her money for *dukkeripen*—saying
the future.

Walking through the maze of stalls, Catherine saw
Pearsa working, selling Jericho flowers—resurrection
plants from the Red Sea. Dominic had shown her once
how the dead, brownish clumps of curled leaves and ugly
dried roots—totally lifeless in appearance—would slowly
uncurl when placed in water, and turn a vibrant green.
The Gypsies told buyers that if you owned one, your life
would change for the better in the same miraculous way.

Catherine laughed, thinking how clever the Gypsy
women were and determined to be just as clever. Some
ways down from Pearsa, she convinced a man to rent her
his stall for just a few hours.

"You're probably hot and thirsty after working so long,"
she said to the short, balding man when he started to protest. "Surely you would like something to eat and drink?
In the meantime, your place will be secure and earning
you money while you aren't even here."

He grinned at that, appreciating her logic. "I will return
in just two hours. I will expect payment then—one way
or another." His eyes fixed on her breasts, his meaning
more than clear.

"You shall have your money," Catherine said, her chin
coming up. But for the first time she felt a little uneasy.
What if no one stopped to have his fortune told? What if
they didn't believe her and made her return their money?
Whatever happened, it was too late to back down now.

Catherine sat down in the booth, smiled, and began to
ask passersby if any would like his fortune told. She discovered she needn't have worried. The first man she
smiled at tossed her a coin and sat down in the chair
across from her. Catherine dropped the money down the
front of her blouse as she had seen Pearsa do.

She studied his face, guessing him to be in his thirties, took in his simple homespun shirt and canvas pants, and spotted the delicate piece of lace he had stuffed into his pocket, probably a gift for a woman. He was old enough and poor enough to have experienced the standard number of problems, she decided. Since she had no beans to cast, she turned his hand over and pretended to read the lines in his palm.

"At one time, you had great trouble with your relatives and friends," she said, praying it was true.

The man searched his memory, his light brown brows knitting together. "Why yes! Once my best friend ran away with the girl I was to marry. How did you know?"

Catherine just smiled. Again she studied his hand. "You have been three times in great danger of death." She held her breath.

The peasant looked thoughtful. "I was very sick as a child ... then there was the time I fell off the barn, and ... and the time my friend and I fought bitterly over the girl I finally married." He regarded her with a look of awe. "Go on," he said, "I must hear more."

And so she told him about the woman he loved and how he wanted to please her, and again he looked awed. When he left sometime later, Catherine was a second coin richer, and the man seemed well pleased. The hour passed with one customer stopping after another. Catherine dropped coin after coin into the bodice of her blouse.

It was working! She had actually done it! Recklessly, she wished Dominic would return a little early, come in search of her, and see for himself what she could do. If he were pleased with what she had done and his mood seemed right, maybe they could discuss their return to England and she could begin to tell him the truth.

With that thought in mind, she dropped another small coin into her bodice, where it clanked against the others, then jumped in surprise as a long-boned, fine brown hand followed it down.

Feeling the sweep of bold fingers on her breast as

Dominic drew the money out, she bolted to her feet in outrage, knocking back the bench she had been sitting on. Hard black eyes fixed on her face, and a look so furious it could have melted stone.

"I thought I told you to get some sleep."

What was he so angry about? "I wasn't sleepy."

His eyes ran over her, insolent and mocking. "Good." One hand locked on her wrist, and he started striding away, jerking her rudely behind him.

"What are you doing? Where are you taking me?" Dominic didn't answer, just kept on walking, making her run to keep up. When they reached his wagon, he climbed the stairs, opened the door, and dragged her inside.

"Dominic, what on earth is the matter?"

"You need money?" he replied, turning to face her as he tugged his full-sleeved red silk shirt free of indecently snug black breeches. He pulled a pouch of coins from his waistband and tossed it in her direction. "I have more than enough, and you have exactly the favors I wish to purchase."

"What?"

"It isn't bad enough you insult the *cobayi* by pretending to practice their trade. No, you had to go behind my back, trying to get your hands on more money."

"I meant no insult. I was doing it for you and the others. I thought I'd found a way to help out."

"Don't lie to me, Catherine. The truth is the money you stole from me wasn't enough for you to get back to England—to your precious betrothed. I told you I would take you, but you didn't believe me. You were determined to get there on your own."

"You're crazy!"

He unbuttoned the cuffs on his shirt then stripped it away, throwing it heedlessly into the corner.

Catherine's unease heightened at the sight of his wide muscular chest. She tried to brush past him, but he caught her up in his arms and tossed her back onto the bed.

"You think you're in love with him, but you're not." He

sat down opposite the bed and pulled off his boots, which landed with a heavy thud against the rough wooden planking, stood up and unbuttoned his breeches.

Catherine's eyes fixed in horror on the narrow line of coarse black hair that angled down from his flat stomach, and the heavy bulge of his sex, pressing hard against the front of his breeches.

"What do you think you're doing?" she asked, her voice shaky with the first real stirrings of fear. When Dominic's only answer was a hungry look that make her mouth go dry, Catherine moved to the side of the bed, tried to edge around him, then ran for the door. Dominic's sinewy arm locked around her waist and he hauled her against him.

"You're not going anywhere. I've waited long enough." His mouth came down over hers, hard and unforgiving. Catherine struggled against him, hating the lies that had brought him to this, fighting for a chance to explain.

She jerked her mouth free of his. "I'm telling you the truth!"

He gripped her shoulder and arched her backward, kissing her more savagely than before. Though she struggled to break away, he lifted her easily and carried her over to the bed. She felt his fingers tugging down her blouse, then the rending of fabric.

"It's time I took what others have already taken."

With a fresh rush of fear, his brutal words sank in. "Dominic, please—you don't understand. Please—you must not do this!"

But he was lost in a haze of passion and pain. Pinning her wrists to the bed, he tried to kiss her, his big body moving over hers. Catherine turned her face away.

"I beg you, please, you must listen!"

It took several long moments more before her words and frantic pleas for him to stop began to sink in. Dominic looked down at her pale oval face, saw the fear, saw the hurt—and not an ounce of desire for him.

What the hell am I doing? He took a steadying breath, and his hold on her wrists grew gentle. He shook his head, trying to clear it, trying to regain control. He let her go and Catherine sat up on the bed.

"You wish to claim that which others have taken," she said softly, "but there are no others." Her green eyes glistened with a mixture of confusion and uncertainty. "There never has been."

Dominic frowned, his heart still hammering the last of its anger, desire still raging through his veins. "You're not telling me you're a virgin?"

Her pale cheeks colored with a slight rush of pink. "Yes."

"That's impossible. You've been left on your own for weeks. There isn't a sane man alive who wouldn't have taken you—except maybe me." Outside the wagon, dusk had fallen. He could hear muffled laughter and singing. He raked a hand through his hair, willing his heartbeat to slow.

"I was meant for the pasha," Catherine reminded him. "I was worth a lot more money untouched. Then Vaclav came along and . . . you know the rest."

Dominic just stared at her, his mind as yet unwilling to accept what she had said.

"What I told you about the money was the truth," Catherine continued. "I did it for you and the others. I wanted to help in some way. I had hoped I would make you proud."

He saw the way her eyes met his and didn't glance away, and a heavy weight lifted from his shoulders—replaced by a sharp stab of guilt.

"Damn." Dominic released a ragged breath. His body, still hard and pulsing, ached for her with every heartbeat. Her breast peeked enticingly from behind the rent he had made in her blouse, and her soft red lips were still swollen from his kisses. God, he wanted her.

Was she really a virgin? he wondered, and felt an unwanted surge of emotion. "I'm sorry. I saw you take that money and something inside me just snapped."

The corners of her mouth curved up in a small forgiving

smile. It made her look vulnerable and all the more desirable. "It's all right. You didn't really hurt me."

"I'd never hurt you," he said softly, and in that moment he knew what he must do. "Believe that, Catherine. Whatever happens, you must always believe that."

Her smile grew warmer, and there was a look of relief in her eyes. Dominic leaned over and kissed her, gently, ever so gently. He brushed her lips, then settled his mouth over hers. Still, he didn't move to touch her. Catherine hesitated only a moment, then softly returned the kiss, her tongue brushing his in a tentative feather-light motion.

When she started to pull away, Dominic deepened the kiss just a little, compelling her to remain. Her lips felt warm and incredibly soft, and his body grew harder still. He wanted to plunge his tongue into her mouth, to cup her breasts, shove up her skirts, and drive himself inside her. He wanted to take her and make her his. Instead, he shifted his position beside her and gently pulled her into his arms.

"I'm sorry, fire kitten," he whispered. "I should have trusted you—or at least let you explain." He kissed her sweetly, an apology, a tender touch that proved how much he cared.

When Catherine slid her arms around his neck, accepting the gesture, returning it, Dominic slid his tongue into her mouth. His hand moved up her body, then slipped inside the tear in her blouse to lift and mold a breast. The heavy weight of it, the way her nipple hardened beneath his fingers, made the ache in his loins grow hotter.

"Catherine," he whispered, his tongue moving deeper, more boldly, willing hers to return his skillful invasion. For a moment she did, and his hand worked its magic on a full ripe breast. Then she pulled away.

"We have to stop," she said, breathing almost as heavily as he was.

"Not yet," he said and started kissing her again. He used every skill he had ever learned, every trick of passion. He could feel her fingers lacing through his hair, feel the rapid beating of her heart. Again she drew away.

"We . . . have . . . to stop," she repeated, her eyes glazed with passion, "before it's . . . too late."

He raked her with a last hungry glance. "It's already too late." Dominic pressed her back down on the bed and Catherine gasped at the feel of his hard male body over hers. Her small hands pressed against his shoulder, but he captured her mouth, and his hand slid under her skirts.

"Dear God," she whispered as his finger sifted through the soft red-gold nest above her womanhood, searched for and found the satiny folds of her flesh and slipped inside. Catherine moaned into his mouth and arched against him. With infinite patience, he moved his finger in and out until her head fell back and he could feel her building passion.

"You would never have come to me, would you?" he whispered, amazed and in a strange way proud of her will. Beneath her garments, his hand stilled its movement. Catherine squirmed, silently begging for more.

"No," she said softly.

"But you want me, don't you?"

When Catherine didn't answer, he kissed her, long and hard. One hand teased her nipple. "Don't you?"

Catherine trembled. "Yes."

Dominic released the breath he had been holding, and the last of his uncertainties fell away. He would take care of her, see she was protected.

Kissing her all the while, he stripped away her torn blouse and tossed it aside, then eased her skirt down over her hips, leaving her naked before him. Her long, flame-colored hair spilled teasingly over one shoulder while her high lush breasts with their tawny nipples, heavy at the base then curving deliciously upward, seemed to reach toward his hand. Her skin looked as pale as alabaster, her waist so narrow he could span it with his hands. Supple thighs and graceful legs tapered down to small feminine feet with delicate high arches. Catherine didn't try to cover herself, just looked up at him as if she sought his approval.

"I knew you would be lovely," he said, his voice husky, "but you are so much more."

Catherine closed her eyes and let his words of praise wash over her. Desire pulsed through her veins with every breath, but until this very moment, she had remained unsure. She was tired, so very tired of pitting her mind against her body.

Now, as Dominic's mouth covered hers and his hands skimmed over her flesh, she knew her body had won and the battle, at last, was over. She felt his touch and knew this was what she wanted—had wanted all along. His fingers moved knowingly, skillfully, with such infinite patience that in minutes she found herself caught up in the dreamlike web he spun.

His fine dark hands cupped each breast, molding it, pebbling the peak into a hard tight bud, then he stroked her thighs, his finger sinking into her as he took a nipple in his mouth, ringed it with his tongue, then began to suckle gently.

Catherine felt the heat of it, the incredible sweetness, and flames of desire shot through her body. His hands and his mouth were everywhere, his fingers probing, knowing exactly where to touch her. When he left her to strip off his breeches, the thought of stopping seemed nothing more substantial than a hazy wisp of smoke.

"Dominic," she whispered as he settled his hard-muscled body between her legs. But no words of protest reached her lips. Instead she traced the sinews across his shoulders, and her fingers splayed on his chest, the smooth skin taut over steely bands of muscle beneath. How long had she wanted to do that? she thought vaguely. How could she have waited one more day?

Dominic kissed her again, and she felt his hardened shaft against her leg. She should have been frightened, but she was not. She was only afraid this would end. As his mouth moved over her breast, he nipped and teased until she squirmed at the exquisite sensations.

"Please," she heard herself whisper, arching against his hand. But he paused.

"The Englishman," he said. "Tell me you love him and this will not happen."

She waited for the inner voice to command the lie, but it never came. She thought of the trouble her untruths had caused, the hurt this new lie would bring.

"Do you still believe you're in love with him?" he pressed.

"No." She felt a slight alteration of the tension in his body.

"Thank God."

Dominic kissed her then, passionately, thoroughly, using his tongue, his hands, the weight of his body to drive her insane. She could feel the rough hair on his legs, the muscles of his chest, and the hard demanding length that sought to gain entrance. Catherine opened her legs, offering herself to him, and Dominic released a soft groan.

"Catherine," he whispered. Nudging her legs apart even more, he settled himself between them and eased himself inside. He stopped when he reached her maidenhead, and the expression he wore was so tender it touched her heart.

"I'll have to hurt you—just this once. I'm sorry."

Catherine twined her arms around his neck and brought his lips down to hers for a kiss. Dominic returned it, teasing, coaxing, then plunging his tongue into her mouth at the same instant he drove himself inside her.

Catherine cried out at the searing pain, and her fingers dug into his back. His lips moved to her temple, he kissed her throat, her cheeks, her eyes as he held himself in check. When she felt his palm gently stroking her breast and realized he wasn't going to hurt her again, Catherine began to relax. The moment she did, Dominic eased himself farther inside.

"All right?" he asked.

Catherine swallowed back her uncertainties and nodded. She felt filled with him, connected as she never would have believed.

"The worst is past," he promised, his voice raw and husky, and began to move slowly inside her.

She could feel the tension in his body and knew the strength of will he must be using to hold himself back. Catherine relaxed even more and began to let the rhythm of his movements sweep her up. Dominic sensed her acceptance and the force of his thrusts picked up speed.

In minutes he was plunging against her, pounding hard and deep, and Catherine was arching into each powerful thrust. Her own muscles tensed as something sweet and sterling swelled inside her, something so elusive it seemed it could not be real. Instead of fighting against it, she gave herself over, clutching Dominic's neck, wrapping her legs around him, crying out his name.

Sensing the precipice she neared, he drove deeper and harder, and Catherine soared over the edge. Bright lights lit the horizon, silver pinpricks, flashes of scarlet, and a taste so sweet she wet her lips trying to capture it before it could fade away.

It seemed the world as she had known it no longer existed, replaced by a starry landscape of sweetness and beauty, passion and serenity. As she began to spiral down, she had the feeling she had captured a tiny particle of that world and that she would never lose it.

Then she felt Dominic's hard arms around her, pulling her against his long, hard-muscled length, and the fine sheen of perspiration that covered his body mingled with that of her own.

It was in those last precious moments of closeness that she knew. Those seconds that she held him and he held her. When the intimacy of what they had shared still clung like a fragrant perfume.

She loved him. There was no more denying it. There was no way to avoid the truth.

And though the knowledge frightened her, it also set her

free. Whatever happened, whatever path in life she followed, nothing could destroy this memory she had captured of what it felt like to love.

"Are you all right?" Dominic smoothed the damp red-
gold hair from her temple.

"Yes. You were wonderful."

"I didn't hurt you?"

"Only a little. I would gladly pay the price again for the
pleasure—dear God, what pleasure you gave me."

Dominic eyed her a moment, taking in the flush in her
cheeks, the smile on her lips still ripe from his kisses.
Drawing himself up on an elbow, he leaned over her.

"You are the most incredible woman I have ever known.
I thought you would be weeping, blaming me for forcing
you. I believed it would take me at least three or four more
such occasions before you would admit that you enjoyed
it, too."

Catherine only smiled. "I shouldn't have done
it—there's no denying that. But I did, and I can't undo it,
nor can I let you take the blame. No matter what happens,
I shall always treasure this moment. I shall always remember it with fondness." *And love.*

"Fondness?" He seemed a bit disgruntled. "Is that all you
can say about what just happened?"

"What would you say?"

What would *he say? What does a man say about the
most poignant moment of his life?* Dominic wouldn't
have believed such a thing could have happened—at least
not to him. Maybe it was the way she had given herself
so completely, or the way she had put her trust in him.

Not that he deserved it.

What kind of a bastard would plot for weeks to take a
young woman's virginity? Of course, at first he hadn't
known, and later . . . well, even now he didn't regret it. She
wasn't in love with the Englishman, and even if she were,
the man was hardly likely to welcome her home.

"I would say it was magnificent—no, better than magnificent. I would call it wondrous."

Catherine smiled. "Yes . . . wondrous. That's a far better word." Catherine ran her finger down his chest, causing the muscles to ripple. Her own body tightened as the memory returned of what it had felt like to enter that strange sweet land Dominic had shown her.

"I was wondering if we could . . . ?"

Dominic grinned wolfishly. "You little minx." Rolling on top of her, he pressed her down in the soft feather mattress. He was already hot and hard. He had just been afraid she would be tender. When she discovered his throbbing arousal, her pretty green eyes went wide.

"I believe, little kitten, you have just found your answer."

Catherine laughed softly, and Dominic covered her mouth with a kiss. Tonight they would make love—until the little vixen's *wonder* came to an end. In the morning he would ease her worries about the future—he would tell her the rest of his plan.

Chapter Eleven

Catherine awoke to the sensual haze of hard arms around her and the musky scent of man. Dominic's chest felt solid and warm, and he looked almost boyish with his glossy black hair tumbled appealingly into his eyes. Thick black lashes made dark half-moons on his angular olive-skinned cheeks.

Catherine wished she could lie there forever.

Dominic groaned in his sleep and rolled toward her, his hold instinctively tightening as she snuggled more closely against him. She wondered what he would do when he woke up, what he would say in the bright light of morning. She wondered what she would say.

Dominic stirred, beginning to awaken. Catherine closed her eyes and pretended to sleep. With a tenderness she wouldn't have expected, he eased himself away from her, swung his long lean legs onto the wood plank floor, and reached for his breeches. He pulled them on, along with his boots, then grabbed up his shirt. Stopping beside the bed on his way out the door, he lifted away her tousled hair, leaned over and kissed her cheek. Still, Catherine did not stir.

She wasn't ready to face him, wasn't sure exactly what to do. She waited until he had left the wagon, striding off to take care of his horses, before she sat up and began to search for her clothes. After mending the tear in her blouse as best she could, she slipped it on along with her skirt, brushed her hair and tied it back with a scarf, then climbed down from the wagon. Pearsa had already started a fire and had the morning meal well under way.

"You are hungry, yes?" There was a knowing look in her aged black eyes, but not the censure Catherine had expected.

"Yes. But I'd like to freshen up first."

"There is water in the barrel, or the trickle of a stream some ways off to the left."

Catherine opted for the latter, taking a small linen towel, and heading in that direction. The marshy earth felt damp beneath her bare feet, and the early morning chill sent gooseflesh over her skin, but Catherine scarcely noticed. She needed time to think, time to decide what to do.

She thought of the wondrous hours she had spent in Dominic's arms. She thought of his strength and compassion, the love she felt for him that she would never feel for another. He was special, this man. So special that for a fleeting moment in time, she considered staying with him. She could survive the life of a Gypsy. She had done it and she could continue.

She remembered all they had shared, the way he had protected her, cared for her. She wanted him. She loved him. How could she leave him?

Catherine's heart constricted, squeezing her insides into a ball of despair. Even if Dominic loved her as much as she loved him, it could never work between them. She could exist in the world of the Gypsy, but she could never be happy living a life with no more purpose than survival from day to day.

She didn't have their wandering spirit—never would have. And she couldn't imagine raising a child to live that way.

Catherine found a secluded spot, took care of her ablutions, bathed as best she could, then sat down on a patch of dry earth behind a tamarisk tree. Whatever happened, she couldn't let things continue as they were. Their one sweet night of lovemaking had already left her heart in tatters and her future in shreds.

There was little she could do about her heart, but the future was still within her grasp. Dominic would be taking her back to England, back to her home and family. She would never forget the man she had come to love, but once they got there she would leave him. She had to get on with her life—she really had no other choice.

Catherine was certain she could mend things—with enough money and influence, other young women of the *ton* who had fallen from grace had been saved.

Though her options would sorely be limited, once she returned to England and the scandal somehow buried, her wealth was bound to attract a number of less fortunate young nobles with the duty of marrying to save the family holdings. Uncle Gil could no doubt find one among them who was willing to accept her loss of virtue for the wealth and power the man would gain.

But what of Dominic? Just the whisper of his name in the silence of her mind set her heart to pounding. She would never forget the passion they had shared, the feeling of oneness. But she couldn't risk other such moments—even now she might be carrying his babe.

Catherine felt a rush of warmth and a tender yearning she hadn't expected. She had known the consequences of succumbing to Dominic's charms, but she hadn't known the heartache she would feel at the thought of giving him up.

Still, there was no other solution and the only way she could convince him of that was to tell him the truth—no matter how much it might cost. After the closeness they had shared last eve, she was certain that he would believe her. And knowing that she was a countess, a member of the nobility, would separate them as if they'd been cleaved apart with an axe.

With a sign of resignation, Catherine walked back toward camp, skirting the dozens of wagons and black mohair tents that littered the open space behind the fortress church. Many had celebrated throughout the night and only now had begun to stir; others crouched on their heels, Gypsy fashion, eating the heavy morning meal; some still drank from bottles of wine or tin cups filled with *palinka*; and a few sprawled in their colorful now-rumpled clothes on the ground beneath their wagons.

Catherine had almost reached Dominic's *vardo* when she heard some sort of ruckus in one of those nearby and recognized young Janos's voice and that of his stepfather, Zoltan. Lifting her skirts up out of the way, Catherine hurried in that direction, arriving just as Zoltan jerked Janos up off the ground, boxed his ears, and slapped his face.

The small boy hit the ground hard and curled into a small protective ball against the swift kick his stepfather dealt to his ribs.

"Stop it!" Catherine commanded. "Zoltan, what are you doing?"

"Stay out of this, *Gadjo*. This is none of your concern."

Catherine kept on walking until she stood between Janos, who crouched behind her skirts, and Zoltan, who towered well above her, his face dark with rage.

"Stand away!" he commanded. "I am warning you!"

"What did he do?" Catherine asked, refusing to budge. "What could be so terrible?"

"He stole money from me. Me! The one who feeds him, the one who buys his clothes!"

Catherine thought the dirty rags little Janos wore could hardly be described as clothes. "Surely there is some explanation."

"You want to know what happened?" Zoltan bellowed. "He spent my hard-earned money on these!" He held up two tattered, leather-bound volumes.

"Books?" Catherine could scarcely believe it. He couldn't even read.

Zoltan grabbed the leather strop he used on those rare occasions when he shaved, which certainly wasn't today. In fact, with his wine-stained clothes and unkempt hair he looked as if he hadn't yet been to bed. "I will give him a taste of this, and next time he will know better than to take what is not his!"

Catherine heard Janos's sharp intake of breath as his small hands tightened on her skirts, but still she did not move. "I'm sure he had a reason," she soothed, stalling for time. *Dear God, where was Dominic?*

"I am warning you, woman!" Zoltan took a menacing step in her direction.

"What the devil is going on here?" Those words from Dominic, who, to Catherine's great relief, had just returned to camp.

"Take your woman, Domini. I will deal with the boy."

"Janos took money from Zoltan to buy books," Catherine hurriedly explained. "Surely if we loaned him the money to pay his stepfather back, then Janos would find a way to pay us back and everything would be all right." She glanced from Zoltan to Dominic, willing him to agree.

"What do you say, Zoltan? If the boy worked to repay the debt, would that be punishment enough?"

"No!"

"What if he paid you back with interest?" Dominic asked.

"Interest? What is interest?"

"The money he owes you, plus money for the trouble he has caused."

Zoltan fingered the thick leather strop, and Catherine held her breath. The big Gypsy's word would stand, and even Dominic would not go against him. Zoltan grumbled something Catherine couldn't hear, looked hard in her direction, saw she wasn't about to move, and finally agreed.

"The boy has been nothing but trouble since the day his mother died. Why should I care if he turns out to be a thief among his own people?" With a shrug of nonchalance he obviously wasn't feeling, he hung the razor strop back on its hook and accepted the coins Dominic tossed him, then he climbed up in the back of the wagon.

Dominic turned his hard gaze on Janos, who stood with

his big dark eyes fixed squarely on the toe of one bare foot. "You know what you did was wrong."

Liquid brown eyes looked up at him. Janos blinked at a well of tears. "Yes."

"What did you want with the books?"

"They were so beautiful—all leather and gold. I saw books in your wagon. I saw you looking through them. I want to learn to read."

Catherine's heart wrenched. Sooner or later, she suspected, many Gypsy children had such notions. They were firmly squelched, just as Zoltan would have done if Catherine hadn't arrived when she did.

"You know how your stepfather feels," Dominic said, "how the others feel. When you're older, you'll be able to choose." There was a hint of regret in his eyes. "For now, you must do as your stepfather says."

"You could teach me."

"I will soon be leaving," Dominic said softly.

"Oh."

Dominic straightened, looking even more stern. "I'll expect you to repay the money I gave to Zoltan."

Janos nodded.

"You may start by cleaning up after the horses. You'll find a shovel and rake near their tether."

Janos started to leave, then stopped and turned. "Thank you, Catrina."

"You're welcome."

"Thank you, Domini."

Dominic only nodded. He watched the child walk away, then turned his attention to Catherine. "You like him, don't you?"

"He's a wonderful little boy. It's a shame he'll never get the chance to be more than—" She broke off, wishing she hadn't voiced her thoughts aloud.

"To be more than just a Gypsy?"

"I didn't mean it that way."

"I know," he said, surprising her. "Sometimes I wish

there were a way I could help them. But it wouldn't work. For the most part, they like their lives just as they are."

"What about you, Dominic? Do you like your life just as it is?"

He smiled at that and took her hand, tucking it into the crook of one strong arm. "Come on. I think it's time we talked."

Not yet, Catherine thought as they started back toward the wagon. Not when their bond of sharing was so new, so precious. But she climbed the stairs and Dominic followed. When she took a seat on the bed, Dominic sat down beside her and once more clasped her hand.

"About last night," he began.

"It was wonderful, Dominic. The most wonderful night of my life, but—"

He looked as if he'd been about to agree, but the last word brought him up short. "But? But what?"

"But . . . but . . ." Catherine swallowed hard. She looked at his beautiful dark thick-fringed eyes, the sensuous curve of his lips. In the deep vee of his shirt, smooth brown skin rippled over taut muscle and she remembered how it felt beneath her hand.

She needed to tell him they could never touch each other as they had last night, that they were from two different worlds and whatever had passed between them would have to end. Instead her fingers came up to touch his cheek. She cradled his face in her hands, bent over, and kissed him. Dominic groaned softly into her mouth, then his arms went around her and he crushed her against him.

"Catherine," he whispered, his hands already moving down her body to cup a breast.

While his tongue fenced with hers, he slid her blouse off one shoulder, reached inside, and used his fingers to pebble a nipple. He was kissing her throat, nibbling her ear, then trailing kisses down to her shoulder. When he took her breast into his mouth and began to suckle gently, Catherine knew a sweetness, a sense of rightness like nothing she had known.

Just this one last time, she vowed, she would give herself over to the feelings of love that would have to last her a lifetime.

"Make love to me, Dominic. I need to feel you inside me."

He raised his head to look at her. "I've never wanted a woman the way I want you." He kissed her again, plunging his tongue into her mouth.

Catherine felt his hand beneath her skirts, gliding up her thigh till he reached the hot damp core of her womanhood.

"You're so wet," he whispered, almost with reverence. "So small and tight."

She opened to him, let him slide his fingers inside, let him work his magic. Nothing mattered but the heat that was building inside her, the feel of his hard-muscled body beneath her hands. When he broke away to shed his clothes, Catherine clung to him.

"No," she whispered, "I don't want to wait that long." Her fingers worked the buttons on his breeches until he sprang free and her hand closed around his thick shaft.

"Easy, little one. We've got to slow down."

"I want you," she told him. "Now. This minute." Knowing the risk she was taking only made her more desperate.

Dominic seemed to sense her need. He covered her with his big body, shoved up her layers of skirts, and settled himself between her thighs. She spread herself wider and felt his hardened length probing for entrance. His hands gripped her buttocks, he lifted her up, and in one deep, powerful thrust, drove himself inside.

Catherine moaned at the feel of it. She clung to his muscular shoulders and arched to meet each driving stroke. In minutes, he was carrying her to the peak of sanity, pounding into her with wild frantic thrusts, urging her higher and higher. She felt a wild need to be joined with him, to be one with him and never let him go.

Dominic's body grew tense, and the rhythm of his movements increased. Catherine's head fell back, she sank her nails into the ridges of muscle across his back, and writhed against him. When she could bear the sweet torture no longer, she cried out his name and soared out over the edge. Brightness swirled around her—and joy and love. She knew such sweetness, such incredible fulfillment.

How could she ever let him go?

Dominic whispered her name and his whole body grew rigid. He gasped as he reached a shuddering release that left both of them breathless and slickly entwined. Then he rolled to her side and pulled her against him.

For moments they lay quiet, the silence filled by the beating of their hearts. "I've been wanting to do that all morning," he finally said, kissing the damp hair at her temple. "I was just afraid you would be sore."

"I feel fine," she told him. "Better than fine."

He smiled at that. "I meant to go far more slowly."

"It was wonderful. You're wonderful."

He softly kissed her lips. "I wish we had time to start over, but I'm afraid we don't. I've got to leave, Catrina. Just for tonight. I'll be back late tomorrow. In the meantime, I don't want you to worry. Everything is going to be all right."

"Where are you going?"

"There's a tavern in the city, the Black Bull. The owner is *Romane Gadjo*, a friend to the Gypsies. He takes messages for us from friends, others who might pass by. Yesterday I got word that a messenger from my father will be arriving at a small town farther down the coast."

"Your father?" Catherine sat up and adjusted her clothes, and Dominic did the same, buttoning up his breeches.

"It's a long story. One I'll tell you when I return."

"Dominic—"

"In the meantime, I want you to know I have everything all worked out."

"Dominic, you must listen."

"I will, I promise. We'll talk everything over and I'll answer your questions just as soon as I return. For now, just know that I have plenty of money to take care of you.

When we get back to London, I intend to arrange a town house for you. You'll have fine new clothes and servants to see to your needs—you'll have everything you've ever wanted."

Catherine's mind spun until she could hardly think. "What are you talking about?"

"I'm talking about being together, just as we are now. At least for the most part. I have other responsibilities, things that will take me out of town, but we'll see each other often and you, my love, will want for absolutely nothing."

Catherine's scattered thoughts were beginning to come together. "You're going to set me up in a town house? You have enough money to do that?"

"Yes."

"In London."

"Yes."

"Are you telling me you plan to make me your mistress?"

"Catherine," Dominic said at the rising tone of her voice, his grip on her hand growing tighter, "the Englishman wouldn't have married you. You've got to face that fact and deal with the choices you have left."

"And what about you, Dominic? You don't seem to be interested in marriage either—or am I missing something here?"

The tenderness left Dominic's face, the hard planes looking even harder. "I told you once, Catrina, I never intend to marry. That fact hasn't changed. What I'm trying to make you see is that it doesn't matter. I'll see that you're protected, cared for—"

Catherine knew such incredulity that for a moment she found it hard to think. Then she started laughing, the highest, most incredible sound that had ever escaped her throat.

"You intend to make me your mistress? To parade me through all of London as your whore? How very kind of you, Dominic. I should have known you would handle things in a most expedient manner." She laughed again, almost hysterically.

"Stop it!" Dominic demanded, beginning to get angry. "I had thought you would be pleased . . . or are you worried someone will know I'm a Gypsy? If you are, you may rest assured they will not."

Catherine kept right on laughing. How could she have believed for a moment that his feelings for her ran deeper than merely lust? How could she have been such a fool?

She thought of Yana and the way Dominic had discarded her. *He will tire of you, just as he has me.* She heard Pearsa's words of warning: *My son will never marry*, and the bitterness of betrayal rose up in her throat.

To Dominic, she was just another conquest, another woman to bed until he grew bored. He had accomplished exactly what he'd set out to from the moment of their first meeting. She thought of the way she had begged him to make love to her—he had succeeded even better than he had planned.

"I'm sorry, Dominic," she said, pulling herself under control, determined to hold back her tears. "It isn't a matter of your heritage. It's just that—" She broke off, laughing softly again, so close to weeping she wanted to run from the wagon. How she had suffered, dreaded telling him the truth that would drive them apart. Now she wouldn't give him the satisfaction.

"You're right of course," she continued. "This is wonderful news. And it will indeed solve all my problems." The first thing it would do, outside of destroying her life and her family, would probably be to get her killed. There was still the matter of the man responsible for her abduction. He wouldn't be pleased when she returned. God only knew what he might do.

"Of course it will," he said, but he looked at her with a face full of doubt. "You'll be happy, I promise you. Just trust me, and this will all work out."

"I trust you, Dominic." Once she had meant it. "I always have."

He watched her a moment, trying to read her, apparently not liking what he saw. "I've got to leave. I want to be back by tomorrow night. If things go smoothly, we'll be ready to leave a day or two after my return."

"Whatever you say."

He looked at her with a hint of concern. "We'll talk about this again when I get back," he promised. "It's going to be all right."

She nodded, forcing herself to appear sincere. "I'm sorry, Dominic. It just came as such a surprise. I'm certain you're right. Once we return to England, everything is going to work out."

He bent down and kissed her, a hard, possessive kiss without a great deal of warmth. "We'll talk again tomorrow. Then I'll take you home."

"Yes," she agreed. "It'll be good to get back home."

Dominic rode Rai, his big gray stallion, along the narrow dirt road toward the meeting place outside Palavas, a small village farther down the coast. The first message from England had arrived several weeks ago, though Dominic had not known it until now, saying his father's condition had worsened and that he should return to England forthwith.

If he *had* known, it would not have mattered. Dominic had been receiving the very same message for the past four years.

The second message said nothing about his return, but asked him to meet a courier from Gravenwold at the Inn of the Seven Sisters near Palavas. The man would arrive on the twenty-sixth and remain until Dominic's arrival. It was crucial that they speak.

Dominic reined the huge gray horse on down the winding road toward the inn. It was just another ploy, he was certain, but the man had come a long way—to say nothing of crossing into a country with which England was at war. Dominic owed him the courtesy of listening to what he had to say.

Besides, the time of his return had finally arrived, and this would give him the chance to make the necessary preparations for the journey.

Dominic almost smiled. Now that he had settled things with Catherine, he found himself looking forward to going home. He could hardly wait to get her settled, could already imagine the leisurely hours he would spend in her bed. He wanted to teach her dozens of ways to make love. He wanted to buy her beautiful gowns then see her wearing them just for him. He wanted to lavish her with presents and pamper her with luxury.

That she hadn't taken the news as well as he had expected shouldn't really have surprised him. Catherine was a proud young woman. He should have eased her into the idea of being his mistress instead of dumping the notion on her all at once. He should have explained why he could not marry. That providing the father he loathed with an heir to the Gravenwold fortune was the one thing in life that he would not do.

Dominic smiled grimly into the darkness. From the moment he had been swept away from his family fifteen years ago, his father, Samuel Dominic Edgemont, Fifth Marquess of Gravenwold, had plotted and planned for his bastard son to carry on the family name. It was a desperate move born of the death of the marquess's eldest son, Gerald, lost in His Majesty's Service.

It was why the marquess adopted his illegitimate half-Gypsy child, why he schooled him, provided for him, why he tolerated him at all. The marquess knew that with the birth of Dominic's son and his son's sons, the Edgemont name would be ensured. Gravenwold would go on as it always had. All he had worked for would not be in vain.

Except that for the past fifteen years, Dominic had sworn that it would not happen.

Reining up in front of a two-story brick building with a faded wooden sign reading Inn of the Seven Sisters, Dominic dismounted, handed the gray to a stable lad, instructing him in French to see the beast well cared for, then opened the heavy wooden door and stepped inside. It was smoky in the dim, low-ceilinged interior lit by blackened whale-oil lamps, and noisy with laughter and bawdy songs.

"Good evening, m'sieur. What is your pleasure?" asked a buxom barmaid with graying once-blond hair. Her light blue eyes ran the length of him, taking in his simple but well-tailored clothes.

Tonight he wasn't a Gypsy. He wore a crisp linen shirt and snug black breeches tucked into a pair of polished riding boots. No flashy silk, no coins, no earring. He didn't want to attract attention to the Englishman his father had sent.

"Wine," he said, "and hurry. The long ride has given me a thirst."

"Oui, m'sieur." The woman walked away, hurried by a pat on her broad behind from a man at a table nearby. As soon as she was gone, a stocky, balding man with careful gray eyes approached.

"Lord Nightwyck?" he asked softly.

"Not in here. In France in these times, a wise man has no name besides his birth one. Dominic will do."

"Yes, sir." The man spoke French as if he'd been born to it, and in his worn woolen breeches and simple homespun shirt blended in well with the peasants and few landed gentry who ate and drank in the taproom. "My name is Harvey Malcom. I've come about your father."

"He isn't dead, is he?"

"No, sir. But I fear he is gravely ill."

"My father's been *gravely ill* for the last ten years. If you've come to urge me home, you needn't bother. My time here is ended. I'll be leaving France in the next few days."

"Thank God," Malcom said.

Dominic arched a brow. "You sound truly concerned. My father's been bedridden off and on for the past four years. Are you telling me he has in truth taken a turn for the worse?"

"I believe he has, sir. As you will soon see."

"Yes, I suppose I will. In any case, you needn't concern yourself further. You may expect me in a fortnight or less."

"I beseech you, sir, to come to your father straightaway. It isn't certain how much longer he will last."

Dominic searched the man's face for some sign of false-hood, but found none. Sooner or later, the old marquess's uncertain health was bound to take its toll. It appeared the time had at last arrived.

"You may convey my impending arrival." Dominic smiled thinly. "I wouldn't want to miss my father's parting words."

Harvey Malcom declined Dominic's invitation to sup and instead climbed the stairs to the lodgings he had let for the evening. Dominic made arrangements of his own, slept a few short hours on a lumpy feather mattress, then saddled the gray and rode hard back the way he had come.

The festivities were in full swing when he arrived late that night. The crypt of Saint Sara had been opened and swarms of Italian, French, and Spanish Gypsies had made their way inside to take up their two-day vigil. Inside the crypt, Gypsies would be sleeping on the floor amidst a sea of guttering candles in front of the statue of Sara.

Outside, mounted Camargue guardians, carrying their three-pronged tridents, escorted throngs of revelers. Wearily, Dominic threaded his way through them, steadily making a path back toward his wagon—and Catherine.

For hours he had replayed the scene in the wagon, this time attributing her odd behavior to the hurt she must have been feeling. *You intend to parade me through the streets of London as your whore? How kind of you, Dominic.* He should have taken the time to explain, should have made her understand that was not the way he felt at all.

His eyes searched the crowd, past flamenco dancers, knife-swallowers, a man playing a mandolin and another who cranked a hurdy-gurdy while a tiny trained monkey turned circles on his shoulder. But he saw no flame-haired minx, even as he neared the wagon.

Instead, his mother met him before he had time to dismount. Dominic saw by the strained look on her face that something was wrong.

"What is it, Mother?" He swung a long leg over the stallion's rump and stepped down to the ground. "What's happened?" But even before she said the words, he knew.

"Catherine!" He started toward the wagon, but his mother caught his arm.

"She is gone, my son. She left just moments after you rode out. I was working, and with the excitement of the festival no one discovered her missing until nightfall."

"Tell me what you know," he said, gripping Pearsa's thin shoulders.

"Thanks to your friend, André, at the Black Bull Tavern, we know a great deal and yet we still know nothing. He came looking for you after she had been to see him—it appears she knew he was your friend—"

"Yes, I mentioned that the owner of the Black Bull often took messages for passing Gypsies."

"She went to him. Told him you had sent her and that you had said he would help her. She was no longer dressed as a Gypsy, my son, but as a *Gadjo* lady."

Dominic swore an oath, crossed to the wagon, and climbed the stairs. The money he kept in his trunk—all of it—was gone. In a way he felt relieved. "She has plenty of money to get home," he said, returning to his mother. "She took what I kept in my trunk."

"André said she hired a young woman from the tavern to go with her. She asked him to arrange safe travel to Marseilles."

Dominic's dark look darkened even more. "She's bound to find a ship there. If I hurry, maybe I can stop her before she sails."

"It is possible. But I believe your Catherine will do all she can to keep that from happening."

"Yes," he agreed. "Damn her treacherous little heart."

"There is more bad news," Pearsa said. "Last night in town, Zoltan got into a knife fight with a big Spanish Gypsy named Emilio. Zoltan is dead."

Dominic closed his eyes against his growing despair. "What of the boy? Who will take him?"

"He wants to go with you."

Dominic hesitated only a moment. "Bring him to me."

"Why did she go, my son?" Pearsa asked. "I thought you had agreed to take her home."

"I handled things badly. I've got to find her. Explain things." He started to turn, but his mother caught his arm.

"This time, my son, I do not think you will."

Chapter Twelve

THE CARRIAGE CATHERINE HAD HIRED rounded the last bend in the lane heading toward Lavenham Hall. Through the trees up ahead, she could just glimpse the huge estate in Dorset where her uncle, Gilbert Lavenham, Duke of Wentworth, reigned supreme.

Beside her on the tufted leather seat, hands folded demurely in her lap, sat the small brown-haired girl Catherine had virtually bought away from the Black Bull Tavern to serve as her traveling companion. She was a thin, frail young woman, delicate in a way Catherine wasn't.

Gabriella LeClerc was hardly a beauty, but there was a softness around her mouth and an innocence in her wide brown eyes that somehow made her attractive. She had jumped at Catherine's offer to escape her life at the tavern, been eager to learn, helpful, and decidedly loyal. Already they had formed a friendship of sorts.

"Mon Dieu," Gabby whispered, her eyes fixed on the three-story structure with its sharply gabled roofs, rows of mullioned windows, dozens of chimneys, and acres of manicured lawns. "Surely, my lady, this is not where we are going?"

Catherine had chosen the girl mostly because she spoke English—a legacy of a British mother who had abandoned her as a child—and as soon as they had left France on the tiring journey home, she had been allowed to speak nothing else.

"That's Lavenham Hall," Catherine told her. "I believe I mentioned it." Catherine had filled the young girl in on who she was and where they were going, but very little else. The subject of her time with the Gypsies—and especially her relationship with Dominic—was just too painful to discuss.

"You mentioned it, my lady. But I could not have imagined . . ."

"Just remember, Gabby. Say nothing to anyone until my uncle and I have had time to talk."

"I will say nothing," Gabby promised, and Catherine knew a knife at the young girl's throat could not pry out the words.

She smiled at the good fortune that had brought the two of them together. One small ray of sunshine among her dark days of despair. Catherine leaned back against the tufted black leather. Soon she would be shed of the simple traveling clothes she had bought for herself and later for Gabby.

She had taken Dominic's money—without a shred of conscience after what had passed between them—then carefully and determinedly set out to elude him.

And this time she had succeeded.

The night of her arrival in Marseilles, she had located a Portuguese brig, *Menina Belo*, bound for Lisbon on the morning tide. From there they had found and boarded another ship, the *Pegasus*, sailing for England, managed to evade Napoleon's warships, and made their way home.

The carriage pulled through the massive iron gates, around the circular crushed-granite drive, and up to the wide stone porch with its huge carved lions. A silver and dark green liveried doorman helped Catherine alight, then helped Gabriella, who was staring so hard at their stately surroundings she stumbled and nearly fell.

The massive carved mahogany doors were pulled open even before they reached them, and Catherine stepped into the foyer. Glistening chandeliers reflected the black and white marble floor and the walls were covered in gold watered-silk damask. It might have been gaudy without the exquisite Chinese vases on their carved mahogany stands, and the simple lines of the high-backed chairs with their subtle ivory inlays.

Recognizing several small knickknacks on the ornate hall table that she had played with as a child, Catherine steeled herself against the feelings of homecoming that welled up inside her. Even then, her throat closed up and her fingers trembled until she had to still the movement by smoothing the front of her skirt.

Just then, Soames, the butler, stepped forward, his watery old eyes assessing her dusty traveling clothes.

"May I be of service, madam?" he asked, lifting his nose as if what she had to say had very well better be important or she wasn't about to get in.

"Yes, Soames. I believe I should like you to fetch my uncle."

Soames's narrow slash of a mouth dropped open. He took a step backward, his thin, veined hand fluttering up to his heart. "Lady Catherine," he squeaked.

"It's all right, Soames. I assure you I'm not a ghost."

"B-but where have you been? We all thought you were . . . that you were dead, milady."

"As you can see, I'm very much alive—and very glad to be home." She smiled at him tiredly. "Now . . . are you recovered enough to fetch Uncle Gil?"

"Why, yes, milady. Of course."

"Soames, this is Gabriella. I'd appreciate your seeing her settled. We've traveled quite far. I'm certain she's exhausted."

"Of course." He showed Catherine into the Tapestry Room, a huge red-walled salon beneath massive hand-sculpted beams, closed the door, then led Gabby upstairs to the servants' quarters.

Catherine sank down on a ruby-brocade Hepplewhite sofa and tried to calm her pounding heart. She had prepared herself for this moment, known it must come, and still she wished there was some way to avoid it. Instead the double doors opened and a pale-faced, tired-looking version of her uncle walked in. He was a stout man, portly some might say, thick of chest and shoulders, with a shock of silver-gray hair and clear green eyes the same shade as Catherine's. The duke was a man of average height, yet somehow he always seemed taller.

Catherine forced a smile in his direction, but her uncle made no move. He just stood there staring, looking as though he'd been sure this was some sort of trick and had just discovered it was not.

"Catherine," he whispered, regaining his composure with his usual alacrity and starting toward her, his arms outstretched. A hard lump rose in Catherine's throat. In an instant, she was on her feet and flying across the room, melting into his solid embrace, clutching him and crying against his shoulder.

"My dearest Catherine," he said, and she heard the unshed tears that clogged his throat. "We all believed you dead."

"Oh, Uncle Gil, so much has happened." She hugged him fiercely, and he hugged her back. For a long while they just stood there, Catherine secure in the circle of his stout arms, Gil thanking God that she still lived.

"Come," he gently urged when her crying had ceased. With an arm around her shoulder, he walked her to the sofa and sat down beside her. For minutes that seemed like hours he said nothing, and neither did Catherine.

"I've felt so deuced guilty," he finally said, surprising her. "I kept asking myself if you might still be alive had I done my duty. Instead I let you go off on your own with only your cousin and his wife for supervision. If I had kept you here with me—"

"It wasn't your fault. How could you have known what would happen? How could anyone have known?"

She went on to tell him about the night of her abduction, how she had been sleeping in her bedchamber after the Mortons' soiree, how a man had come in through the window, rendered her unconscious, and carried her away.

"There was a young woman's body discovered in the river," the duke said. "She was . . . no longer recognizable, but she appeared to have been about your age. Everyone believed it was you."

Catherine shook her head at the awful image. "Maybe that was what people were meant to believe." She told him how she had been sold to a band of Gypsies and taken across the channel to France, how she'd been intended for a Turkish pasha, been traded instead to a Gypsy named Vaclav, and finally ended up with the Pindoros.

"What you must have suffered," her uncle said, squeezing her hand.

"In the beginning, I didn't believe I could survive it. In the end, I knew I was strong enough to survive almost anything."

Her uncle looked grim. "And this band of Gypsies," he said, "the Pindoros, was it?"

"Yes."

"They helped you get home?"

This was the part she had dreaded. "There was one among them. A man they called Domini. He looked after me, watched out for me. He would have brought me home, but I——" Catherine glanced away, for a moment unable to go on.

"It's all right, my dear. You don't have to tell me any more than you want to. You're home and safe. Nothing else matters."

"I want to tell you, Uncle Gil. I have to. It's going to be hard enough mending things as it is."

Nearly impossible, Gil thought, but didn't say so. Right now his beloved niece had returned from the grave, a gift from God he would never be able to repay. When he had walked into the room, he almost hadn't recognized her, so much had she changed. No more the little girl, this Catherine was a woman—self-assured and strong. She would need that strength to draw on in the difficult days ahead.

"Tell me about this Domini," he said, gently urging her on.

Catherine smiled faintly. Gil noticed the look that crept into her eyes, a mixture of fondness and pain.

"In most ways, Uncle, he was a fine man." The memory seemed to warm her. "He was tall—very tall—and his skin was smooth and dark. He was so handsome—the most handsome man I've ever seen. Not foppish, mind you. Not like the dandies in London. But handsome in a masculine sort of way. In truth, he was only half Gypsy. I think his father may have been English, though he never really said so. It seems they did not get along."

"I see."

"Believe it or not, he was educated—very much so."

Gil grunted. "An educated Gypsy."

"Oh yes. And far more intelligent than most of the men I've met in England."

"What did he say when you told him who you were?"

"I didn't. I had tried that before, you see, and all it got me were beatings and mistreatment."

Gil's chest felt tight. Good God, what she must have endured! He thought about the man who had stolen her away from the town house. Why? he silently demanded. Who could have done such a thing? They were questions he had asked a thousand times, but still remained unanswered. He would find out, he vowed again as he had before. And when he did there would be bloody hell to pay.

"Surely if you had told him, the man would have helped you," Gil said.

"Oh, he did. He bought me away from Vaclav when he would have beat me. He provided for me, taught me things about nature, about the Gypsies. He protected me—even at the risk of his own life. . . ." She looked away, her eyes drifting to the small fire blazing in the hearth at the end of the room.

"I fell in love with him, Uncle Gil," she said softly, sounding more like the little girl she had been when she left. "I didn't want to. I knew I shouldn't—I did everything in my power not to, but . . ." Catherine gazed down at her lap and toyed with the folds of her skirt.

"And this man, this Gypsy," Gil said softly, "did he also love you?"

She shook her head. "No." She raised her eyes to his. "But it wasn't his fault. Not really. I was angry at first. I thought he took advantage. Now I believe that in some way he cared for me. And he was honest in his intentions from the start."

"He told you he didn't love you?" Gil felt the heat of anger, but firmly tamped it down.

"No. But I knew he had vowed not to marry. And even if he had wanted me, it would never have worked. I'm meant for the life of a countess, not the wandering existence of a Gypsy."

"That's my girl," Gil said with pride, patting her hand. "You've always had a head on your shoulders."

Catherine met his green gaze squarely. "I'm afraid, Uncle Gil, that for one small moment I lost it." Her cheeks turned scarlet, and the duke inwardly groaned.

He'd known from the moment she began her story, she could not possibly have remained untouched and yet . . . "Are you telling me, my dear, that this Gypsy . . . took your innocence?" He'd find the bloody bastard and have him horsewhipped!

"Not exactly. It was more like I gave it to him." Catherine didn't look away. Gil searched hard but could find no trace of regret. He sighed, in a way more proud of her than he had been before.

He gently squeezed her hand. "You aren't the first young woman to stumble on the difficult road to womanhood. Whatever has happened is past. We've money and position on our side. We'll think of something."

Catherine merely nodded. She'd had plenty of time to think and she had come up with an idea she thought just might work. But she felt bone-weary, and Uncle Gil needed time to get used to her return.

"I hoped we might discuss it at supper," she said. "I know the servants will be buzzing, but surely we can hold them at bay for a little while longer."

"Good idea. Leave the servants to me." His determined expression dared them to open their mouths. "Until then, I suggest you get some rest. Your bedchamber is just as you left it. I hadn't the heart to remove your things."

Catherine breathed a sigh of relief. After her father had died, she'd spent a great deal of time at Lavenham Hall. She kept a wardrobe of clothing, which, thanks to Uncle Gil's sentimentality, meant she would at least have something to wear.

She smiled tiredly. "I'm certain to feel better after a bath and a rest."

"Of course, my dear. And you mustn't worry. Somehow things will work out."

Catherine just nodded. Wasn't that what Dominic had said? She wondered as she had these long days past exactly where he was and what he was thinking. She wondered if he missed her or if he had already settled on another to warm his bed.

"I'm so glad to be home, Uncle Gil." She leaned over and kissed his cheek. "I can't tell you how glad."

Gil cleared his throat. "Not nearly as thankful as I am to have you."

With a last brief smile in his direction, Catherine crossed the thick Persian carpet to the door leading out to the hall. Ignoring the odd looks she received from the servants, she wearily climbed the stairs.

Catherine slept longer than she had intended, her dreams troubled by images of Dominic. She was running from him, trying to hide, yet hoping he would find her. She felt torn in two by the thought of separation, yet something pulled her away. She could hear him searching, calling her name, begging her not to go. Then she heard Yana's laughter, brittle and mocking, branding her a fool.

Then he was there, tall and imposing, pulling her into his arms, holding her, kissing her, molding his mouth to hers, his fine dark hands roaming her bodice. Fiery warmth spread through her.

"Dominic," she whispered, clutching him against her.

"Don't leave me," he said softly, and she knew this time she could not go.

A movement in the room, and Catherine bolted upright in the small daybed at the foot of the huge four-poster. Her heart still pounded fiercely, and it took a moment for her to discern where she was.

"I—I am sorry, my lady. You told me to wake you no later than seven." Gabby looked regretful, but determined to do as she had been told.

Catherine smiled and worked to slow her speeding heart. The last fleeting vestige of Dominic's warm embrace faded away and suddenly she felt empty. Dear God how she missed him.

"Thank you, Gabby."

"Shall I have your bath brought in?"

"Please." She'd been so tired she had fallen asleep in her chemise. "It's a luxury I shall never take for granted again."

Catherine lounged in the warm copper tub until the water began to cool, then stepped into the crisp linen towel Gabby held. A search of the carved mahogany armoire in the corner provided a pale blue watered-silk gown, high-waisted, the bodice not nearly so low as those she had worn in London, but with its small puffed sleeves and delicate seed-pearl trim, fashionable just the same.

Gabby, who had already become a passable coiffeur, twisted Catherine's hair into a thick, sleek coil at the back of her neck, and she made her way down the wide spiral staircase to the drawing room where Uncle Gil poured her a glass of claret.

In his immaculate dark blue frock coat with its high turnover collar, burgundy striped waistcoat, and pale gray trousers, he seemed much more relaxed and far more in charge of himself than he had just hours ago.

"You look lovely, my dear." He seated her on a cherrywood sofa not far from the marble-manteled hearth.

Catherine shifted a bit on her chair. Used to the freedom of her Gypsy clothes, she felt a little uncomfortable in garments more confining than any she had worn since she'd left England.

"Thank you, Uncle." She sighed. "In a way it feels good to be beautifully gowned again, but in another way . . . It's difficult to explain, but after the freedom I've known, I feel a tiny bit awkward dressed as I am."

Gil sat down in a wing chair across from her. "Like all things in life, there are advantages and drawbacks to everything. The Gypsy knows possibly the greatest freedom on earth, yet at the same time, he is limited by that very freedom as to what he may achieve. On the other hand, our society is quite rigid in most things, but it is that very structure which helps us define our place in life and achieve our greatest accomplishments."

Catherine smiled. "Having lived both ways, I believe I know what you mean." She took a sip of claret and set it aside. "Which brings us to the problem at hand."

"Yes," Gil said with an even deeper sigh, "you've quite gone outside the bounds of propriety, I'm afraid, even if it wasn't at all your fault."

"I've had a good deal of time to consider this, Uncle. Are you willing to hear my plan?"

"Since I've drawn little more than a blank so far, I'd say I'm more than willing."

Catherine leaned forward, eager to learn his thoughts on the matter, yet fearful he might uncover a flaw she had somehow overlooked.

"I haven't yet gotten the details all worked out, but so far it goes something like this: Lady Catherine and her cousin Edmund argued terribly the night of her disappearance. In a fit of pique, Catherine stole away to the solitude of a convent near her home in Devon. She had no idea about the young girl's body that was found in the Thames, therefore no idea that anyone thought she was dead. She meant to teach her cousin a lesson, but now regrets most heartily all the trouble she has caused."

Catherine looked at him hopefully. "Of course we'd need Edmund and Amelia's complete cooperation."

"That certainly isn't a problem," Gil said, still mulling the idea over. "The man was utterly grief-stricken by the whole affair. Blamed himself, you see."

"Did he? I wonder how stricken he'll feel when he discovers I've returned?"

Gil fixed his gaze on hers and saw her look of suspicion. "I realize he had a good deal to gain, but surely you don't believe . . . ?"

"I presume his grief was lessened somewhat by his assumption of the Arondale title and fortune."

"The bloody bastard!" Gil swore, surging to his feet. "He wouldn't dare!"

Catherine stood up, too. "Cousin Edmund has been like a brother to me since I was a girl. I'm not accusing him of anything—at least not yet."

The duke took a hefty swig of brandy from the delicate crystal snifter he held in one thick hand and began to pace in front of the fire. "I had considered it, of course, so did others. But the man was so despondent no one gave the notion much credence for more than an instant or two. Why, Edmund could barely hold up through the funeral."

"Funeral?"

The duke flashed the wisp of a smile. "Quite an occasion it was, you being a countess and all. Cost your cousin a fortune."

"You mean it cost *me* a fortune."

Gil chuckled at that. "Yes, I suppose it did."

Catherine sat back down, urging Gil to do the same. She picked up her glass and took a sip of claret. "If Edmund isn't the culprit—and I tend to agree that he is not—then who do you think it was?"

"There are men who do villainy just for sport—that was

of course a consideration. Edmund and I thought maybe it had something to do with your involvement in that damnable Friendly Society."

"The Society for the Betterment of the Poor? But what would that have to do with this?"

"For years those groups have been becoming more and more unpopular. Lately, they've come even more heavily under fire."

Catherine had known that a goodly number of people believed educating the children of the poor would encourage revolution. They were afraid what had happened to the nobility in France might happen again in England.

"But my involvement in the group was so remote. Surely, since I lived as far away as Devon, very few people knew anything about it."

"Your father made it no secret. He came under attack more than once. And some of the opposition has become quite radical in their views."

"I suppose it is a possibility."

"Yes, well, a remote one, but not to be overlooked. I've had men looking into the crime for weeks. Nothing's turned up yet, but I intend to keep after it."

"Thank you, Uncle. I should like very much to see the matter put to an end." Catherine sipped her drink. "As to the problem at hand," she said, "what do you think of my plan?"

"I think it has definite possibilities. When do you intend to give Edmund the good news of your return?"

"I doubt Edmund will qualify giving up his earldom as a bit of good news. I had hoped that you would speak to him, get him over the shock, then gain his cooperation."

"That you may count on, my dear." He set his glass aside, reached for hers and set it aside, then both of them stood up. Gil took her arm and looped it through his. "You may also rest assured that the Convent of the Sacred Heart in Devon, to which the Earl of Arondale and the Duke of Wentworth have both contributed heavily throughout the years, will also agree to assist us."

"Then you think my plan will work?"

He led her into the dining room and pulled out one of twenty high-backed carved walnut chairs. Catherine seated herself, and the duke took a seat at the head of the table not far away. Gold candelabra gleamed against gold-rimmed porcelain plates and the scent of white roses filled the air.

"It's better than anything I've come up with. But even if all goes well, you'll still risk the cut direct for your supposed foolhardy behavior."

"I know."

"Unless, of course, we can recruit several of the more powerful families to our cause." Gil looked thoughtful. "Sommerset is most certainly in my debt for a favor I granted his eldest son, and Mayfield . . . I believe he's a close enough friend we may count on his wholehearted support. Hornbuckle, of course, will side with us—Ozzie's well liked, though he hasn't much clout. We'll convince the women that you're drowning in guilt for what you have inadvertently done to your poor dear cousin and me, and kindhearts that they are, they'll probably see you as the injured party. With them and a handful of others on our side, we've a chance to succeed."

Catherine began to breathe easier. Of course, even if her social position was once again secure, there was still the problem of finding her a proper husband—one by whom her lack of innocence would be quietly overlooked.

What kind of a man would that be?

At the prospect of actually marrying someone, Catherine's stomach tightened. She thought of Dominic, and his handsome face rose up before her almost as if he had entered the room. Where was he? she wondered. Had he gone on to England as he had planned? Or with Catherine no longer urging his return, had he decided to stay in France?

"Are you all right, my dear?" Gil looked at her with a worried frown, and Catherine realized he had been speaking to her for quite some time.

"I'm sorry, Uncle. I guess I'm not precisely back to normal."

"It's all right, my child. I quite understand."

I'm glad someone does, she thought. For the hundredth time since she had left France, Catherine forced thoughts of Dominic aside. Her uncle seemed to understand what was wrong with her. Catherine only wished she did.

Chapter Thirteen

DOMINIC EDGEMONT STALKED the sconce-lit halls of Gravenwold Manor, headed for the master's bedchamber on the second floor of the west wing.

He had been in residence for the past two weeks, leaving France on a Spanish ship from Marseilles. Once he had reached England, via Morocco, he had made just one brief stop. In London, to hire a Bow Street runner to track down the whereabouts of a certain young woman with red-gold hair—last name unknown.

He felt somewhat the fool for the latter. After all, he knew the exact location of the dimple behind her knee that made her squirm when he touched it. He knew the slightly apricot hue of her nipples, and the precise curve of her shapely little bottom. But her name? He wasn't completely certain the one she had given was correct.

Why hadn't he found out more about her? he cursed himself, not for the first time. But in truth, he knew. When he was Domini, he was Gypsy—to his very bones.

Names didn't matter, time didn't matter. Nothing seemed important but the here and the now, and with Catherine beside him, that time had been exquisite. So much so that he had followed her to Marseilles the day he had discovered her missing, but as his mother had predicted, found only the merest trace.

A woman of Catherine's description had been seeking

passage aboard a ship. It was assumed she and her traveling companion had found one. None knew anything more.

Dominic believed she had made it back to England. It
was difficult to stop a woman as determined as Catherine—that he had discovered firsthand. Still, he needed to
know she was well and safe, that she wasn't in some sort
of trouble.

More than that—he wanted desperately to see her
again.

"The marquess is awake and asking for you, milord."

Dominic nodded to his valet, Percival Nelson, a gaunt,
rapidly aging old man blind in one eye and slightly hard
of hearing. The marquess had wanted him retired years
ago, but Dominic knew how much Percy, a man whose
family numbered only those in the household staff he had
served with for the past forty years, dreaded that day.
Against his father's wishes, he let the old man stay on and
in return gained a loyalty so strong no man could break
it.

"I'm on my way there now," Dominic said. Two weeks
ago, just hours after his arrival, the marquess had slipped
into a state of unconsciousness. Yesterday he had roused
himself, seeming to rally his strength for a final assault on
his son.

Every conversation since then had ended in a bitter
debate about the future of Gravenwold—the old marquess demanding his son marry and produce an heir,
Dominic thinking of his mother, his years of mistreatment
at the hands of his father, and more determined than ever
that this was not to be.

He entered the massive royal-blue bedchamber and saw
his father, hollow-eyed and sunken-cheeked but still recognizable as a man of power and will. He rested beneath
white satin sheets; his skin, once healthy and tanned nearly
as dark as Dominic's, had faded to the sheets' same alabaster hue.

"My son has arrived," he commanded the servants in a

voice much stronger than his body. "One of you lazy fools help me sit up!"

By the time Dominic reached the marquess's side, the valet had accomplished the task, and his father sat propped against the pillows, a determined look on his face.

"Well?" he asked, as if that one word should be more than enough.

"Well what, Father? Have I changed my mind about the Cummings girl? I told you yesterday, her fortune means nothing to me. Nor do your threats of disinheritance should I decline to follow your wishes. I'll not marry the girl. Now or in the future."

"Why? At least tell me that. Her holdings would nearly double the size of Gravenwold. It's your duty as my heir to make the best possible marriage for the sake of the family." His voice, though raspy, still held a note of command.

"You know why. We've been through this a dozen times."

"Because you're determined to seek revenge for the wrongs you've suffered? For the wrongs you believe I've done to your mother?" He leaned forward on an elbow, a bit of color infusing his cheeks. "I don't give a fiddler's damn about all that. We both know I made mistakes. I should have dealt with you better. Should have seen you protected from mistreatment. But all that is behind us. You've your whole life ahead of you and all the wealth I command to make that life the best it can possibly be. All I ask in return is for you to guard that which I bequeath you—" he coughed behind a withered hand then rallied—"to see that the future of Gravenwold is secure."

Dominic watched his father's face. As always there was the harshness, the driving determination to get his way. Nothing or no one else mattered. Not now—not ever. "No," was all he said.

His father fell back against the pillows. "You're a hard man, Dominic, but you are not a fool. Agree to this marriage. Let me go to my final resting place in peace."

Peace, Dominic thought. What peace had his mother

been granted? She'd been foolish enough to fall in love with the newly titled marquess when the Pindoros had stayed on his family's estate in Yorkshire. She had slept with him and produced a son. A year later, she'd been even more foolish. On a return trip to England, she had told the man she loved about his child, showing him the boy, who bore the Edgemont crest, a small purple mark in the shape of a waning moon that had darkened every Edgemont male thigh for six generations.

She had been foolish enough to expect him to rejoice.

Instead he had spurned her. Wouldn't acknowledge the child as his and drove the Gypsies from his land. Pearsa had been crushed. Though she had never expected marriage, she had always believed he loved her, that he would be as proud of the son she bore him as she was herself.

"Any peace you find will be between you and your maker—or the devil. I have nothing to do with it."

The marquess's pale face grew red with rage. "Get out!" he ordered in his raspy voice, jabbing a bony white finger toward the door. "Don't come back in this room until you've agreed to marry—or I'm dead and gone!"

"Then this is our final good-bye," Dominic said with equal harshness. A last hard glance in his father's direction and Dominic strode out the door.

Two days later, his words became truth. The fifth marquess of Gravenwold passed away in his sleep.

Dominic leaned back in the tufted red leather chair in front of the dying fire in the library, his fingers drumming unconsciously on a row of brass tack trim. Usually, he felt comfortable in this wood-paneled room filled with books, a haven he came to whenever he spent time at Gravenwold. It was a place of warmth in a hostile environment, a place to escape his fiery confrontations with his father.

Today it brought him little peace.

Weeks had passed since his father's death. Weeks which should have carried a cleansing breath of freedom into his world. Instead he'd been oddly depressed. Though the weather outside had been pleasant, flowers blooming, the sky clear and blue, Dominic had scarcely noticed, remaining indoors, the curtains drawn against the bright light of day.

He took a sip of his brandy and stared into the low flames of the fire he'd had built against the chill which came mostly from within. He felt brooding and empty, more so than ever before in his life. His father was gone and with him a receptacle for his anger and contempt at the world. Now the rage just ate at him, little by little, gnawing his insides like acid, seeping into his very bones.

Dominic sighed and leaned his head back against the leather chair. Since his return to England, it seemed as if his world had somehow dimmed. His time of abandon with the Gypsies was past, a chapter of his life which, except for his mother, had finally come to an end. There was Gravenwold to consider, people to care for, responsibilities he must deal with. Though he would never provide an heir, for as long as he lived it was a duty he would not shirk.

And Catherine was gone. Even though he had sought out Harvey Malcom, the man his father had sent to him in France, and hired a dozen more Bow Street runners, no trace of her had been found. He was beginning to doubt she had ever reached England, and it tortured him to think of what she might be suffering even now.

Or what she might have found if she *had* reached her home. Had the man she once loved turned her away? Or refused her marriage but forced her into his bed?

What if, after Dominic and Catherine had lain together, she had conceived his child?

The thought of his babe growing up as he had, fatherless and struggling each day for survival, or of Catherine sharing another man's bed, made his insides churn.

Damn you! he swore. But it wasn't her fault, it was his. He had botched things from the beginning. If he had taken a firmer hand with her right from the start, none of this would have happened. How had such a slip of a girl been able to bend him to her will? It wasn't like him. In his future dealings with the fairer sex, it would not happen again.

Still, he missed her. He remembered every moment he had spent with her as if it had only just occurred. He recalled the scent of her, clean and womanly, and the exact silky texture of her hair. He remembered making love to her, and every time he did his body grew hot and hard.

Damn her, where was she?

Dominic started at a knock at the door. He swung his long booted legs off the leather footstool and onto the Aubusson carpet just as Blythebury, Gravenwold's towering butler, opened the door.

"It's the boy, milord," said the long-nosed, thin-faced man.

Dominic stood up. "What's happened?"

"Nothing serious. Just a nasty cut and a bit of a lump on the head, but I thought you would want to know." Oliver Blythebury watched the concern that crossed the young marquess's face. A few years back, Oliver wouldn't have bothered to tell him what had happened. He'd have tended the little boy's bruises and put him to bed, certain the master's son wouldn't have a care.

It was His Lordship's kindness to Percy that had convinced him differently. As far as Percival Nelson, His Lordship's valet, was concerned, the young lord walked on water—or very nearly did—and his old friend's staunch defense of the marquess's son, disliked by most of the staff in the beginning, had finally broken through the harsh wall of disapproval they had erected.

"Where is he?" Dominic strode toward the door.

"His room, Your Lordship. Begged me not to tell you, but I thought it best you know."

"You did right," Dominic assured him, following the tall, erect butler out the door.

They climbed the broad stone staircase then traveled the long stately corridor to Janos's bedchamber. The little boy lay beneath an ice-blue satin canopy on the big four-poster bed, his dark eyes huge with worry. The skin around one looked purple and swollen, there was a scratch across his cheek, and a lump the size of an egg above his right ear.

"God's breath," Dominic softly swore, guessing easily what had happened.

"Please do not be angry." Janos cast a guilty glance at the blood on his expensive white linen shirt and sat up straighter in the bed.

"The clothes are of no concern," Dominic soothed. "We can get more of those. Just tell me what happened."

The boy looked away, his big dark eyes fixed on the wall. "They called me names . . . ugly names. They said bad things about my mother."

"I told you they might." Dominic turned Janos's chin with his hand, forcing the child to look at him. "You must learn to ignore them." Though no one had mentioned the boy's Gypsy blood, and he had been dressed in expensively tailored clothes by the time they reached Gravenwold, the darkness of his skin, darker by far than Dominic's, and his strange way of speaking had immediately set him apart.

"It is not easy," Janos said.

"I know." The boy had surprised him in one way. He'd been determined to see his decision through. He had wanted to come to England, and since his arrival, not once had he complained at the demands being made of him.

Though he fussed at the uncomfortable clothes, his small linens, short coat, and tight leather shoes, he never asked to remove them. Instead his attention was absorbed by the strange new delights of the world around him, as if he would gladly pay the price of his discomfort for the wonders being revealed.

"Who did this to you?" Dominic asked.

Janos looked down at the pale blue satin counterpane, but did not answer.

"Tell me."

"One of the other children," he answered evasively.

There were children by the score on Gravenwold. Off-spring of servants, stablehands, men who tilled the fields.

"Exactly which one of the other children?"

"What will you do to him?"

"I'll have his father take a switch to him, which he sorely deserves."

Janos said nothing.

Dominic waited. Still nothing. Finally, he sighed. "You're certain this is what you want?"

"I do not wish to bring trouble. I only wish to learn."

Dominic's jaw hardened, memories of his own bitter years as an outcast hovering far too close. "You belong here just as much as the rest of them, maybe more. Remember that, even if you can't come out and say it."

The boy knew better than to speak of Dominic's heritage, or his own. He nodded then smiled, his small face lighting up at Dominic's words. "I will remember."

"Percy will see to your bath. After that Mr. Reynolds will continue with your lessons." He was the tutor Dominic had hired.

Janos brightened even more. "Thank you, Domin-nic." Occasionally the boy still fumbled over the English pronunciation of Dominic's name, but he was determined to master it, to adjust to his new home in every way.

Dominic felt a surge of pride. Unless he spawned a bastard, the boy was as close to a son as he would ever have. He imagined how the old marquess would have cringed at the notion and felt a perverse sense of satisfaction.

Then the triumph faded, replaced by a sudden memory of Catherine holding on to the little boy's hand. Dominic left the room. He found himself wandering aimlessly back downstairs, then sitting down in his chair in the library. In minutes his dark mood returned and he stared once more into the flames.

"Sometimes I can still scarcely credit it." Tears touched Amelia's gentle blue eyes as she looked across at Catherine.

Though Edmund and Amelia had been at Lavenham Hall

three different times over the past several weeks, Amelia occasionally lapsed into emotional moments such as this one.

"If only there was a way to change what has passed," she said with a catch in her crystalline voice.

"Nothing can change things, Amelia." Catherine wasn't even sure she would want them to change. "If I've learned anything, it's that the best course of action is simply to go on."

"Yes, I suppose it is."

All this fuss over the burnished hue of Catherine's once-pale skin. Amelia had come this time to help her select just the proper ball gown to make her return to Society. But the sun-browned color of her flesh against the whiteness of the gown had brought to mind once more all Catherine had suffered in her months away from home.

Catherine looked into her cousin's pretty face, saw the regret Amelia felt, and just as it had the moment of their reunion, something fragile stirred in Catherine's breast. Amelia Codrington Barrington was her closest friend. She and cousin Edmund, Edmund Jr., and Uncle Gil were the only family she had left. From the instant Catherine had seen Amelia and Edmund, all her suspicions about them had flown right out the window.

No two people could have looked more relieved to see her alive.

And no one who looked that way could possibly have meant her harm.

"My dear, dear child," Edmund had said, drawing her into his arms, tears streaking wetly down his cheeks. "God has returned you to us. It is a miracle."

Not quite, Catherine thought, but didn't say so. In fact, she didn't say much at all, just gave them the barest details about what had happened, certainly made no mention of Dominic, and neither did her uncle, bless his heart.

It was strange in a way, since she and Amelia had always been so close. It almost seemed that telling her story to Uncle Gil had caused as much grief as she was prepared to deal with at the moment. Besides, the memory of her dark Gypsy lover was hers and hers alone. When she was older, wiser, she would take it from its secret place inside her, examine it, and savor it. Until then, it would stay locked in her heart.

"Whatever shall we do?" Amelia asked, referring once more to the slightly golden cast of Catherine's skin. "We can try to bleach it, but I'm not certain how much good it will do."

Catherine rolled her eyes at the thought of the harsh, foul-smelling liquid against her tender flesh. "I think we will simply ignore it. At least the color is fairly even on the parts that show. The rest doesn't matter."

Oddly enough, until Amelia had pointed it out, Catherine hadn't even noticed. During her stay with the Gypsies, she had enjoyed the warm sunshine as she never had before. Now the custom of hiding one's skin from the slightest chance of color seemed silly and far more trouble than it was worth.

"And your hands," Amelia was saying with a frown, picking one up to examine it. "You've freckles on the backs. You must remember to keep on your gloves."

"Just tell Edmund and Uncle Gil to hasten their efforts to find me a husband. Once I'm married, my freckles will hardly be of concern."

Amelia fussed with the gown, an ethereal creation of gauzy white tulle over a background of embroidered white satin. "No, I don't suppose it will." The gown was the third of five that had been purchased for this and future occasions, and each seemed more beautiful than the last.

Amelia surveyed the gown and shook her head, her glossy short blond hair bouncing around her face with the movement. "This just won't do. You'll have to wait to wear this until your skin fades out a bit more. Put on the gold."

"Are you certain? It's really quite lovely."

"The gold," Amelia said with authority, and knowing her cousin's impeccable taste, Catherine obeyed.

In an instant she saw Amelia was right. The golden glow of her skin looked perfect against the shimmering hue of the high-waisted gown. It rode off one shoulder, emphasizing her graceful carriage, dipped low in front, fit snug beneath her breasts, then fell in a slim, straight line to the floor. There was a slit up the side that showed a bit of ankle. Even Catherine was impressed.

"It's beautiful," she said, suppressing a flash of yearning that Dominic could have seen her in it.

"It's perfect." Amelia adjusted the metallic gold swag that drew the gown up to Catherine's shoulder. "We'll weave golden ribbons into your hair. You'll wear your mother's diamond and topaz earbobs—nothing more. One look and the men will forgive you anything. Once that's happened, their wives will have no choice but to follow in their stead."

"I hope you're right," Catherine said, knowing she had a great deal more to be forgiven than Amelia understood.

Something clattered in the hall, and Catherine turned just in time to see the door to her chamber burst open and little Edmund Jr. rush in.

"Mama! Mama! Look what I've found!" He was an exact miniature of his father, brown-haired and blue-eyed, with a fair complexion and delicate bones. He would probably be taller than Edmund, though at four years old it was really too soon to tell.

"What is it?" Amelia asked, peering down at the small hand being held out to her, then leaping back with a shriek when Eddie opened his fingers to reveal a palm-sized frog.

"I found it in Uncle's fountain. His name is Hector. He won't hurt you."

Amelia rolled her eyes in exasperation. "Take it outside immediately! You know better than to bring something like that into the house."

Eddie looked chagrined, but only for a moment. He knew his mother well—she indulged him overly in just about everything. Catherine really didn't blame her, he was such a darling little boy.

"Want to come out and play?" he asked Catherine, ignoring his mother, just as he usually did.

"I'd love to, but it seems your mother has plans for me here."

His bottom lip stuck out. "She's no fun at all."

"Eddie," Amelia warned, but the child just grinned.

"Maybe my frog would like a dragonfly to play with," he said. "I think I shall go and see if I can find him one."

"You listen here, young man," Amelia scolded, "don't you dare bring either of those horrid creatures back inside this house—"

But Eddie had already gone. Catherine wondered if Amelia would swoon when the dragonfly arrived—which she was certain it would.

Amelia sighed. "Sometimes I worry about him," she said, shaking her head.

"He's just a boy. I'm sure he'll learn to behave himself as he grows older."

"That wasn't what I meant," Amelia said with a hint of indignation.

"Oh."

"I worry about his future. How he'll manage when he grows up."

"Manage?" Catherine asked.

"His holdings, I mean, his lands and income. He certainly won't have the kind of wealth you have."

"I can't see where that is a problem. Edmund is far from penniless, and Eddie will carry on the Northridge title. Besides, he's my cousin and I love him. I certainly don't intend to see him go without."

Amelia smiled a bit more easily. "Thank you, Catherine. Of course he can count on you. I don't know what I was thinking. . . . At any rate, it's your problems we need to be concerned with here."

She looked Catherine over once more, moving to survey her from every angle. Amelia smiled again, this time with warm satisfaction. "You look lovely. I believe, my dear friend, your terrible ordeal is about to be over—once and for all."

Catherine thought about Dominic and the ache for him that would not leave her heart. "Yes," she said softly. "Once and for all."

"It's the Viscount Stoneleigh, my lord." The butler held open the library door, Blythebury's black coat immaculate, his posture, as always, perfectly correct. "Shall I show him in?"

Dominic came to his feet. "By all means." Spotting his friend standing just outside the door and knowing he would have come in anyway, he flashed the briefest of smiles.

"Hello, Rayne." Dominic set his brandy snifter on the drum table near the fire as the tall broad-shouldered man stepped into the room.

"You're looking as grim as ever," Rayne Garrick said, clasping Dominic's hand in a grip just as solid as the man. He had thick dark copper-brown hair, which he never trimmed quite short enough, intelligent dark-brown eyes, and a passion for the out-of-doors that always kept him unfashionably tanned.

"It's good to see you, too," Dominic mocked with a grin that felt all too rare these days.

Rayne glanced around the room, noting the unopened curtains, taking in the slightly musty smell. "I see you're still brooding. I presume it's over the woman and not the late marquess."

"Strangely enough," Dominic admitted, "it seems it's a little of both."

Rayne arched a dark-brown eyebrow. They had known each other since their days together at Westholme Private Academy, then later at Cambridge. "What's the matter?" he asked, with his usual perception. "No one left to fight with?"

Dominic thought of the anger that stayed bottled up inside him. "So it seems."

"How's the boy?"

"Worrisome. I know what he's going through. I have no idea how to help him."

"The children giving him trouble, I take it."

"They know little about him. Just that his skin is dark and that he's somehow different. They're determined not to like him."

"Children can often be cruel, especially when they've no one to teach them anything different."

"Just one more reason to brood," Dominic said darkly.

"Well, I've come to put an end to it. It's time, my friend, you got out of this place and back into the stream of things. The Duke of Mayfield is having a lavish affair the end of the week—the opening of his newly built mansion on Grosvenor Square. It's going to be quite an occasion. I'm certain if you sift through that pile of letters on your desk, you'll find an invitation."

Dominic's gaze shifted to the stack of unopened postings he had received, condolences at first, then later invitations.

"The recently anointed Marquess of Gravenwold," Rayne drawled in that husky way of his, "and his roguish friend, the Viscount Stoneleigh, are going to be in attendance." He grinned, a flash of even white teeth that set hearts aflutter all over England. "You've dozens of female admirers waiting to lavish their approval on the new marquess in the most agreeable manner. It's time you stopped disappointing them."

Dominic had to smile. Stoneleigh was right. He needed to get away from Gravenwold, if only for a little while. He needed to end this dismal brooding and get on with his life.

He needed a warm willing woman in his bed.

"When do we leave?" he said, and Rayne looked a little surprised.

"How about tomorrow?" Rayne had traveled from Stoneleigh, his estate a long day's carriage ride away. "A good night's sleep will see me through, then we'll be on our way."

"I'll have Blythebury show you upstairs and tell Cook you'll be staying for supper. Why don't you join me for a drink in the Stag Room about seven-thirty?"

"I look forward to it, my friend." Rayne clapped Dominic on the back. "A lusty romp between the covers ought to improve your disposition. It won't be long before you forget all about your fiery little redhead."

"I'm bloody amazed it's taken me this long," Dominic admitted. And damned unhappy about it. In fact, he was beginning to look forward to his return to London. With any luck at all, he'd find a willing wench, take her hard and often, and get Catherine out of his blood—once and for all.

Chapter Fourteen

"J UST STAY CLOSE to Edmund and me, and everything will be all right." Gilford Lavenham, Duke of Wentworth, extended a stocky arm, and Catherine rested her golden-gloved hand on the sleeve of his burgundy brocade tail-coat. Beneath it he wore a white silk waistcoat, frilled white shirt and cravat, and perfectly tailored pin-striped burgundy breeches.

"God in heaven, I hope so," she said, pasting a smile on her face. She was bloody well tired of hearing how right everything would be.

"Whatever happens, just keep smiling," Amelia put in, brushing a fine piece of lint from her pale blue satin gown as she took Edmund's arm.

"Gil and I have seen to everything," Edmund said with confidence, leading the small procession forward. A fine-boned, far thinner man than Gil, Edmund, with his blue eyes, well-defined brows, and patrician features, cut a dashing figure in his bottle-green frock coat and yellow silk breeches.

"Watch your step, Catherine dear." Gil guided Catherine unerringly up the broad front steps through the carved mahogany doors. Servants in red and gold livery lined the way, and as Catherine stepped into the Great Hall, one of them took her satin-lined cloak.

The magnificence of the duke's new residence made her

draw in a breath. Rising over sixty feet high, the ceiling of the Great Hall arched above towering alabaster columns, the walls had been painted in rococo-style murals of cherubic angels, and she stood upon gold-streaked white marble floors. Statues of Greek and Roman emperors surveyed their domain with fixed stares of arrogance.

Catherine assessed her surroundings with nothing short of awe. Just a few brief months ago, she would have paid little attention. She had been raised to think nothing of such extravagant displays of wealth. Now she couldn't help comparing the ragged plight of the Gypsies, who lived at the barest level of subsistence, to the absurdity of so much gilded spendor.

Off to the left, the Duke of Mayfield and his thin wife, Anne, were surrounded by the party who had entered ahead of them, but their eldest daughter, Georgina, a tall, lanky girl with wide sea-green eyes and curly strawberry-blond hair saw them and hurried in their direction.

Noting her welcoming smile, several heads followed the tall girl's movements, their eyes coming to rest on Catherine. There was whispered conversation, Catherine felt Gil's reassuring grip on her arm, saw Edmund's studied nonchalance, and Amelia's look of composure.

"Lady Arondale!" Georgina said. "How good it is to see you." She clasped Catherine's cold hand between her warm ones. "Good evening, Your Grace," she said to Gil, "Lord and Lady Northridge."

"It's good to see you, Lady Georgina." Catherine smiled warmly as greetings were exchanged. She had met the girl during her London Season, and finding they shared a passion for books and riding, they soon became friends.

"I hope your journey was not overly tiring," Georgina said, working hard to ignore the whispers around them. There was a hint of concern in the tall girl's eyes, but also determination. The Mayfields were making their sympathies clear. Catherine was to be forgiven her folly. The power of two dukes, several viscounts, and an earl—as

well as the once-again Baron Northridge, and the Arondale
title and fortune—would surely be felt this eve.

As if to confirm the message, Georgina's father and
mother appeared.

"You look radiant, my child," the duke said to Catherine.
"Your father would have been pleased."

"Thank you." Catherine smiled, more easily this time.

"Positively charming," the duchess agreed, squeezing
Catherine's arm in a gesture of affection. Anne assessed the
golden gown, the coronet of red-gold hair atop Catherine's
head that made her look almost regal, and smiled. "A stint
in the country does wonders for one's complexion."

So much for Amelia's worry about Catherine's burnished
skin. With those few words, hats would be tossed aside
and the rays of the sun enjoyed by fastidious members of
the *ton* for at least the next several weeks.

"Yes," Catherine said, "Devon is a lovely place in the
spring."

Gil smiled at the subtle innuendos carefully being
exchanged. The pattern was set for Catherine's return to
the fold. All should be well if the evening continued to
progress as smoothly as it had started.

He guided her into the ballroom, a huge black and gold
affair where the fashionable elite were outshone only by
the magnificent crystal chandeliers hanging in a glittering
row above their heads.

Catherine accepted Gil's hand, and he led her onto the
dance floor, his movements graceful for a man of his stout
build. Edmund claimed the next dance, and Sir Osgood
Hornbuckle, her uncle's closest friend, the next. A dance
with His Grace, William Bennett, Duke of Mayfield, and
Catherine's acceptance was set.

She continued to dance, smiled until she thought her
face would surely crack—and prayed that nothing would
go wrong.

Dominic accepted the glass of champagne the red-liveried
servant had offered, part of him wishing for something

more stout. He had forgotten how crowded and airless one of these garish affairs could be, how utterly tiresome.

Still, as Rayne had promised, even their late arrival had not daunted the women, who continued to flutter around them, each one bolder than the last. Lady Campden was the boldest, her husband, the earl, obviously not in attendance.

"Surely, milord," she was saying, her smile overly warm, "now that you're in London, you'll find yourself vastly more entertained. The country can be so tiresome, and you've always been a man to keep himself . . . occupied."

She fluttered her hand-painted fan, moving tendrils of shiny sable hair beside her shell-like ears. The scarlet silk gown she wore dipped so low in front he could almost see her nipples.

He smiled faintly. "London can certainly cure one's boredom—though some diversions are obviously more pleasant than others." He fixed his eyes on her breasts. "Some far more pleasant, indeed."

Genevieve Morton, Lady Campden, had shared his bed on more than one occasion. It was obvious she wished to share it now.

"I also am prone to occasional boredom," she confessed with a smile that made clear her welcome. Azure-blue eyes, thick-fringed with long soot-black lashes, drifted to the front of his snug gray breeches, their bold gaze almost a caress.

Dominic watched her pale pink tongue slide wetly across her mouth and felt his blood begin to stir. He remembered well the last time they had made love—in the lady's West End town house, her husband just downstairs.

Genevieve had given a house party. While her husband imbibed too much rum and pushed his unwanted presence onto his guests, Genevieve led Dominic upstairs to a room off the hall. With privacy a concern, he had simply bent her over the back of the sofa, shoved up her expensive silk gown, unbuttoned his breeches, and taken her right there.

He looked at her now, saw the too-bright flush that stained her cheeks, saw that her glance had caught the swelling in his breeches before he could bring it under control, and knew she remembered it, too.

Damn, but he needed a woman. The weeks he had spent wooing Catherine had hardly been satisified by their two brief encounters, pleasant as they might have been. Pining away for her had done him no good, just made life hell for the people around him.

Catherine was gone from his life for good. Genevieve was here, warm and willing. So what if she'd slept with half the men in the room? She was a lusty wench who could set his body and soul free of another he could not have.

He leaned forward to whisper in her ear a time and place for their meeting—tonight, if it could possibly be arranged.

"I say, is that you, Gravenwold? When did you get back to London?" It was Gilford Lavenham, Duke of Wentworth. He wasn't a man to be ignored.

"I think I'll catch a breath of air," Genevieve said with meaning, tipping her pretty head toward the terrace. "If you gentlemen will excuse me . . . ?"

"Of course, my dear," the duke said. Both men bowed slightly, and the sable-haired beauty slid gracefully away. Dominic smiled to think of the welcome he would find on the terrace.

He turned his attention to Wentworth. "I only arrived from the country this week." He shook the duke's offered hand. Wentworth was a man he respected. Not pompous and arrogant, but forthright and, he had heard, a man one could trust.

"My condolences on the death of your father," Wentworth said. His glance slid to Dominic's arm. He saw no black band of mourning but made no mention.

"Thank you."

"I heard you've been out of the country."

"Yes. I travel a bit every year—which isn't all that easy with Napoleon and this damnable war going on."

"No, but one must make do." Wentworth sipped his champagne, glanced briefly toward the terrace, then back in Dominic's direction. "Will you be staying long in London?"

"At least a week or two. I needed to get away from Gravenwold for a while."

"Yes, that's probably a very good idea." Through an opening in the crowd, Wentworth spotted someone leaving the dance floor and a smile of warmth crossed his face. "If you've a moment, there's someone I'd like you to meet."

He didn't have a moment. Genevieve was waiting. Still, he respected the duke, and it shouldn't take that long to be cordial.

"Certainly." He followed the stout older man across the black and white marble floor toward a circle of ladies and gentlemen, one of whom he recognized as Edmund Barrington, Baron Northridge. There was a lovely blond creature, Northridge's wife as he recalled, and a brown-haired young man in his early twenties.

"Lord Gravenwold, I'd like you to meet my niece," the duke said, "Lady Arondale."

At the sound of her name, a woman he hadn't noticed before stepped from behind the young man. When she turned with a smile and looked up at him, Dominic's breath froze somewhere in his chest.

She was an image he had conjured in his dreams. A vision of fire and beauty, of passion and gentleness. A woman who with that single soft smile could heat his blood and take his breath away. His black eyes fixed on her startled green ones, pinned them, wouldn't let them go.

Catherine's pretty face paled. The glass of champagne in her hand began to tremble, then her fingers slowly opened and it crashed to the floor. With the shatter of crystal against marble, several pairs of eyes swung in their direction.

Dominic recovered first. "Lady Arondale," he said, bowing formally over her golden-gloved hand. "It's a pleasure to meet you." He squeezed it in silent warning, his mind spinning, trying to fit the pieces together.

Lady Arondale, he repeated to himself. He had heard the name before; Rayne had mentioned her. She was the daughter of the late earl, a man with no male heirs who had petitioned the crown to bestow the title on his unmarried daughter. Barrington—that was her name.

Catherine Barrington. Countess of Arondale. One of the richest women in England.

"How do you do?" she managed at last.

"You know Northridge, of course," the duke was saying, "and his lovely wife, Amelia. And this young man is Jeremy St. Giles. Jeremy, this is His Lordship the Marquess of Gravenwold."

"A pleasure to meet you," the young man said.

It took all his control, but Dominic made the appropriate responses, and only then followed St. Giles's gaze back to Catherine, who still looked shaken and pale.

"Is something the matter, milady?" the young man asked with a look of such concern Dominic's jaw instantly hardened. Was this then her Englishman? This unseasoned pup who would bow and scrape to her every command?

"You *are* looking a bit pale, my dear," her uncle said. "Maybe you should take a breath of air."

"Yes . . . I believe I should." Catherine looked as though she had just been granted a respite from the hangman.

"Allow me," Dominic said, taking her arm and sliding it through his with such authority that the duke took a step backward and young St. Giles just stood there with his mouth gaping open.

"Thank you," Catherine said, finally under control enough to pick up his lead. "I'm sure it's nothing. Probably just the heat. It's terribly stuffy in here."

Dominic led her toward the terrace, his surprise already

fading, replaced by a mounting rage. Little liar! Why the hell hadn't she told him who she was? What the devil game did she play? No wonder she had laughed at his grand scheme to keep her as his mistress. What a fool he had been!

He could feel her beside him, no longer trembling, her head held high as they strode through the glass-paned French doors. She was working hard to maintain her control, and the fact that she was succeeding only angered him more.

The moment they reached a darkened corner where they could find a moment's privacy, he turned on her with all the wrath he had been storing these past few weeks. Gripping her shoulder, he started to speak, but Catherine jerked free and whirled to face him.

"My God, Dominic, what in heaven's name do you think you're doing?" Dominic blinked. "Do you have any idea the risk you're taking?" Green eyes flashed with a fury to equal his own, and the scathing remark he'd intended to make died on his lips.

"God in heaven," she raged, "when they find out who you are, they'll toss you in Newgate and throw away the key!"

"Newgate? What the hell are you talking about?"

"What the hell am I talking about?" she repeated incredulously. "A marquess, no less. You couldn't have been satisfied as a viscount or a baron." Her eyes ran the length of him, taking in the perfect cut of his black silk tailcoat, burgundy waistcoat, frilled white shirt, and striking black cravat. His dove-gray breeches fit him like a second skin, a fact which brought a pretty flush to Catherine's cheeks. In her shimmering golden gown, her hair a fiery wreath above her head, she looked like the goddess he had once called her.

God, how could he have forgotten how lovely she was?

"Dominic—you're not listening!" Her eyes met his once more. "You've got to get out of here."

It dawned on him then, what she was talking about. She

thought he was pretending, that this was just some grand Gypsy scheme. Maybe she thought this was how he got his money—a means to fleece rich English *Gadjos.* As angry as he was, it was all he could do not to laugh.

"I'm listening. But you needn't worry. No one here but you can give me away. Unless of course, that's what you're planning."

She looked as if he had struck her. "Of course not. How could you even think such a thing?"

He didn't miss the worry in her voice, and at the sound of it, some of his anger began to fade. "Is that concern I hear, Catrina? After the way you left me, I find it a little hard to believe."

"Of course I'm concerned. I—" She stopped, the rosy flush returning, her expression far more tender than her words. "I owe you a great deal, Dominic." Her eyes moved over his face, as if she drank in the sight of him. "Maybe even my life. I've certainly not forgotten. I'll help you get out of here and—"

Dominic reached for her. His fingers encircled her arm and he hauled her against him. "Hush," he said softly. "I've been wanting to do this since the moment I saw you—we've wasted too much time already."

His mouth came down over hers and for an instant she went still. Then she clutched his shoulders. He had wondered if she would fight him—to her he was still just a Gypsy. Instead her arms slid around his neck and she kissed him back, softly breathing his name.

Dominic's hold grew tighter. He kissed her again, and Catherine's world spun out of control. She knew she should stop him—that this could ruin every carefully laid plan she and her family had made. But from the moment she had seen him, tall and so beautifully handsome, she had wanted nothing more than to feel his hard arms around her, to slide her fingers into his hair.

She did that now, feeling the corded muscles of his neck, the smoothness of his fine dark skin. He smelled of a musky cologne mingled with the scent of male she remembered so well. His tongue worked its magic, touching, tasting. When she parried it with her own, Dominic groaned into her mouth.

Just like her dream, his hands slid up her bodice to cradle her breasts, his thumb budding her nipple even through the fabric of her gown. Catherine felt the heat of his long, hard body, and her heart thundered wildly against her ribs. She could feel his maleness pressing against her and remembered it plunging inside her, claiming her, possessing her very soul.

When footsteps sounded in the distance, they ended the kiss, their breathing far too rapid, Catherine's hands still clutching the velvet lapels of Dominic's coat. Just as she stepped away, Lady Campden approached, a woman in scarlet with the face of a dark-haired angel. To Catherine's amazement, she flashed Dominic a look of contempt.

"I didn't know the two of you were . . . acquainted," the beautiful woman said, after a curt hello.

"Why, yes," Dominic answered smoothly. "Lady Arondale and I were introduced just this eve. Her uncle, the duke, suggested I escort her outside for some air."

For a moment she seemed to weigh his words, searching for the truth, Catherine guessed. Why it was so important, she wasn't quite sure.

"Yes . . . ," Lady Campden finally agreed, "it is rather sultry tonight. So much so, I believe I shall go home early. Unfortunately, Lord Campden has been called out of London on business, so I've only the servants for company." Her full red lips curved upward. "I suppose I'll just have to make do."

Dominic's mouth lifted, too. "I suppose," he said, far too blandly. There was something in the look he flashed her that gave Catherine pause. Was the lovely Lady Campden, a married woman and high-ranking member of the *ton*, extending an invitation? Catherine had heard of such things, but had never really seen the occurrence firsthand.

"Then again," the woman said, looking more than a little bit vexed, "the hour isn't really all that late. Perhaps I shan't

leave after all." Her too-bold glance confirmed it—she had
meant for Dominic to follow her home!

The dark-haired woman waited for a moment, as if she
expected Dominic to say something more. When he
didn't, she smiled thinly, made polite farewells, and turned
to take her leave.

"Supper is served, in case you hadn't noticed," she
called over one pale shoulder. "Surely you wouldn't want
to miss it." With a seductive sway of her hips, she turned
the corner out of sight.

Catherine rounded on Dominic, who had already
tucked her hand into the crook of his arm. "It didn't take
you long to find a replacement—I presume that's what she
is."

Dominic's black brows drew together, his expression
thunderous. "Lady Campden and I have been . . . friends
for some time. As to her or any other woman warming my
bed, I've been far too busy worrying over you. Now it
seems I needn't have bothered."

He was angry again, yet something eased in Catherine's
breast. He had worried about her, just as she had worried
over him.

"We'd better go back inside," he said, his voice cold as
he urged her off toward the door. "The scandalmongers
will be having a field day. Besides, I'm getting hungry all
of a sudden."

She noticed the way his hard black eyes had turned
slightly opaque and shifted to the curve of her breast. She
knew that look, and it wasn't food he wanted. She thought
of what he had said about the gossips and shuddered. Wag-
ging tongues were the last thing either of them needed.

Dominic had almost reached the house before Catherine had gathered her wits enough to stop him.

"Surely you can't mean to go back in there? Dominic,
you must get out of here before someone discovers the
truth."

He studied her a moment, jet-black eyes raking her. "I
told you once, *Your Ladyship,* a Gypsy can play any role

from a beggar to a king. Now maybe you'll believe me."
His lips curved up in a mocking half-smile that made her
stomach tighten. "Unless of course you'd prefer to remain
outside and continue our ... *conversation.*"

Catherine's eyes went wide. "No! Of course not." She
lifted her chin. "As you can plainly see, I no longer belong
to you—this is England, not one of your Gypsy camps."

His grip on her arm grew tighter. "No, Catrina, sadly it
isn't. If it were, you'd already be lying beneath me, not
primly sitting at my side eating a supper I'll scarcely be
able to taste."

Catherine flushed. Then it dawned on her what he had
said. "Sitting beside you?" For some insane reason she had
foolishly believed he would let her walk away.

"What's the matter? Surely you don't want to miss my
performance?" His expression grew even darker. "Or had
you planned to sup with your Englishman?"

"My Englishman?" Why couldn't she stop inanely
repeating his every word?

"The man you love—or had you forgotten? Surely it isn't
young St. Giles."

So many lies. They swirled around them as thick as a
London fog. "Lord Jeremy is just a friend."

By then they had reached the door to the state dining
room, a lavish high-beam-ceilinged chamber with leather-
covered walls hand-gilt with gleaming fleur-de-lis. Pictures
of English kings hung above endless silver platters of
steaming trays served by red-liveried servants. Linen-cov-
ered tables set with silver candelabra and huge bouquets
of lush red roses had been set up to seat hungry guests,
and additional tables of equal magnificence filled the sev-
enty-foot-long gallery just outside the opposite door.

"There you are!" Uncle Gil called out as they
approached. Beside him stood his friend Sir Osgood Hornbuckle. "I was beginning to worry."

Catherine didn't know whether to be relieved or
alarmed. Her uncle was scarcely a fool. How long would
Dominic be able to deceive him?

"Your lovely niece charmed me into forgetting the time," Dominic told him. "I hope you'll forgive me."

"Of course." The duke smiled warmly. "I often find myself equally charmed."

"Gravenwold, ain't it?" Ozzie said to Dominic. "Friend of Stoneleigh's, I hear. Pleasure to meet you."

Who in blazes was Stoneleigh? Catherine wondered. Another Gypsy in disguise? She groaned inwardly just to think of it.

"The pleasure is mine," Dominic assured him, looking as though he meant it. His confidence amazed her. She had known he was intelligent and well schooled, but to this degree she never would have guessed. Still, there were a dozen ways he might slip up, the chances greater with every passing moment.

"Good evening, Your Grace." A woman Catherine recognized as Lady Agatha James approached her uncle; along with a friend of hers, Lady Elizabeth Morton, Lady Campden's sister-in-law.

They made pleasant conversation with the two older men for a while, then Hornbuckle said, "Why don't we all go in to supper? I ain't had a thing to eat all day."

Catherine smiled. Sir Ozzie was one of her favorites, a short, balding little man with a quizzing glass who, though it was hard to believe, had been quite a hero in his day. During the Rebellion in the Colonies, Ozzie had saved the life of several of his superior officers, earning the king's favor and a knighthood into the bargain. He and Uncle Gil had met shortly thereafter, nearly thirty years ago, and remained staunch friends ever since.

"You still look a little peaked, my dear," the duke said to Catherine. "Are you certain you're all right?"

"Quite all right, Uncle. It's probably just the excitement." He scrutinized her a little harder than she would have liked, but Catherine merely smiled.

"I hope you don't mind if I join you," Dominic said, though it was hardly a question. "With such lovely company, I find it difficult to tear myself away."

"A pleasure to have you," the duke said, and Catherine silently pleaded for strength. Did his arrogance know no bounds? But then she knew very well that it did not.

The conversation continued as they progressed toward the front of the buffet. There were gleaming silver platters decorated with flowers and fruit, each laden with sole, whitings, or lobster. A huge haunch of beef, artfully sliced to order by a white-hatted chef, sat beside trays of pullet, woodcock, and partridge, pheasant stuffed with pecan and oyster dressing, sweetbreads of veal, sliced leg of lamb, steaming vegetables, custards and puddings by the score. When one tray emptied, another took its place, the array of delicacies endless.

Catherine, who had earlier been hungry, now felt mildly nauseated just at the sight of so much food. She could sense Dominic's powerful presence, though he stood several feet away, knew others must surely feel it, too, and her worry for him increased.

"Why don't we sit out on the terrace?" she suggested, away from prying eyes. "It's so much more pleasant out there."

Dominic smiled blandly. "I'm certain the gallery would be far more comfortable—unless, of course, you really aren't feeling all that well."

She wanted to kill him. Instead she smiled. "The gallery will be fine." Ozzie and the duke looked relieved. Balancing a silver plate full of food on one's lap was hardly their forte.

Catherine let Dominic seat her, waited for the others to be seated, then sat down himself. Several chairs down on the opposite side, Lady Campden sat beside a tall, handsome man with thick, dark copper-brown hair. Apparently, she had decided not to go home.

"I see Lady Campden has found someone else to entertain her," Catherine said with a falsely warm smile.

"Stoneleigh." Dominic looked more amused than disappointed, which pleased Catherine no end though she was loath to admit it. "He should be able to keep her mind off her loneliness for a while."

From behind him, a servant poured each of them a goblet of wine then set the crystal decanter on the table in front of them. It wasn't the good French wine they drank at home. Since the war, one never drank French wine in public. This was Portuguese, rich and dark.

Catherine spoke once more to Dominic. "Are you certain you don't wish to keep the pleasure of Her Ladyship's company for yourself?" she pressed, knowing very well she shouldn't.

"I might have . . . earlier. Now I find myself vastly more entertained." One corner of his mouth curved up, and Catherine's heartbeat quickened.

"That may be true for the moment. But I'll soon return home with my uncle. Where does that leave you?"

"Certainly not where I'd like to be, Catrina—resting between your shapely little legs."

Catherine blushed fiercely and glanced away. Furious at Dominic yet somehow strangely pleased, she picked at her food in silence. It seemed hours before they had finished, but eventually they did, and were about to quit the table when the Duke of Mayfield strolled up.

"Sorry I missed your arrival, old boy," he said to Dominic, who stood up and clasped his large hand. "Didn't want you to leave without a chance to say hello."

"It's good to see you, Mayfield." Dominic smiled. "How are the duchess and Lady Georgina?"

"Very well, thank you. Sorry to hear about your father. He could be a mean old bird but, under it all, he was always a decent sort."

Dominic's jaw tightened, and with it Catherine's stomach. Though she pretended an interest in the others' conversation, her breath caught on every other word. *Dear God, don't let him make a mistake.*

"So they say," Dominic replied tightly. "Personally, I wouldn't know."

"Yes . . . well, I guess it no longer matters. You've Graven-wold to consider now."

"So I've been told."

"You'll do well with it, I'm sure."

Dominic's tension seemed to ease. "I've been in London less than a week and I find myself missing the place already."

Catherine relaxed at the duke's easy smile. She couldn't help admiring Dominic's skill at conversation. He said a polite farewell as Mayfield and his party left, then sat back down in his seat. It was as if he really knew these people, that he wasn't just pretending. It was as if his father had really been the Marquess of Gravenwold, as if—

Catherine's mind froze. Suddenly she remembered another night, another gala party. There had been a tall, dark man there that evening, too. She hadn't seen his face, but she could still recall his glistening blue-black hair, the incredible width of his shoulders.

"They say he's a Gypsy," one of the women had said, and with the memory of those words it all became horribly, unerringly clear.

"You're him," she whispered, drawing his attention, her eyes huge and fixed on his face. "You're Nightwyck."

Dominic smiled grimly. "I *was* Nightwyck, until my father had the good grace to die and leave Gravenwold into my care."

She wet her lips, which suddenly felt dry. "You're a member of the aristocracy, a nobleman. Why didn't you tell me?"

"I had hoped it wouldn't matter."

"You're supposed to be a gentleman. How could you have behaved the way you did? How could you have *done* what you did?" Green eyes burning with angry tears she refused to shed, Catherine slid back her chair and made ready to leave. Beneath the table, Dominic caught her wrist and gripped it in a deathlock.

"Sit down."

"In case you haven't noticed," she gritted between clenched teeth, "you're through giving orders."

"I said, sit down." He jerked her back into her chair, every bit as angry as she, yet his face showed little emotion. "Smile," he warned, so only she could hear. "It appears your family has miraculously put our little adventure to rest. I suggest you keep it that way."

"Go to hell," she whispered, but she knew that he was right. Pasting a smile on her face, she slid her chair back up to the table. Though she forced herself to speak and nod politely, inside she was seething. She wanted to lash out at him, to claw his handsome face. She wanted to weep for hours.

Of course, she would do neither. She would simply pretend he did not exist, that sitting there next to him wasn't the meanest form of torture she had ever endured. Dominic seemed not to notice. Catherine feigned equal nonchalance, but as soon as everyone had finished their meal, she politely rose to her feet, sending the men to theirs.

"I'm sorry, Uncle, but I find I'm a bit off my feet after all. If you wouldn't mind leaving early, I should like to go home."

Gil shoved back his chair, the sound grating on the marble floors. "Certainly, my dear. I was about to suggest the same thing."

"I believe I shall rub on, myself," Sir Ozzie said. "Dashedly splendid affair, though, if I do say so."

"I'll see Lady Arondale out to your carriage," Dominic offered, taking her arm in an uncompromising grip and turning her toward the door. With a nod of agreement, Gil and Ozzie made their way around the table, intending to tell Edmund and Amelia of their departure, then join them out front.

"You're a cad and a bounder," she said beneath her breath as Dominic walked her toward the entry.

"You should have told me who you were," he countered,

accepting her satin-lined cloak from a servant, then engulfing her in its folds. "None of this would have happened."

"No? Why is it that I don't believe you?" She stood woodenly in the entry, torn between anger and despair. Dominic's handsome face betrayed a hint of anger, too. Dear God, he blamed her just as much as she blamed him!

Catherine felt a wave of heat as she began to consider her own scandalous behavior. True, he had seduced her, but Gypsy or lord, she had let him. Maybe even encouraged him. She had wanted Dominic almost from the start. Some of her anger began to fade.

Dominic looked at her, seemed to read her thoughts, and his hard expression gentled. He called for the Wentworth carriage with its blazing silver crest, then waited beside her on the broad stone steps for her uncle to arrive. A soft breeze blew in from the Thames and a full moon shone, yet on the wide veranda, they stood in shadow beneath a tall cypress.

Dominic's hand came up to touch her cheek. "I wish, little one, that I could say I was sorry. In truth I am not. My only regret is that we ever had to leave the Gypsy camp." There was a gentleness in his words, a tenderness she hadn't expected. His thumb brushed lightly across her jaw, making her skin grow warm.

The last of Catherine's anger slipped away. What had happened was past, the present was all that mattered. "Surely England is your home as well. You intended all along to return, did you not?"

His hand fell away, and his voice held a note of regret. "That may be true. But here I am no longer free to do exactly as I wish. You are a young lady of quality. My intentions are strictly dishonorable. You are more lost to me now, my love, than you ever were in France."

Catherine fought to make sense of his words. "Dishonorable?" she repeated numbly. "Dominic, what are you saying?"

"That you have escaped me more completely than you ever could have dreamed."

Though her thoughts remained in turmoil, Catherine began to understand. Now that he had returned to England, Dominic didn't want to see her again. He had wanted her as a woman to warm his bed, nothing more. The anger she had felt returned, more powerful than before. She felt sick and used, and she wanted to lash out at him.

Then again, what more should she have expected? Surely not marriage. She could still recall Pearsa's words of warning, Yana's bitter predictions. Yet, in truth, she expected exactly that.

Dominic had ruined her. As the son of a nobleman, a high-ranking member of the *ton,* a marriage contract was only right and proper.

She scoffed. Since when had Dominic done anything right and proper?

A tide of bitterness welled up inside her. "There was a time, Lord Gravenwold, when I believed you one of the finest men I had ever known. How could I have been so wrong?" She tried to brush past him, but he caught her arm.

The lines of his face turned grim, his voice hard-edged and remote. "You will come to me if there are any unforeseen . . . problems?"

Catherine frowned. "Problems? What sort of problems?"

One corner of his mouth curved up, making him look more like the handsome dark Gypsy he had been in the camp. "So, milady countess, not so much has changed. You are still the charming innocent you were in France, and I'm still a black-hearted bounder."

It struck her then that he spoke of her carrying his babe. Cheeks flushed crimson, Catherine moved back into the shadows.

"You needn't worry, milord," she said tartly. "There is no . . . problem." She waited for his breath of relief—there was none.

"Then this is farewell, fire kitten," he said softly, bowing over her hand. "I am glad that you are safe."

"Are you ready to go, my dear?" At the duke's approach, Dominic handed her into her uncle's care, turned and walked away. She watched his tall, imposing figure return to the house and an ache rose up inside her.

She had left him in France, suffering a loss far greater than any she had known. Now, just when her heart had begun to mend, she had lost him again. It hurt just as much this time—more because now she knew the truth.

As she had once feared, she had only been his plaything. A passing fancy to idle away his time in the camp. Even as a countess she held no appeal for him.

The ache swelled and grew, knifing her insides, goading her once more to anger. How dare he use her and toss her away! She wasn't a woman of easy virtue like Lady Campden—she wasn't some light-skirt casting about for a lover. She was a woman of principle who didn't need Dominic Edgemont or any other man. If it weren't for the heir she must produce, the freedom and respectability a husband could give her, she would do without one!

At the very least, she intended to find a man who would be malleable to her wishes. Someone whose every glance couldn't set her blood on fire and nearly drive her insane. Someone who wouldn't break her heart.

As the carriage rolled along, Catherine squared her shoulders and stared into the darkness. To her bitter chagrin, a single tear rolled down her cheek.

She wiped it away with the back of her hand and swore there would be no more.

Chapter Fifteen

"I BELIEVE YOUR RETURN to Society was at least a passable success," the duke's voice rumbled from the opposite side of the carriage. In the darkness, Catherine could not see his face.

The city had finally begun to quiet, the clip-clop of the horses' hooves a hollow echo against the cobblestone streets. In the distance, she could hear the nightwatch calling out the hour. A fog had begun to set in, and the air smelled damp and musty.

"It was wise of Edmund and Amelia to remain," her uncle continued. "Their presence should help stifle the last of the gossip."

"They've been wonderful," Catherine said. The coach moved beneath a streetlamp, illuminating for a moment her uncle's side of the carriage. The lines of his face appeared more deeply etched than they had earlier in the evening, and his eyes strained into the darkness, assessing her, it seemed.

"What did you think of Gravenwold?" he asked mildly, but there was an underlying tension in his voice.

God in heaven, surely he couldn't know. "He's handsome in the extreme," she replied with as much nonchalance as she could muster. "He seems quite the rage with the ladies."

Gil leaned forward in his seat. "He said nothing unto-ward to you, did he?"

"No, no. Of course not. His Lordship was entirely the gentleman." That was a lie. Dominic was as far from a gen-tleman as any man she had ever met.

"Yes ... well, I should hope so. Probably shouldn't encourage his association. He clearly has no intention of entering the marriage mart, and we've got to find you a husband."

Catherine felt a tightening in her stomach. "I've been told he has vowed never to marry. Whyever not? I should think he'd be concerned with gaining an heir."

"Something to do with his father. A long-running feud of some sort. He's determined the Edgemont name shall not carry forth."

"But his father is dead. Surely now—"

"I'm afraid that's all I know. In any case, he seems most intent on the matter. Doubt even you could stay him from his course."

Catherine ignored what might have been a note of chal-lenge. "Gravenwold is the last man I would choose."

Her uncle shrugged into the darkness, the expensive fabric of his burgundy tailcoat rustling against the tufted green velvet seat. "Probably right about that. The man would be demanding as blazes and a devil to live with."

"Exactly," Catherine said.

"Bound to be other men who would far better suit. What about young St. Giles?"

"Jeremy?"

"As a second son, he won't inherit, but at least his father is an earl. He's intelligent and forthright. Aside from that, he's obviously feet over the mark for you. I should think, with a bit of theatrics on your part, he would probably for-give you anything."

Catherine thought of Jeremy. She had liked him from the moment of their first meeting. He was kind and gentle and sincere. "No," she said softly. "Jeremy deserves a woman who loves him. I never could.

"But—"

"What about Litchfield? He's penniless, obviously casting about for a propitious match. Do you think he might suffice?"

"Surely you've no interest in Litchfield—the two of you would hardly suit."

"Whether or not we would suit is scarcely the issue. Beyond that, I have no interest in any man. Litchfield seems as good a candidate as anyone else."

The duke fell silent.

"Well, what do you think?" Catherine prodded.

Gil made a disgruntled noise in his throat. "Litchfield is hardly the man for you. He's attractive enough, I suppose, in a rather dandified way, but you'd be bored with him in a fortnight."

Sooner than that, Catherine thought but didn't say so. Richard would be easy enough to manage, would do his husbandly duty but afterward probably be willing to leave her alone—as long as he had his mistresses—and he was in desperate need of her money.

"I should think on it, Uncle," she said. "It seems to me, a baron would do well enough."

"It seems to me you would run the poor beggar ragged." He sighed. "At any rate, we've time enough to look further."

Catherine smoothed the front of her gold brocade gown, her mind returning to her unpleasant encounter with Dominic. "I suppose that is so, but in truth, I should prefer the matter settled quickly. It's my fondest wish to return to Arondale. I worry about its management, and there's the school to think of. I miss the children terribly."

"I've been meaning to discuss that with you ... your school ... what was it?"

"We named it the Christian Barrington Charity School. It was originally called the Arondale School for the Betterment of the Poor, but it was Father's idea, so when he died, Edmund and I renamed it. The children were doing so well when we left. I can't wait to see how they're progressing."

Arondale. Just the name conjured thoughts of a haven from her turbulent emotions. If only she were there now, away from London—away from Dominic and all the longings he stirred.

"I know it's deuced unpopular," Gil said, "but I've been considering such a school at Lavenham. I could easily arrange enough time for the children's studies. Your father and I spoke of it several times, but once he was gone, I never seemed to get things going."

Catherine brightened. "That's a wonderful idea, Uncle. Of course, you'd have to find a schoolmaster, and there's the matter of convincing the parents—which is often the most difficult part. But it would surely be worth it."

"I may need a little advice."

"I'd be delighted to help. We can start looking for a teacher while we're staying here in London."

Gil smiled into the darkness. "It shouldn't delay your plans to find a husband for more than a couple of weeks."

Dominic paced the floor of the study in his town house on Hanover Square. Unlike the library at Gravenwold, this low-ceilinged, wood-paneled room was one he usually avoided. It had been a favorite of his father's, whose massive smiling portrait looked down on him from its place of honor above the black marble mantel.

Last night after his return from Mayfield's soiree, Dominic had come to the room to sit and stare at the portrait. Seated in the chair behind his father's carved rosewood desk, he had wanted the marquess's haunting, mockingly arrogant presence to jeer at him and harden his heart.

In the dismal gray hours before dawn, he had drunk himself senseless on *palinka,* which he saved for just such morbid occasions, and thought of his mother, reminding himself of her years of hardship without a man's protection, of the loss of her son at the hands of his father, of the hours of soft weeping he had heard in her wagon.

He thought of the lonely nights he had spent in his barren room at Yorkshire, the brutal canings he had endured, the endless punishment for not mastering his lessons as quickly as his tutors expected, or for some imagined slight he had made in front of his father. He remembered how he had wanted to run away but didn't because he knew it would only bring more sadness to his mother. He thought of how the two months each year that he spent with the Gypsies were the only weeks of happiness he knew in all the time he lived with his father.

Dominic forced himself to remember—willed himself not to think of Catherine—and drained the last of the liquor, tossing the fiery contents back in a single swallow. Unfortunately, after a few hours' sleep, his head cradled in his arms on top of the desk, a bath and a shave, he had little more than a pounding headache to show for his efforts—he had too much on his mind.

"He is here, Your Lordship," the butler said. "Shall I show him in?"

"Yes."

The sound of footsteps echoed in the hall outside the door, and Harvey Malcom walked in. He wore an ill-fitting brown broadcloth frock coat and nervously adjusted his neckcloth as he walked across the room to where Dominic stood in front of his desk.

"You sent for me, Your Lordship?"

"I did. I wanted to tell you that you may call off your bloodhounds. I've found her."

Malcom's sandy brows shot up. "Here?"

"Practically under our noses. It seems we should have been searching somewhat higher up the social ladder—our lady is a countess."

Malcom's eyes went wide. "A countess!"

"Catherine Barrington, to be precise, Countess of Arondale. I want to know everything you can discover about her—down to the way she butters her scones, if that is possible."

"Now that we know who she is, that shouldn't be much of a problem."

"You understand, Malcom, your discretion must be considerable."

"Have no fear, milord. Your father trusted me completely. I'll not let you down."

"Good. I'll expect to hear from you no later than three days hence."

"That should be more than sufficient."

As soon as Malcom had left, Dominic returned to his high-backed chair behind the carved rosewood desk. As he had through the long hours of the night, he stared up at the portrait of his father.

"I won't let you win," he said with soft menace. "Not even for Catherine." But he had to know the truth about her, had to put things to rest. Once he had done that, he could get on with his life.

He looked at the portrait and smiled.

"We'll be attending the Sommersets' soiree this eve," Edmund said. "Litchfield is certain to be there, since he and the earl are close friends."

"Good," Catherine said. "I'm not certain how many more of these dreary affairs I can stand. Dear God, how I miss the country."

Edmund scowled, but the duke smiled. "I'm glad to hear it," he said. "I've accepted an invitation for us to spend a week at Rivenrock, Mayfield's country home. It isn't far from the city, but at least we'll be able to catch a breath or two of fresh air. Poor little Eddie is about to go crazy with no place to play but the park."

"A week, Uncle Gil?" Catherine said. "I had hoped to conclude our . . . business . . . and start planning my return to Arondale by that length of time."

"I'm afraid that's out of the question. Have you forgotten so soon, my dear, the attempt that was made on your life?

You can hardly return to Arondale until the matter is laid to rest."

"But that's ridiculous! The man might never be apprehended. I shall simply continue to do as you have done— hire men I can trust to protect me."

The duke had hired the best men he could find to provide for Catherine's safety. They traveled as footmen whenever she left the town house, and guarded the residence around the clock while she was at home. Her chamber had been secured, and the trellis below her window neatly cut down, leaving no way for an intruder to reach her.

"Similar precautions at Arondale," she continued, "should suffice until I'm married. Once that's happpened, I doubt anyone would dare to threaten my life."

"Especially should you marry Litchfield," Edmund put in. "He's superb with sword and pistol. He's won at least two duels that I know of."

Catherine's head came up. "He hasn't killed anyone?"

"Not that we've heard of," the duke grumbled. "I think he chooses his opponents rather more by their skill—or lack thereof—than their imagined indiscretions."

Catherine ignored this last. "You see, Uncle. With Litchfield I'll have nothing to worry about."

"The man who abducted you was probably just some ruffian looking to fatten his purse," Edmund added. "After all, he must have gotten a very tidy sum for you."

"If that's the case," the duke said, "why didn't the man ask for ransom? It would have meant a greater sum by far."

"I haven't been able to credit that one," Edmund admitted.

"Well, he must have singled Catherine out for some reason—it wasn't as though she were easy prey. Why, the culprit must have had a devil of a time getting her out of that room."

"Who can say for sure?" Edmund said with a shrug of his shoulders. "Maybe the man had seen her somewhere and gone feet over the mark. She's just lucky the fellow didn't take liberties with her himself."

"That's enough, Edmund," Amelia said from the doorway, having just walked into the room. "I'm sure Catherine would rather discuss something more pleasant." Edmund Jr. tugged free of his mother's hand, turned, and raced back out the door.

"Thank you, Amelia, I would indeed." Catherine ignored her friend's weary sigh as she glanced down the hall to her small son's retreating figure. "As a matter of fact, we were earlier discussing the matter of Litchfield's imminent proposal—of course he doesn't know about it yet."

"Are you certain it's Litchfield you want?" Amelia asked. "Why not take a little more time, get to know him a bit before you decide?"

"I don't need to know him. All I need from him is the use of his name and the delivery of an Arondale heir. Once that duty is complete, I shall live my life quite separately from my husband."

"Catherine dear," the duke said softly, but a knock at the door interrupted his next words.

"The modiste has arrived," she said brightly, lifting her rose-sprigged muslin skirts and heading toward the door. "I'm due for a final fitting on the gown I'm to wear this eve. If Litchfield's to attend, I want everything perfect." She swept from the room with a radiant smile on her face.

Radiant, indeed, Gil thought with a frown. *All* too *radiant.* He alone knew of her tragic affair with the Gypsy. The *educated* Gypsy, he corrected. The one whose father might have been English. Catherine's gay demeanor didn't fool him for a moment. She was hurting inside and nothing she could do or say could make him believe any different. Worst of all, he had a sneaking suspicion the ache in her heart had grown worse these past few days—and a terrible hunch he knew why.

Dominic could hardly see the front of Sommerset's town house for the number of gigs, phaetons, curricles, coaches, and carriages already lining the street. He had come to the extravagant soiree in a determined effort to put his life forward and prove to himself once and for all that he was immune to Catherine.

Once he got inside, he found himself praying she wouldn't attend. Unfortunately, his hopes were dashed in that regard when she arrived with her uncle and her cousins, looking decidedly regal in her emerald silk gown shot with silver. Though he did his best to avoid her, and she had acknowledged his presence with only the briefest of nods, for the past several hours he had found himself searching her out in the crowd, his black eyes drawn to her as if by some powerful spell.

"Gravenwold!" It was Wentworth. Thank God, Catherine was not in tow. At least that was what he thought until he saw her dancing with Litchfield—again. "Haven't seen you about, old boy. Thought maybe you'd left town."

"As a matter of fact, I intend leaving shortly. I'm spending a week in the country then heading back to the manor."

"Mayfield's, I imagine. Heard you might be going. Should be quite an extravagant affair."

Dominic felt a flicker of unease. "Are you and your lovely niece planning to attend?" If they were, he wouldn't be.

"Doubt it. Too much going on here."

Dominic inwardly sighed. As determined as he was to sever his feelings for Catherine, seeing her tonight had been far more difficult than he would have believed. Half of him wished he had returned to Gravenwold after their first encounter, but the other half refused to let his regard for a woman rule his life.

To that end, he had taken Lady Campden up on her offer of companionship and spent several hours in her bed. Unfortunately, he found his interest in her had waned considerably. His lovemaking was at best halfhearted, with little thought to her pleasure, and not much more to his own. In the morning he had left her, wishing he hadn't gone in the first place and feeling less content than he had before.

"Well, if it isn't the elusive Lord Gravenwold. Heard you were here. About time you saw fit to grace us with your presence." Lord Litchfield, a lean blond man, fair complected, well dressed if a bit of a dandy, extended a hand, and Dominic shook it. It took all his will not to look at Catherine, who smiled at him serenely from a place on Litchfield's arm.

"Lady Arondale," he finally said, with a slight bow over her hand. "I trust your evening has thus far been pleasant?" *No doubt,* he thought. Every man in the room had been fawning over Catherine since the moment of her arrival. To his amazement, only Litchfield had garnered any attention in return.

Dominic felt the heat at the back of his neck. What the devil did she see in that rake? The man was near penniless, a womanizer of the worst sort, and not nearly her equal in intelligence.

"The evening has been extremely amusing," Catherine told him with a haughty little lift of her chin. "It seems Richard loves to dance almost as much as I do."

Richard! So that was the way of it. Well, he certainly wasn't the Englishman she had spoken of—as near as Malcom could discover, that was just another of the lady's fabrications—at least it was until tonight.

The group of musicians at the far end of the room struck up a new tune.

"I say," Litchfield said, "they seem to be daring a waltz." His eyes fixed on Catherine with an unspoken request. Two dances in a row—three altogether—it was highly unseemly and both of them knew it—unless his intention was marriage.

Dominic flashed him a sharp look, and Catherine the thinnest of smiles. "I was hoping Lady Arondale would allow me the honor."

When it appeared she might refuse, Dominic's fingers tightened about her wrist, the threat in his hard black eyes more than clear.

Catherine smiled up at him sweetly. "Why certainly, milord." But her gaze remained cold.

Dominic led her onto the dance floor and took her into his arms. The moment he did, he realized he had made a mistake. The feel of her tiny waist reminded him of the lush, sweet curves beneath her gown, the length of the shapely legs moving so gracefully next to his. He remembered every smooth inch of her skin, the apricot hue of her nipples. He wanted her naked, wanted her writhing beneath him, calling his name as she had before. He wanted to hold her and kiss her and make sweet love to her forever.

"I've missed you," he said softly, wishing it wasn't the truth.

"Well, I have not," Catherine said tartly. "I've been far too busy to think of a treacherous, deceitful blackguard like you."

"Too busy thinking of Litchfield?" he mocked, arching a thick black brow.

"Richard is a very attractive man, in case you haven't noticed."

"*Richard,*" he sneered, "is a driveling dandy."

Catherine's chin came up. "Lord Litchfield is more of a gentleman than you'll ever be. Thus far, he hasn't pressed his suit, but I believe he soon will. When he does, I intend to accept. We'll be married just as soon as propriety allows."

Dominic's step faltered, causing Catherine to stumble. He recovered quickly and forced himself to smile. "I believe you're overly tired," he taunted, drawing her toward the double doors leading outside. "Why don't we get some air?"

"But—"

He hauled her around the corner out of sight, her posture stiff and unyielding. "I want the truth, Catrina. You aren't in need of a husband because of what transpired between us?"

Catherine gasped. "Certainly not! Marriage is simply a

means to gain my freedom. I've had a healthy dose of it, and I find I miss it sorely. Once I've produced an heir, I'll have the same independence other married women have. In short, I'll not have to answer to anyone but myself— ever again."

Dominic watched her a moment, noting the flush of color in her cheeks, the way the moonlight reflected off her flame-colored hair. He reached for one of the silky tendrils that curled softly beside each ear and smoothed it between his fingers. "Was answering to me really all that bad?"

Catherine's eyes lifted to his, their emerald brightness softening. She watched him, remembering, it seemed, just as he was, other nights they had spent beneath the stars. "Nay, my lord Gypsy, it was not. But you are not the man I will marry. And I am loath to do another man's bidding."

"Yet you will submit to him in the marriage bed."

Catherine's lips thinned into a disapproving line. "I'm no green girl, milord, thanks to you. I know exactly what is required. I will endure it."

Dominic worked a muscle in his jaw. "Is that the appeal Litchfield holds? Surely you're not foolish enough to believe he can make you feel the way I can?"

Before she could answer, he swept her into his arms, his eyes holding her captive just as surely as his hands. Then his mouth closed over hers in a fiery, sweet, passionate kiss that said what his words had not.

"Catherine," he whispered into her mouth, and felt more fire from the brush of her lips than he had thrusting into another.

Her hands slid around his neck, and she returned the kiss, but only for an instant. Then she broke free. "Please, Dominic. Please don't do this."

For a time he just stood there, holding her in his arms, feeling her tremble, her soft curves molded against him. His body felt tense and rigid, his shaft hot and hard where it strained against the front of his breeches. God, how he wanted her.

"Please," she whispered, and he let her go.

Catherine touched her kiss-swollen lips, her eyes overly bright, her expression uncertain and more than a little accusing. Then she turned and hurried away. Stopping a moment at the door, she smoothed her hair and straightened her gown, lifted her chin and went in.

Dominic raked a hand through his hair. Bloody hell! What the devil did he think he was doing? He would ruin her, if he wasn't careful. He scoffed. What the hell did he think he'd already done? Malcom had uncovered the story of her supposed drowning and the ruse she'd employed to return to Society—the months she had spent in a convent—and it had been brilliant. The last thing he needed was to cause trouble for her again.

On top of that, she might be in danger. Malcom had yet to verify the truth of her abduction, but the presence of the guards the duke had hired seemed to lend credence to the tale. At least she was well protected. And Dominic had directed Malcom's efforts to discovering the man behind the deed. Though he knew now the folly of being near Catherine under any circumstance, he would rest a lot easier knowing she was well and truly safe.

Giving Catherine and her party a wide berth, Dominic skirted the house and in minutes stood out front, awaiting his carriage.

So much for his plan to exorcise his feelings for her.

From now on, he'd just have to stay out of her way.

"Where the devil is Catherine?" The duke surveyed the dance floor, but saw neither his beautiful niece, nor Gravenwold, the man with whom she'd been dancing. "Every time those two get together, they seem to disappear."

"The man is a notorious rake," Edmund said. "Shouldn't be allowed anywhere near. I had better go find her." He made his way through the crowded, tittering throng out through the doors that led into the garden.

But it wasn't Catherine he sought.

"Cave!" he whispered into the darkness. "Where in blazes are you?"

"Right 'ere, Yer Lordship." Like an oversized genie, Edmund's personal manservant, Nathan Cave, a huge, brawny man with a thick black mustache and long black hair pulled back in a queue at the nape of his neck, appeared at his side from behind the trunk of a tree.

"Well?"

"The chit come out here, all right, but she 'ad some big bloke with 'er. Kissed 'er, 'e did. Right there on the porch."

"Bastard," Edmund said.

"Too many people 'ere to get 'er alone. Best to wait a little longer. Find someplace else. Sooner or later, she'll go off on 'er own. When she does, I'll be waitin'. Promise you, Yer Lordship, this time I'll finish 'er off, like I shoulda done before."

"You and your conscience," Edmund muttered. "You nearly got us both a trip to the three-legged mare with that little stunt."

The big brawny man hung his head. "Her Ladyship's always been kind to me. It just didn't feel right, puttin' an end to 'er that way. Still don't, but I guess there ain't no 'elp for it now—not by 'alf."

"The men you've chosen can be trusted?" Edmund asked.

"Couple o' gallows birds, but they're brothers o' the blade. Enough quid, they'll keep their mouths shut."

"Time's getting short," Edmund said. "Once she's married, her death won't help us—her fortune will go to her husband and we'll all be well and truly shagged."

"No need to worry. Once we get 'old of the mort, the job'll be done in a wink."

"We've got one thing in our favor—that little story she concocted covered up your bungled attempt. If we succeed this time, we're home free. You'll be living like a king, instead of spending the next twenty years doing my bidding." Edmund smiled. "Yes, sir, Nathan my boy, you'll be able to forget those ugly days in Newgate forever."

Nathan visibly cringed, as Edmund knew he would. Just a reminder of his years of living in the filth and stench of debtor's prison were enough to keep him in line.

It had been several years after his imprisonment that a relative of Nathan's had gone to work for Edmund as a coachman. When Edmund had run up a gambling debt he could not pay and been in need of someone to discourage the gentleman he owed from calling him out, he had quietly spoken to one of his more trusted servants. Billy Cave had mentioned his cousin, assuring Edmund that if he paid Nathan's debt and freed him from Newgate, the man would give Edmund his unwavering loyalty.

He also said that Nathan, though somewhat bird-witted, was an excellent shot, good with a knife, and could brawl his way out of the meanest situation.

Edmund took a chance, paid Cave's paltry debt, and won the man's loyalty. There was no task Edmund could not ask of him. Which was not to say, the big looby didn't occasionally make a mistake.

"Got to get 'er away from them guards. Get 'er off somewheres alone."

"Wentworth may have solved our problem. We'll be spending the week at Rivenrock, Mayfield's country house. Could be just the opportunity we've been seeking."

Nathan sighed. "Wish there was some other way."

"Well, there isn't. You tried it your way—now we'll do it mine."

Scuffing the toe of his boot in the dirt, Cave hung his head in resignation. "You've got me word."

Edmund just nodded. "I've got to go in. Nothing's going to happen here, so you might as well go back home."

The brawny man nodded and lumbered off toward the carriage house, which faced a street in the rear.

Edmund shook his head. God's teeth, but things had gotten muddled. He had never wished Catherine ill, but damn it all, he couldn't expect his wife and child to continue living on Catherine's crumbs. His own fortune had dwindled considerably. What would be left for little Eddie when he grew up?

The only way he could properly see to his family was with his cousin out of the way.

Life could be deuced hard sometimes.

Chapter Sixteen

CATHERINE CLOSED THE HEAVY MAHOGANY DOOR to her elegant bedchamber in the east wing of Rivenrock and leaned against it for support. "God in heaven, he's here!"

"Who is 'ere, my lady?"

"Dominic. The man's like a shadow. Everywhere I go he appears. Surely he isn't following me on purpose?"

Catherine had finally confided in Gabby. There was no one else she could turn to, and she knew her little French maid would never betray her secret. Gabby had long ago succumbed to the fires of passion, she understood them only too well.

"But 'e must have followed you. Why else does 'e go wherever you go?"

"I don't know. The way he feels about me, it just doesn't make sense." Catherine paced the thick Aubusson carpet. Outside the window, sheep grazed in the distance and sunlight reflected off small blue ponds. Mayfield's sumptuous estate sprawled on eight thousand rolling and forested acres just a two-day carriage ride from London.

"Maybe 'Is Lordship cares for you more than you know."

Catherine shook her head. "He wants me—that he's made clear. But only to warm his bed. Since I'm still unmarried, we'd both be ruined and Dominic knows it." She sighed and sank down on the peach moiré counterpane beneath the matching silk bed hangings on the four-poster bed. "I've got to talk to him. Find out the truth."

"Do you think that is wise? If things are truly as you say, being seen wiz 'im might cause problems with Lord Litchfield."

Catherine fidgeted on the bed. "Perhaps you're right. The most important thing right now is to wring a proposal from Litchfield. The sooner I'm away from London"—*and Dominic*—"the happier I'll be."

Catherine dressed for the evening ahead with infinite care, choosing a cream silk gown with a gauzy tulle gold-flecked overskirt. She wore the Arondale emeralds, enhancing the color of her eyes and hoping to dazzle Litchfield with the lure of her money. She intended to lavish him with her attentions and ignore Dominic in the extreme.

It didn't go quite the way she had planned.

Richard, who had been in attendance since she had first entered the drawing room, had gone to fetch her a sherry, leaving her alone for a moment next to the pianoforte. Dominic had not yet appeared.

At the sound of footfalls beside her, she turned, sure that Richard had returned, only to discover the tall dark figure she had been dreading.

"What the hell are you doing here?" Dominic did nothing to hide his displeasure, his stance rigid, the smooth dark skin across his cheekbones taut. "I'm beginning to think you're following me."

"What! You're the one who's following me!"

He smiled slowly, but there was no warmth in his eyes. "Is that so?"

"Yes. My uncle and I made plans to attend this outing some time ago. I assure you, if I had known you would be here, I would not have come."

"Your uncle informed me just last week that he had more important goings-on in London."

Catherine frowned. "That's odd. Well, maybe he hadn't quite decided. At any rate, I'm here and I'm not leaving.

If my presence disturbs you so much, why don't you leave?"

Dominic's jaw clenched. "You should know by now, Catrina, neither you nor any other female is about to run my life. I'll stay as long as I like. You just keep out of my way."

Catherine wanted to slap his handsome face. "You are the most arrogant—"

"Save your breath, love. We both know exactly what I am—what I'll always be." Spotting Litchfield's return from the corner of his eye, Dominic bowed formally over her hand. "Behave yourself, little one. You wouldn't want His Lordship to see your true colors, would you?" Turning, he walked away, joining the man he had come with, Viscount Stoneleigh.

It took all Catherine's control, but she forced herself to smile at Litchfield and accept the glass of sherry he had brought her.

"Thank you, milord."

"Richard," he corrected.

"Richard," she said warmly, trying not to glance in Dominic's direction.

"So glad you could make it. Should be a dilly of a time—Mayfield never spares the expense."

That was the truth. As sumptuous as Lavenham was, Rivenrock was at least three times as large, and magnificent in the extreme. The room they stood in had been done in majestic shades of purple and gold, the floors were of inlaid marble, the carpets of silk in a pattern depicting the Crusades.

"There's the hunt on Wednesday," Litchfield was saying, "and a masque tomorrow night—and that's only for starters."

"A masque?" Catherine said, "but I didn't bring a costume."

Just then Lady Georgina approached, catching the last of her words. "You needn't worry about the ball, Catherine. As usual, Father's thought of everything. Some of the ladies were told about it ahead of time, but it was rather a last-minute idea, so for those who weren't informed, he's brought in half a dozen seamstresses and dozens of yards of fabric. They'll be able to whip you up something in no time at all. You just have to decide what it is you wish to be."

Catherine looked across at Dominic, saw his splendid dark eyes looking back—and knew *exactly* what she wanted to wear.

"I am not certain this is such a good idea, my lady." Gabby slid the sequined white peasant blouse over Catherine's head.

"Perhaps it isn't. But the look on Dominic's face will be worth any risk I might be taking." She lifted her arms and ducked her head into the gathered red silk skirt, also heavily sequined, pulled it down, and fastened it at her waist, adjusting the layers of petticoats she wore beneath.

"Oh, 'e will be surprised," Gabby said, "I 'ave no doubt about that." She walked over to the dressing table and stood in front of the mirror. "Come. Let me brush out your hair."

Catherine smiled with anticipation. She would wear the fiery mass hanging loose down her back, pulled up on one side and laced with the small gold coins Dominic had given her what seemed eons ago. At her wrist more coins jingled from a bracelet Gabby had fashioned, and a wide gold band surrounded her upper arm. Thin hoops of gold dangled from her ears, and her blouse dipped shamelessly low.

All in all, she looked much as she had in the Gypsy camp. Except that the shimmering red silk fabric was far more expensive than any she could have afforded back then.

"Mon Dieu," Gabby breathed. "'Is Lordship will be mad for you."

"I don't know about that." But secretly she hoped Gabby's words proved true. It would serve the bounder right. She hoped he recalled every moment they had shared, every heated kiss. She hoped he burned with remembered passion.

"Are you sure I look all right?" Catherine asked, suddenly a little nervous. Any minute Uncle Gil would arrive to escort her, and he wasn't going to like this—not one bit.

"You look lovely, my lady."

Impulsively, Catherine reached out and hugged her. "Thank you, Gabby. For everything." A knock at the door told her the duke had arrived. When Catherine opened the door, Gil sucked in a breath.

"Have you gone insane?" he roared.

"There's no need to worry, Uncle Gil, you're the only one here who knows anything about my past."

"Indeed?" he said, arching a bushy silver-gray eyebrow.

"Why . . . yes," Catherine said, but a guilty flush crept into her cheeks. "Shall we go?"

"I don't like this, Catherine."

"You're getting upset for nothing. It's only a costume."

"Costume," he grumbled. "Indeed."

The masque was held in the lavish red and silver ballroom up on the third floor. By the time Catherine and Gil arrived, most of the other guests had, too. Besides those who were staying at Rivenrock, wealthy members of the local gentry had been invited, and any friends of Mayfield's who lived within easy traveling distance.

All in all there were dozens of revelers, all gaily costumed. Everything from knights in armor and their pretty damsels to Egyptian pharaohs and Roman soldiers. There were Greeks in togas, characters from Shakespearean plays, and even a fairy princess, all safely hidden behind their satin masks.

Uncle Gil had dressed as a barrister, wearing a curly white wig. Edmund wore a black patch over one eye, a bright red sash and sword at his waist, and a scarf tied around his head. Amelia was dressed as a lady of the court, with wide panniers under her plum brocade skirts and a tall white wig with small stuffed birds roosting in the top.

"My," Amelia said, her eyes skimming Catherine's gaudy Gypsy clothes, "one would almost think you a peasant in truth."

"Thank you, Amelia, I think." Catherine smiled and accepted the glass of champagne a liveried servant handed her. She was about to say something more when she felt an odd tingling at the back of her neck. Someone was watching her, and she knew who it was even before she turned to look at him. When she did, her breath caught and the rest of the room seemed to dim.

Dominic stood no more than six feet away, wearing the snug black breeches he had worn in the camp, tall black boots, and his embroidered tapestry vest trimmed with spangles and gold. Beneath the vest, his broad dark chest remained bare, and a small silver earring curved around the lobe of one ear.

Tall and incredibly handsome, he was no longer Nightwyck or the Marquess of Gravenwold. No longer some forbidding stranger. He was the man she had loved, and Catherine longed to go to him, be caught up in those powerful arms and carried away.

Beneath the flickering candelabra, the room cast a warm bronzed glow to his skin as he moved forward, his eyes, so impossibly dark, fixed on her face.

"Good evening," he said, "milady Gypsy."

"Good evening," Catherine replied, her voice little more than a whisper.

"Since we are both of the same mind this night," he said formally, "I think it only fitting that I should claim your first dance."

It was supposed to be Litchfield's, but Catherine no longer cared. "All right." He took her hand and led her onto the dance floor.

A dozen musicians began to play, filling the ballroom with the heady sound of violins. Dominic drew her a little closer than he should have, his hand warm and firm at her waist. They danced as they hadn't before, each lost in memories, thinking of another time, another place, yearning to be there again.

Dominic's gaze held hers, no longer harsh but intimate and possessive. "I wish I could see you dance once more as you did that night in the camp. You were wild and beautiful. You danced for me alone that night—I saw it in your eyes."

Catherine's cheeks grew warm. She would never forget that evening, or the wild abandon she had felt.

"I wish we were back there now," he said softly. "I wish I could carry you off to my *vardo.*"

His deep male voice brought thoughts of the passion they had shared, the feeling of oneness she would never know with another, and a hard lump swelled in Catherine's throat. "I've missed you," she said softly. "Sometimes I wish I had stayed."

Dominic's eyes held a tenderness she hadn't seen since she'd left the caravan.

"That's what I wish each time I return to England. But never more than this time. . . ." His words touched her, reached into her heart and compelled her toward him. He *had* missed her, as he had once said. "I wish things could have been different . . ." he said. "I wish *I* could be different."

Catherine watched him from beneath her lashes, studying the hard planes of his face, remembering the feel of his skin beneath her fingers. "I loved you," she said. "I loved Domini, the man you were in the *kumpania.*"

For a moment he said nothing, but his hold on her waist grew tighter. "I'm the same man now."

Catherine shook her head. "No. Here you are different. Harder. Unforgiving. Is it the hatred you feel for your father that makes you this way?"

Dominic glanced off in the distance, his eyes turning slightly opaque. "What do you know of my father?"

"Nothing. Only that he is dead. That whatever there was between the two of you is past."

A muscle tightened in Dominic's jaw. "It isn't past. It will never be past."

Catherine saw the bitterness, the grim determination, and a painful sadness stole into her heart. "Then the man you are now has only my pity."

"Catherine—" The dance ended abruptly, halting any further words he might have said.

In silence, Dominic led her from the floor. A roundelay began as he returned her to her uncle, who stood scowling, a black look etched on his face. Catherine started to ask him if something was wrong, but Litchfield appeared to claim the next dance and her uncle wandered away.

She tried to focus her attention on the attractive blond man who held her, but even as she smiled into his face, her thoughts spun away to another. From the corner of her eye she could see him, so tall and imposing, and whenever she did, she found him watching her as closely as she watched him.

She danced with him only once more, but just as before the magic swept over them, the spell of their masquerade returning them to their wild Gypsy nights, the memories that bound them together and would not let them go.

After that, for Catherine the hours became a blur. Litchfield remained solicitous, and Catherine believed he meant to press his suit. She gave him not the slightest chance. Not tonight. Not with Dominic so near.

Tomorrow would be soon enough to face the future. Tonight she would make her excuses and slip away from the others. Just this one last time she would seek out her beloved Gypsy.

And then she would let him go.

As the hour grew late, Catherine bid her good-nights to Edmund, Amelia, and her uncle, and pretended to retire upstairs. Instead she moved off into the darkness, following Dominic, who had walked off into the garden. Beneath a silvery moon, he wandered the dimly lit paths leading away from the house, silently heading into the night.

It occurred to her that he might be making an assignation with one of the women he had danced with, but she didn't really think so. He had been just as disturbed as she by the memories they had conjured this eve.

She watched him now from a distance, leaning against the garden wall, one booted foot propped behind him. He drew on a thin cigar, exhaling a plume of smoke into the still night air, and absently searched the darkness with his eyes. Catherine wished she could search his soul.

"Good evening, my lord Gypsy," she said softly as she approached.

"Catherine . . ." He straightened, tossed away the cigar, and glanced around her, saw that she was alone. "You should not have come out here."

"Where you are concerned, there is a great deal I should not do."

"Why did you?"

Catherine smiled softly. "Because Domini is here this eve, and I know I will not see him again."

Dominic hesitated, then stepped toward her out of the shadows, a panther of grace and stealth. He stood in front of her, watching her eyes, studying her face, warring with himself, it seemed. Then his hand came up and laced through her hair, sifting the heavy strands between his fingers. Tilting her head back, he drew her into his arms, then slowly brought his mouth down over hers.

Catherine rejoiced in the feel of his long hard body. Parting her lips beneath his, she accepted the onslaught of his tongue, her own coming up to parry its sensuous movements as she slid her arms around his neck. She tasted the wine he had been drinking and the bittersweet taste of his cigar. Mostly she tasted the maleness of him, felt it in the corded muscles across his shoulders, the hardness of his desire, pressing against her with such demanding force.

"You truly are a witch," he whispered against her ear, breaking away from her lips to rain kisses along her jaw and down her throat to her shoulders. He reached inside her blouse and filled his hands with her breasts, lifting them, molding them, pebbling the crests to hard, throb-bing peaks. "I try to forget you, but I can't. I try to sleep, but you come to me in my dreams. I want you as I've never wanted another woman."

"Dominic," Catherine whispered, "dear God, Dominic, I've missed you so."

His hands moved down her body, cupping her buttocks, molding her more tightly against him. "I need you, fire kit-ten, and yet I cannot have you." He kissed her then, with such longing Catherine felt overwhelmed by it. She kissed him back with equal yearning, probing his mouth with her tongue, her hands sliding over his chest, feeling the sinew and muscle, wanting to be naked beneath him.

"Dominic," she whispered, and at the sound of his name, he lifted her into his arms, his long legs striding farther away from the house.

"This shouldn't be happening," he said as he turned down the path to the gazebo and climbed the wooden stairs into the darkness. He sat down on one of the cush-ioned seats and cradled her in his lap. "I've told you I can-not marry. No good can come of this."

"I don't care."

"You do care. You've always cared. Stop me, Catherine. Make this madness end."

"Tomorrow," she said. "Tomorrow I'll care again. Tonight you are mine and I am yours and nothing else matters."

Dominic cupped her face in his hands, then he kissed her, long and deep. "God, I want you."

"Make love to me, Dominic. I need to feel you inside me one last time." She kissed him and Dominic groaned, the sound almost anguished.

He settled himself on the seat and worked the buttons on his breeches until his hardened length sprang free. Catherine reached for him, her fingers closing around his thick shaft. "Please," she said softly.

Dominic kissed her, a fiery, thorough kiss that left her weak and trembling. Then his mouth burned a path down her throat. *"Mi cajori,"* he whispered, so low she almost didn't hear. His lips and his hands worked their magic, heating her blood, blazing a trail of fire that led straight to her loins.

When Catherine moaned and dug her fingers into the fabric of his coat, Dominic positioned her astride him, his hands cupping her buttocks beneath the layers of her skirt. She was wet and slick when he slid himself inside her, filling her with his hot thick length and making her heart beat so fast she found it difficult to breathe.

Catherine threw back her head at the feel of him, her heavy red-gold hair cascading toward the floor. Dominic withdrew almost fully, then impaled her. She had to bite her lip to keep from crying out.

"You're mine," he said softly. "In my heart you will always be mine." Gripping the back of her neck, Dominic forced her mouth down to his, searing her lips, driving his tongue inside. Catherine laced her fingers in his hair and began to move against him, feeling his rigid shaft thrusting in and out, plunging into her until the blood in her veins seemed to burn. She was writhing against him, moaning into his mouth, clutching his neck while he gripped her hips and drove into her again and again.

In minutes she was soaring over the edge, careening through a world of brilliant stars and shimmering pleasure, tasting a sweetness so poignant her tongue ran hotly over her lips.

Dominic followed her over the edge, his hardness pumping into her, spilling his seed. She found herself praying the seed would take hold, that the child she would bear would be his and not that of another.

She didn't realize she was crying until Dominic gently brushed the tears from her cheeks with his fingers. "Don't," he whispered. "Please don't cry."

"I'm not," she lied, "I never cry."

Dominic held her then, rocking her back and forth, his cheek pressed against hers while she clung to his neck. They sat in the darkness, holding each other, wishing these last few moments would not end. Eventually the night sounds intruded: an owl in a nearby elm tree, the croak of a bullfrog in one of the garden ponds, the whirring rhythm of the crickets. Distant strains of the orchestra reminded them poignantly that their time together must end.

"If I could, I would marry you," Dominic said against her cheek. "I cannot."

Catherine said nothing.

"I owe it to my mother. I owe it to myself. I will not let him win."

Still she said nothing, just slid off his lap and began to straighten her clothes.

"It doesn't mean I don't care."

Catherine looked at him, saw the anguish in his beautiful dark eyes, and cradled his face in her hands. "You must do whatever it is you feel you must."

"Catherine . . ."

"And I must go," she said. "Tomorrow this will all seem only another dream."

Dominic shuddered to think of it. More nights haunted by her image, more hours of feeling alone as he never had even in his youth.

"My marriage to Litchfield should solve any unforeseen . . . problems," Catherine said with false lightness. "You needn't worry about that."

A knife in his heart couldn't have pained him more. "Has he offered?"

"No, but he soon will."

"Surely there is someone who would better suit."

Catherine's smile held a trace of bitterness. "Have you someone else in mind? Stoneleigh, perhaps? How far does your friendship extend?"

Stoneleigh in Catherine's bed. Dominic felt sick at the thought. "Rayne would grant you no more freedom than I would. Maybe Litchfield *is* the answer. Once you've borne him a son, he'll have his mistresses to keep him company—if that's truly what you want."

"It is," Catherine said.

"Perhaps . . . once you've married . . . things could be different between us." A year or more at least, all the while, Litchfield taking his pleasure with Catherine. Dominic's insides churned.

"Perhaps," she said, but he knew she didn't mean it. He doubted very much this cavalier attitude she had taken toward marriage. Once she was committed, odds were she would remain faithful, no matter whom she wed. Catherine was just that way.

"You had better go back before you are missed," he said softly.

"Yes."

"I've promised Mayfield my presence at the foxhunt. I can't leave before then without being indiscreet. In the meantime, I'll stay well out of your way."

"That would be the wisest course." She kissed him on the cheek, and never had he sensed a more definite farewell. "Good-bye, my Gypsy lover. I will never forget you." She started to leave, but Dominic caught her wrist.

"Catherine . . ."

"Don't," she said, jerking her hand away. "Please." With that she turned and started running back down the path. Dominic watched her go, feeling as if he were being torn in two. He wanted her, but he could not have her—not and be able to call himself a man.

He leaned back against the cushion and stared into the darkness. Feelings of desire and rage and yearning all roiled and seethed inside him, warring with guilt and duty, and vows he meant to keep no matter the cost. *Catherine,* he thought, *if only I had never met you. If only things could be different. If only you weren't the woman you are.*

But she was. She was the woman whose passion and beauty were surpassed only by her kindness and compassion. The woman he respected and desired above all others—a woman he could not have.

It seemed even in death his father could cause him pain.

*There are two things an Englishman
understands—hard words and hard blows.*
W. Hazlett

Chapter Seventeen

STARING OFF INTO THE DARKNESS outside the gazebo, Dominic fixed his gaze on the place where Catherine's retreating figure had just disappeared around a tall box hedge out of sight.

Already he missed her.

He raked a hand through his thick black hair and released a weary sigh. He shouldn't have taken her, shouldn't have given in to his desires the way he had. It wasn't fair to Catherine—it wasn't fair to himself.

How was it, he wondered, that one small woman could so disrupt his life?

Dominic tensed. Something had stirred in the darkness; he worked to determine what it was. A second sound reached him, this one clearly that of a man's deep voice whispering among the shadows—then Dominic heard Catherine's muffled scream.

He was on his feet in an instant, racing down the path, his heart slamming hard against his ribs. When he rounded the corner, he saw Catherine fighting a man wearing a heavy woolen stocking pierced with holes to form a mask, his hand clamped over her mouth as he dragged her into the bushes.

Dominic closed the last few steps between them, his jaw clenched in fury. Grabbing the back of the man's homespun shirt, he whirled him around and hit him—hard.

Catherine sprinted to safety, and the man went down in a heap. Dominic jerked him up and drove a hard blow into his ribs, knocking him backward and making him groan. Dominic bent over him, ready to hit him again, but a second man stepped from the shadows, this one taller, more powerfully built. Dominic caught the flash of a pistol arching downward, tried to sidestep the blow, then felt a crushing pain at the side of his head that sent him reeling.

"Dominic!" Catherine cried out, running toward him as his world spun crazily and he sagged to his knees.

"Run!" he commanded. "It's you they're after, not me!" He fought the throbbing inside his skull, his blurred and dimming vision, fought the swirling circles behind his eyes, and began to push them away. Gaining his feet a bit unsteadily, he threw a hard punch that connected with the first man's jaw, knocking him into the flowers at the base of a tree. Feet splayed against the second attacker, he glanced around to see Catherine a few feet away, wielding a pair of garden shears as if it were a bludgeon.

"Bloody hell!" the second man cursed, caught between Catherine's razor-sharp blades and Dominic's stalking approach. "I ain't signed on for no cobbing—let's get our arses outta here!"

Both of them started to run. Dominic staggered after them, but the spinning circles returned and with them the blinding pain. His steps slowed and he swayed against the trunk of the tree.

"Dominic!" Catherine tossed the shears away and ran to his side, her arms going protectively around his waist to steady him. "Are you all right?"

"Why the hell didn't you do what I told you?" His blue-black hair hung forward into his eyes as he massaged the swelling near his temple. A trickle of blood dampened his fingers.

"I wasn't about to leave and let you get killed!"

If his head hadn't hurt so much he would have smiled. "You might have brought back some help. Where the devil are those guards your uncle hired?"

Catherine's head came up. "You know about them?"

Dominic merely nodded. "I know just about everything there is to know about you, my love. In case you haven't noticed"—his black eyes shifted to her breast—"I'm a very thorough man."

Catherine blushed and rolled her eyes. "If you know so much, then you should know that I didn't go for help because I didn't want any more scandal. Now let me have a look at your head." Her fingers probed the nasty cut near his ear and he winced.

"I'm fine," he said gruffly. "We've got to find your uncle, tell him what's happened." He grabbed her arm and started back toward the house.

"Are you insane?" Catherine jerked free, stopping him. "I can't tell Uncle Gil I was out in the garden in the middle of the night with you! As for the guards, we didn't expect anyone to be bold enough to try anything this close to the house—they're posted farther away. Tomorrow I'll make up some feather-brained story and convince my uncle to move the men in closer."

He watched her a moment, weighing her words, knowing there was really no other choice. He also knew he'd hire men of his own to watch over her.

"Have you any idea who's behind these attacks?"

Catherine shook her head. "Uncle Gil thought it might be someone with strong feelings against my work with the Friendly Societies, but I really can't credit that. I don't think someone opposed to my political views would go to such extremes."

"Neither do I," Dominic said, "which puts your dear cousin at the top of the list."

Catherine arched a brow. "You *are* thorough."

"It doesn't take much to figure that out. He has the most to gain."

"Do you really think Edmund is to blame?"

"The only other motive I can think of is ransom."

"They didn't ask for ransom the last time."

"Perhaps they decided the risk was too great and took the safer route."

"And this time?" she asked.

"They're afraid you know too much. That sooner or later you'll piece together who it was. I doubt they expected your untimely reappearance."

Catherine's brows drew together. "I suppose that would explain it. I certainly don't believe it's Edmund. He and Amelia are my dearest friends."

"Perhaps . . . but we can't afford to take any chances. I'll have someone keep a watch on your cousin."

"That's hardly your responsibility. I shall hire someone myself."

Dominic slanted her an impatient scowl. "This is not a matter to be dealt with lightly, Catrina. Your life is at stake."

"I'm well aware of that. You may be certain I will take the proper precautions."

And you, little kitten, may be certain that I will. "Then I'll leave it to you," he said, without the slightest intention. He would hire an army if he had to—the more protection she had, the better he would feel. He hated the idea of leaving Rivenrock with Catherine still in danger, but there seemed no other choice. "You had better get back inside and up to your chamber. Lock the doors and latch the windows."

"I will."

Unconsciously Dominic clenched his fist. "I wish we'd caught the bastards."

Catherine's worried look softened. "So do I." She started back to the house, then stopped and turned. "You're certain you're all right?"

Dominic smiled, a flash of white in the darkness. "Thanks to a forgetful gardener and you, little tiger."

"Good-bye, Dominic," she said.

"Good night, my love."

"I say, Gil, old man, you may be right." Sir Osgood Hornbuckle sipped his brandy, one hand clasped behind his back as he paced in front of the small fire burning in the marble-manteled hearth in the drawing room of the duke's east wing Rivenrock apartments.

"Then again," he mused, "the rogue might just be dallying with her affections—or trying his deuced best. He's got that reputation, you know, though I ain't heard it said he would trifle with an innocent."

"I tell you it is he," Gil said, "the man Catherine was involved with in France. You've heard the stories about him—why, it's often been bandied about that he's Gypsy blood in his veins. Never believed it myself, but I damned well do now." Gil had confided in Ozzie, a man he could trust with his life, to say little of the welfare of his niece.

"Can't you simply ask her? It would seem the straightest course."

Gil sighed. "If she intended to tell me, she would have done so by now. The rogue knew her well enough, he's counted on her integrity right from the start. She isn't about to force a marriage with a man who doesn't want her."

"But you believe he does."

"By God, I do indeed. Never seen a man watch a woman the way Gravenwold watches Catherine. God help the man who slights her, however inadvertently. The marquess will have his head served up on a silver platter."

Ozzie chuckled. "Reminds me of a young duke I once knew. Fell feet over the mark for the daughter of a baron. Nearly got himself killed dueling over her."

Gil flushed, recalling his wild passion for his late wife, Barbara; Bobbie he had called her when they were alone. Ten years she had been gone and still he missed her, probably always would.

"Yes . . . well, if I'm correct, Gravenwold feels that same grand passion for my niece. Hasn't sense enough to see it, is all. His hatred of his father, his damnable need for revenge, is too far-reaching. He'll destroy himself if he continues along the path he has chosen."

"Still, you can't be sure the marquess is the chap who snatched her innocence," Hornbuckle pointed out.

"Not without a thorough investigation—and there isn't time for that."

"So what do you propose?" Ozzie asked.

"We'll put him to the test. Whatever his heritage, Gravenwold seems a chap of the first water. Once the issue is forced, if he is her damnable Gypsy, he'll do what's right—what he should have done all along."

"Ten to one, Catherine ain't going to like this."

"Catherine intends to marry Litchfield. That coxcomb would hardly do her justice. Catherine needs a man of strength and intelligence, a man who can handle her, tame her fiery spirit without breaking her."

"Can't say for certain, but Gravenwold looks a rum sort." Ozzie sipped his brandy. "Once he's leg-shackled, I can't credit he'd treat her badly."

The duke grinned, thinking of his fiery-tempered niece. "Not unless she has it coming." Both of them laughed at that. "She's a handful, Ozzie. Strong-willed, determined. And very precious, indeed. I want to see her happy—and by God, I'll do whatever it takes to make that happen."

Hornbuckle set his brandy snifter aside. "Tell me what it is you want me to do."

"What does it say, my lady?"

Catherine read the note a second time. She had found it folded and shoved beneath her door when she awoke that morning. "'Must see you. Break away from the others and meet me in the old stone cottage in the woods beside the east lake.' It's signed with a *D*."

"Is the writing 'Is Lordship's?"

"I've never seen Dominic's writing."

"Then 'ow can you be certain it is from 'im and not the men who attacked you? It is too dangerous. You must not go."

"The men my uncle hired will follow at a distance. They'll come to my aid if something is wrong."

"I do not like this."

"Neither do I, but Dominic wouldn't have asked me to come if it weren't important." Besides, he was leaving today, and she hadn't seen him since the night of the masque. True to his word, he had stayed well away.

"Maybe he cannot bear to let you go."

"Maybe he wants to say good-bye." The evening of the ball, he had purposely avoided such final parting words and the lack thereof had swelled her heart with hope. "Whatever the case, I must go."

Gabby sighed. "Then we 'ad better 'urry. Dawn is beginning to break. If you expect to hunt with the others, you 'ad better get dressed."

Catherine nodded. She and Lady Georgina and two other women were the only ones joining the men on the foxhunt. Most women rode only a little, enough for an outing, a gentle gallop through the park. Catherine and Georgina loved the sport and both were excellent horsewomen, something Catherine was extremely proud of. She would use that skill today to elude the others—maybe even the men her uncle had hired.

The more she thought about it, she realized she could easily survey the cottage from a place in the woods as long as she got there early. If Dominic didn't arrive, she wouldn't go in, just return to the hunt and catch up with the others. If he did, she had nothing to worry about, she would be perfectly safe in his care.

She scoffed at that. When had she ever been safe with Dominic?

With Gabby's assistance, Catherine completed her morning toilette and dressed in a high-waisted burgundy velvet riding habit. Crisp white ruffles formed a vee in the bodice and surrounded her wrists and throat. Gabby brushed her hair into a sleek golden-red coil that rode at the nape of her neck, and placed a miniature burgundy high hat, flat-crowned and narrow-brimmed with a small black veil, at a jaunty angle atop her head.

"Do I look all right?"

"Perfect," Gabby said, sensing how badly she needed reassurance.

Already she was so nervous her palms had begun to sweat. Her heart was beating wildly, and she hadn't even gone downstairs. What did he want? she asked herself for the thousandth time, but still no answer came.

With a sigh of resignation that her question would have to wait, she made her way out the door and down the magnificent spiral staircase.

At the rear of the mansion, the hunters were already assembled, black and white hounds baying, horses neighing and pawing the earth in their urgency to be away. Though Catherine had little appetite, the others had earlier eaten a light meal of coffee or chocolate, biscuits or toast, and would return for a huge hunt breakfast. In the meantime, for the next three or four hours, the hunters would follow the track of the fox over hill and dale, jumping hedges, stone walls, fences, and ditches, chasing the elusive small red animal and riding to the sound of hounds and horn.

Catherine's nervousness grew. As she climbed the mounting block and settled herself on the heavy padded sidesaddle on one of Mayfield's sleek bay hunters, she searched the throng for Dominic. Amidst the lively chaos of horses, riders, and dogs, Dominic's tall frame and the ease with which he sat the duke's big black stallion stood out among the others. Already he wore a dark look, as if he didn't approve of her joining the hunt, yet knew he had no means to stop her. Was that his reason for the meeting—just a diversion to keep her safe from the dangers of the open fields? Whatever it was, if the note were real, she would soon find out.

She met his gaze, holding it overly long, until she received a nod that told her he would indeed arrive at the meeting place he had chosen.

Certain now of seeing him, Catherine relaxed for the first time and let herself be caught up in the excitement of the hunt. She would meet Dominic at the appointed spot, but first she would enjoy herself—and nothing would give her more pleasure than leaving Dominic Edgemont to trail in her dust.

"I wish you would reconsider this nonsense." This from her uncle, who stood worriedly beside her, one hand patting the sleek bay's neck. "Until the men who accosted you in the garden have been apprehended, it isn't safe for you to be off on your own."

She had told Gil about the men—merely changed the time of the encounter from night to day, and even gone so far as to give Dominic credit for saving her.

"There are at least thirty people here—that's hardly alone—to say nothing of the men you've hired who'll be following a stone's throw away."

"I still don't like it," he grumbled.

"And I don't like you worrying so much. I'll be fine—I promise."

Gil nodded and Catherine smiled at his departing figure. He was a fine rider himself, but apparently had awoken a bit under the weather. He and Ozzie had decided to stay behind.

Catherine took a deep breath, enjoying the smell of leather, new-mown grass, and horseflesh. Around her, riders began to stir, the big bay's ears went up, and Catherine's heartbeat quickened. The shrill of the hunting horn sounded, a whip cracked, and the hunt cantered off, horses' hooves pounding against the earth. The master of the hounds led the field, the pack of long-necked, thick-chested animals baying their excitement.

It took only minutes for the first of their quarry to be spotted. The tiny red animal darted from beneath a box hedge somewhere in the distance, and the hunt began in earnest. As horses and riders thundered across the open fields, Catherine leaned over the big bay's neck and took the first jump with ease, a low stone wall brightened by patches of buttercups. She didn't know where Dominic was, but a sixth sense told her he wouldn't be far away.

She passed Lady Georgina at the second jump, a small

grassy pond that dropped off rapidly before a second stone fence. One of the riders went down, but came away laughing and hurried to remount his horse.

They spread out after that, Catherine passing the slower, less proficient riders, leaving the other two women, and riding now with the leaders. From the corner of her eye, she saw Dominic moving up beside her, his jaw still tight with disapproval.

She jumped a tall row of hedges, clearing them neatly, and Dominic did the same, drawing closer still.

"If you're bound and determined to come out here," he called to her, "at least have the good sense to ride with the others. You're much too easy a target up here."

Catherine merely smiled. "What's the matter? Having trouble keeping up?" She brought her riding crop down on the horse's flanks, leaping ahead, then collected him and sailed over a difficult water jump that most of the men went around.

At Dominic's look of astonishment—or was it actually admiration?—she laughed and drew back on the reins until he once more rode beside her. "The old stone cottage," she said. "Give me fifteen minutes."

"Try not to break your neck in the meantime," he called after her, watching her trail off among the others, working to lose herself without calling anyone's attention.

Fifteen minutes later, she had left the pack behind, eluded in the woods the men her uncle had sent to guard her, and picked her way back toward the east lake, easily spotting the small stone cottage that nestled among the trees.

Catherine breathed a sigh of relief to find the big black stallion Dominic had been riding tethered out of sight beneath a willow. She tied her own animal off in another direction, then made her way back to the house.

Dominic stood in the parlor, looking breathtakingly handsome in his navy-blue pin-striped coat, tight buckskin breeches, and gleaming high-top black Hessian boots. His shoulders looked so wide they seemed to fill the room, and his snug-fitting breeches outlined his powerful legs and thighs and rode provocatively tight against his manhood. Catherine's heartbeat quickened at the sight of him, and even the scowl on his face could not dampen her mood.

"You little minx," he said, walking toward her, "what the devil did you think you were doing?"

Catherine merely grinned. "Having some fun for a change."

"You might have broken your neck—or worse yet, someone might have shot you."

Catherine shrugged. "Well, I didn't and they didn't. Besides, it's no concern of yours."

Dominic sighed. "All too true, Catrina."

When he didn't go on, she started to ask him what he wanted, why he needed to see her so urgently, then decided to bide her time. There was no hurry. The hunt would go on for hours. She wouldn't give him the pleasure of knowing how curious—and hopeful—she was.

"We shouldn't be here," he finally said, surprising her.

"No, we shouldn't," she agreed. "Then again, when has that ever stopped either one of us?"

He smiled at that, a flash of white so beautiful it made her heart turn over.

"Also true." But he made no move to close the distance between them and neither did she. "Your uncle thanked me for intervening on your behalf in the garden. Since he didn't call me out, I presume you didn't tell him what we were doing out there."

"I merely changed the story from night to day."

"Very clever," he said, but a muscle tightened in his jaw. "As a matter of fact, my sweet, you're extremely good at fabrications. I'm particularly fond of the tale you told me about your betrothed. May I ask why you went to such extremes?"

She didn't like the blandness of his tone—it didn't match the hardness in his eyes. So much for Gabby's theory that he couldn't bear to let her go.

"If you must know, I was trying to stay out of your bed. I naïvely believed that if you thought there was someone I was in love with, you wouldn't force your intentions upon me."

"Is that what I did, Catrina, force you?"

Catherine glanced down at her hands, found them trembling a bit and clasped them together. She lifted her eyes till they fixed on his face. "No. I believe I could have stopped you—even at the end. By then I didn't want to. I don't want to now."

His only response was the slight elevation of one thick black brow. For a moment he just stood there. Then he moved closer and reached for her hand, freeing it from the other, and bringing her palm to his lips. "I have never known a woman like you. I doubt I ever will."

Catherine searched his face, admiring the sharp planes and valleys, the sensuous curve of his lips. His eyes reflected the same stark longing she knew shone in her own. But in Dominic's eyes there was more, a tightly leashed resolve, an all-consuming bitterness that made her shudder to think of the depths he was prepared to go.

Watching him there, Catherine felt a surge of pity well up inside her. Against her will, her hand came up to his cheek, and she cradled his face in her palm. Raising on tiptoes, she kissed him, tenderly, sweetly, wishing she could cleanse him of his bitterness, his anger.

"Catherine . . ." It was a sound of anguish, of a pain that darkened his soul.

Dominic swept her up in his arms, his lips searing hers, his tongue delving inside her mouth until her own tongue hotly responded. He carried her over to the sofa and began to unbutton the back of her burgundy velvet riding gown. In minutes it slid off her shoulders and she felt his lips on her flesh, trailing a fiery path from her throat to her breasts. His tongue flicked over a nipple, then he took it into his mouth, suckling it gently, a slow drugging pull that reached down deep inside her.

"I want you," he whispered, "I know I shouldn't, but God help me, I can't seem to stop myself."

Catherine laced her fingers in his hair and pulled his mouth to hers, willing him to continue. Feeling her urgency, he drew back a moment.

"If this is to be the last, then let us make the most of it. We have hours before we're missed. Let me love you as I should have done before, slowly and completely. Let me show you the way I feel."

At Catherine's soft smile, Dominic bent his dark head to the task, laving her breast with his tongue as he worked the last of the buttons on the back of her riding gown.

"Good God, Ozzie, are you all right?" Gilford Lavenham knelt beside Sir Osgood Hornbuckle, who sat in the grass at the base of an old stone wall, his short legs out in front of him, rubbing the knot on his head.

"Should have gone round, I guess. Getting too old for this sort of rubbish."

Gil chuckled and helped his friend to his feet, careful to stand clear of Ozzie's sorrel hunter, which stood just a few steps away. When the horse had refused the jump, Ozzie had held on to the reins like the trooper he was, even as he flew over the animal's head.

"You're not too old, my friend," Gil said. "You just never were much of a horseman."

Ozzie laughed softly and climbed unsteadily to his feet. "Not like that niece of yours, that's for certain. Gel's got a seat like a man."

The duke merely grunted. "She can ride, I'll grant you. But her lovely little bottom is far too feminine by half. She's caught more than Gravenwold's eye, if I'm not mistaken—and thanks to your untimely landing, we've left them alone far too long."

Ozzie climbed up in the saddle. "By Jove, we'd better get crackin'. She's compromised well enough as it is—no need to embarrass her any more than we have to."

Gil grumbled, stuck his foot in the stirrup, and swung

his leg over the rump of the stout white gelding he rode. Damned but he hoped he and Ozzie hadn't made a mull of things. Aside from the possibility that the pair had discovered they'd been duped and already left the cottage, there was the danger Catherine was in being out here on her own. He had weighed all that and decided to go forward with his plan. Now he prayed he had made the right decision.

"Hurry, Ozzie, time's a-wasting." With that both men dug their heels into their horses' flanks, skirted the wall, and rode hard for the cottage.

Chapter Eighteen

FROM A DISTANCE, the small stone house looked deserted, and Gil's mouth thinned into a disgruntled line. Then he spotted the big black stallion Gravenwold had been riding, and across the way, a further search turned up Catherine's sleek bay.

"They're here, all right," Gil said.

"Could be deuced embarrassing," Ozzie muttered. "Damnable luck that fall."

"Embarrassing or not, we're here and we're going to see this through. I owe that much to Catherine—whether she sees it that way or not."

Gil dismounted in front of the cottage, making as much noise as he could, speaking to Ozzie loudly about his worry for Catherine's safety, then pounding fiercely on the door. He didn't miss the low muttered curse from Gravenwold or the rustle of fabric coming from inside the room.

He knocked more loudly. "You had better open this door," he demanded. "I most definitely intend to come in!"

"A moment, Wentworth," Gravenwold called back, his voice low and hoarse.

Gil did just that—waited only a moment. He was determined not to let the rogue escape the consequences of his actions. "I'm coming in," he said, lifting the latch and bursting into the room. Hornbuckle entered a few paces behind.

Gil found exactly the scene he had imagined: Catherine a disheveled mass of rumpled burgundy velvet, her fiery hair streaming down her back, her bodice only half buttoned. Her pretty cheeks flamed scarlet, and her small hands trembled against the front of her gown. Gravenwold looked little better, his shirt hanging open to his waist, leaving his wide chest bare, his black hair mussed and hanging over his forehead. At least his riding breeches were buttoned and he had pulled on his boots.

Gil stared in silent condemnation. "Well," he said gravely, "what have the two of you to say for yourselves?"

Catherine lifted her chin and met his hard gaze squarely. "I believe, Uncle, you and Sir Ozzie are acquainted with Lord Gravenwold."

Gil harrumphed. "Obviously, my dear, not nearly as well as you are." Catherine's cheeks flamed brighter, but it was Dominic who spoke.

"Your arrival is quite timely, Your Grace. May I ask what exactly it is the two of you are doing out here?" The look he flashed seemed far more forbidding than Gil's. "I believe you were under the weather when we left—or will you bother to deny you and your conniving little niece arranged this entire little drama."

"What!" Catherine whirled on him, her big eyes flashing green fire. "You're the one who sent the note asking me to meet you. You're the one who arranged this, not me!"

"I sent no note," Dominic countered, "as all of you well know. I received one—from you."

"That's not true!" Catherine turned away from Dominic's hard, accusing features to stare at the duke. "What *are* you doing here, Uncle?"

Gil stood firm. "The men I hired returned to the mansion frantic that you had turned up missing. Ozzie and I joined them in their search, of course, and one of the riders pointed us in this direction, said it was the last they had seen of you."

It was plausible, Catherine conceded.

"Then who sent the note?" Dominic asked, still glaring at Catherine.

Gil interrupted her response. "What brings you both here is hardly the issue. The fact is you are—and half dressed into the bargain. You've compromised my niece, Gravenwold. I'll expect you to do the right thing."

"No," Dominic said simply. "I've no intention of marrying Catherine or anyone else. Not now, not ever."

Gil felt a jolt of heat to the back of his neck. "You will, by God, or I swear I shall call you out. I may be older than you are, but I can still shoot a pistol with the best of them. You'll marry my niece or wind up a dead man."

"No!" Catherine cried, grabbing her uncle's arm. "I won't let you do it. Dominic might kill you."

Dominic's mouth thinned. "What's the matter, my love, no worry for me?"

"You!" She whirled on him. "You're a blackguard and a bounder. You care for nothing or no one but your damnable revenge. I wouldn't marry you if you were the last man on earth!"

"Good, then we've nothing more to discuss." He turned and reached for his coat, slung over the back of a chair.

Hornbuckle caught his arm, his expression steely for a man of his small stature. "I don't believe the duke's quite finished with you." Dominic stiffened and Hornbuckle let go of his arm.

"I meant what I said, Gravenwold," the duke continued. "You'll accept your due like a man, or you'll face the consequences. Which is it to be?"

Dominic worked a muscle in his jaw, his fury barely contained. Though Catherine looked shaken and pale, he silently cursed her and her uncle for the scheming trap they had laid. Still, in a way he could not fault them. Any man of honor would have owned up to his responsibilities long ago. He had ruined an innocent young girl. He should have married her and been done with it.

And there was Wentworth to consider. He didn't want to kill the man—in a way he respected him, even admired him. He was only doing what he thought was right and proper, what any man in his position *ought* to do.

Dominic clenched his fists. He could almost hear his father's mocking laughter, the smug satisfaction that dripped in his cold, cruel words.

"Who do you think you're fooling?" the marquess had once said. "You're a hot-blooded young buck—same as I was. Your yard'll be your undoing. You can't keep it in your breeches any more than I could."

Dominic swore an oath beneath his breath, trying to block the taunting voice that rang in his ears until his head began to throb. There had to be a way around this—there had to be.

And suddenly he knew what it was.

Dominic turned his attention to Wentworth, a grim smile playing on his lips. "All right, Your Grace, you win. I'll marry the chit on one condition—"

"And that is?" the duke pressed.

"It will be a *mariage de convenance*—a marriage in name only. I've vowed there'll be no issue to carry forth the Edgemont name, and that is exactly the way it will be."

"I won't listen to this," Catherine broke in, "not for another moment." Lifting the hem of her riding dress out of the way, she started for the door.

"You stay right where you are, missy." Her uncle's voice cracked like a whip across the room. "You'll see this through, just as he will."

Catherine had never seen her uncle so determined. She swallowed hard, but made no further move.

"Now then, what kind of nonsense are you spouting?" the duke said to Dominic. "Am I mistaken, or is there not at this very moment every possibility that a child of yours might already have been conceived?"

Catherine flushed and Dominic bristled. "Good of you to point that out. Since that is indeed the case, the marriage will have to wait until such time as it's determined Catherine is not with child. Once we're certain of that, we may proceed."

Even Gil looked stunned. "Are you telling me that if my niece is carrying your babe, you will abandon her?"

Dominic faltered. Hearing it put that way squeezed his insides into a hard, tight knot. "Obviously, I would accept full responsibility for both Catherine and the child—it just would not carry my name."

Catherine felt like weeping. Dear God, was this the man she had believed she loved? "How kind you are, Dominic. I can hardly fathom such benevolence. But where, may I ask, does all this leave me?"

"You, my sweet, will be the Marchioness of Gravenwold, a position even a countess should not scorn."

"Your title means nothing to me. I have Arondale to consider. Do you intend to take my fortune without giving me the heir my family needs?"

"You may keep your money," Dominic said with a mocking glance. "I have more than enough of my own. As to the question of an heir—there will be none—at least not of my loins. If you're willing to accept that, then so be it. If not . . ."

Catherine felt a fury so great she could barely speak. "You are a devil! A hard-hearted bastard with the conscience of a snake. I want no part of you—not now, not ever!"

Gil watched the two of them as he had from the very start. God's teeth, he was taking a terrible risk—one that could ruin Catherine's life. Yet whenever he looked at her or at Gravenwold, he could almost feel the powerful spark that flashed between them.

In truth, he believed, the marquess might be bent on revenge, but he was still just a man. And Catherine was a beautiful, desirable woman—one the duke believed Gravenwold loved beyond measure.

Forcing them together was a terrible gamble indeed—greater than any he had ever undertaken. Failure would mean hatred and despair for them both. Success would mean the greatest reward a man and woman could ever reap. A rare and precious love that others spent a lifetime seeking and very few ever found.

The Duke of Wentworth believed that kind of love was worth the risk.

He steeled himself. "Agreed," he said.

Catherine turned her anger on him. "You cannot be serious. I won't do it—you can't make me."

"You will do it. I am still your guardian. You will do exactly as I say." Catherine stared at him as if he were a stranger. "Now I suggest you make yourself presentable while the rest of us await you outside." He gestured toward the door, and Ozzie pulled it open. "Gentlemen?"

His posture stiff and unrelenting, Dominic stepped through the opening and into the sunlight. Wentworth followed him out, and Ozzie closed the door, leaving Catherine to stare after them in silence.

"You understand my niece is still in danger," the duke said to Dominic. "I believe, with you as her husband, the threat will be lessened somewhat."

"I shall attend to it myself," Dominic promised, but his mind remained fixed on the one word the duke had said that he had never expected to hear. *Husband.* Catherine's husband. He ignored the tiny flicker of pleasure that word produced and concentrated instead on the rage he felt at being so well and truly snared.

Catherine descended the wide mahogany staircase at Lavenham Hall, making her way to her uncle's book-lined study. She found him bent over his ledgers, immersed in his work as he had been most evenings of late.

Head held high, she knocked lightly on the open door to attract his attention, and the duke glanced up. When he saw who it was, he flashed her a weary smile.

"Good evening, my dear."

"Good evening, Your Grace," she said formally, her tone much as it had been since the day he had come to the cottage.

"Would you care to join me for a sherry? The hour is still early after all, and I could use a little company."

"I'm afraid I'm a bit too tired," Catherine lied, determined to maintain her distance. "I've merely come to tell you that you may inform His Lordship that his worries have been set to rest." Catherine felt the heat creeping into her cheeks, still she kept her chin up and her shoulders squared. "I do not carry his child."

Gil cleared his throat and came to his feet. "I see."

"I presume you are still determined that I'm to go through with this farce of a wedding?"

Gil stiffened. "I am."

"Then I should prefer it done in all haste. Dwelling on it only makes the task more distasteful."

"Catherine, my dear," Gil said with a sigh. "I wish I could make you understand that I'm doing this for your own good."

"You are forcing me to marry a bitter, hateful man who doesn't want me."

"The latter remains to be seen. As for the man's disposition, a loving wife can often make changes."

Catherine pondered that.

"You were in love with him once," the duke said gently. "Surely you don't deny it."

Catherine's gaze shifted down to the Aubusson carpet. "That seems years ago."

"True love can survive a great deal," her uncle said, "believe me, I know."

Catherine raised her eyes to his. "Dominic feels too much hate to love." She turned and made her way out the door.

Dominic sat at a rough-hewn table in the Knight and Garter Tavern, Covent Gardens. It wasn't White's or Boodles, it wasn't Brooks, St. James. It was a seedy, raucous, boisterous inn crowded to the rafters with thieves, pickpockets, prostitutes, and drunkards. The place reeked of gin and cheap perfume, and the smoke hung so thick it burned the eyes of its patrons, who were too far into their cups to care.

It was the last place a gentleman of the *ton* would come, and exactly where Dominic wanted to be. He felt surly and out of sorts, itching for trouble and well on his way to a brawl.

He wasn't drunk, though he'd been drinking rum for the past two hours. He also wasn't a nobleman—at least he didn't appear to be—just a man in a full-sleeved linen shirt, tight black breeches, and scuffed black boots. When a drunken sailor jostled into him, spilling part of the drink in his hand, Dominic surged to his feet, grabbed the man's thick shoulder, and spun him around.

"Watch what the hell you're doing, man!"

The big sailor knocked his hand away. "You don't like it, mate, why don't ye do somethin' about it?" The accent was right off the docks. He had the look of a man who'd been pressed into service, worked aboard ship every day till he dropped. If he was, he'd be tough as boot leather and hard as the hubs of hell.

Dominic didn't really care. He threw the first punch and it landed with a crunch against the huge man's jaw. The red-bearded man only grinned.

"Now you're in fer it, mate," one of his friends called out.

Several staggering blows later, Dominic stood over him, wiping the blood from his mouth with the back of his hand. He worked his jaw back and forth to see if it was broken, found to his relief that it was not, and nudged the boot of the unconscious man. Thank God the big oaf didn't move.

"Satisfied?"

Swaying a bit on his feet, Dominic turned at the sound of the familiar voice. "What the hell are you doing here?" he said to Rayne Garrick. The tall viscount stood grinning among the throng who'd been watching, an eye open for anyone who looked as if he might interfere.

"Looking for you." The men seemed to have guessed his intent, having caught the bulge of the pistol he carried beneath his frock coat, the way his wary brown eyes assessed them. Now that the fighting had ended, they muttered a few disgruntled phrases, wandered back to their tables, hoisted their mugs, and began to swill their liquor again.

"How did you find me?"

"It wasn't too hard," Rayne said. "If you'll recall, we've come here a few times together, whenever a black mood struck."

Dominic nodded and pushed his thick black hair back off his face. Reaching for his tankard of rum, he tossed the last of the fiery contents back and finished the drink in one long swallow, the liquid searing his stomach.

He set the tankard down on the scarred wooden table and turned his attention to the door.

"Leaving *would* be the wisest course," Rayne said by way of agreement, mindful of several pairs of sullen eyes that still watched them.

"My thoughts exactly." They headed for the door and out into the night, making their way along the narrow lane toward a street in the distance lit by a few oil lamps, hoping to hire a hack.

"I presume your need for a little ... diversion ... had something to do with your recent betrothal," Rayne said.

"I've set myself up for a lifetime of hell," Dominic muttered.

"You're in love with the girl, you know."

"Don't be absurd."

"No?" Rayne's wide shoulders lifted in a gesture of nonchalance. "Then you've nothing to worry about. You can simply carry on as you always have, taking your pleasure wherever you can find it. A lot of women would be grateful not to be forced to submit to their wifely duties."

"Not Catherine," Dominic said, and Rayne worked hard not to smile.

"No, that one looks to be a woman of some passion. And with you for a teacher, I'm certain you've initiated her quite thoroughly."

"Not nearly as well as I would have liked."

"Nevertheless," Rayne said, "you may go on as you wish, taking your lovers from wherever you choose—simply turn the other way when Catherine does the same."

Dominic's hands balled into fists. "Can't we speak of something else? I came out here to forget about my forthcoming nuptials. My sham of a marriage is the last thing I wish to discuss."

"Has the date been set?" Rayne asked, ignoring Dominic's words.

"According to the duke, Catherine's monthly has come—she is definitely not with child. The wedding will take place the end of the week."

"If the girl had conceived, would you really have refused to claim the babe?"

Dominic glanced off in the distance. "The question is moot. Catherine does not carry my seed. She never will. Now, unless you wish to return to the Knight and Garter and take up where we left off, I suggest we discuss something more pleasant."

Rayne saw his friend's dark scowl, thought of the women Dominic had bedded, the hot blood he would have to control, and the beatiful woman who would soon be living beneath his roof. Rayne thanked God that *he* had thus far escaped the parson's mousetrap. He had no intention of winding up in a marriage muddle like his friend, though considering Dominic's absurd obsession with revenge on his dead father, in this case it might just be for the best.

Thinking of the fiery pair and the battle of wills that lay ahead, Rayne chuckled to himself and grinned into the darkness.

"I don't care about the danger, you fool. Can't you understand, time is running out!" Edmund spoke to Nathan Cave in the stables behind Catherine's West End town house, Catherine having, several weeks ago, returned to Lavenham Hall.

The big black-mustached man looked chagrined. "I know, Yer Lordship, but—"

"But nothing. You and those bumbling fools you hired have botched things at every turn. My cousin's to be married at week's end, for God's sake. This could be our last chance." He brushed viciously at an errant piece of straw that had settled on his immaculate royal-blue frock coat.

"Me and the lads kin 'andle things," Cave said. "This time there won't be no problems."

"There won't be any problems," Edmund said, "because I'm going to handle things myself."

"But—"

"I'd advise you, Nathan, just to keep your fat mouth shut and listen. I'll tell you exactly what we're going to do."

As Edmund divulged his plan, one of the horses nickered softly and an owl hooted in the rafters above them. Nathan hung his head and did as he was told.

Catherine stood before the ornately carved and gilded cheval mirror in her bedchamber at Lavenham Hall, staring at her reflection. How could she look so good when she felt so bad?

Wearing a high-waisted cream silk gown, the slim skirt overlaid with embroidered pink roses, she looked radiant. Her hair had been coiffed in a glistening mass of red-gold ringlets atop her head, and her skin appeared healthy and glowing as it hadn't since the slight bronze hue of the sun had faded. Only the lackluster dullness of her eyes betrayed her inner turmoil, the painful coil of hopelessness she felt within her breast.

"Ready, my dear?" Uncle Gil stood in the open chamber door, looking elegant in his dark blue velvet tailcoat, white linen waistcoat, and wine-colored trousers.

Catherine nodded. "As ready as I can manage."

"You look lovely, my dear. You make me very proud."

How could she stay mad at him? He was doing what he thought best. "Thank you, Uncle Gil." Catherine crossed the room to take his arm, raised on tiptoe and kissed his cheek. Gil cleared his throat and looked away, a slight flush coloring his features.

She let him guide her down the sconce-lit hall then they descended the wide mahogany staircase and crossed the marble-floored foyer. Soames handed Gil her cloak, a hedge against the early morning chill, and he wrapped her in its billowing folds. Soames held open the massive front door.

"You shall dazzle him, milady," the aging butler said.

"Thank you, Soames." Catherine forced a smile in his direction. No use mentioning that Dominic had no intention of being dazzled—now or ever.

They descended the wide front porch to the Wentworth carriage, which waited out front, silver crests blazing in the sunlight. Two liveried coachmen sat atop it while two overly large guards disguised as footmen stood at the rear. A pressing business engagement had forced Edmund and Amelia to remain in London until the very last moment. With time a problem, they would be traveling straight to the church.

Catherine held her uncle's arm as they crossed the gravel drive and one of the footmen opened the carriage door. Gil helped Catherine inside, and she settled herself against the tufted green velvet, smoothing her cream silk gown out in front of her. With its high waist, gently scooped neckline, and softly puffed sleeves, the gown was the height of fashion. Catherine straightened one of the pink embroidered rosebuds that matched the fresh ones laced in her hair and tugged up her long kid gloves.

A glance out the window told her the countryside, with its rolling green hills, puffy white clouds, and clear blue skies, matched her outward appearance far better than her dismal mood. Forcing down her nervousness as best she could, she heard the slap of the reins against the horses' rumps, and in minutes the carriage was bowling along the lane toward the small parish church in the village where Dominic would be waiting—though Catherine had an uneasy feeling he might not.

Deep down, she believed he was less of a gentleman than he was a Gypsy. She had lived with them long enough to know they were rarely coerced into doing something they didn't want to do.

Would Dominic simply leave the country, return to his people, and never return? With his wealth and position, it seemed absurd—and yet . . . ?

Lost in her musings, it took a while for Catherine to focus on the sound of approaching riders. Not, in fact, until she heard pistol shots and the thundering echo of horses' hooves.

"God's blood!" her uncle roared, grabbing her arm and shoving her down to the floor of the carriage. "The black-guards are upon us!

"Whip up the horses!" he commanded his driver, though the man had already cracked his whip above the animals' heads, sending them into a flying gallop. A second crack had them running, their long necks stretched out, their muscled chests straining against their collars, but the angle of the highwaymen's approach still cut them off.

The Wentworth horses, matched blacks, the best of their breed, raced flat out, all four animals surging forward, the carriage wheels spinning, the guards at the rear returning the highwaymen's fire. Still, the riders closed the distance, drawing nearer with every passing second. There was no way to avoid them, and on this vacant stretch of road, no one to hear the outlaws' shots or the volley returned by the guards.

Catherine felt her uncle's hand on her head, forcing her lower, felt the carriage careening wildly, heard more shots fired and the shrill neighing of horses as the riders surrounded the coach in a whirl of dust and forced it to a halt.

"Here," Gil whispered, thrusting a pistol into her trembling hands. "Use it if you have to. They won't be expecting it coming from a woman."

He turned away from her then, grim-faced and fearsome, his fists clenched in rage. When the duke shoved open the carriage door, he found himself surrounded by five mounted horsemen, all masked, each wearing a variety of dirty, ill-fitting clothes. Each held a pistol trained on one of his men—and one of them pointed at his heart.

He stepped down from the carriage and turned to see a guard slumped over the rear, the front of his silver-trimmed livery covered in blood. The other looked pale and shaken, having taken a ball in the arm.

"Those pistols be spent, ye whoresons," said one of the highwaymen, a thick-set man with cold green eyes. "Ye best be tossin' 'em down." Masks covered their faces, and all wore hats pulled low on their foreheads.

"Bloody cutthroats," the driver sneered. The other coachman cursed, but eventually each of them did as he was ordered.

"Tell the lit'l sauce box to git 'erself out 'ere."

"She stays where she is," Gil said, taking up a stance in front of the carriage door. "I'd advise you *gentlemen* to abandon this foolhardy scheme of yours. You've already killed a man—you've a trip to old Jack Ketch in store if you're caught. Every moment you delay makes the chance more likely."

A tall thin man with a reedy voice chuckled behind his mask. "Get outta the way, gov'nor. Her Ladyship's been spoken for. We mean to see she's delivered."

"Spoken for? What do you mean?"

"Get outta the way."

"No."

"Uncle Gil, don't!" Catherine cried, jerking open the door just as the man's pistol erupted, spitting smoke and flame. With a grunt of pain, Gil clutched his shoulder and pitched forward into the dirt.

"What have you done?" Catherine jumped down from the carriage, her hands trembling, the pistol gripped against her side, hidden in the folds of her cloak. She rushed to her uncle's aid to find him breathing heavily, blood seeping through his coat as he tried to get up.

"Just lie still," Catherine begged him, with a look of concern then one that told him she still held the gun.

"I'll fetch the wench," the thin man said. Hearing the reedy timbre a second time, Catherine recognized the voice as belonging to one of two men who had attacked her in the garden. She waited until he dismounted and walked toward her, obscuring her from the others for a moment, then she thrust the barrel of the pistol against his heart.

"Don't move," she said with soft menace. "Not a muscle."

Above the mask, pale, thin-lidded eyes went wide, and she heard his sudden intake of breath.

"If you want this man to live," she said to the men still mounted, "I suggest you turn those horses around and ride out of here."

For a moment, no one said a word. Then, "Calvin knew whot 'e'd bought into when 'e signed on."

"What!" Calvin squeaked, but he very clearly made no move.

The others grumbled among themselves, but didn't openly disagree. They kept their pistols held at the ready.

"Do it if ye've the brass, miss," said the one who seemed to be the leader. "End will be the same." He chuckled. "She's a rum blowen, ain't she? Shame we 'ave to give 'er up."

"I'll kill him," Catherine threatened, "I swear it!"

"Do it, wench," he countered, "and I'll pick the 'ead off your driver." He raised the pistol and aimed it squarely at the coachman's head.

"Dear God." Catherine's hand began to shake. She was about to give in and toss the pistol away when the first shot rang out behind them.

A second exploded and then another. "Bloody constable's comin'!" one of the highwaymen roared, wheeling his horse and digging his heels into the animal's heaving sides. "Purse's yours—I'm away!"

The other four seemed to agree, taking in the fast-approaching riders crossing the heath in a cloud of dust. "Let's ride, lads!" the leader commanded.

Even the man Catherine held at gunpoint spun round, catching her off balance, the pistol firing into the air. While the coachmen scrambled toward the weapons they had tossed on the ground, eager to reload them, he raced to his horse, swung into his saddle, and urged the scrawny animal into a run.

He had almost reached a nearby thicket when a stocky, sandy-haired man Catherine had never seen before thundered up, his horse lathered and panting. He leaped across to the fleeing man, knocking him out of his saddle and into the dirt. The two of them rolled, one on top and then the other, until the slightly balding, stocky man sat astride the thinner man's chest. Drawing back a stout arm, he landed a vicious punch to the highwayman's jaw, snapping his head back. The man lay unmoving in the dirt.

With a sigh of relief, the sandy-haired man came to his feet and strode to where Catherine knelt beside her uncle. "Lady Arondale," he said, "thank God you're all right." He squatted on his haunches at her side.

"I—I'm afraid my uncle has been wounded," Catherine told him, her voice unsteady.

Gil groaned, but with their assistance, finally managed to sit up. "Took a ball in the shoulder," he said. "Could have been a lot worse, Constable, if you and your men hadn't routed the bounders."

"My name is Harvey Malcom, your grace. I'm in the employ of His Lordship, the Marquess of Gravenwold."

"Gravenwold? How the devil did he know about this?" The duke allowed Catherine and Malcom to help him to his feet, swaying a bit unsteadily.

"He doesn't." Malcom unbuttoned the duke's frock coat to take a look at the wound. "In fact, right now he's awaiting his bride at the church, probably a most disgruntled groom."

Even with the worry for her uncle, Catherine found a trace of humor in that, remembering how she had worried about *his* arrival. She glanced uncertainly toward her uncle. "How is he?" she asked.

Malcom stuffed his handkerchief against the small round hole where the lead ball had entered. "Shot went all the way through. Wound appears to be nice and clean and not too serious."

"Thank God," Catherine said.

"Then how *did* you know?" the duke pressed, ignoring both of them.

Malcom opened his mouth to explain, but was brought up short by the thundering arrival of the rest of his men. They held two of the five fleeing highwaymen in check, their arms bound behind them as they sat atop their horses. Another man lay draped across his saddle, his limp arms hanging nearly to the earth, his chest unmoving.

"Two of them got away, damn their bloody hides," said one of Malcom's men, adding an embarrassed, "beggin' your pardon, Your Ladyship," when he saw Catherine. "Caught this chap up on the hill." He pointed to the dead man. "When I went after 'im, he made to escape. Fired on me, 'e did. As luck would 'ave it, I was the better shot."

Even in her dazed and worried state, Catherine noticed the dead man's horse was of far better ilk than those that had been ridden by the others. Then she noticed the clothes—finely tailored fawn-colored breeches, polished Hessians of soft brown leather, and a fine lawn shirt.

"Let me see his face," she whispered, hardly able to make her voice work, fighting to deny the neatly groomed hair, the thin-boned fingers that told her who the villain was.

"I would advise against it, milady," Malcom said gently, but the other man complied before he had time to stop him.

"Good Lord," Gil said, "it's Edmund."

Catherine pressed trembling fingers against her lips to stifle the cry that lodged in her throat. "God in heaven," she whispered, "I prayed it was not so."

Gil's hand closed over hers. "We both did, my dear, we both did."

"The marquess ordered him watched some time ago," Malcom was saying, but Catherine could barely focus on his words.

Edmund, dear God, Edmund. The smiling young boy who had played with her as a youth. He had been there when her mother died, helped her survive the death of her father.

Edmund. The man behind her abduction, the man who wanted her dead. How could he have done such a thing?

Then again, during the weeks since her return, she had sensed a subtle change in him, a withdrawal Catherine had attributed partly to her own suspicions. Remembering them now, she felt a twinge of guilt that she had not hired someone to watch him as she had promised. She just hadn't been able to bring herself to spy on him.

Her uncle said something Catherine missed, but his voice drew her attention, and Malcom spoke again.

"He nearly got away from us today. Didn't think he'd try anything, what with the wedding and all. But when he left his wife and son at an inn in the village, one of my men got suspicious. Came to me and we tracked him here. Thank God, we weren't too late."

Gil nodded his agreement, then gave Catherine's cold hand a comforting squeeze. "It's time we were off, my dear," he said gently. "There is nothing more to be done here. Besides, my shoulder is beginning to pain me, and we've your disgruntled groom to attend."

"Yes, yes, of course." She turned to Harvey Malcom, intending to ask his assistance, but the man had already pulled open the carriage door and begun helping Gil inside. He took Catherine's arm and helped her up, then closed the door behind them.

"Leave everything to me," Malcom said with a glance toward Edmund's body. He turned to the coachman. "There's a surgeon in the village. Make all haste to see His Grace arrives there safely."

"Nonsense," Gil called up to his driver. "Get us to the church, and have a care to hit as few ruts as possible."

"But your shoulder," Catherine protested as the whip cracked and the carriage lurched forward.

"We'll send for the surgeon just as soon as we arrive."

"But—"

"I'll be fine, my dear. Suffered far worse than this in the war."

Catherine didn't bother to point out that that had been years ago when he was a far younger man. She knew it would do no good, and at any rate, her thoughts had shifted to what lay ahead. Poor Amelia. How could they possibly tell her? What could they say? And what of Dominic? He was certain to be relieved to have the wedding postponed. There would be funeral arrangements to consider, as well as a suitable period of mourning.

Thinking of the delay, Catherine felt a wave of relief herself. She would have time to deal with her grief and weeks to spend back at Arondale. Maybe her uncle would finally see reason and allow her to cry off this entire disastrous affair.

"How are you feeling, Uncle?" she asked, her worry for him resurfacing.

"I told you, my dear, I'll be fine."

She gave him a smile of encouragement. "Once you're home, it shan't take long for you to mend, and I promise to pamper you every moment of your recovery."

Gil's bushy gray brows drew together. "In case it's escaped your notice, my dear, I have dozens of servants who see to my welfare. Besides, you'll be living at Gravenwold, attending your husband. You'll hardly have time to be worrying yourself about me."

"But Uncle, surely you can see that the wedding must be postponed." She thought of Edmund's lifeless body, carelessly slung over his horse, and swallowed against the tightness in her throat. "There are . . . arrangements . . . to be made, dear Amelia to consider, as well as—"

"I see nothing of the sort. Your cousin did his damned-est to ruin your life—I'm not about to let him succeed."

"But—but, it's impossible."

"Today is your wedding day, my dear," the duke said, his voice growing firm. "You may as well resign yourself. Now if you don't mind, my shoulder is aching to beat the devil. I think I'd better rest until we get there." He closed his eyes and leaned his head against the seat.

Catherine just stared at him, torn between worry about his still-bleeding shoulder, and fury at what he intended to do. Her one hope lay in Dominic. He alone had the courage to stand up to her uncle. It shouldn't take much pleading to get him to delay.

Yes, she thought, Dominic would be easy enough to convince. Insanely, part of her resented the fact that he would.

Chapter Nineteen

"$\mathcal{S}$O YOU SEE, DOMINIC, with all that's happened, the only sensible course is to put the wedding off." Shaken and pale, Catherine faced him in the small vestibule off the main chapel, her wedding gown slightly rumpled, several strands of fiery hair having come loose from its pins.

Working to remain composed, her hands clenched together, she looked forlorn and disheartened—and as beautiful as Dominic had ever seen her.

"What does your uncle have to say?" After relaying the story of Edmund's failed attempt on Catherine's life, the duke had been taken to another small room where the surgeon could attend him. Wentworth's condition appeared favorable, thank God.

"My . . . uncle," Catherine hedged, "has been injured. He really isn't thinking too clearly right now." She fidgeted under his close regard, then glanced away, her pale cheeks coloring faintly.

"Which means," Dominic said flatly, "he damned well intends for you to go through with it."

"But I can't possibly! Don't you understand, my cousin is dead!"

Dominic saw the way her lips trembled, how huge and green and desolate her eyes looked. She needed to put this whole sordid business behind her, needed to set the gossip

to rest before it started all over again. No doubt the duke
had seen that as clearly as he did.

"I believe, my love, the vicar awaits us. If your uncle is
up to it, I shall see that he's in attendance. If not, he may
pay his well-wishes later."

"Dominic, you can't mean to do this. What about
Amelia? She and Edmund were coming here straight from
London. God only knows where she is right now, or what
story Edmund concocted before he left her. When she
finds out what's happened, she'll be devastated. She'll need
me and I'll have to—"

"We'll see to Amelia as soon as the deed is done." He
started toward her, determined to finish what her uncle
had started.

"What about you?" Catherine countered, backing away
from him. "This is the chance you've been wanting. If we
postpone the wedding, maybe you won't have to marry
me at all."

Dominic shook his head. "Your uncle was right. You
were my responsibility from the moment I took you to
my bed. I should have seen to matters long ago. I intend
to see to them now."

"Damn you! You're bound and determined to ruin my
life!"

Dominic paused, but only for a moment. "I'm afraid,
Catrina, the die has been cast. My mother taught me years
ago, it is best to play out the cards fate has dealt." He
offered his arm. "Shall we go?"

Though Catherine's mouth thinned in resentment, she
stiffly placed her hand on his coat sleeve. Dominic
straightened a rose that threatened to tumble from her
slightly mussed hair, then led her toward the door.

Just outside, seated on a carved walnut pew in the small
high-ceilinged chapel, Rayne Garrick came to his feet as
they entered. A moment later, the duke stepped out of a
small room down the hall.

"I see we're all here," Gil said, his face a bit pale but his
smile well in place. "I hope I haven't kept you waiting."

His wound had been bandaged, his arm placed in a sling, and his dark blue tailcoat draped over his injured shoulder.

"You're certain you're all right?" Catherine asked as if her last hope for reprieve had just blown away.

"I'll be a good deal better once I've seen my duty done." He pinned a hard look on Dominic, who didn't even flinch.

"Your niece and I are more than ready." Dominic flashed a false smile few could miss. "Aren't we, my sweet?"

When she opened her mouth to protest, Dominic's grip grew hard on her arm. "Yes, Uncle."

"You have the papers we agreed on?" the duke asked.

Dominic reached into the pocket of his waistcoat and removed the documents which gave Catherine control of her lands. He handed them to the duke, who gave them only a cursory glance. "Shall we get on with it then?"

As Wentworth followed Dominic and Catherine up the aisle and took a seat in the front pew, Rayne moved to Dominic's side and turned to face the vicar, who stood across from them holding an open Bible.

"Without Amelia, I've no one to stand up with me," Catherine said in a very small voice.

"Have no fear, milady." The vicar's plump matronly wife came forward with a smile. "I would be honored to stand at your side."

Catherine swallowed hard and stared straight ahead. "Thank you."

In minutes it was over. Dominic could hardly focus on the vicar's words until Rayne nudged him gently and handed him the beautiful emerald ring he had bought for Catherine. He slid it onto her shaking finger, his eyes touching hers for an instant before she glanced away.

"You may kiss your bride," the vicar said.

Catherine tilted her face up but didn't close her eyes. Dominic gripped her chin and barely brushed his mouth across her lips. They felt as cold as marble and he fought the urge to warm them, make them melt against his own as he knew he could. His loins tightened at the thought, and he stepped away, an unspoken oath on his tongue.

"Congratulations." Rayne shook Dominic's hand, then swept Catherine into his arms for a kiss that was far less brotherly than his own. Dominic's stomach clenched, but he forced himself to smile.

"Sweet as nectar," his friend said, breaking away. "You're a very lucky man."

At the taunting grin on Rayne's handsome face, Dominic wanted to hit him.

The duke hugged Catherine, whispered what appeared to be words of encouragement, and the vicar and his wife wished them well.

"What of Amelia?" Catherine asked.

Dominic turned to face her. "As soon as Malcom arrives, I'll set him the task of finding her."

"Once we know where she is," the duke said, "I'll go to her, explain what has happened."

"You're not up to it, Uncle. I must go to her myself. She's going to need a friend very badly."

"Has it occurred to you, love," Dominic said gently, "you may be the last person the lady will wish to see?"

"You must go home with your husband, my dear," Gil told her. "In a few days' time, if Gravenwold sees fit and Amelia wishes your presence, you may return to care for her."

"Your uncle is right, Catrina. Give Lady Northridge some time."

"But the burial—it wouldn't be right not to be there."

The duke grumbled something unpleasant. "Considering the circumstances, I had thought to have a small private service on the morrow. No one need know you did not attend."

"I would know."

The duke turned to Dominic. "I would prefer she return with you to Gravenwold, but I cannot find it in my heart to force her. I shall leave the decision to you."

Dominic looked hard at Catherine. "You've given Edmund enough. We'll take our leave."

Catherine caught his arm, her hand looking small and pale against the black of his superfine coat. "Please, Dominic. He meant a great deal to me once."

Damn, but he wanted her out of there. Even with the resentment he felt, he wanted her safe and secure and away from all this sadness. Still, these people were her family. He knew how important that could be.

He glanced at her again and caught the subtle lifting of her chin, the squaring of her shoulders. If he tried to stop her, he would probably have to tie her up to do it. Another time, he might have smiled.

Instead he swung his attention to Wentworth. "No one need know the truth of the baron's death. A simple fall from his horse could have killed him. If we all stand together, that explanation should suffice."

The duke nodded.

"Catherine and I will leave on the morrow, just as soon as the burial is over."

"Thank you," Catherine said.

Her eyes found his and the gratitude in them sent something warm through his veins. It was the last thing he wanted. "My carriage awaits," he said, his tone growing cold. "Let us go."

Dominic settled an arm around Catherine's shoulder and guided her toward the entrance. Before they could reach it, the heavy plank door swung wide, lighting the foyer with a ray of sunlight that glistened on the top of Amelia's blond head. Little Eddie stood at his mother's side, clutching her hand, his blue eyes huge, his cheeks streaked with tears.

"Is it true?" Amelia asked, her voice high-pitched and nearly hysterical. "Is my Edmund really dead?"

"Why don't you sit down, my dear?" the duke said. He glanced at Eddie. "Maybe the boy should wait outside."

"He knows already." Amelia came forward, the delicate crystal beads on her elegant blue gown shimmering like the tears that welled in her eyes. "Your man Malcom stopped our carriage a ways up the road. He wanted us to go back to the inn, but I refused. I made him tell me what happened." She pressed a white lace handkerchief against a fresh fall of tears.

"I'm sorry, my dear," the duke said.

"We arrived a little bit earlier than we had planned so we stopped for a bite at the inn. Edmund said he had some errands to run . . . that he would be back in plenty of time for the wedding. We waited and waited. . . . When he didn't return, we set out on our own. We thought he must have been delayed . . . we thought . . . dear Lord, he can't be dead." Amelia swayed unsteadily, and Rayne stepped in to catch her against his thick chest.

He led her over to one of the empty pews then turned to Eddie, lifting him up beside his mother, who hugged the boy to her breast.

Catherine crossed the room and knelt beside her. "Amelia, I'm so sorry . . . so very, very sorry."

The women embraced, and Catherine hugged Eddie.

"He did it for us, you know," Amelia said tearfully. "He was worried about our future . . . little Eddie's future. I still can't believe he really meant you harm."

Catherine said nothing to that. "He could have come to me, surely he knew that."

Amelia twisted her white lace hanky. "He should have. You've always been kind to us . . . I just don't understand. . . ."

"Neither do I. But I want you to know you have nothing to worry about. You never did."

Tears streaking her lovely pale cheeks, Amelia stared at the emerald ring on Catherine's hand. "It would seem that is now up to your husband—though I assure you we are not destitute, as Edmund seemed to think."

"My husband has left me in control of my wealth and the Arondale title. You and Eddie are family—I love you both very much."

Amelia's eyes lowered to the hands she clasped in her

lap. "Most people would have spurned us for what my husband did. You are a very dear friend."

Her own cheeks damp, Catherine embraced her, then Dominic's hand touched her arm.

"I think it would be best for everyone if we were away."

He was right. Though the church was empty, the vicar and his wife stood nearby and there were servants moving about. All of them had ears, and the fewer people who knew the truth of what had happened the better off they would be.

"You and Eddie will come to Lavenham," Gil said to Amelia. "The fresh country air will help you forget all this sadness."

"Thank you, Your Grace." For the first time, Amelia noticed his wounded shoulder. "Dear Lord, you're injured. Did . . . did my Edmund do that?"

"One of the highwaymen," Gil said. "I'm going to be fine in no time."

"I'll look after you, Your Grace. I'll see to your recovery myself."

Gil smiled faintly.

"Ready, love?" Dominic asked. He wished there was something he could do to ease Catherine's grief, but there was nothing. Only time could make her forget and once again be happy.

He frowned. The life she faced with him would hardly make her happy. A husband in name only. A barren, childless existence that would stretch on through the years. Still, she would be safe and well cared-for, a woman of wealth and power envied by most of the *ton*.

With the Gravenwold household to manage and the Arondale lands she still owned, she would have plenty to occupy her time, and maybe little Janos could take the place of the child he denied her. He refused to imagine her taking a lover, carrying a babe sired by somebody else. By Sara Kali, he wouldn't allow it! No matter how much she might wish it. The bargain had been struck—she would have to learn to accept it.

He prayed to God that he could.

Catherine could scarcely recall the burial, just a hazy memory of a handful of mourners lining the graveside in the Lavenham family plot. That Edmund, as her father's brother's son, should have been buried at Northridge or Arondale crossed her mind, but only briefly. Edmund had brought this end upon himself; it was his wife and child who mattered now—and that meant silencing the truth.

At least she'd had time to spend with Amelia. Over and over, her friend had begged Catherine's forgiveness for the evil her husband had done, and again and again Catherine had assured her that she was not to blame. In the end, the two women had wept together, the first real tears Catherine had shed since her abduction. It felt good to cleanse herself, but the temptation to cry for her loveless marriage was far too strong. She wouldn't give in to the urge again.

Though her memory of the burial was hazy, her recall of what should have been her wedding night wasn't much clearer. Just more hours in the Lavenham bedchamber she had always slept in—her husband wasn't there. Dominic spent the night in a room down the hall, "in respect for her grief," he said to the others.

But Catherine knew the truth. That night was only the beginning of a thousand other lonely nights she would spend by herself through the years. She wondered what her uncle had been thinking when he had seen her retire alone. She hadn't missed the disgruntled twist of his lips when he looked at Dominic or the guilt in his eyes when they settled on her.

She wondered if he regretted his decision, but something in his posture told her he was not yet daunted. She knew he still believed Dominic would eventually put aside his anger at the past, that he would turn to Catherine and become the husband he believed she needed.

Catherine wished with all her heart that she could share her uncle's conviction. But she knew Dominic far better than he did, knew his bitterness—and his determination.

He would do exactly what he had vowed to do—just as he always did.

As soon as the burial was over, Dominic settled Catherine in his coach and he and his party left Lavenham Hall to begin their travel to Catherine's new home. It was an unpleasant journey of little conversation and curt replies, the tension between them growing stronger with each passing day. The nights on the road were exactly as she had envisioned. Dominic solicitous of her comfort, then leaving her alone.

There was an air of aloofness between them now that had never existed before. An almost absurd abundance of formality.

"Are you warm enough, madam?" he would ask, or "Are you hungry, milady?" He bowed over her hand, rarely smiled, and his eyes remained vague and distant. His perfect manners and terse conversation made her furious. She wanted to reach out and slap him, to shake him and rail at him and make him see that whatever his feelings for her, they would be thrown together for the rest of their lives—they had to make the best of things.

Instead she said nothing. Just behaved like the lady she was and replied just as formally as he.

The following day they reached Gravenwold, a huge estate in the rolling countryside of Buckinghamshire. Built of great gray stones and standing four stories high, it looked impressive from the outside but inside was cold and musty. What kind of man had lived here? she wondered. Had he been as dark and dreary as the house itself? Would Dominic be that way, too?

The butler took her cloak, and Dominic made introductions to members of his staff, who all seemed surprisingly pleasant.

Then an aging valet approached. "Welcome to your new home, milady." With his thin, veined skin and brittle, bowed legs, he looked so frail it seemed a miracle that he could stand up.

"This is Percival Nelson," Dominic said, "my valet and my friend."

The introduction might have surprised someone else—a marquess claiming the friendship of a servant. Not Catherine. To a Gypsy, no man was beneath him—except maybe a *Gadjo* aristocrat.

"Call me Percy, milady," the old man said with a watery smile. "Everyone else does."

Catherine smiled, too. "It's a pleasure to meet one of Dominic's friends."

Standing a few feet away, the stately butler coughed behind his hand, but Percy fairly beamed.

"Blythebury will introduce you to those of my staff you haven't met," Dominic said, referring to the tall, very proper butler she'd been introduced to earlier. "I'm afraid I've several pressing matters to attend."

Catherine forced herself to smile. "Of course."

"Milady." Dominic bowed slightly, turned, and walked away.

And so it had gone, all very proper—all very dreadful. Catherine had felt such a yawning despair only once before—the night she had awakened aboard a ship bound for France. The night she'd been sold to the Gypsies. Yet even their harsh treatment had somehow been better than this.

Seeing the bleak and lonely future stretched out before her, Catherine followed the butler up the stairs, her footfalls echoing on the wide stone stairs. *Resign yourself,* she repeated. *Learn to make the best of things.* He would never forgive her for their marriage; she had known that from the start.

Again and again, as she had for the past long weeks, she fought to convince herself to accept what she could not change and had almost succeeded when the butler led her past the master's bedchamber to a chamber down the hall.

"Surely my room adjoins that of my husband," Catherine said without thinking.

Blythebury's face turned red. "His Lordship thought you

would be more comfortable in here—just while you're in mourning, of course."

"Well, His Lordship is wrong." What possessed her in that moment to turn and make her way to the sumptuous room that obviously belonged to the former marchioness she would never know. Maybe it was the rush of humiliation she felt that the servants should know her husband's feelings toward her. Maybe it was the dark walls and hollow sound of her footsteps, tolling like a bell the empty years that lay ahead.

Whatever the reason, that was the moment she decided she wasn't about to sit idly by and let Dominic ruin their lives. She wouldn't meekly accept this dreary house, this dreary life of loneliness and despair. She was Catherine Barrington Edgemont, Marchioness of Gravenwold—she would fight back!

Blythebury surprised her by grinning—quite out of character for him, she would guess.

"Quite right, milady," he said, following her into the empty room. "I should have suggested this chamber first." He began to fuss with the draperies, drawing them open, fluffing the pillows on the huge gold silk canopied bed. "I shall have the chambermaid freshen the room immediately. Should have seen to it myself."

"Thank you, Blythebury."

He busied himself with her trunks until Gabby arrived to take over the task. "I'm going to have this room redone," Catherine said firmly, noting the slightly mustard hue of the carpets, the too-gaudy luster of the heavy silk bed hangings. The walls were partially paneled in rich warm wood, but the ornate gold-flocked paper overshadowed its simple beauty.

"It's entirely too dark and depressing. When Dominic sees how much better it looks, maybe I can convince him to let me do something with the rest of the house." It could be beautiful, she thought, remembering the ornate carvings she had seen downstairs, the incredible architecture overshadowed by poorly chosen fabrics and carpets.

Being built of stone, in a way it reminded her of Arondale. She wondered at the last marchioness and vowed to see the house better cared for than it had been.

"But of course your 'usband will agree," Gabby said. "A man needs a woman to put things in order. 'Is Lordship will see what a wonderful marchioness you make, and 'e will fall even more in love with you."

Catherine didn't bother to explain that Dominic wasn't in love with her at all. She hadn't been able to tell even Gabby the circumstances of her marriage. It was just too embarrassing to admit her husband didn't want her in his bed.

Catherine worked beside Gabby, rearranging the room and unpacking, until a soft knock sounded at the door.

"It is probably your 'usband," Gabby said, crossing the room to let him in, "eager for 'is bride."

Catherine rolled her eyes. Sooner or later she would have to tell Gabby the truth—unless, of course, she could somehow make things change.

As Catherine had guessed, when the French girl opened the heavy wooden door, it wasn't Dominic but Percy who stood in the opening. What she hadn't expected was the little boy standing there holding Percy's hand.

"Janos!" Catherine dropped the lacy chemise she held and raced across the room in his direction.

"I hope we aren't disturbing you, milady," the old valet said. "Janos was supposed to let you rest until His Lordship returned, but you know how little ones are."

With a warm smile, Catherine knelt beside the dark-skinned boy. When she opened her arms, he stepped into them, and she hugged him against her. "Dominic didn't tell me you were here."

Janos hugged her back, clinging to her a little longer than she would have expected, then he moved away. "Maybe he wanted to surprise you."

"Yes . . . that must have been it." In truth they had spoken so little since their betrothal, and never of anything important. Still, she wished she had known; she would have had something to look forward to.

"We came back together from France," the boy said, in answer to her unspoken question. "My stepfather died in a fight."

"I'm sorry," Catherine said, remembering Zoltan, the huge brutish man Janos had lived with. She assessed the fine fabric of the little boy's clothes, the polished sheen of his shoes. It was obvious that Dominic intended the boy to stay. "I'm so happy to see you. I was afraid I'd be lonely here. Now I have you to keep me company."

His fine dark brows drew together. "I will be studying a lot. But you will have Dominic. He can be very entertaining."

Catherine worked hard to stifle a grin. What a pleasure the child would be. Dominic, on the other hand, would hardly be *entertaining*. Most likely he would be as sullen and remote as he had been from the moment of their marriage. Unless . . .

"I am learning to read," Janos said proudly.

"That's wonderful."

"Maybe one day I will return to the caravan to teach the others."

"I think that's a fine idea." Catherine couldn't help thinking that in the weeks since she had seen him Janos seemed older somehow. "Do you miss them?"

"Mostly I miss the children. There is no one here to play with."

"But that's not true. The servants have children—there must be dozens of them living on Gravenwold land." Too late, she saw Janos's stricken face and felt Percy's gentle nudge.

"'Fraid they haven't got used to the boy quite yet," the old man said. "He's different, you know. Takes them some time."

"They'll never like me," Janos said, "and I'll never like them."

"But Janos—"

"I have to go now, Catrina—I mean Lady Gravenwold."
He turned to Percy. "Mr. Reynolds will be waiting."

"He's the boy's tutor," Percy explained.

Catherine squeezed Janos's hand. "I'll be very upset if
you don't call me Catrina—at least while we are alone."

Janos smiled.

"Promise?"

"I promise."

"Good. Now, off you go. We'll talk again later."

Taking Percy's hand, Janos led the old man off down the
hall. Catherine wondered just exactly who was looking
after whom?

Thinking back to their conversation, she frowned. It
didn't surprise her that the little Gypsy boy was having
trouble with the other children. Before her father had
started the Charity School at Arondale, there had often
been problems of prejudice or jealousy among the children. Education was the answer—her work at the school
had taught her that. It was one more subject she intended
to discuss with Dominic.

At the thought of their coming confrontation, Catherine
squared her shoulders. She certainly had her work cut out
for her.

For the first time in weeks, Catherine smiled.

Chapter Twenty

DOMINIC HEAVED A LAST weighty shovelful of dirt over one bare shoulder and set the long-handled instrument aside. The final dim rays of the sun had escaped him, leaving only the chirping of the crickets to keep him company. He had sent the rest of his workers home several hours earlier but remained to finish digging the trench himself.

Jerking a handkerchief from the pocket of his breeches, he mopped at the sweat on his brow. It covered his chest and ran in rivulets down his arms, but he didn't care. It felt good to be away from the house—away from Catherine.

It felt good to exhaust his body—so he wouldn't think of hers.

Dominic grabbed up his shirt and shrugged it on, then walked to his horse. Swinging up into the saddle, he rode the animal back to the stables, dismounted, and handed the reins to one of the grooms.

"Evenin', Yer Lordship."

"Good evening, Roddy."

"Lady Gravenwold's been lookin' for you," the lanky boy said, surprising him.

Dominic tensed. "Is something wrong?"

"No, sir. She just said you'd been gone so long she was beginnin' to worry."

"Thank you, Roddy. I'll make a point to see she understands I often work late." And intended to continue, now more than ever.

"She's a very nice lady." The gangly lad grinned. "Pretty, too."

More than pretty, he thought, but forced the notion aside. "See Chavo gets an extra bucket of oats. He's had a long day, too." All the horses bred at Gravenwold carried Romany names, though nobody recognized the fact. Dominic took secret pride in the animals' triumphs, the credit in a very small way going to the Gypsies who had taught him the knowledge of the *grai.*

He started back toward the house, wondering why Catherine would have come looking for him. Since the day of their wedding, she had kept as far away from him as he had from her. He intended to keep it that way.

He entered the house and went straight up to his bedchamber. By now Catherine should have eaten and retired. He hoped so. The less he saw of her the better.

Not so with Janos. He looked forward to the time he spent with the child, and right now he felt a little guilty. Janos had been thrilled to learn of his marriage to Catherine. He had wanted to see her as soon as she arrived, but wanting to give her time to settle in, Dominic had made the boy wait.

Wait, he thought, feeling the pull of a smile, *for exactly how long?* No doubt by now, the little Gypsy boy had found a way to see her. Janos was as headstrong as he had been at the same age—he could bet that one way or another the two had been reunited.

"You're home, milord," Percy said, catching him as he crested the top of the stairs. "I saw you ride in. Your bath has been drawn, and Her Ladyship awaits you in the Blue Room."

"What?" He felt as if someone had punched him in the stomach. "Surely she's tired and in need of her rest. What's she doing down there?"

"Why, she plans to join you for supper, of course. Cook

has prepared something special. We expected you sooner," he said with a hint of censure, "but sometimes those things happen."

"They'll be happening quite often, Percy—as you of all people should know."

"She's seen the boy, sir. He's been put to bed."

Dominic nodded. "Very well." Opening the door, he strode into his chamber. A dark blue frock coat, white piquet waistcoat, and light gray breeches had been laid out on the four-poster bed. He never wore small linens. There were some concessions he just would not make.

"Is there anything else you'll be needing, milord?"

Dominic eyed the steaming bath and thought of his weary muscles. He needed his rest a whole lot more than a confrontation with Catherine. What the devil was she up to?

He sighed and began to tug off a boot. He wouldn't know until he went downstairs—by then it would be too late.

Wearing a burgundy brocade gown trimmed with satin and lace, Catherine paced the Aubusson carpet in front of the hearth in the Blue Room. Damn him! She had known he would avoid her, but she thought he might at least make some pretense of a marriage for the sake of the servants.

Then again, she had known the task she had undertaken would not be easy. She had best prepare herself for the battle ahead and get on with it.

As if those thoughts had conjured him, she turned just in time to see Dominic stride through the door. With his black hair damp and curling over his collar, his skin sunbrowned even darker than before, he looked as handsome as ever, and Catherine felt a rush of warmth.

"Good evening, milord," she said, coming toward him with a smile. "Since your day was overly long, I've arranged for supper to be served in here. I hope that suits you."

Dominic eyed her warily. "It suits me well enough, madam. But from now on you needn't bother. I'll often be working late. You may take your supper whenever you wish."

Catherine merely smiled and handed him a glass of claret. "I assure you, husband, it's no bother at all."

Though his expression reflected indifference, maybe even displeasure, when he reached for the glass, their fingers brushed and Dominic's hand tightened unconsciously around the stem. Catherine felt the jolt of contact as surely as he must have, and it pleased her to know she still held some measure of attraction for him.

"Come . . . sit down. I know you must be tired." She rested a hand on his arm, guided him over to the sofa, and sat down beside him. As tall as he was, he could easily look down the front of her low-cut burgundy brocade gown. Two soft mounds of cleavage bulged invitingly upward, just as she had planned.

"Where did you get that dress?" His eyes, like jet-black shards, fastened exactly where she wanted them.

"You don't like it?" she asked with feigned innocence. In truth, it had taken Gabby several hours to alter the dress so sinfully low.

"It's practically indecent," he growled. "I hope to God you don't intend to wear it out of the house."

"I thought I might wear it to the supper the St. Giles are giving next month." That was a total fabrication, but watching Dominic's reaction, she was beginning to enjoy herself. "The color would be nice for that time of year . . . of course, if you really don't like it—"

A muscle twitched in his cheek. "St. Giles already follows you around like a lovesick puppy. You needn't encourage him. I'd prefer you wear something more modest."

Catherine shrugged. "You were hardly concerned with my modesty when we were traveling with the caravan. I'm surprised it concerns you now."

"That was different."

"Really? How?"

"You're my wife now, that's how. And I suggest we discuss something else."

Just then one of the servants, a lean man named Frederick, came in carrying a silver tray laden with their supper. The succulent aroma of a rich meat stew drifted up from beneath the silver dome.

"Just set it on the drum table, Frederick," Catherine instructed. The thin man nodded, set the heavy tray down, and left the room.

Drawn by the mouth-watering smell, Dominic lifted the lid and smiled. *"Gulyds,"* he said, unconsciously licking his lips. "My favorite. How in the world did Cook know how to make it?"

"I know how, remember? I merely told her how much you loved it, and she all but fell over herself wanting to get it just right. I hope it's to your liking."

He picked up a spoon, dipped it in, and tasted. "Delicious." Dominic started to serve up their portions then stopped, his thick black brows coming together in a frown. "All right, Catrina, what game do you play?"

"Game, milord? I play no game. I act the part of wife, that is all. I'm sorry if I have not pleased you."

In spite of himself, he *was* pleased. Catherine could see it, even if he tried to deny it.

"It pleases me," he finally admitted, "as you knew it would." He pinned her with a glance that could have cut steel. "But your presence here—dressed as you are—does not."

"You would prefer I joined you at supper wearing rags?" she asked.

"I would prefer you dressed as a monk and stayed as far away from me as possible. Since that will hardly do, I suggest you do the next best thing."

"Which is?"

"Finds ways to entertain yourself which do not include me."

"But surely, as your wife, it is my duty to serve you."

Dominic smiled but it was not warm. "Since when have you ever desired to serve me, Catrina? Certainly not in France, when I wanted you to."

Catherine said nothing to that.

"You know the terms of our agreement. I expect you to abide by them."

"You and my uncle agreed—I did not. I am married to you, Dominic. I shall behave as a proper wife should. What you do is your business." She smiled even more pleasantly. "I'm really quite hungry. Shall we eat?"

Dominic grumbled something unpleasant beneath his breath, but said nothing more, and Catherine was unwilling to press him further. The battle had just begun. Her strategy called for a long and dedicated campaign; there was no need to hurry.

Still, she believed she had won this first small skirmish.

The next night Dominic found Catherine waiting for him just as she had been the night before, though the hour of his return was even later. She sat with him through supper, making polite conversation and looking far too lovely in a beautiful dusty-rose gown whose bodice was also too low.

This time he made no comment, just did his best to ignore the fact, which wasn't easy to do. They spoke of Janos, and Dominic could see the affection she already felt for the boy.

"I'm worried about him, Dominic. We've got to find a way for him to be accepted."

"If you think of something, let me know," he said darkly.

She opened her mouth to speak then seemed to think better of it. "I'll give it some thought," she finished.

When he made no further attempt to converse, nor allowed his gaze to rest more than a moment on her indecent display of bosom, she retired with a polite "good night," apparently annoyed at his indifference.

Sitting alone in front of the fire, he finished a brandy, poured himself another, then carried the crystal snifter upstairs to his room. When he opened the door, he found Percy waiting as usual, but the old man had fallen asleep in a chair in the corner. Dominic smiled at the sound of Percy's snoring, sat down on the bed and tugged off his boots.

After he had stripped off his clothes and pulled on a dark green dressing gown, he leaned over and shook the old man's shoulder.

"Go on to bed, old friend."

"What?" Rheumy blue eyes, one filmed over, tried to focus and finally fixed on his face. "But surely you'll be needin' some help."

"I'm fine. You just get some sleep." He wouldn't know what to do with a valet who actually helped him undress.

Percy stumbled groggily toward the door, waved good-night, and pulled it closed. Dominic started toward the big four-poster bed in the center of the room, but a sound in the chamber next door drew his attention. No one had used that room in years, and yet . . . There it was again—footsteps—he was sure of it.

Furious that one of the servants should be prowling the empty room this time of night, Dominic grabbed the latch to the adjoining door and yanked it open. He sucked in a breath at the sight of Catherine sitting at the gilded dressing table dressed only in a thin chemise, brushing her fiery hair.

"What the devil do you think you're doing?" Dominic's mouth felt dry.

"The house is so new, I found it difficult to sleep." She smiled softly. "I was just enjoying the breeze coming in through the windows."

He glanced to the open balcony doors. The scent of roses drifted up from the gardens below and the curtains billowed gently. "This isn't your room," he said.

"It isn't?" Catherine's pretty green eyes went wide. "But this is the marchioness's chamber, is it not?"

"Yes, but—"

"And I am the marchioness, am I not?"

"Yes, but—"

"Unless, of course, you and my uncle made some sort of agreement about that, too."

Dominic bristled. "You know very well we did not."

"Then this *must* be my room. At least it will be once I've removed those dreadful dun-colored draperies and hung something cheerful. You have no objection to that, do you?"

"No—I mean, yes. I mean no, I have no objection to anything you do to this dreary old house, but I have every objection to you being in this room—especially dressed like that."

Catherine glanced down at her breasts, straining against the front of her thin chemise, the tawny peaks barely concealed. She reached for her blue silk wrapper, stood up and slipped it on. Lifting her hair up out of the way, she straightened the robe, then let the long silky mass slide heavily down her back, firelight dancing on the golden-red strands.

Dominic groaned. With the flames behind her, even through her robe he could see the outline of her body. How could he have forgotten how shapely her legs were, how narrow her waist?

"I'm sorry if I've offended you," she said. "Next time, if you'll only just knock, I promise I shall be properly clothed."

Clothed or unclothed, it didn't matter. Just looking at her made him want her so badly he ached. Beneath the folds of his dressing gown, his manhood pressed hot and hard against his belly, his pulse raced, and the room seemed suddenly airless and overly warm. It was all he could do not to stride across the room and take her right there on the floor.

"You can't stay here," he said instead, his voice thick and husky.

"Oh? Why is that?"

"You know very well why. I believe I demonstrated the fact quite clearly in the back of my wagon."

Catherine flushed prettily. "I won't be put out of my own room, Dominic. I won't be made a fool of in front of the servants."

She was right, dammit. He should have thought of that himself. "All right, you may stay. But lock your door." He turned to leave.

"I suggest you lock yours, if that is what you wish."

Dominic spun to face her. "You little vixen, you're enjoying this!"

"A woman has . . . needs . . . my lord, the same as a man. It was you who taught me."

"Bloody hell!" The little wench was stalking him with the same force of will he had used on her! His mouth thinned to a narrow line. "This isn't going to happen, Catherine. A week from tomorrow, I'm leaving for London. I suggest you find a means to entertain yourself while I'm gone."

"A gentleman caller, perhaps?" she taunted.

Damn her! In four long strides, Dominic reached her. He gripped her arm and hauled her against his chest. "You're my wife, dammit! You'll behave like it or suffer the consequences."

Catherine jerked free. "That, you may rely on—from the moment you begin to behave like my husband." She whirled toward the open balcony doors, her back ramrod straight, her lips pressed tightly together.

Dominic cursed soundly, turned and strode from the room, slamming the door behind him.

The wench was in league with the devil—he would swear it. The devil or his father—they had always been one and the same.

Catherine spent the next three days letting Dominic's temper cool. Her own as well. She hadn't meant to get angry, but his damnable high-handedness had sent her over the edge. Of all the nerve! While he was off to London—doing God only knew what—she was supposed to sit idly in the

country. Well, she wouldn't do it—curse his bitter soul—
she wouldn't!

Then again, perhaps his leaving was a sign that her plan
was working. Perhaps the temptation to make love to her
was stronger than he would admit.

Catherine almost smiled. Now that she thought about
it, there were a dozen other things she could do to stir his
passions. What would happen if she did? And if she succeeded in her game of seduction, would Dominic accept
their marriage as a marriage in truth?

She didn't know, but she had four more days to find out.
And Catherine intended to do just that.

With that aim in mind, she headed off toward the stables, hoping Dominic might be somewhere near.

"Are you going riding, Catrina?" Little Janos raced
toward her from a door at the rear of the house.

Catherine smiled, thinking how adorable he looked in
his ruffled white shirt and velvet breeches—his stockings
off and his shoes in his hands. "Would you like to join me?
Cook has prepared a picnic basket." Catherine lifted the
embroidered white linen cloth and Janos leaned forward
and took a sniff.

"Mr. Reynolds said we were through for the day." He
grinned, flashing small white teeth. "I would love to go."

"You had better go change. I'll wait for you in the stable."

He turned and raced away.

"Saddle a horse for Janos," Catherine instructed the
lanky youth named Roddy, once she'd arrived.

"Primas?" he asked with a hint of disapproval.

"If that's the horse he usually rides." He left to do her
bidding and returned a little later leading the tall bay
horse.

"Primas is my favorite," Janos said, walking up beside
them.

"Lot of 'orse for a lit'l boy," Roddy grumbled.

"Janos is an excellent rider." Catherine well remembered the skill with which all of the Pindoros children rode.

The groom merely grunted. While they waited for the horses to be readied, Catherine glanced around, hoping to see Dominic. Instead she spotted little Bobby Marston, Roddy's younger brother, both sons of Dominic's head groom.

"Hello, Bobby," Catherine said.

"Hullo, Yer Ladyship."

"I'm sure you know Janos."

Bobby's expression turned sullen. "I know 'im."

Janos's dark face betrayed nothing. Gypsy through and through.

"Maybe you two could play together sometime," Catherine suggested. Though the boy was a few years older, she was determined to breach the problem she knew Janos faced every day.

Bobby looked horrified. "'E 'it me, 'e did. Blacked me eye. Me pap woulda strapped him good weren't fer 'Is Lordship."

Janos said nothing.

"Why, Bobby? Why did Janos hit you?"

"Me'n the boys was only teasin' 'im a bit. Didn't mean 'im no 'arm."

"You were teasing him because he's different, isn't that right?"

"Talks funny. Acts funny, too." Bobby stuck his chin out.

"How would you like to go to school, Bobby?" Catherine asked, changing the subject and surprising him. "How would you like to learn to read?"

He eyed her warily, scuffing his shoe in the dirt. "Pap says school's a waste o' time."

"Oh, he does, does he?"

"Book learnin' won't put food on the table," he repeated, spouting more of his father's words.

"Maybe it won't and maybe it will," Catherine countered. Turning, she tugged Janos toward the waiting horses.

"Going riding?" Dominic's deep voice boomed from the door of the tack room.

"Yes." She felt a sudden increase in the tempo of her heart. "Why don't you join us?"

"Please, Dominic. Come with us," Janos pleaded. "It is such a beautiful day. We can ride into the *vesh*—the woods," he said to Catherine. "We can be Romany again for a day."

Dominic shifted his stance in the doorway, leaning one wide shoulder against the jamb. For a moment he looked uncertain, as if he warred with some part of himself. "Not today, little one. I have too much to do."

"Why don't you go on?" Catherine said to Janos. "Wait for me under the trees at the top of the hill." She smiled. "We'll race to the stream."

After the boy had mounted and ridden away, Dominic turned in her direction. "You shouldn't encourage him to be so reckless." His eyes touched her face and one corner of his mouth curved up. "Or is it the other way around?"

Catherine flashed an impish grin that told him he'd hit on the truth. "He's a wonderful little boy. I just wish he wasn't so lonely."

Dominic sighed. "Sometimes I wonder if I've done the right thing in bringing him here."

Catherine pulled a golden piece of straw from the front of his sweat-stained shirt, then twirled it between her fingers. "I think I know a way to help him."

"Help him? How?"

"I want to give the children a school, the kind my father built at Arondale. I can use my own money, but I'll still need your help."

"I'm not sure that's a good idea. You know how people feel. Some of them will be certain you're sowing the seeds of revolution."

"Surely you don't believe that."

"Hardly. But even the children's families won't approve. They'll worry you're setting them up for disappointment, that they'll want things they can never have."

"I know it won't be easy, but I also know it's the right thing to do. If you want Janos to find a place here, let me build my school."

Dominic pulled the straw from her hand, ran his fine brown fingers along it. Then he smiled, and Catherine felt as if the sun had come up. "Will it keep you out of trouble while I'm gone?"

She eyed him a moment. "It might . . . if you promise to stay out of trouble as well."

"What *I* do, Catrina, is none of your concern. But you may build your school."

Catherine ignored a pinprick of anger. For the moment, the school was all-important. "And you'll help me persuade the families to let their children attend?"

"The children will attend, I promise you."

She forced herself to smile. "Thank you."

Dominic walked her to a tall chestnut gelding and lifted her up on the sidesaddle, his hands warm and strong at her waist.

"I wish you would come with us. It would make Janos happy."

"Sorry. Too much to do."

"Of course," she said with a last tight smile, "how could I have forgotten how busy you are." Digging her heels into the horse's flanks, she turned and rode away.

As he had promised, Janos waited at the top of the hill. They didn't return until dusk, much later than they had intended. But the day had been warm and lovely, and the picnic basket filled with succulent meat pies and fresh baked puddings. They had raced to the stream, Catherine letting Janos win, though she wouldn't have beaten him by much. He could ride like the wind itself, she thought, remembering the way Dominic had looked astride his big gray stallion.

Back at the stables, a groom took the horses and Catherine sent Janos inside while she lagged back, hoping for another chance to see Dominic.

She'd had all afternoon to think about him, plenty of

time to imagine what might happen once he left for London. She couldn't bear to think of him with another woman. She had to do something, and she had to do it fast.

She heard him before she saw him, his deep rumble of laughter rich and warm. She hadn't heard him laugh that way since they had left the Gypsy camp. Noticing several other voices, she realized he was standing out in back, talking to some of his men. He was always at ease with them, and they loved him for it. Why couldn't he be that way with her?

Catherine stood in the shadows of the stable, listening to their easy conversation. If she walked out there, the others would leave, but so would he. Unless . . .

It was an old ploy, but all she could think of at the moment. Catherine glanced around, saw no one was near, picked up a handful of straw and a bit of dust, and tossed it over the front of her riding habit. Several more handfuls dirtied the bodice. Leaning down, she lifted the hem and tore the fabric, then pulled several pins from her hair.

"Dominic?" Catherine called out as if she had just begun searching for him, then she cried out as she pretended to trip and fall. Dominic came at a run, several grooms in his wake.

"What is it? What happened?" He knelt beside her. "Someone get a lantern."

"It's all right," Catherine said, "I just tripped. Silly really. I'm usually not so clumsy." One of the stable boys brought the lantern, and Catherine tried to stand up. Easing her foot down, she winced and nearly toppled over. Dominic caught her up in his arms and carried her toward a low wooden bench.

"It's my ankle," Catherine said weakly, leaning against his hard chest. God, it felt good to be there. "I must have sprained it."

"It's all right," Dominic told the others. "I'll take care of her."

The men walked away, leaving them alone, and Dominic lifted the hem of her riding skirt. "Which leg is it?"

"The right one."

He worked it gently, probing for the source of the injury. Catherine flinched just a little.

"It doesn't look too serious." He pulled down her skirt. "I'll carry you back to the house."

"I think I may have pulled something a little higher up," Catherine said with a glance away.

"Higher up?" he asked, once more lifting the fabric. "You mean your knee?"

"A little higher than that."

Dominic's hand skimmed over her white-stockinged leg. He glanced around, afraid someone would see. "We'd better get you back to the house, so I can have a look."

Catherine merely nodded. Her throat had closed up at the thought of Dominic removing her stockings, his strong brown hands touching her flesh. When he lifted her up, Catherine wrapped her arms around his neck to steady herself, and he carted her up the gray stone walkway to the house.

"What were you doing out there in the dark?" he asked, halfway there. "As a matter of fact, what the hell were you doing staying out so late? And where's Janos?"

"Janos already went in. We stayed out because it was a beautiful day, and we were enjoying ourselves."

"And?"

"And what?"

"If the horses were already stabled, what were you doing out there in the dark?" Dominic stopped on the path, waiting for her to answer.

Catherine hesitated only a moment. "If you must know, I was listening to you. It's been so long since I've heard your laughter. I don't know . . . I guess I just missed hearing it."

Dominic didn't move. But his hold on her grew tighter. She could feel his eyes on her face. She looked up at him, praying he would kiss her. Instead he started walking again, kicked open the door with the toe of his boot, and strode in.

Taking the stairs two at a time, he carried her up to her chamber and placed her on the wide canopied bed. Reluctantly, she let go of his neck.

"I'd better call Gabby," he said, assessing the bulky velvet riding habit she would need to remove.

"I can do it myself if you'll help me."

Dominic hesitated, then watching Catherine struggling with the buttons at the back of her dress, pushed her hands away and worked them himself. With a practiced skill she forced herself to ignore, in minutes he had stripped away her riding habit, always careful of her leg. Catherine lay on the bed in only her stockings and chemise.

"Maybe I should call the surgeon," Dominic suggested, staring at the length of white silk that covered her calf, the smooth white flesh that disappeared beneath her chemise.

"I—I'd rather have you look, if you don't mind. I mean you've already seen me. I'm not embarrassed with you. Besides, it's probably nothing . . . and the surgeon's hours away."

"All right," he agreed with a certain amount of reluctance. Dominic took a deep breath, unfastened and rolled down her stocking. One hand slid under the edge of her chemise, moving upward, probing gently along her flesh. Catherine felt the heat of his hand, the way his fingers had begun to tremble, and moaned.

"Did I hurt you?" he asked, jerking away.

"No! I mean, yes . . . just a little."

"You must have strained something when you fell."

"Yes . . ."

Dominic set his jaw. Lifting the edge of her chemise, he stared at her bare thigh for several seconds, then once more ran his hand the length of it.

"Oh, God," Catherine whispered, unable to stop herself.

Dominic didn't seem to notice, just shoved up her chemise until her entire leg and hip were exposed. His hand traveled from her thigh up over her buttocks. He squeezed it gently and Catherine squirmed. His eyes fastened on the rounded slope of her bottom, the curve of her leg.

"Dominic . . . ," Catherine said softly.

At the sound of his name, he pulled away, and Catherine cursed herself roundly. With brisk, efficient movements, he pulled her chemise back down and lifted his eyes to her face.

"I'm sure it's nothing serious," she said a bit breathlessly, wishing she could somehow disguise the flush in her cheeks.

"No," he said thickly. "You'll probably be fine in the morning."

"Yes."

"I'd better go," he said, but didn't move.

Stay, she wanted to shout, but knew she did not dare. "Thank you."

"You're welcome." He turned and walked out of the room.

Catherine leaned back against the pillows and released a sigh of both frustration and relief. It's working! she thought. Dominic had wanted her—fiercely. She had no more doubt about that. But time was her enemy. One more night was all she had before he left for London. Tomorrow she must succeed.

Chapter Twenty-one

Dominic raced Rai, his big dapple-gray stallion, across the rolling heath. A wind had come up, bending the damp green grasses beneath them, and flat gray clouds streaked the dark sky overhead.

He'd been riding for hours, running the big horse flat out until its coat glistened with lather and its sides heaved with the effort. When he finally brought the animal to a halt beneath a dogwood tree at the top of the hill above the stream, Rai's nostrils flared and his ears swung forward. As tired as the animal was, it was obvious he had enjoyed the run.

Dominic wished he had. Instead, no matter how far from the house he rode, no matter how weary his bones or how hard he worked to busy his mind, his thoughts returned to Catherine.

He was beginning to think he'd go mad.

Last night had been the worst. When he had heard her cry out, something had torn loose inside him. He had raced into the barn to find she had merely tripped and fallen, yet he couldn't stand the thought of her hurting, even from something as minor as a simple sprain.

That she had stood in the shadows listening to the sound of his laughter made an ache well up in his heart. He had never really believed she had cared for him that much. She had left him, hadn't she?

The fact that she had given herself to him meant only that she desired him. Plenty of women had. But none had stood alone in the darkness listening to the sound of his voice.

He tried to remember when last he had heard *her* laugh. An occasional smile, somewhat wistful at that, was the best he could remember. Yet there were times when the sound of it rang in his mind. Times when they had laughed together in the Gypsy camp.

He thought of the way she had come to care for little Janos. Already she felt protective of him. What a wonderful mother she would make. She had a way of taking charge that never offended, yet she always seemed to get things done. In the days since her arrival, the house felt more like a home than it ever had before. Just a few simple changes here and there, heavy drab curtains removed, a window or two left open to let in fresh air.

Even the servants seemed different, as if their routine tasks mattered more because Catherine was there to appreciate whatever it was they had done.

Until Catherine had come, he had never thought of Gravenwold as his home. It was a symbol of all he had learned since he'd left the Rom, things he had accomplished, things he meant to accomplish still. Now, with Catherine's arrival and the changes she had wrought, it tormented him with possibilities. Dreams of love and family he had never allowed himself before. Dreams he refused to allow himself now.

Dominic dismounted and walked Rai along the streambed, letting the horse blow and cool down a little. The wind ruffled his hair, and he raked it out of the way with his fingers.

He glanced down at them, thinking again of the scene last night in Catherine's room. Even now his body burned with the memory of his hand on her flesh, her skin warm and soft beneath his. A minute or two more and he would have been lost. Only the memory of his father's bitter laughter, the sound of his mother's lonesome weeping, had kept him from taking her there and then.

How had he ever gotten himself into such a coil? How could he extract himself without breaking his vow of revenge? He didn't understand why staying away from her had become so difficult. He didn't understand the feelings she stirred—the longings—and he didn't want to.

Leaving for London was the only means he had of keeping his sanity. He wouldn't return until he had whored with half the wenches in the city and slaked his seemingly insatiable lust.

Married or not, he would rid himself of his hellish desire for Catherine. When he returned, he would send her back to Arondale. If anything would make her happy, that would.

Then his life could go on as he had planned. Catherine would have her independence—to a point. And he would be able to live with himself.

"None of them understand, do they, boy?" he said to Rai, gathering the stallion's reins and swinging up into the saddle. "And there is nothing I can say that could possibly make them see."

They in this case meant Catherine. How did a man explain to a woman reasons for his actions born over a score of years? How could he ever make her see that his Romany pledge to honor his mother by his revenge against his father could not be broken?

There was no way.

Dominic pressed his knees into the stallion's sides and the huge horse galloped off toward the beckoning fields in the distance. Tomorrow he would leave for London. Maybe there he could find some peace.

Catherine paced the room, her small feet wearing a path in the carpet in front of the hearth. Everything had to be perfect—there would be no second chance. Darkness had fallen hours ago, but the moon was full and tiny white stars sparkled like jewels in the heavens. Dominic would be home soon. At least she prayed he would.

Surely he wouldn't have changed his mind and left without saying good-bye?

Hearing a knock at the door, Catherine crossed the room and pulled it open. Gabby stood beside two servants who carried a big copper bathing tub and steaming pails of water.

"Set it in front of the fire," Catherine told them. She had waited till the last possible moment, worried the water would cool. "Hurry, Gabby, help me get undressed." She turned to the girl as the servants had left.

"*Mon Dieu,* 'Is Lordship will be mad with lust."

"I hope so," Catherine muttered. She still hadn't told Gabby the truth, just that she planned an evening of seduction and she wanted it to be perfect.

"What did you say?" Gabby asked.

"I said I'm certain he'll be wildly overcome." She just prayed he wouldn't be so furious he wouldn't even come in. "You won't forget to leave the note beside his supper tray?"

"I will not forget." It read simply, *Need to speak with you tonight. C.*

Catherine glanced out the window for the dozenth time in the last ten minutes. Only this time she saw Dominic riding down the hill toward the stables. "It's him. He'll be here any minute."

"I will fetch 'is supper."

"Don't forget—"

"I will put the note where he cannot fail to see it."

Catherine nodded. A few minutes later, she heard Dominic enter his room. Pressing her ear against the heavy door between their bedchambers, Catherine could hear Percy's faint conversation, then the thud of boots as they hit the floor.

"I've taken the liberty of ordering your bath, milord," Percy told him, and Catherine groaned. How long would that take? Her own bathing water was growing colder by the minute.

Naked beneath the flimsy emerald silk dressing gown that Gabby had fashioned just for the occasion, her hair piled loosely atop her head, Catherine began to pace the floor again. Too easily she could imagine Dominic's powerful naked torso as he sat in the water of the bathing tub, his long muscular legs bunched beneath him. Maybe she should simply go in and start washing his back. She was his wife, wasn't she?

Catherine shook her head. Percy might still be in there. She had better stick to her plan. She walked to the door again and pressed her ear to the heavy wood. Percy was leaving at last. She heard the thump of the door closing behind him, then Dominic's footsteps crossing the floor. Now he would find the note.

She waited, holding her breath. He must have found it, because his light knock sounded at the door. Catherine tossed her wrapper over a chair and stepped into the water, which now felt tepid at best. At least the suds still rose in tempting white mounds to scantily cover her breasts. Ignoring a shiver, she sank down into the suds.

Dominic knocked on the door again, this time louder. "Catherine?"

When she didn't answer, he lifted the latch as she prayed he would and strode into the room.

"Dominic!" Catherine said with feigned surprise, rising to her feet and reaching for the white linen towel on the table beside the tub. Soapsuds slid down her body and clung to the peaks of her breasts. Droplets of water cascaded down her legs to pool on the floor as she wrapped the scanty towel around her.

"I'm sorry," she said, "I'm afraid I didn't hear your knock."

"No?" His dark eyes raked her. "What about the note you left me? I believe it said you needed to see me tonight."

"Oh, yes, the note. I wrote it early in the evening. I believed quite wrongly that since you'd be leaving on the morrow you would probably be getting home before dark. Would you mind handing me my wrapper?" She indicated the emerald silk robe draped across the chair just a few feet away from him. Dominic picked it up and strode in her direction, his arm outstretched. Catherine reached for it, but when she did, her towel slipped loose and floated to the floor.

"Oh my." Catherine clutched the lush green silk to her breasts. One tawny nipple peeked from between her fingers.

"What is it you want?" Dominic asked, his jaw taut. He was speaking to her, but eyes like glittering jet slid to the juncture of her thighs, covered only by a small swatch of fabric.

"It would probably be best if I put my robe on first. Why don't you help me?"

Dominic's sensuous mouth thinned. Though he wore no shirt, he had pulled on his boots and a clean pair of breeches. Now a hard masculine ridge pressed firmly against the buttons up the front.

With one deft movement, he snatched the robe from Catherine's grasp, leaving her naked. In the light of the fire and the glow of the candles, beads of water glistened against her skin. Her heavy, upturned breasts rose and fell with each breath, and fiery red-gold hair formed a delicate triangle at the apex of her thighs.

He stared at her with a mixture of hunger and pain.

"I'm your wife, Dominic," Catherine said. "I belong to you, just as I did at the Gypsy camp. I'm yours to do with as you wish." She stepped forward, sliding her arms around his neck. Dark bands of muscle pressed into her paler breasts, his skin felt hot, and wavy strands of ink-black hair spun softly around her fingers.

"I want you," Catherine whispered, and Dominic's solid arms crushed her against his chest. His mouth came down hot and hard over hers, searing her with its demand, and the heat of his body inflamed her. His fingers slid into her hair, pulling it free of its pins, and it swirled around her shoulders. She could feel his rigid shaft, pressing against her, and wanted more than breath itself to feel it deep inside.

Dominic's tongue plunged into her mouth and his hands cupped her buttocks, dragging her against him, molding her to his hard length and firing her blood even more. Her tongue parried his, seeking, searching, demanding he claim her.

Dominic kissed her savagely, fiercely—then he tore himself free.

"You planned this, didn't you?" The fury in his eyes was unmistakable.

"Yes."

"And last night—you didn't fall."

"No."

"You know how I feel about this, yet you care nothing for my wishes, only your pleasure."

"I'm your wife," she defended.

"My wife?" he taunted, still gripping her arm. His eyes ran over her nakedness, making clear his displeasure, and for the first time she felt ashamed. "It isn't as my wife you've behaved this eve—but as my whore."

Catherine flinched at the cruelty of his words and the venom with which he spoke them. When she fought to break free, Dominic let her go and she stumbled. He tossed her the green silk robe. Catherine pulled it on with shaking fingers.

His dark eyes raked her. "You have played the wanton well, my sweet, but it's another of your kind whose bed I'll seek this eve." Turning, he strode toward the door.

"Dominic!" Catherine caught up with him before he could reach it. "Please," she whispered, "please don't do this."

"It would have happened sooner or later. Perhaps it is better this way." He jerked his arm free and strode through the door, slamming it loudly behind him.

Catherine stood transfixed, staring at the place he had been. Time seemed to swell as she listened for the slamming of his door, then the echo of his footfalls as he strode down the hall.

Clutching the lovely silk wrapper around her, fighting to block out the chill she suddenly felt, Catherine moved woodenly toward the window, fixing her eyes on the road leading out of the estate. It wasn't long before she caught sight of him atop his big gray stallion, riding like thunder toward the village not far away. She watched him till he rode out of sight, then sank down on the window seat and curled her legs up under her chin. From her place in the window, she could see well up the road, but there was nothing but a silvery path of moonlight to mark the place where he had been.

Still, she sat there staring, wondering what she had done wrong, telling herself over and over that she'd had to try, then lashing herself for acting like a harlot. Until tonight, she hadn't realized that a man expected his wife to behave differently than his lover. Now she knew—and it was too late.

She rested her chin on her knees but kept her eyes fastened on the desolate stretch of road. The fire had begun to die down, and the room had turned cold, but Catherine didn't care. She thanked God for the numbness, the icy chill that matched the coldness in her veins. Where was he now? she wondered, what was he doing? But there was no way to avoid the truth.

He had scorned her affections, even the use of her body. Now he gave himself to another, wrapped himself in her arms and shared with her his need. Catherine closed her eyes against a wave of pain, but she could not fall asleep. Not when the clock on the mantel struck one, not even when it struck three. She just kept staring down the empty stretch of lane Dominic had traveled to sever the last of his affections—if he had ever felt any at all.

What Catherine felt went far beyond that. She knew that now. Her uncle had been right—she loved him still. She would die for him, if it came to that, yet he felt nothing but contempt for her. How could love be so one-sided?

she thought vaguely, wondering how life could be so
unfair.

Catherine swallowed the bitter lump that swelled in her
throat. She had never felt more like crying and yet the
tears would not come. She hurt too much to cry.

Or at least so she thought until she saw Dominic riding
back down the road.

That was the moment it hit her. Raw scorching pain so
deep and abiding that for a moment she thought she might
be sick. An image of him lying naked, so beautifully dark
and male, rose up before her. But the woman he kissed was
another. Some dark, sensuous, nameless woman with lush
curves, full, ripe breasts, and a moist mouth bruised from
his kisses.

She watched him ride through the massive front gates,
his pace much slower than before. But she could barely
see him. Tears welled in her eyes and slipped down her
cheeks, blurring her vision. She had lost him—she
accepted that now as she hadn't before—and the terrible
ache she felt inside finally overwhelmed her.

Resting her head on her knees, she began to cry. Not
soft, gentle tears, but deep, wracking sobs that mirrored
the pain she felt in her heart.

She cried for his loss, cried for the love she felt that
would wither and die just as surely as it had grown. She
cried for her family, for the children she would never hold.
For Edmund and his betrayal, for Amelia, for little Eddie,
who would now grow up without his father. Mostly she
cried for Dominic. For the bitter, empty life he had chosen
over the boundless love she had wanted to give him. The
happiness neither of them would ever know.

She cried though she wished she could stop. She cried,
and wondered if she would ever stop crying again.

Dominic stood at the bottom of the massive stone staircase that led to his second-floor chamber. His hand shook
as he gripped the banister and forced himself to take the
first step. Above him, he could hear Catherine weeping,

an eerie lament that even through the thick gray walls seemed to accuse him. He had never heard her cry that way—never. He had rarely heard her cry at all.

He climbed the stairs, his feet leaden, each step harder than the one before. He had done this to her; he had brought her this terrible sadness. He might have been able to go back to his room if he hadn't heard her. He might have been able to pretend that tonight had not happened.

Now he could not.

So instead of shutting himself inside the protective walls of his chamber, instead of pretending, denying what he felt inside, what the hours he had spent in the tavern had made so achingly clear, he crossed the dimly lit hall, went into his room, and lifted the latch on her bedchamber door.

It was dark inside, except for the single white candle that sputtered in the deepening wax, and the last orange-red embers of a dying fire. It was cold in the room, he realized, his heart clenching as he stepped in, his eyes seeking, searching, then glimpsing her shadowy figure huddled on the brocade cushion in the window. And her thin silk robe offered no protection at all.

Catherine wept even as he stood there, unseen in the darkness, and knowing that he was the cause, he could not make himself cross the floor. Instead he kept thinking of the women in the tavern, remembering how he had looked into their vulgar painted faces and red-rouged mouths and thought of a lovely gentle face filled with inno-cence and compassion.

He remembered how he'd meant to follow one of them up to her room, to strip her naked and plunge into her ripe, overused body. How he'd intended to take her roughly again and again, until he cleansed his mind and heart of his hellish need for Catherine.

Instead as he sat there drinking, all he could see was an image of her facing up to Vaclav. Catherine—a countess scrubbing pots without complaint beside his mother. Catherine, who worried for Medela and loved little Janos, who tried to protect a counterfeit marquess from being tossed into prison.

He saw her eyes flashing, her fiery hair tumbled loose around her shoulders as she came to his rescue with a pair of garden shears. He saw her standing there this eve, gloriously naked, soapsuds trailing wetly down her body. He thought of the courage it had taken for her to face his rejection again and again, to offer her warmth, though he didn't want it. To offer her body, though he offered nothing in return.

He had sat in the tavern, trying to deny what he felt for her, needing her as he had never needed a woman—as he ached with need for her now.

She sensed him then more than heard him, for her head came up and she brushed at her tears with the back of a hand.

"Get out of here." Her voice sounded strained and uneven as she sat up on the seat pulling the silk robe closer around her, her small feet sliding onto the cold wooden floor.

He deserved her scorn, and yet his heart lurched painfully at the sound of it. He watched a tiny yellow flame among the coals burnish her skin to that same golden glow and thought of what his madness had cost him.

"What do you want here?" she asked. "Go back to your w-whores."

Her small hands trembled more fiercely than his own, and he wanted to reach out and touch her, to soothe away her tears. He wanted to beg her forgiveness and carry her away. "There were no whores," he said softly.

Catherine came to her feet, her fiery hair swirling around her, the green silk clinging to her as Dominic wished he could, reminding him that earlier she would have let him take it from her, would have removed even that small barrier, if he had but asked. Now a world of sadness lay beween them, a mantle far heavier than her thin silk robe.

"You needn't bother to lie," she said on a ragged breath.

"Not when you went to so much trouble to be certain I would know."

How could he have done it? How could he have treated her worse than any whore? His stomach clenched in bitter self-disgust, and his eyes slid closed against the pain. He deserved her wrath, the terrible loss of her affections. He had taken something fragile, something beautiful, and ground it into dust beneath his heel.

When he made no move to leave, just stood watching from the shadows beside the door, Catherine picked up a silver-handled hairbrush and hurled it in his direction. It slammed against the wall above his head.

"There were no whores." His soft words echoed in the stillness of the room. He wished there was more he could say, something he could do . . . but what words were left to a man who had destroyed the very thing he cared for most?

"I want you o-out of my room. I'll be gone from here in the morning."

Ah, God. He had lost her, and yet he could not bear to leave.

Catherine took an unsteady breath, the tears on her cheeks still glistening in the glow of the candle. She hefted a heavy crystal perfume bottle and hurled it across the space between them. He saw it coming, but didn't try to avoid it, just let it bounce off his shoulder, the jolt of pain almost welcome. The bottle shattered on the floor, scattering small crystal shards that glittered in the faint red embers of the fire. They reminded him of the fragile bond they'd once shared that he had shattered this eve.

"There were no whores," he whispered, his voice rough and husky as he started toward her, his boots crunching harshly on the fragile broken glass. In the flickering light of the candle, Catherine's face looked pale, her eyes desolate. She looked vulnerable and defeated as he had never seen her. He had accomplished with his harsh words and ill care what others could not accomplish with their cruel treatment or their pain.

When he reached her side, he just stood there, his chest tight, his heart aching. His gaze took in her trembling lips, the liquid pools that still welled in her eyes. He tipped her chin with shaking fingers and looked into her face.

"The woman I wanted this night was my wife," he said softly. "I discovered no other would do."

Catherine's breath stilled, her green eyes watching, the hurt in them clear, the pain.

He brushed a drop of wetness from where it clung to her lashes. "You are the woman I wanted . . . all I've ever wanted."

He thought he heard a tiny noise in her throat, some small acknowledgment of his words. Wary green eyes moved over his face, seeking the lie, but unable to find it. Silently he willed her to believe him, then held his breath and prayed that she would.

"I don't want you to go," he said softly. "I need you. I always have." He knew the very moment she accepted his words as truth, the instant the hurt began to dim. He saw it in the subtle shifting of her lips, the merest blink of an eye. He saw it—and something blossomed inside his chest.

That was the moment he knew for certain, though he had long suspected the truth and it had forced itself on him full-blown this eve. Still, the feeling was too new, too raw, for him to speak the words.

"Forgive me," he said instead, praying she would know how much her forgiveness meant to him. How much *she* meant to him. "I never intended to hurt you. I . . ." His hand came up to cup her cheek. "Nothing . . . no one . . . can make me hurt you again."

From beneath her thick dark lashes, Catherine watched him, assessing, weighing, deciding whether or not she should trust him, aware of the risk she would be taking. Dominic closed his eyes, willing her to take the risk, praying to God that she would, yet afraid of what would happen if she did.

"I love you," she said softly, her green eyes brimming

once more with tears. "My beloved Gypsy, I have loved you for so long."

Dominic swept her into his arms, clutching her against him, his face buried in her silky red-gold hair. The tightness in his throat made it hard for him to speak. "Catherine . . . ," he whispered, his chest aching, his own cheeks damp. "Say you'll forgive me," he begged, "say it."

"I love you," she said. "What has happened does not matter. I want to be your wife."

"Ah, God." Dominic bent his head and took her lips, feeling her soft mouth trembling beneath his, thanking God again and again that she was still his. Sliding an arm beneath her knees, he lifted her up, feeling her icy skin, her cold stiff fingers. He had done this to her. God, how could he? He kissed her again, with all the tenderness he felt for her, all the yearning.

"It's all right, *mi cajori,* everything is going to be all right." He carried her over to the bed and kissed her eyes, her nose, her mouth. "You're so cold," he said, when he felt her shiver. He pulled the covers up to her chin, but left her only long enough to stoke up the flames in the hearth.

"Dominic?"

"Yes?" he said, returning to the place beside her.

"I'm sorry, too, for what happened. I should have known wives were supposed to behave with more—"

"Don't," Dominic said, cutting her off, hating himself for the way he had made her feel. "Don't even think it. You did nothing untoward this eve. It was my fault—all of it."

"If you wish it, I could try to be more—"

"There is nothing about you I would change. I—" *Love you just as you are.* "Any man would count himself lucky to have a wife who desires him."

"Any man but you," Catherine said, echoing the thought he had firmly pushed away.

"What I want no longer matters. It is your needs that concern me now."

When Catherine started to protest, Dominic kissed her,

long and tenderly, then he drew back the covers. The green silk robe did little to disguise what lay beneath, yet that the robe was there reminded him of the barrier he had set between them. Bending down, he kissed the peak of her breast through the delicate fabric then carefully drew it open.

"You're lovely," he said, "so incredibly lovely." Heavy apricot-tipped breasts swelled above a tiny waist and lushly curving hips. His shaft, already pulsing and thick with desire, rose up and hardened even more.

Dominic cupped a breast then bent over to take her nipple into his mouth.

"Dominic?"

He laved the peak with his tongue, then pulled away to look at her.

"You don't have to do this. If you will just hold me, it will be enough."

One corner of his mouth curved up. "Do you have any idea how much I want you?" He took her small hand and rested it on the bulge at the front of his breeches. "Never have I desired a woman the way I do you."

"But—"

"Hush," he said softly. "It's time I made you my wife."

Dominic covered her lips with a kiss. Catherine felt the heat of it, felt the slick warmth of his tongue, and gave herself over as she never had before. Nothing mattered but his touch, the warmth of his hand—nothing mattered but that he had come home.

"I love you," she whispered as his mouth moved hotly along her throat and down her shoulders to once more suckle a breast. He drew it into his mouth, his tongue teasing, his strong teeth tugging, firing an ache that made her fingers clutch the fabric of his shirt.

It didn't matter that he didn't repeat the words. That he was there, for now, was enough.

Dominic traced a path of fire from her breasts to her belly, his mouth and tongue burning away the last of the cold. His lips trailed wet heat across the flat spot below her navel, his tongue darting in, ringing it, his hands sliding beneath her bottom to gently lift the rounded globes.

"Open for me, *cajori*," he whispered, bending over her as he coaxed her legs apart. "Let me love you."

She couldn't have done any less, not when his hands asked as softly as his words. Not when his fingers slipped through the thatch of golden-red hair above her womanhood, then moved with quiet determination to separate the sensitive folds below and slide inside.

"God in heaven," Catherine whispered, feeling his heated strokes, feeling his tongue move along her thigh. There was something of penance in the way he caressed her, taking no pleasure for himself, just settling between her legs, parting them until he had the access he wanted. Then his mouth moved over her flesh to suckle the sensitive bud at her core and his tongue slid inside.

Catherine moaned, and her body went up in flames. How long she had ached for his touch, if only just the merest caress. This—this was ecstasy she couldn't have dreamed. In minutes she was writhing beneath his mouth, calling his name over and over, consumed by the flames of her passion. She clutched the bedsheets, her hands balled into fists, and in the eye of her mind, a bright wave rose up to sweep her away. Light and touch became one, pleasure and passion and love. A tender sweetness rolled over her until she thought she would surely die of it.

He knew the right time to leave her, spiraling down, lost in a hazy cloud of pleasure that hadn't yet faded away. Before she could miss him, he returned to her naked, covering her mouth with his, his tongue thrusting between her teeth at the exact moment his hard shaft filled her in one deep savage stroke.

Catherine clutched his neck, her fingers biting into the muscles across his shoulders, her body arching as he plunged inside her. He felt huge and heavy, and he filled her again and again, making the sensuous wave of pleasure return, different this time, but just as fierce and heady. She let the sweetness roll over her, lifting her, carrying her, and savored the warm taste of passion, of the love she felt for the man who held her captive with both his body and his heart.

She felt him trembling just as she was, felt him stiffen, and arched against him, ready to accept his seed.

Instead he pulled away, his hard body jerking, his seed spilling wetly against her belly. She knew only a moment of sadness for the child they might have conceived, then it was gone.

Fifteen years of hating was a very long time. Dominic had come to her when she needed him most. He had proved that he cared. It was all she could ask, more than she had dared to hope for.

"Are you all right?" he asked, brushing damp strands of hair from her cheeks.

Catherine nodded. "Thank you," she said softly.

He arched a thick black brow. "For what?"

"Coming home."

His eyes flashed a moment of pain, then it was gone. Dominic smiled gently, lighting her world as no one else could. "I never knew how much I needed such a place until tonight."

She brushed his mouth with a kiss. "What you said earlier . . . ," she ventured, though part of her warned her she shouldn't, "it was the truth?"

Dominic cupped her cheek and turned her face with his hand. "There isn't another woman in this world that I want."

Catherine felt a lump rise in her throat and a lightness of heart that nearly overwhelmed her. "I've missed you," she said softly.

"Not nearly as much as I've missed you."

Catherine snuggled against him, feeling as if her world had finally begun to right itself. Dominic drew her into the circle of his arms, and she felt the same possessiveness he had shown toward her in the Gypsy camp. With a sense of hope she hadn't allowed herself before, she smiled into the darkness.

In minutes the heat in the room and that in her body made her eyelids grow heavy and she drifted to sleep. But when she woke in the morning, Dominic was gone.

Chapter Twenty-two

CATHERINE DRESSED HURRIEDLY and left her chamber. She was terrified Dominic had gone to London after all. What had he felt when he woke up? Did he resent her for what had happened between them?

His room seemed undisturbed; his clothes still hung neatly in his huge carved armoire. Still, he was certain to have more than enough in his town house on Hanover Square. Downstairs, she asked of him briefly, but she didn't want to seem anxious. If he had indeed gone, the servants would have more than enough to gossip about.

She found him soon after, working in the stables, his shirtsleeves rolled to his elbows, the front open nearly to his waist. He looked up when she walked in, and Catherine forced herself to smile.

Dear God, let everything be all right. Did he feel bitter and resentful? Would he be more determined than ever to construct a wall between them? Every moment since she awakened had made her uncertainty soar.

Instead when he saw her, he stepped from inside the stall, walked toward her, and opened his arms. Catherine went into them with a feeling of relief so heady it made her weak.

"You were exhausted," he said as if reading her mind. "I thought I should let you sleep."

She felt like weeping again. "I feel fine," she said a little too brightly. "Wonderful, in fact."

Dominic took her hands and stepped back to look at her. Her fingers were trembling and she knew he could feel it.

"What's wrong?" His eyes went dark with concern.

Too many lies had already passed between them. "I— I was afraid you would regret ... that you would be angry. ..."

"If I'm angry at anyone, I'm angry at myself. He tipped her face up and captured her mouth in a tender, loving kiss. "I'm not going to tell you this is easy for me because it isn't. Everything inside me rebels at the thought of breaking my vow, the idea of his winning—everything."

Catherine touched his cheek. "Will you tell me about it? What he did to you?"

Dominic took her hand and led her outside the stable. They crossed to a grassy knoll beneath a broad-leafed tree. Catherine leaned back against the trunk, and Dominic stared off in the distance, his gaze fixed on some imaginary point among the clouds.

"What he did to me was little compared to what he did to my mother. I can never forget the day his men came for me ... riding into our camp in a great cloud of dust ... jeering at my people. 'Get the damnable Gypsy bastard,' one of them said. They laughed when they saw my ragged clothes. 'Gravenwold must be mad,' someone said to my mother."

"What did Pearsa do? Why did she let them take you?"

"She thought my leaving would be for the best. She knew I would one day be rich and powerful—just like my father. I begged her not to make me go, but she wouldn't listen. Still, when we said good-bye, she clung to me as she never had and cried so hard she made me cry, too. After that, whenever I came to visit, she wouldn't touch me. She never held me at all—not even once. She knew if she did she would cry as she had before and that I would not leave her. She knew—and she would have been right."

Dominic turned away.

"You must let what happened pass."

"I vowed to her I would make him pay. I took an oath of blood. Now . . ."

"Now because of me, you will fail."

He tried to smile, but faltered. "You deserve more from life than what I meant to give you. You're beautiful and desirable, and I care for you as I never have another. I just need time, Catrina. Can you give me that?"

Catherine's heart ached for him. "As long as I know you care, nothing else matters."

He brought her hand to his lips and kissed the palm. "Thank you."

They spent hours together after that. A different kind of time than they had ever shared before. A loving, giving, gentle kind of time. Dominic spoke of his dreams, plans he had for the future of Gravenwold, though Catherine very carefully said nothing of family or heirs.

They talked about Catherine's school and Dominic seemed pleased by her efforts.

"I'll find a site for a small school building," he promised. "We can post notices in the *Public Advisor* and the *Morning Chronicle* that we're looking for a schoolmaster, and we'll build his quarters above."

"That would be wonderful. I should like Janos to attend as often as possible. Once the children see that he isn't really different from them, he'll be able to make new friends."

Dominic squeezed her hand, leaned over and kissed her cheek. "I know you're convinced this will work, but you mustn't be disappointed if it does not. No matter how much time he spends with us, Janos will always be a Gypsy. You must let him follow his heart."

Catherine smiled and nodded. Though in some ways Dominic remained distant, she could often feel his eyes on her, their black depths warm with affection, and more often than not—desire.

Catherine shoved her own desires away. Dominic needed time—she intended to see that he got it. Instead, she worked to build the foundation for their marriage that up until now had never been laid down, coming to know each other in ways they hadn't before.

She asked him about his horses and he told her his plans to breed great racers, proudly showing her Rai and Sumadji and some of the stallions he intended to put at stud.

Standing in the drawing room after luncheon one day, she asked him about his friendship with Stoneleigh, and he grinned.

"Rayne and I met through a wager at Whites nearly five years ago. We'd both been drinking heavily, boasting about our conquests as we shouldn't have been. Someone said we were the two most notorious rakes in London and that we should have a go at seeing which of us could best the other." Another devilish grin. "As a gentleman, I'm not at liberty to mention the lady in question, but suffice it to say ... we both won."

Catherine poked him in the ribs. "I trust your wagering days are through, milord ... at least in regard to the ladies."

Dominic slid a hand around her waist and drew her back against his chest, wrapping her in the circle of his arms as he bent to nuzzle an ear. "I've my hands full with you, love. You've had only the briefest taste of the pleasures I've in store for you."

Catherine felt his breath warm and promising against her cheek, and a jolt of desire slid through her body. Even through the fabric of her gown, she could feel his shaft grow hard, and her nipples tightened in response. When she turned to look at him, she found his dark eyes smoldering, then his mouth came down hard over hers.

He took her lips with fiery demand, his tongue sliding inside, touching, tasting. Then Blythebury walked through the open double doors, and Dominic pulled away, careful

to stand discreetly behind her to hide the bulge in his
breeches.

"Sorry to bother, milord," the stately butler said, his
somber face glowing an odd shade of pink. "The post has
arrived with a letter for Lady Gravenwold. It appears to
have come from London. I thought it might be important."

"Thank you, Blythesbury," Dominic reached for the letter then handed it to Catherine. "That will be all."

The tall butler bowed formally and left the room while
Catherine tore open the letter. "It's from Amelia." She sank
down on the tapestry sofa as she hurriedly scanned the
lines.

"Is everything all right?" Dominic sat down beside her.

"She's moved back into my town house. She says we
should let her know if that is inconvenient." Catherine
glanced up. "She doesn't need my permission. Amelia is
family. I wish she understood."

"What else does she say?"

"That Uncle Gil is almost completely recovered. He was
devilishly difficult for a while, but he's fine now. He's
opened the charity school we started and he's more than
pleased with the progress the children are making." She
read a few more lines. "Poor dear. Amelia says she's dread-
fully lonely without Edmund. She asks if we would consider coming to London for a visit." Catherine looked up
at him, the question unspoken.

"Would you like that?"

"Very much so."

"Then we'll go just as soon as we can get things settled
here."

Catherine smiled. "Why don't we take Janos? He and little Eddie aren't that far apart in age."

Dominic's black brows drew together. "Are you certain
Amelia would approve? After all, the boy's still a Gypsy."

"Don't be silly. Amelia isn't that sort of person. She'll be
delighted to have another child in the house."

Dominic didn't seem convinced, but he said nothing
more.

Several days later, during supper, Dominic spoke his feelings about the war, a subject Catherine had long been curious about, but hadn't as yet pursued.

She was wearing a very modest taupe silk gown scattered with seed pearls while Dominic wore a burgundy frock coat and light gray breeches. Cook had served a meal of roast partridge with oyster stuffing, candied carrots, and perigord pie.

"The British have tightened the blockade," he said, in response to an item about Napoleon she had seen in the London paper. "It's a good thing you're not still trying to escape from France."

"And what about you, milord? Wouldn't it be just as difficult for you to leave?" He grinned, beautiful white teeth flashing in a face so handsome Catherine's stomach fluttered.

"A Gypsy has little trouble going anyplace he wishes. We have a knack for blending, fitting into our surroundings whenever we choose to."

"Is your Gypsy heritage the reason you've never become involved in the war?"

"Partly. My father lost his firstborn son in His Majesty's Service. Since he didn't believe he owed them another, he went to great lengths to see me spared. As I'm a Gypsy first and an Englishman second, my own beliefs never entered into it. Besides . . . who says I haven't been involved?"

Catherine swallowed her last bite of partridge, which went down a little harder than it should have. "Are you?"

"On my return from the Continent each year, I've reported my observations to the authorities—troop movements, information I picked up here and there."

"You were a spy?"

"Hardly. What I did was little, but I believe it may have helped. In truth, it was all I was willing to do—more than most of my people would have done. It's the nature of the Rom to remain outside petty squabbles."

"Petty squabbles!" Catherine gasped and Dominic chuckled.

"I suppose it depends on one's point of view."

They took tea and cakes in a small drawing room off the Long Gallery. Catherine noticed Dominic had grown distracted, occasionally rubbing the bridge of his nose or the skin at his temples.

"Are you feeling unwell, milord?" All evening he had been watching her, his eyes moving over her body with the same dark hunger she had come to know so well. *He wants me,* she thought with a feeling of exhilaration. It wouldn't be long till he took her to his bed.

"I'm afraid my head has begun to pound."

Catherine walked behind the sofa and began to massage the back of his neck. "You're far too tense, milord." She worked her fingers into the muscles and sinews. "You should learn to relax." He leaned his head forward, letting her ease the tightness, then leaned back against the sofa and closed his eyes. Catherine continued to work over him, kneading his shoulders, easing the stiffness away.

"I know exactly what will cure my tension." He opened his eyes and flashed a heated look that left no doubt as to what he was thinking. "But . . ."

"But you still need a little more time," Catherine finished.

Dominic caught her wrist and brought it to his lips, then turned his head to look at her. "I know you don't understand. I wish there was a way to explain what I feel, but there isn't. I've got to work this through, Catrina."

Catherine kissed his forehead. "We've a lifetime to love. Years from now these few days will hardly matter."

With a sigh that said he wished he agreed, he stood up. "Since things remain as they are, if you don't mind, I believe I'll go on up to bed."

Catherine nodded. "I find I'm weary, too."

They crossed the room and climbed the wide stone staircase to their bedchambers on the second floor.

Dominic kissed Catherine good-night, then retired to his room next door.

After readying herself for bed, Catherine dressed in one of the high-necked white cotton nightgowns she had taken to wearing of late and started to draw back the covers. It occurred to her that with the tension he'd been feeling, Dominic might be in need of a sleeping draught.

Pulling on a heavy quilted wrapper, she picked up a small vial of sleeping powder from its place on the bureau, crossed to the door between their rooms, and rapped lightly on the heavy wood. Dominic bade her enter, and Catherine opened the door. She found him lying on his huge four-poster bed, naked except for the sheet he had pulled to his waist.

A candle flickered on the bedstand, turning his dark skin a gleaming brown-gold. Bands of muscle rippled on his chest as he turned toward her, and at the sight of his hard-muscled body, Catherine's heart began to pound.

"I-I'm sorry to bother you, but I thought you might be in need of something to help you sleep."

Dominic's eyes ran over her. "Come here," he said softly.

Catherine forced herself to move, stopping when she reached the edge of the bed. Dominic's gaze took in her heavy quilted robe, the ruffle of her high-necked nightrail peeping from beneath. She had plaited her long red-gold hair into a single thick braid, which fell over one shoulder.

Dominic's mouth twitched in amusement. "Your lovely green silk robe has given way to this?"

"I shall be happy to wear the other . . . anytime you wish it, milord."

"I look forward to the day when your green silk robe shall find a permanent place on the floor at the foot of our bed."

Catherine ran her tongue over her suddenly dry lips. "How is your head?"

"Better." He shoved his hands behind his neck as he leaned against the headboard.

"Then you don't want the sleeping draught?"

"You're the only sleeping draught I need." Onyx eyes moved over her body, as if he could see through her thick layer of clothes. "Soon you'll have no need of a nightrail to warm you."

Catherine flushed and turned to leave, then stopped short and turned back. Her eyes fastened on the width of his shoulder, his muscular arms, narrow hips, and firm, flat belly. She could well remember what lay below the edge of the sheet.

"I was wondering, Dominic . . ."

"Yes, love?"

"About . . . the last time we made love . . . about the pleasure you gave to me. I was wondering if a man could receive that same sort of pleasure from a woman?"

When he spoke at last, Dominic's voice sounded rough and husky, and there was no mistaking the hard ridge swelling beneath the sheets. "It is the same, yes. But many women find the idea . . . distasteful."

Catherine's palms began to sweat. "I believe, milord, I should not find it so. In fact, quite the reverse." She moved toward him. "I believe I should enjoy giving you pleasure. That is . . . if you would enjoy it, too."

"If I would enjoy . . . ? Ah, God." Dominic reached for her, slid his hand around her neck, and drew her mouth down to his for a long, fiery kiss. By the time he had finished, Catherine was breathing as raggedly as he.

She shed her heavy robe and tossed it over a chair, then approached the bed and gently drew back the covers. Dominic's arousal rested hot and thick against his belly. Catherine reached for it, touched it, and heard him groan. Bending over, she trailed soft, wet kisses along the inside of his thigh, then stopped.

"What is this?" For the first time, she noticed the small brown spot in the shape of a waning moon that marked his upper leg.

"That, my love, is the Edgemont crest. It's the way my father knew I was his son. I call it the Edgemont curse."

Catherine leaned forward and carefully placed her lips

on the spot. Beneath her mouth she felt him tremble. When her small hand wrapped around his shaft, Dominic drew her toward him and kissed her, cupping a breast in his long brown fingers.

Catherine pulled away. "I want you to promise that you will let me do this for you . . . that you will let me love you."

"What of you, fire kitten? Will you not allow me to soothe your passions as well?"

Catherine shook her head. "Tonight is yours, my love. My gift to you, if you will but take it."

With a hint of reluctance, Dominic's hand slid away from her breast to settle once more upon the bed. Catherine moved forward, her heavy braid falling across his chest. Dominic's muscles grew taut as her lips covered his and her fingers curved once more around his thick shaft. In minutes he was breathing hard, his hips straining, his head thrown back. When Catherine's mouth followed her hand, her lips tasting, coaxing, then drawing him inside, Dominic whispered her name.

It was heady this feeling of power, this seemingly limitless control she held over him, the pleasure she was giving. His breathing was rapid, his body bathed in a fine sheen of sweat, his lean hips grinding against the soft feather mattress. Still, she did not stop.

When she knew he was close, she felt his grip on her arm.

"Catherine . . . if you don't stop now—"

"Hush," she said, leaning over him, her long braid skimming his belly. "This I do for me as well."

He came then, in wracking spasms that shook his body and forced her name from his lips. Again and again, he reached that plateau of sweet pleasure she had carried him to and Catherine exulted in the heady sense of control.

When he reached for her, she stopped him. "Close your eyes, my love. Let the last of your worries fade."

She left him a moment then returned with a cool, damp cloth to cleanse away the remnants of his seed. Catherine pulled the sheet up to his chin, bent over and kissed his lips. She could hear his even breathing, and knew that he was sleeping.

Smiling into the darkness, she returned to her room confident that in some small way she had helped him battle the unseen foe that ate at his heart—and the problems that until tonight he believed he faced alone.

Chapter Twenty-three

DOMINIC AWOKE BEFORE SUNUP, feeling rested as he hadn't in days. He lay still for a moment, recalling the events of the evening ... recalling Catherine.

Dominic's whole body tightened. What the hell kind of a man was he? In a room on the other side of that door was a woman whose beautiful body and fiery nature had called to him from the very first moment he saw her. Catherine slept just a few feet away, her warm, willing body waiting to accept his, needing the release he had needed last eve.

Dominic thought of her soft pale skin and ripe lush breasts, and muttered a savage oath. He was no longer just that "damnable Gypsy bastard." He was lord of the manor and the lady was his wife! On top of that he loved her—it was time to stop dwelling on broken commitments and vows he could not keep, and make this madness end.

Ignoring the tension that suddenly churned in his stomach, Dominic tossed back the covers and strode naked across the room, but stopped as he reached for the heavy iron latch. Catherine deserved more from him than a quick morning tumble. She deserved an elegant supper, fine French wine, and whispered words of passion. She deserved a night of seduction.

He would see that she had it. And when the evening came to an end, he would claim her. Make love to her for hours on end and plant his seed so deep it would have no choice but to take root and grow.

The churning in his stomach grew stronger, but Dominic ignored it. Instead he set his jaw, his expression an odd mixture of anticipation and grim determination. Tonight he would make her his wife in truth—and never sleep alone again.

"Wear the burgundy brocade," Dominic said to her softly, his gaze searing as his eyes moved slowly down her body.

Catherine felt a warming in her cheeks. It was the gown she had altered so scandalously low, the gown she had worn to seduce him. "Yes, milord," she said breathlessly.

"Cook will be making something special. I hope you will enjoy it." His eyes suggested that what would follow would be far more pleasant, and Catherine's cheeks grew warmer still.

"I'll be home early," he promised as Catherine followed him into the entry. His smile almost a caress, he turned and bent over her hand. "Until tonight, my love." Firm lips brushed her fingers and the heat of his mouth sent a honeyed warmth through her veins.

"Until tonight." He left her then, striding off toward the stables, his broad shoulders and narrow hips disappearing out the door.

All day she waited, the hours creeping slowly as they never had before. Only the time she spent with little Janos passed quickly, though that had left her more worried for him than she'd been before.

"I miss them, Catrina," he had said. "So much it hurts in here." His small hand came up to rest on his heart.

Catherine hugged him. "I know, Janos, but soon you will come to love us just as much."

"I love you now. But I miss Medela and Pearsa and Stavo. I miss the children and the dancing and the violins. I miss waking up in the wagon, traveling to new and different places...."

"You'll come to love it here," she promised, praying the

school and making new friends would help, but she was no longer sure.

They read a bedtime story together, then Catherine left Janos with Percy and returned to her room. When she glanced at the clock on the mantel and saw how late the hour had grown, wings of anticipation fluttered in her stomach. She bathed and dressed with care, pinning her hair up in a simple wreath above her head, and donned the shamelessly low-cut burgundy gown.

She blushed when she looked in the mirror, and wondered if she really ought to wear it, but the look on Dominic's face when she walked into the drawing room told her she had pleased him.

"You look beautiful," he said, brushing her cheek with a kiss. "I used to wonder what you would look like dressed as a lady."

"You did?"

"Often, though as a Gypsy, I was loath to admit it."

Catherine smiled. "Now that you've known the two, which of us do you prefer—Catrina, the sun-haired Gypsy, or Catherine, the lady?"

"I prefer, my love, that you are a little of both." Dominic's warm smile, white against his dark skin, stirred a second flutter of wings.

Supper was a lavish affair served in the dining room. Golden goblets, gold-rimmed porcelain plates, and gold candelabra crowned a table as elegant as any she had ever seen.

"It's lovely," she said. "You've gone to a great deal of trouble."

He brought her hand to his lips and kissed the palm. "To me, love, you are far more precious than gold."

They ate a meal of creamed sole and sweetbreads of veal, asparagus, spinach, sausage and pepper pie. Dessert was a sweet, molded in the shape of a hedgehog and stuck with almond quills, served with a sweet white wine. They took tea and cakes in the drawing room.

As delicious as the food was, neither of them ate very

much. The flutter in Catherine's stomach wouldn't allow it, and Dominic seemed far too intense to be able to even taste it. Aside from the hunger in his eyes and the overall tension he couldn't quite disguise, he was more charming than she had ever seen him, flashing heart-rending smiles and lavishing her with compliments. No wonder the London ladies thought him all the vogue!

Through it all, Catherine felt his desire for her in every look, every heated glance. There were moments when she wanted to push back her chair, grab his hand, and race upstairs.

Of course, she did not. Just waited like the lady she was—though she'd scarcely behaved like one of late—smiled and conversed and waited for Dominic to make his wishes clear.

"My lady wife," he finally said, the last word spoken with some authority and what might have been a hint of trepidation, "I believe it is time we retired." Hot black eyes fixed on the bulge of her breasts, nearly exposed in the burgundy gown, and Dominic reached for her hand.

Catherine wet her lips. "Yes, milord."

"Dominic," he corrected, his thumb making warm, tingly circles on her shoulder.

"Dominic," she whispered.

They climbed the stairs hand in hand, Dominic guiding her past her room to the master's bedchamber down the hall. He opened the door, bent down and lifted her into his arms. Carrying her into the room, he set her on her feet, her body sliding slowly the length of his, kissed the nape of her neck, and began unfastening her gown.

In minutes she stood naked before him, her hair loose from its pins and tumbling around her shoulders. With trembling fingers, she reached for a button on Dominic's coat, and in that same short span of time he stood as naked as she, his broad shoulders and narrow hips gleaming bronze in the glow of the candles.

Dominic's mouth covered hers in a searing kiss that left her weak and breathless. More kisses followed as he carried her to the deep feather mattress and began making slow, beautiful love to her.

"I need you, fire kitten, as I've never needed a woman."

They were the last words he spoke before he took her, sliding inside, heavy and hard, to join them and make them one. Catherine rejoiced in the feel of him, letting him lift her to the fiery heights of passion he had taken her before.

"Catherine," Dominic whispered, moving faster and harder, pounding into her welcoming body, his own so tense and hot he felt he might explode. God, she felt good moving beneath him, her small hands clutching his shoulders, her head thrown back as she neared the summit of her passion. He meant to say *I love you,* to whisper the words she needed to hear, words that would bind them as nothing else could.

But as he watched her small pink tongue run wetly across her mouth, saw her thick dark lashes drift down to her cheeks, his eye caught the carving in the headboard above the bed.

The Gravenwold crest. It had been etched in the polished wood a hundred years ago, just as his hatred of it was etched into his heart. *The Gravenwold crest.* Six generations of wealth and status and all-consuming power. Six generations—and tonight perhaps another. An heir to the Gravenwold title and fortune, a child to take over the lands and property his father had loved above all else.

Part of him welcomed the thought, yearned for it. But another, deeper part heard his father's triumphant laughter echoing across the room almost as if he stood there. Dominic blocked the haunting image as best he could and pounded into Catherine. He felt her grip tighten on his shoulders, knew she had found release, and worked to find his own.

Instead, his loins clenched in agony, refusing to let go his seed. Muscle and sinew screamed in protest, bone and blood seemed at war with his will. As he drove himself on in a frenzy of need, Catherine moaned and her body shook once more. Dominic thrust into her like a madman.

But his body only tightened, every corded muscle straining, every vessel, every fiber, and still no release would come.

There would be no child this eve, he thought bitterly, an agony of despair washing over him. He had once more bested his father, but in winning he had lost himself.

Catherine felt the last of the second hot wave begin to fade and tensed as she waited for Dominic to follow. Instead she felt his hardness dragged from her body, taking its heat and leaving her empty as Dominic rolled away.

"Dominic?" she whispered, uncertain what had happened, feeling suddenly afraid. She came up beside him, a hand on his shoulder. His muscles were as rigid as steel, his hands balled into white-knuckled fists. "What has happened? What is wrong?"

Dominic turned to face her, his handsome face ravaged. "It seems, my love, that my mind and my heart have accepted you as my wife . . . but my body has not."

Dear God. "Let me help you." Catherine reached for him. "Let me . . ."

Dominic caught her wrist. "No." He shook his head. "No." Rolling from the bed, he padded across the floor and picked up his dressing gown, shrugging it onto his broad shoulders. "I was afraid something like this might happen." He reached the door and pulled it open. "I'm sorry." Then he stepped into the hall and drew it closed.

Catherine climbed out of bed in a state of numbness. When had things gone wrong? What had happened? Her experience with men was sorely limited. She didn't know exactly what Dominic had suffered, but she intended to find out. As she stooped to pick up her garments, her brocade gown and cast-off slippers, she worried about her husband, remembering the desolate look on his handsome face. What was he thinking? What would become of him now?

Her movements wooden, Catherine carried the clothes into her bedchamber, her heart aching for the man downstairs. Was there nothing she could do to help him?

But she knew this time there was not.

In the hours and days that followed, Catherine saw a remote, hostile, guarded man she scarcely recognized as the one she had married. Though he was always gentle and considerate to her, to the servants and the people he worked with, he had turned into a demon. He criticized their every task, shouted orders until his voice grew hoarse, worked until it seemed he would drop, then drank himself into a stupor.

There were smudges beneath his eyes and his powerful body looked gaunt. God in heaven, if only there was something she could do!

She tried to show him her love, tried to be gentle and understanding, but in truth, in a way he frightened her. She would rather he railed at her as he did the others. She would rather he shouted his frustration than to grace her with a tender smile that did not reach his eyes. How long could he hold himself in check? she wondered. What would he do when he finally let go?

"I'm so worried about him, Gabby," Catherine said as she watched him early one morning from the window of her upstairs chamber. "I hardly know him anymore." Desperate to understand what had happened, Catherine had told Gabby everything, even what had occurred the last time they had made love.

"I know of such things," Gabby had told her, her delicate features turning pink. "When a man's mind and body are not in accord, sometimes 'e is not even able to . . . 'ow do you say? 'E cannot perform the act of love."

Oh, God, no wonder he wanted to wait, to work things out in his mind.

"You must remember," Gabby said softly, "'e is Lord Gravenwold, but 'e is also a Gypsy. At the tavern, I knew many of them, enough to know they think differently about love and honor . . . about revenge. If 'e has made this vow, as 'e has said, breaking it cannot be easy. You must try to help him."

And she had tried. She had shown him her love in every small way she could think of, but when she saw his temper snap at one of the servants, saw him lash out for no apparent cause, she wondered what else lay beneath the surface of his troubled mind and heart.

"If only there were something I could do," she repeated, speaking her thoughts aloud, her gaze fixed on the path that led to the stables.

Standing beside her, Gabby swung her light brown eyes to Catherine's face. "Why do you not tell 'im about the babe?"

"Babe?" Catherine repeated. "What babe?"

Gabby's slender fingers came to rest on Catherine's stomach. "The one you carry in 'ere."

"Don't be silly, I'm not with child."

"No?"

"Of course not. It isn't possible."

"What of your last monthly?" Gabby pressed. "Why 'ave your gowns begun to grow snug?"

Catherine's mind whirled. "It isn't possible. I can't be pregnant. It's been months since we ... since he's ..." *And she'd had her woman's time only once.* "Dear God in heaven."

Catherine sank down on the window seat, her fingers clutching the front of her sprigged muslin gown. She thought of the subtle changes in her body, the slight thickening at her waist, the tenderness in her breasts she had noticed of late, but until now thought little about. With a flash of certainty, she knew Gabby spoke the truth. "Dear Lord, it's true."

"What will 'Is Lordship say when 'e finds out?"

"I don't know." She glanced back out the window, saw him disappear into the stable, then ride out a few moments later atop his big gray stallion. "A child is the last thing in the world Dominic wants. He wouldn't have married me in the first place if he'd known I carried his babe." A hard lump swelled in her throat. "He would rather I bore him a bastard."

"Mon Dieu," Gabby whispered.

"I can't imagine what he'll say . . . what he might do."

"'E would not make you get rid of it?"

"Get rid of it? What do you mean?" Catherine came to her feet, her heart starting to hammer uncomfortably.

"It is not uncommon for a man to take 'is mistress to a woman who can . . . rid 'er of 'er problem."

Problem—that was what he had called it once. Catherine splayed her fingers across her stomach, touching the slight curve, discovering an instinct that was sweet and poignant. "This child is mine, as well." Unconsciously, she squared her shoulders. "I love children. I would especially love his." She smiled. "I just wouldn't go."

Gabby covered Catherine's hand where it rested on her stomach. "It would not be the first time a woman 'as been forced."

"What!" Catherine's insides churned. "He—he wouldn't!" But thinking of the hostile man she had seen these past few days, a man torn nearly in two, she wasn't really so sure. "I've got to get out of here. I need time to think."

"You will go to your uncle?"

"No." Catherine strode toward the bed. "I need a woman's guidance in this. I shall go to London, to Amelia. London's closer . . . and I need a friend."

"I will go with you, of course."

"Yes." She bent and dragged a heavy tapestry carpetbag from beneath the high canopied bed. "Dominic will be away till late this eve. We can be gone before his return."

"You do not intend to tell him you are leaving?"

"The way he's been behaving, I'm afraid he might not let me go." Catherine drew open the satchel. "Get your things together quickly, then come back here. I'll order the carriage brought round. If we hurry, we can make London by nightfall."

"Oui, My Lady." And Gabby was gone.

Percival Nelson eased the door to the marchioness's chamber silently closed. Straightening the young lord's clothes, he hadn't meant to eavesdrop, but the plaintive note in Her Ladyship's voice had reached even his deaf old ears. He wrung his thin, veined hands. God's bones, His Lordship was hardly an ogre. Did Lady Catherine really believe he would wish her babe harm? Why, the boy would more likely crow like a rooster, once he came round to the notion.

Percy left the room and shuffled down the hall, worry etching his aged face, his good eye darting around to find the stairs. So the boy had a bit of a temper—always had—always would. God's teeth, a black mood once in a while wasn't reason to hie off to London!

The young lord would put things in order—he'd been through worse and weathered the storm. In time, he'd be just fine.

Percy started down the stone stairs, his bony fingers gripping the polished mahogany banister. He had just reached the landing when a covey of servants flew past him to collect the mistress's trunks. Below him someone shouted for the Gravenwold carriage.

God's bones! She'd be gone in a thrice—and His Lordship still out in the fields! He glanced around for Blythebury, thinking to ask his assistance, then thought better of it. His Lordship would scarcely appreciate his gossiping among the servants. He would have to attend to the matter himself.

With that thought in mind, Percy creaked toward the rear of the house, heading for the stables in search of a lad to fetch His Lordship home. Behind him, after a moment's conversation with Blythebury informing him of her departure, Catherine headed out the front door.

"For God's sake, Percy, what is it?" Dominic swung down off his big gray stallion even before the animal slid to a halt. It had taken hours for the stable boy Percy had sent to discover where Dominic had gone. But the urgency in the old man's message had him riding as if he were chased by the hounds of hell.

"Seems best, Your Lordship, if we speak in private."

"Yes, of course." Dominic handed the reins to a groom and followed Percy's aged movements toward the house.

"You'll be wanting a change of clothes and something to eat," Percy went on, his brittle old shoulders hunching forward, a scarecrow in black and gray.

"Clothes?" Dominic repeated, gripping the old man's thin arm and turning him around. "Where is it you think I'm going?"

"Why, after your wife, sir."

Dominic bristled. "Catherine is gone?"

"To London, milord. You see, she feared for the babe."

"Babe? What babe? Percy, you are hardly making sense."

"Your babe, sir. The one Her Ladyship carries."

Dominic only shook his head. "Catherine isn't carrying my babe. We haven't . . ."

"That's what she thought, too, milord. But it seems you are both mistaken."

Dominic's breath left in a rush. "What are you saying? That Catherine conceived before we were wed?"

Percy's ears turned pink. "You would know more of that than I, sir. Whatever the case, Her Ladyship carries your child, and she is afraid you would see it destroyed. It seems she believes you would not have married her a'tall, if you had known. She said you would rather she bore you a bastard."

Dominic's chest grew so tight he could barely breathe. "Ah, God." How long ago had he said that? It seemed to him now so farfetched an idea he couldn't quite grasp it. "How do you know all this? Surely Lady Gravenwold didn't tell you."

"I overheard her speaking to her maid, sir."

"Then you believe it's the truth?"

"Yes, milord, without doubt. She was quite upset about it."

Dominic halted abruptly. "She didn't want the child?"

"Oh, no, milord. Quite the contrary. She said she would love to have your babe most of all."

Some of the tightness eased in his chest.

"And you, milord?" Percy asked. "How do you feel about it?"

Dominic stopped on the gravel path. How did he indeed? He had worried about this very occurrence, agonized about it, done everything in his power to prevent it. Now that it had happened, how *did* he feel?

Standing there on the path, Dominic heard a mockingbird call from the trees, making the sound of a whippoorwill. He saw how bright and clear the sky was, how light and fluffy the clouds.

How did he feel? He felt unburdened, lighter somehow, like a terrible weight had been lifted from his shoulders. After all his anguish, his determination—his failure—God had made the choice for him. Fate had decided, the stones had been cast, the future laid out in a path he could not—would not—change.

For the first time in days, Dominic smiled. "Like a prisoner freed of his chains. Like a blind man who can once again see." His father had won—and yet he felt as if he had. He didn't understand it, but he didn't care.

He felt joyous, exuberant.

A child of his loins grew in Catherine's womb. For Dominic, it seemed he'd been granted a new life as well. "Where has she gone?"

"To her cousin, Amelia."

Dominic clapped his friend on the back. "Thank you Percy, for everything." He started striding toward the house, then stopped and turned. "Tell the others their purses will be the fatter for putting up with me these past few days." He grinned devilishly, the old man grinned back, and Dominic strode away.

"Are you quite certain you're all right?" Amelia stood at the door to Catherine's bedchamber, her slender silhouette backlit by the flickering light of the sconces down the hall. The walnut clock on the mantel struck half past one.

Wearing her high-necked white cotton nightrail, Catherine climbed up on the high four-poster bed. "Now that I'm here, I'm fine. Thank you for listening." They had sat in the drawing room downstairs, sipping chocolate and talking for hours, but in truth, she had told Amelia very little.

She couldn't bear to speak of Dominic, of their problems, or her fears. She just told her friend that she was with child and that she'd been frightened of what was to come. She had needed a woman's guidance, needed Amelia's help and friendship, and so she had set off for London.

"I can't begin to tell you how good it is to see you," Amelia said from the doorway. "I'm terribly glad you came." With a last warm smile, Amelia closed the door.

Catherine lay in the darkness, listening to the heavy ticking of the clock, thinking of the long, tiring journey she had made from Gravenwold Manor. What had Dominic done when Blythebury told him she was gone? She'd told the butler that her cousin wished her to visit, and that she thought this was a good time to go.

Would Dominic come after her? She didn't really think so, at least not right away. He would probably appreciate the time alone.

Catherine rolled over and plumped her thick feather pillow, trying to get comfortable, hoping to fall asleep. Unconsciously, her hand drifted down to her stomach and she pressed against the small life growing there. What would have happened if she'd told Dominic the truth about the babe? Now that she was away from him, she wondered if she had done the right thing in leaving. Dominic loved children as much as she did. Surely he would love the child she carried. And yet she still wasn't sure.

Catherine felt a hard lump swell ·in her throat. So much had happened between them. So much . . . and not enough.

Tomorrow she would write to her uncle, ask him if there was a way to dissolve their marriage. If Dominic was determined not to claim his child, then she would not force him. She would find a way to give him his freedom; after all, that was what he had wanted all along.

The ache in her throat grew more painful. She might have cried, if it hadn't been for the tiny living creature that grew in her womb. She had the child to think of now, and she would protect that child with every ounce of her will. Dominic's grim Gypsy oaths and vows of revenge had no place in her life from now on.

Yet she loved him still. No amount of time, no words, no amount of pain could change that. She wouldn't tell him about the babe until she had spoken to her uncle— until she felt safe. Then she would set him free.

"My beloved Gypsy," she said softly into the darkness, "I have loved you for so long." Words she had spoken before and never meant more than she did in that moment.

Love and hate, passion and sorrow—emotions so far apart yet so close together it seemed they often were one. For Dominic, it had been that way since their first turbulent encounter. She suspected he had felt those same conflicting emotions even about his father.

Joy, sorrow, loneliness, heartache—which had Dominic felt for her? Did he love her—or hate her? And how would he feel about the babe?

If only things could have been different.

Catherine feared that they could not.

Chapter Twenty-four

HOW LONG HAD SHE SLEPT? Catherine wondered, straining to hear the sound in the darkness that had dragged her from a restless sleep. It came again, so soft she barely heard it, yet it was there, followed by a sliver of yellow light as the door drew silently open.

She started to call out, to ask who it was, but some inner voice, some vague memory of another such night last year, warned her not to. Instead she shifted quietly on the bed, her hand slipping out, groping the bedstand for something to use as a weapon. There were few servants in the house; most had retired early to their quarters out back, over the carriage house, allowing the women an evening of privacy.

Now Catherine wished fervently that they were still there. Her fingers searched the bedstand until her hand closed over a heavy brass candlestick. In the darkness, she slid it toward her then dragged it beneath the linen sheets.

For an instant, the door swung open, and in the light that lit the room before it closed, Catherine glimpsed a cloaked and hooded figure. It was too dark to make out who it was, but the figure was too tall to be a woman, and his shoulders were so broad they seemed to fill the room. It was a man, she knew, though she could not see him clearly, and because she could not, Catherine did not cry out.

"Dominic?" she whispered, half of her praying it was he, the other half praying it was not. Had he come because he loved her and wanted her to come back home? Or had he somehow guessed the truth about the babe, something overheard by one of the servants?

And if he knew, what would he do?

Catherine's chest constricted. "Dominic?" she whispered again as the intruder approached, her heart thumping hard against her ribs. When the man moved closer, Catherine saw the glint of moonlight on the blue-black hair at his temple, then his arms went up. She caught the outline of a long, heavy iron poker gripped in his hands and screamed, rolling out of the way an instant before the smoke-blackened rod smashed the carved wooden headboard into splinters.

"God in heaven!" she cried out, trying to avoid the second heavy blow. "I love you, Dominic. Please don't do this." With trembling fingers, Catherine lifted the tall brass candlestick and hurled it at the figure looming above her. It bounced off his shoulder and crashed on the floor.

"Amelia! Somebody help me!" In an instant, he was on her, gripping her arms, his hands digging into her flesh until she winced. Big hands, powerful hands, she realized dimly, not fine brown fingers—not Dominic.

Relief and fear combined in a rush that made her heart beat even harder, but if she died on the spot, she would not die of despair. *Dominic wouldn't hurt me,* she realized in some distant corner of her mind, and wondered how she ever could have believed he would.

"Who are you?" she demanded, working to keep her voice from shaking even as the tears slid down her cheeks. *Not Dominic, not Dominic, not Dominic.* The knowledge that her attacker was not the man she loved renewed her strength, and Catherine fought him like a tigress, clawing his face, scratching and biting. *Not Dominic, not Dominic.*

Then he was there, almost as if he had heard her. Stopping an instant in the doorway, taking in her struggles, then striding across the floor with a savage curse.

"Catherine!" he called to her as he gripped the man's lapel and spun him around, then slammed a fist into his ribs. The huge man flew backward, his hood falling off to reveal a mustached man far bigger than Dominic, with thick black hair drawn back in a queue.

Though the cloaked man outweighed him a good fifty pounds, he was no match for Dominic's fury. Blow after blow rained down on the beefy man's head, blood flew from a cut in his lip, then a powerful right smashed his nose, sending a spray of red across the front of his white linen shirt.

In minutes the man lay gasping on the floor, Dominic standing over him, his hands still balled into fists.

"My God, what's happened?" That from Amelia, who stood in the doorway.

A sleepy-eyed Gabby rushed in next. *"Mon Dieu."*

Dominic pulled a small-caliber pistol from the inside of his frock coat and aimed it at the man slumped on the floor. "See that someone goes for a constable," he said to Gabby.

"Yes, My Lord."

As she hurried to do his bidding, Dominic jerked the big man to his feet. "Who are you?"

He teetered precariously, groaning, his huge hands cradling his battered face. He leaned against the wall for support.

"His name is Nathan Cave," Amelia supplied. "H-he worked for Edmund."

"Yes," Catherine said, "I remember him quite clearly."

"Edmund is dead," Dominic said to Cave, gripping him by the shirtfront. "Who is it you work for now?"

When the man didn't answer, Dominic shook him. "Who, Nathan?"

Still nothing.

"H-he must have done it for Edmund," Amelia said. "He must have somehow been involved in Catherine's abduction."

Dominic eyed the huge man with speculation. "Are you

as big a fool as you look?" he pressed. "You realize you'll spend the rest of your life in Newgate for this—if you're lucky enough to avoid the hangman. Is it your wish to go there alone?"

The man seemed to wither before their very eyes. Nathan swallowed hard. "I ain't goin' alone. I ain't rottin' in that bloody bog house by meself, not when it were 'er idea in the first place." He pointed a thick callused finger toward the door. "If I go, *she* goes."

"Amelia?" Catherine gasped.

"He's lying," she said. "Surely you don't believe him."

Careful to keep the pistol leveled at Nathan's chest, Dominic let go of the big man's shirt and turned his attention to the pale-faced woman clutching the front of her blue silk robe. "It was you all along, wasn't it? Edmund did it for you, but it was your idea, yours—not his."

"H-he did it for Eddie and me, yes, but I-I was not involved." She turned beseeching eyes on Catherine. "Surely you believe me. We're friends, after all. We've always been friends."

"Have we, Amelia?" Catherine asked. "Or have you been so worried about your son's inheritance, about your own position and wealth, that you would see me dead?"

"No—no . . . I . . ."

"The time has come, madam, for you to admit the truth." Dominic fixed hard black eyes on her face. "If you don't, you may be certain it will go the worse for you."

Amelia's blue eyes welled with tears which trailed in glistening droplets down her cheeks. "I had no choice—can't you see that? If you hadn't let Catherine keep her title and inheritance, it might have ended with Edmund's death and your marriage. But once I knew my son could still inherit . . . that with Catherine out of the way, he would become the next earl, I-I had to do it."

She swung her eyes to Catherine's. "Tonight, after you told me you had conceived, I went to Nathan. It was supposed to look like an accident, as if you had fallen down the stairs and hit your head. I thought this might be our last chance."

Catherine stared at Amelia as if seeing her for the very first time. "What I had was also yours and Eddie's. I tried to tell you that. I tried to make you see, but—" Catherine's voice broke on the last, and Dominic moved to her side and slid an arm around her shoulders, drawing her against him.

Footsteps sounded on the stairs and a constable and several other men swept into the room. While Catherine pulled on her wrapper, Dominic filled them in on what had happened, promising to give them a more complete statement on the morrow.

"Get the two of 'em outta here," the constable said to his men, who led Nathan, bound securely, and a tearful Amelia away.

"What about little Eddie?" Catherine asked, once they had gone, leaning wearily against Dominic's chest. "He's lost both his mother and father. I know Amelia deserves to go to prison, but . . . I can't bear the thought of her being in there. I can't bear to think of her suffering like that."

Dominic tipped her chin with his warm brown fingers. "Gravenwold interests are extremely far-reaching. We've several sugar plantations in the West Indies. If Amelia will agree to take Eddie and go there—and never set foot on English shores again—I shall see she's released."

Catherine smiled, her eyes soft with gratitude. "Thank you."

"Get dressed," Dominic ordered. "We're getting out of here."

"Where are we going?"

"To my town house. It isn't far. I want you away from all this sadness."

"What about little Eddie?"

"I will stay with the boy," Gabby said from the doorway.

"All right," Catherine agreed.

They left in the Gravenwold carriage, the horses' hooves a noisy echo on the empty cobblestone streets. The hour was late, the streets nearly vacant except for a hired hack or two. They passed a small tavern and the bawdy laughter of its patrons drifted in through the open window. A milk girl passed in front of the carriage, heavy wooden buckets slung over her slender shoulders.

In minutes, they reached Hanover Square and the carriage drew to a halt. Dominic alighted and helped Catherine down, then they climbed the steep stone steps to the town house. Once inside, it was apparent by the fire in the hearth and the tray of cold meats, wine, and cheeses sitting on a drum table near the sofa that Dominic had sent word of his pending arrival.

When the butler, sleep-tousled though he appeared, took Catherine's cloak, she turned to face her husband. "It's been a long night, milord. I'm sorry for the trouble I've caused, but there are things I have to tell you . . . things we need to discuss."

"You're right, my love. We've a good deal to discuss, and we will . . . but not this eve. Not after all you've been through." He smiled softly. "Tonight it's enough that you're safe and that we're together."

There was something about him . . . something different. The haunted look had left his eyes, and though it was obvious he'd had a long, tiring journey, his shoulders looked straighter, his skin more robust. He seemed at ease as he hadn't in days—as he hadn't since his time with the caravan.

"What is it, Dominic?" Catherine asked. "What has changed?"

Dominic flashed such a heart-stopping smile her heart turned over. "My wife is having my babe. What could change a man more than that?"

"You know?" Catherine gasped.

"I know and I'm grateful. More thankful than you'll ever know." He kissed her soundly on the lips. "Thank you, love." Before she could protest, Dominic swept her into his arms and took the stairs up to his chamber two at a time.

"What—what are you doing? Where are you taking me?"

"To my bed, wife of my heart. To finish the task I set for myself several nights ago ... though it appears the deed has already been accomplished." He flashed a roguish grin that warmed places she had tried to close off.

The door latched behind them, and he set her on her feet, his bright smile fading as his gaze ran over her face. Thick black brows came together over eyes that looked suddenly uncertain. "I know why you left," he said softly. "I know you believed I would hurt the babe."

Catherine felt an ache rise up in her throat. "You've been so distant ... so angry ... I didn't know what to believe."

"I know I was behaving like a madman, but sooner or later, I would have worked things out. God, I'm sorry for what I put you through."

"I knew how strongly you felt about not having an heir. When that man came into my room, I thought it was you. I thought ..."

Dominic's face turned ashen. "What?"

"I saw his hair ... the same blue-black as yours. He was tall and broad-shouldered—"

Dominic swept her into his arms. "Don't. I can't bear to think that I drove you to believe such things."

"I saw his hands," Catherine said against his chest, "I knew then it wasn't you—I also knew in that moment that I had been wrong to leave—that you would never have hurt me."

Dominic's hard arms tightened around her. "You'll never know how much I regret the things I've said, the things I've done. If I could do it all over I would ... but I can't. I won't deny I'm a difficult man to live with. I'm demanding and possessive and sometimes bad-tempered. But you are my life and my heart. You mean everything to me ... everything. Never believe for a moment that I would hurt you."

"Dominic ..." she said softly, feeling the sting of tears. He cupped her cheek with his hand, his fingers warm

and strong, his black eyes searching, beseeching, touching
her very soul. "I love you," he said softly. "My beloved
Catherine, I have loved you for so long."

Epilogue

Gravenwold Manor
October, 1806

OUTSIDE THE MULLIONED WINDOW, autumn winds rattled the panes but a fire burned brightly in the marble-manteled hearth. From where he lay in his huge four-poster bed, Dominic watched red- and gold-leafed branches scrape against the glass, his body warm as it pressed the length of Catherine's.

The branch shook in the gusty breeze, the leaves shimmering in the early morning sun, their fiery hue the same as Catherine's hair. Dominic's fingers sifted through the silky strands beside her cheek, one errant curl drifting around his finger. Idly his hand roamed lower, moving over her sleeping figure till he touched the heavy fullness of her breast, the tawny crest soft until his finger began to trace the outline in lazy circles and it rose to a high, stiff peak.

Dominic's loins stirred, his shaft growing hard beneath the blanket.

Catherine's bottom snuggled against his hips, and he felt her shapely legs brush the muscular length of his own. Beneath the curve of her breast, her belly swelled invitingly. She blossomed a little more each day, the babe she carried snug within her womb. Other men might feel little desire for a woman with child, but Dominic's own desire had not lessened. She looked beautiful. Ripe and womanly.

363

He wanted her every time he looked at her. He wanted her now.

He listened to her gentle breathing, leaned over and pressed a soft warm kiss on the nape of her neck. Catherine stirred, pressing even closer, drawing her knees up slightly, shifting her position until they fit together perfectly, her bottom against his loins, his shaft pressing hot and hard against the soft damp petals of her sex.

Dominic groaned. He should wake her, kiss her, whisper words of love before he took her. Yet when he moved closer, easing himself inside, he found her wet and ready.

"Minx," he whispered, leaning over her, knowing she had been awake from the start and wanting him as much as he wanted her.

Catherine smiled softly as he massaged another breast, bringing the nipple to the same pouting peak of awareness. He nibbled an ear, sucking the lobe, then trailed soft kisses along her neck and shoulder. His hands moved to her hips, lifting them a little to slide himself inside.

She gasped as his stiff arousal filled her, and Dominic chuckled softly. "Such a tasty little wench," he whispered, his teeth gently nipping an ear. She arched her back, deepening the position of his shaft, then began to wriggle slowly against his hips.

"God, you feel good." In minutes, he was gripping her buttocks, plunging against her, and she was working to meet each powerful thrust. He could feel it coming, a spiraling wave of pleasure that he fought to hold at bay. With long, measured strokes, he built that same hot feeling in Catherine, stoking the flames of passion until she trembled, driving into her until she cried his name.

His own release came just seconds after hers, rocking him with its sweetness, seeping through his limbs with incredible warmth. He slid his arms around her as it dimmed to a feeling of contentment, of joy, a beautiful feeling of at last being home.

They might have slept and made love again—he had been working hard with his horses, she with her school—

they deserved a day of rest. But a knock at the door set that idea away. Muttering a curse at what could not be, Dominic bade the door opened and saw Percy standing in the hall.

"You've a visitor, Your Lordship. Lady says she is your mother."

"My mother?" Dominic swung his long legs to the floor and grabbed up his dressing gown.

"Pearsa is here?" Catherine asked.

"I don't know." In all her years, she had never come to the manor. Could she have traveled so far just to see him? Would she come to a place she'd for years forsworn to avoid? "Show her into the small salon. Tell her I'll be down in a moment."

"Take your time," he said to Catherine. "You can join us for chocolate and cakes whenever you're ready."

Catherine nodded, knowing he was asking for a moment alone. He wasn't certain what his mother wanted. He wasn't even sure it was really she.

Dressed in polished black boots, tan breeches, and a forest-green frock coat, he descended the wide stone stairs and went straight to the small salon. Pearsa sat with her back to him, her bright yellow skirts fanned out on the mohair sofa. When she shifted her position, the shiny gold coins on her wrists and those around her neck made a jingling sound that skittered across the room. The blouse she wore had been decorated with glittering beads, and a long red sash circled her too-thin waist.

She sat tenuously on the edge of the sofa, surveying her elegant surroundings, a hand reaching toward a fragile Wedgwood porcelain doll, coming close but not quite touching, afraid to pick it up for fear she might break it.

She looked like some small, delicate bird with bright-colored feathers, a tiny creature caught in a gilded cage. She seemed to be watching, waiting for the cage door to open, meaning to take wing and fly away.

"It's good to see you, my mother," Dominic said with a smile as he approached. Pearsa returned the smile, coming to her feet, letting him envelop her thin body in his warm, protective embrace. "Is everything all right?"

"Yes, yes. Things are as they always are." She took a step backward. "Let me look at you, my son." She surveyed him from head to foot, taking in his perfectly tailored clothes and polished Hessians, his white stock and frilled linen shirt. A soft smile curved her lips, and a look that might have been wistful crept into her eyes. "You see, I was right. You are his son, as you were meant to be from the start."

For an instant, Dominic bristled, then the tension drained away. "There was a time when those words would have stirred my anger. That time is gone."

Pearsa nodded. "That is why I have come."

"You got word of my marriage?" He had sent news through the *Romane Gadjo,* friends of the Gypsy who relayed messages for them.

"Yes, my son. I also heard that you have refused to break your pledge. That you do not sleep with the woman who is your wife."

A faint smile played on his lips. He started to speak, but Pearsa stopped him.

"Hear me out, my son. I know of the oath you have taken. I know also of the part I play in that vow."

"Mother, I—"

"There are truths you must learn."

Dominic's thick black brow shot up. "Truths? What truths?"

"I have come to tell you something I should have told you long ago. It is about your father."

The muscles in his shoulders grew taut. "My father." He scoffed. "I know all I care to know about him."

"You are right in your feelings. He was a hard, cold, selfish man. There was little to love about him."

"Yet you loved him. When I was a boy, you told me how much."

"I loved him."

"Even though he abandoned you, abandoned both of us."

Pearsa glanced away, a grave, worried look on her face. "That is what I told you. For years I let you believe that your father abandoned us, that I went to him and he cast me away. It was not so. More than once, he came to me when you were a baby, offering me his protection. He would have given us a home, a place for you to grow up. I did not want it. I was lonely for him . . . I loved him as I've never loved another . . . but I was happy with the caravan—it was my home. After a while, he understood and left me in peace."

"Why didn't you tell me?" Dominic asked. "How could you let me believe the worst?"

"I cannot tell you I am sorry. If it meant having you with me, having your love all those years, then I would do it again."

"But—"

"I was afraid of losing you completely. I knew the lure he offered. I knew your quick mind would soak up the knowledge he could give you . . . I feared you would never return—and that I could not bear."

Releasing a weary sigh, Dominic stood up and walked to the hearth a few feet away. "Why didn't *he* tell me? He knew what I believed."

"I would like to think it was because of the love we once shared."

He returned to the sofa, sat down, and put his arms around her. "It's all right, Mother. There were many reasons for my hatred—too many to count. His treatment of you was only one. Still, I am glad you told me."

"He was a hard man, Domini. Foolish and unforgiving. One who did not know how to show he cared. But I believe, in his own way, he loved you."

Some old bitter hurt welled up in his chest, then it slipped away. "Thank you for telling me."

She shifted on the sofa and he realized how much her confession had cost her, how worried she had been that he would not forgive her. The unpleasant task over, she straightened her narrow shoulders.

"Now about the *Gadjo* woman—"

Dominic smiled. "You may rest easy, Mother. Catherine carries my babe."

Pearsa grinned. "She is the woman of your heart. I saw it in your eyes whenever you looked at her."

"Yes . . ." he said softly. "She is all that and more."

Pearsa's weathered hand touched his cheek, her eyes knowing, seeing things unspoken, as she had since he was a boy.

"How long can you stay?" Dominic asked, but she only shook her head.

"My home is a wagon beneath the stars, just as it has always been. I will go back as soon as I can."

Dominic said nothing to sway her. His father had seen it—the colorful bird would not be happy, even in a gilded cage.

They sat on the sofa for a while, Pearsa telling him stories of her travels, both of them laughing over some new form of *janjano* that had fleeced a *Gadjo*'s purse.

They drank coffee, which Pearsa complained was far too thin, Dominic spoke of Rai and Sumadji and his plans for the horses at Gravenwold, then Pearsa glanced toward the door and Catherine walked in.

"Good morning, my love," Dominic said, striding toward her, taking her arm and drawing her over to the couch.

Catherine's hand slid self-consciously to her gently rounded belly. She hesitated a moment, then smiled somewhat tremulously in Pearsa's direction. "It is good to see you . . . my mother." The uncertainty on her face was more than clear.

Pearsa's jet-black eyes moved to her swollen stomach. "It is good to see you, too . . . my daughter." There was a mist of tears in the old woman's eyes and an answering mist in Catherine's.

Dominic felt his own throat close up.

For a moment in time no one moved.

"Leave us, my son," Pearsa finally said, breaking the

spell. "There are things my daughter should know. The child is Romany, after all. There are spells she must cast, stones she must throw."

Dominic chuckled softly, and Catherine grinned.

They started talking, and he headed for the door, but a soft knock sounded before he reached it. Janos stood framed in the opening.

"Come in, Janos," Dominic said to him. "A friend of yours is here." He noticed the boy wore his oldest shirt, a pair of stained breeches, and no shoes, his small bare feet digging nervously into the carpet. Slender brown arms clutched several volumes of books against his narrow chest.

"Percy came to my room," he said as he approached. "He told me that Pearsa had come." He turned big dark eyes in her direction. "If she will take me, I wish to go with her when she leaves."

"Janos—" Catherine came to her feet. "Surely you can't mean to leave us. What about your schooling? I know it's been hard for you, but in time—"

"We've discussed this, love," Dominic said gently, halting her next words. "I told you from the start the boy might not stay. He must follow his destiny as surely as we have followed ours."

"I know how to read, Catrina," Janos told her, resting his small hand in hers. "I will not forget, and I will remember that you and Domini made it so."

"I would take the boy," Pearsa said. "He would be a great joy to me."

"Janos?" Dominic asked. "You are sure this is what you want?"

"I love you and Catrina. But I am not happy here. I miss the *kumpania* . . . I would go with Pearsa."

"You will always be welcome here," Dominic said, "no matter how far you travel." His gaze swung to Catherine, whose expression looked forlorn. Dominic reached for her hand. "You mustn't be sad, love. You'll soon have a child of your own."

Catherine smiled softly, her hand coming up to her stomach. "Yes."

"A son," Pearsa said. "It will be a boy—dark and handsome—just like these two."

Catherine didn't argue and neither did Dominic. Something in the old woman's eyes said it would be so.

Dominic sent Janos to collect his things—and all the clothes and books he could carry—and left the women to their conversation.

Wandering out toward the garden, he plucked a fading flower from a bush beside the fountain, then turned to look out on the grassy hills around him. On a knoll among the trees, the Gravenwold family plot watched over the fields in the distance. Dominic found himself walking in that direction. Only once had he been there, on the day they had buried his father.

He stood there now, inside the low wrought-iron fence beside the grave, looking down at the cold gray stone. *Samuel Dominic Edgemont, Fifth Marquess of Gravenwold. May He Rest in Peace.*

Dominic stood in silence for a moment, pondering the words, then he tossed the faded flower onto the grave. They would never share the joys of a father and son, but at least they were no longer enemies.

A leaf drifted down from the branches overhead and a rustling sound drew Dominic's attention. A gyrfalcon flew from its perch, winging its way toward the heavens, its flight a study in grace as it moved away from the earth. His thoughts returning to his father, Dominic followed its upward journey until it disappeared among the wispy clouds on the distant horizon.

Perhaps, as his father had wished, he was finally at peace.

Dominic smiled softly. With Catherine and the child they soon would share, at last so was he.

Author's Note

During the course of my research on Gypsies, it became apparent that the elusive quality that makes them so fascinating carries through as well in what has been written about them.

Since their language is only spoken, the spelling of each word varies from text to text, country to country. Words for male and female are often the same, and legends differ, depending upon who is telling the tale. Still, their culture is, at the very least, intriguing, and spinning the tale of Catherine and Dominic, and of Dominic's Gypsy family brought me endless hours of pleasure and an insight into a people and culture I never had before. I hope you'll bear with any liberties I might have taken, and that you enjoyed their story, too.

Stoneleigh. Jocelyn could scarcely believe it. For three long years, the huge stone mansion on the edge of Hampstead Heath just north of London had haunted her nightmares and piqued her temper. *Stoneleigh.* She had dreamed of going inside, been fascinated by its awesome beauty—and appalled by its vicious, cruel-hearted master.

Stoneleigh. She looked at the man who carried that same name, and it occurred to her that the house and the man both exuded the same combination of beauty, strength, and cruelty. She had studied the viscount's movements for the past two years; she knew the man was handsome, but up close he was more than that. There was a power about him, a raw, sensual, masculinity that made other men seem frail in comparison. There was a danger about him, too. A lethal quality that emanated from every muscle and sinew in his tall hard body.

She wouldn't have guessed it from the ease with which he moved in his impeccably tailored frock coat and breeches, the casual way he wore his elegant white cravat. She hadn't guessed it, and now it was too late.

She twisted beneath him, then shuddered at the ease with which he held her.

"I'm twice your size, you might as well quit struggling."

She could feel his strength in the bands of muscle across his chest as he pressed her down on the velvet seat. The large powerful hands that gripped her wrists held her immobile, yet oddly she felt no pain. He hadn't hit her, though she had certainly given him cause. Still, his actions meant nothing. She knew the kind of man he was, the crimes he had committed, and nothing on the face of this earth could keep her from making him pay.

"I'll let go of your wrists," he said, "if you'll promise to stop fighting me."

Jo glared up at him coldly. "Go to bleedin' 'ell." She surged against his hold, then winced when he easily forced her back down.

"I warned you before, you had better behave."

"Why should I?"

"Because if you don't, I shall unleash my formidable temper and give you the thrashing you deserve."

"I'd expect a beating from a man the likes of you."

One corner of his mouth curved up in a smile that wasn't. "Then you won't be surprised when I turn you over my knee and blister your scheming little bottom."

Jo's eyes went wide. He could certainly do it. And she would be powerless to stop him. In the past three years, she had suffered all manner of indignation—but fortunately not that. And the thought of the hated viscount being the man to administer such a blow to her dignity made the idea all the more repugnant.

She nodded stiffly. "All right, you win." *For now*, she thought. Besides, why shouldn't she do as he asked? He wasn't taking her to Fleet Street or Newgate—at least that's what he'd said. Instead, as she had fantasized since childhood, Jocelyn Asbury was going to Stoneleigh.

She raised her eyes to his face and found him

watching her, trying to see if she intended to keep her word.

"Don't think for a moment, I won't do exactly as I promised—and I assure you, I shall relish every blow." He released his grip on her arms, and Jo eased away from him until her back pressed into the tufted velvet seat on the opposite side of the carriage.

"The blond boy called you Jo. Is that your name?"

"None 'a your soddin' business."

His sensuous mouth turned into a thin grim line. "You had better start watching your tongue, you little minx, or I'll make good my threat just for sport."

Jo felt the blood leave her face. "Just because you're bigger than someone doesn't give you the right to bully them."

His brow shot up. Realizing she had spoken without a trace of her usual street slang, Jo cursed him beneath her breath. "Go to bleedin' 'ell."

"At the rate you and your friends are going, I believe you shall precede me by some years."

Jo said nothing. Perhaps his words would prove true. Especially if she succeeded in her plans for revenge. Not that she intended getting caught.

Then a different thought occured to her. It was entirely possible her untimely capture by the viscount might prove a boon instead of a boggle. Once she reached Stoneleigh, if she bided her time and the viscount let down his guard, her failure tonight might well turn into a triumph. Notwithstanding the fact it had been far more difficult to pull the trigger than she had expected, her vow to kill Stoneleigh could at last be fulfilled.

Just then, the viscount's hard dark eyes moved over her body. He was appraising every inch of her, assessing her slender curves and the peaks of her breasts. Jo shivered. Stoneleigh was a villainous, heartless man. She couldn't begin to guess what he might have in store for her once they reached his mansion.

She schooled her features into a mask of calm. She wouldn't let him win, she wouldn't!

One thing was sure: The next few hours would decide her fate. They would also decide who the victor of this deadly game would be. ...

**BE SURE TO LOOK FOR
SWEET VENGEANCE—
ANOTHER EXCITING HISTORICAL
ROMANCE FROM KAT MARTIN
AND ST. MARTIN'S PAPERBACKS!**